THE GOD
OF THE
WOODS

THE GOD
OF THE
WOODS

LIZ MOORE

THE BOROUGH PRESS

The Borough Press
An imprint of HarperCollins*Publishers* Ltd
1 London Bridge Street
London SE1 9GF

www.harpercollins.co.uk

HarperCollins *Publishers*
Macken House,
39/40 Mayor Street Upper,
Dublin 1
D01 C9W8

First published by HarperCollins*Publishers* 2024

4

Copyright © Liz Moore 2024

Liz Moore asserts the moral right to
be identified as the author of this work

A catalogue record for this book is available from the British Library

Hardback ISBN: 9780008663797
Trade Paperback ISBN: 9780008663803

This novel is entirely a work of fiction.
The names, characters and incidents portrayed in it are
the work of the author's imagination. Any resemblance to
actual persons, living or dead, events or localities is
entirely coincidental.

Typeset by Palimpsest Book Production Ltd, Falkirk, Stirlingshire

Printed and bound in the UK using 100% Renewable Electricity by CPI Group (UK) Ltd

For my sister, Rebecca,
who also knows these woods

Contents

Many a pedestrian on reaching these woods is incredulous of the danger which he is told will menace him if he ventures out alone to indulge in his favorite pastime. But let him rest assured that there is no question as to the reality of this danger—the danger of losing himself in the forest. That is the only thing to be dreaded in the Adirondack woods!

—From "Lost in the Adirondacks: Warning to Visitors to the North Woods; What Not to Do When You Lose Your Way and How Not to Lose It," *The New York Times*, March 16, 1890

How quickly, I reflected, peril could be followed by beauty in the wilderness, each forming a part of the other.

—From *Woodswoman* by Anne LaBastille

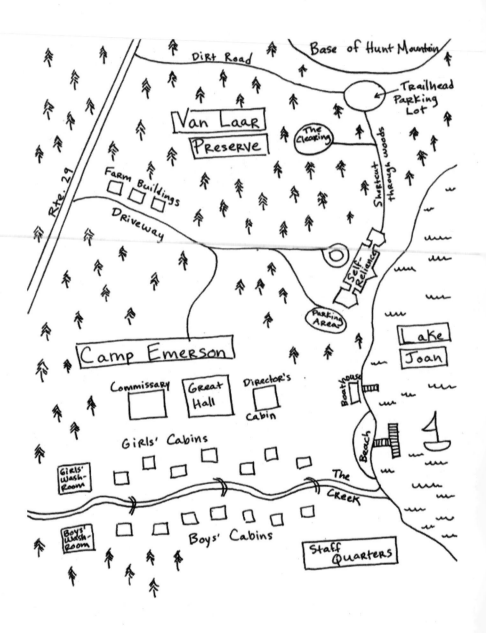

I

Barbara

Louise

August 1975

The bed is empty.

Louise, the counselor—twenty-three, short-limbed, rasp-voiced, jolly—stands barefoot on the warm, rough planks of the cabin called Balsam and processes the absence of a body in the lower bunk by the door. Later on, the ten seconds that pass between sight and inference will serve to her as evidence that time is a human construct, that it can slow or accelerate in the presence of emotion, of chemicals in the blood.

The bed is empty.

The cabin's single flashlight—the absence of which is used, even in daylight, to indicate that campers have gone to the latrines—is in its home on a shelf by the door.

Louise turns slowly in a circle, naming the girls she can see.

Melissa. Melissa. Jennifer. Michelle. Amy. Caroline. Tracy. Kim.

Eight campers. Nine beds. She counts and counts again.

At last, when she can no longer defer it, she lets one name bob to the surface of her mind: *Barbara*.

The empty bed is Barbara's.

She closes her eyes. She imagines herself returning, for the rest of her life, to this place and this moment: a lonely time traveler, a ghost, haunting the cabin called Balsam, willing a body to appear where there is none. Willing the girl herself, Barbara, to walk through the door. To say she has been in the washroom, to say she forgot the rule about taking the flashlight, to apologize disarmingly, as she has done before.

But Louise knows that Barbara won't do any of these things. She senses, for reasons she can't quite articulate, that Barbara is gone.

Of all the campers, Louise thinks. Of all the campers to go missing.

At 6:25 a.m., Louise walks back through a curtain into the space she shares with Annabel, the counselor-in-training. She's seventeen, a ballet dancer from Chevy Chase, Maryland. Annabel Southworth is closer in age to the campers than she is to Louise, but she stands upright and infuses her words with irony and in general works to ensure that everyone recognizes the firm line between thirteen and seventeen—a line made manifest by the plywood partition that separates the main part of the cabin from the counselors' corner.

Now, Louise shakes her awake. Now, Annabel squints. Crooks an elbow over her eyes dramatically. Sinks back into sleep.

Louise is becoming aware of something: the smell of metabolized beer. She had assumed it was coming from her own body—from her own skin and mouth. She certainly drank enough last night to feel the effects this morning. But standing over Annabel, she wonders whether the smell, in fact, has been coming from Annabel's side of the room.

Which concerns her.

"*Annabel*," Louise whispers. In her tone, she suddenly recognizes the sound of her own mother. And in some ways she feels like her mother—her bad mother, her irresponsible mother—in relation to this girl.

Annabel opens her eyes. She sits up and winces immediately. She meets Louise's gaze and her eyes widen, her face becomes pale.

"I'm gonna be sick," she says—too loudly. Louise shushes her, grabs at the first vessel she can reach—an empty bag of potato chips on the floor.

Annabel lunges for the bag. Retches. Then raises her head, panting, groaning lowly.

"Annabel," Louise says. "Are you hungover?"

Annabel shakes her head. Scared.

"I think I," she says—and again Louise shushes her, sitting down on the girl's bed this time, counting to five in her mind, the way she has done since she was a small child. Training herself not to react.

Annabel's chin is trembling. "I think I ate something bad," she whispers.

"Did you go out last night?" asks Louise. "Annabel?"

Annabel watches her. Calculating.

"This is important," says Louise.

Normally she has patience for her CITs. She is practiced in guiding them through their first hangovers. Doesn't mind when they indulge a little on a night off. As head counselor this year, she generally turns a blind eye to behavior she deems harmless. Partakes in it herself, when the moment feels right. But she otherwise runs a tight ship; earlier this summer, the first counselor to fail to wake up on time after a night of carousing was banned from the next several parties, and that seemed to set enough of an example that no one has repeated the mistake.

Until now. Because last night, while Louise went out, it was Annabel's turn to be on duty. And Annabel, apparently, wasn't.

Louise closes her eyes. Runs through the events of last evening.

There was a dance in the community room: the end-of-session dance, which all campers, counselors, and CITs were required to attend. She recalls noticing, at a certain point, that Annabel seemed to be absent— she couldn't set eyes on her, anyway—but Louise is certain that she was back by the end of the dance.

Because at 11 p.m., when Louise did a quick head count, Annabel was there, along with nine campers—yes, nine—who waved to Louise sweetly as they said good night. She can still see the back of them, walking in little clusters toward Balsam.

This was the last time she saw them. Louise, assured that Annabel was in charge, went off on her own.

Next, she tries to picture the campers' beds as she tiptoed into the cabin at the end of the night, well after curfew. This would have been at—what—two in the morning? Three? Images return to her in fragments: Melissa R's open mouth, Amy's arm hanging down toward the floor. But Barbara herself is nowhere among these memories. Nor is the absence of Barbara.

A different memory asserts itself instead: John Paul, in the Clearing, as he windmilled his arms, first in her direction and then in Lee Towson's. John Paul with his rich-kid approach to the fight, brandishing his fists as if he were entering a ring. Lee, wild and scrappy, still in his apron from dinner service. He made short work of John Paul, left him on the ground, blinking absently up toward the branches overhead.

There will be trouble today. There always is when John Paul gets the notion that she's fooling around on him.

For the record: she isn't, this time.

*   *   *

Annabel comes up for air. Puts a hand over her eyes.

"Do you know where Barbara is?" asks Louise. Cutting to the chase. There's not much time: soon the girls in the other room will be waking.

Annabel looks confused.

"Van *Laar*," says Louise, and then she says it again, more quietly. "Our camper."

"No," says Annabel, and collapses backward on her bed.

It is then, of course, that reveille sounds over the speakers mounted on trees throughout the campground—meaning that on the other side of the plywood partition, eight twelve- and thirteen-year-old girls are reluctantly waking up, making their small noises, exhalations, and sighs, propping themselves up on elbows.

Louise begins pacing.

Annabel, still horizontal, now watches her—beginning to understand the problem.

"Annabel," says Louise. "You need to be honest here. Did you go back out last night? After the campers were in bed?"

Annabel appears to hold her breath. Then she exhales. Nods. Her eyes, Louise notices, are filling with tears.

"Yes, I did," she says. There's a childish tremor in her voice. She has very rarely been in trouble in her life: of this Louise is certain. She is a person who has been told, since birth, about her value in this world. The ways she makes others happy. She is crying openly now, and Louise struggles not to roll her eyes. What does Annabel have to be afraid of? There's nothing at stake for her. She's seventeen years old. The worst thing that could happen to Annabel is that she might be dismissed, sent up the hill to her rich parents—who are friends, in fact, with the owners of the camp. Who are, at this very moment, guests at their house on the grounds. Meanwhile, the worst thing that might happen to Louise—an *adult*, thinks Louise, castigating herself— the worst thing that might happen is—well. Don't make too many leaps, she tells herself. Just stay in the present.

Louise walks to the curtain. Pulls it back ever so slightly. In doing so, she catches the eye of Tracy, Barbara's bunkmate, a quiet girl who stands paused on the bunk's ladder in mid-descent, having noticed, apparently, the issue.

Louise drops the curtain.

"Is she missing?" Annabel says. Again, Louise shushes her.

"Don't say *missing*," says Louise. "Say she's not in her bunk."

Louise scans their little room, looking for evidence of their behavior last night. She gathers what she finds into a brown paper garbage bag: an empty bottle of beer that she drank on the walk back from the Clearing; the end of a joint that she smoked at some point; the vomit-filled potato chip bag, which she handles with two stiff fingers.

"Is there anything else you wouldn't want someone finding?" she asks Annabel, who shakes her head.

Louise closes the garbage bag, folds it, makes it compact.

"Listen to me," she says. "You might have to be in charge of the campers this morning. I'm not sure yet. If that happens, you need to get rid of this. Just put it in the garbage enclosure on the walk to breakfast. It needs to be gotten rid of. Can you do that?"

Annabel nods, still green.

"Right now," she says to Annabel, "just stay here. Don't come out for a while. And don't—" She hesitates, searching for words that sound serious but not self-incriminating. She's talking, after all, to a child. "Just don't say anything about last night to anyone, yet. Let me think a few things over."

Annabel goes quiet.

"Okay?" says Louise.

"Okay."

She'll fold immediately, Louise thinks. She will unswervingly tell every authority figure everything that happened and everything she knows. She'll cry on the shoulders of her mother and father, who probably didn't even understand the poem they named their daughter for, and she'll be comforted by them, and resume her ballet lessons, and next year she'll be pipelined into Vassar or Radcliffe or Wellesley by her prep school, and she'll marry the boy her parents have chosen for her—already, she has confessed to Louise, they have one in mind—and she will never, ever think of Louise Donnadieu again, or the fate that will befall Louise, or the trouble Louise will have, for the rest of her life: getting a job, getting housing, supporting her mother, who for seven years now has been unable or unwilling to work. Supporting her little brother, who at eleven has done nothing at all to deserve the life he has been given.

In front of her, Annabel gags. Recovers.

Louise puts her hands on her hips. Breathes. Slow down, she reminds herself.

She squares her shoulders. Pulls back the curtain. Begins the work of feigning ignorance and surprise for this small group of girls who— she swallows her shame like a pill—who look up to her, admire her, frequently come to her for advice and protection.

She steps into their room. Pantomimes scanning the beds. Furrows her brow in a show of confusion.

"Where's Barbara?" she says to them, brightly.

Tracy

Two Months Earlier
June 1975

Three rules were given to the campers upon their arrival.

The first concerned food in the cabins, and the way it was to be consumed and stored (neatly; tightly).

The second pertained to swimming: an activity that was not, under any circumstances, to be undertaken solo.

The third—the most important, as evidenced by its display, in capital letters, in several communal locations—was WHEN LOST SIT DOWN AND YELL.

At the time, this admonition struck Tracy as almost funny. It would be repeated later that night, at the opening campfire; its logic would be explained. But presented as it was in that moment, forthrightly, succinctly, by a tall male counselor who spoke the words without punctuation or emotion—the phrase made her look away, swallow a nervous laugh. WHEN LOST SIT DOWN AND YELL. She tried to imagine it: Sitting down right where she was. Opening her mouth. Yelling. What noise, she wondered, would escape her? What word, or words? *Help? Help me?* God forbid—*Please find me?* It was too embarrassing to consider.

Her father had paid her to attend.

This was what it took, after a week of negotiations that had concluded with a weekend-long standoff in her room: cold hard cash, a hundred dollars of it—fifty percent of which would be waiting for her upon her return.

What she had wanted to do with her summer was simple: she wanted to spend all day in the living room of the Victorian in Saratoga Springs that her family had rented each racing season for a decade. She had wanted to lower the blinds halfway and open the windows halfway and point all the fans in the house in her direction and lie on the sofa, only rising to prepare herself elaborate snacks. And she wanted to read: reading was the main thing.

This had been her routine for five summers in a row. She had hoped that the summer of 1975 would be no different.

Instead, her father—divorced from her mother for less than a year—had, in quick succession, gotten a girlfriend, a fancier rental house, and the notion that Tracy shouldn't lie around all summer with nothing to do. This was what he said to her, anyway, on their ride up from Tracy's mother's house on Long Island in mid-June. (She couldn't help but notice that he'd waited to reveal the plan until they were more than halfway to Saratoga.) The real reason, she thought, was so that she would be out of his hair for two months. So that he and the aforementioned girlfriend could have the run of the place without a sulking twelve-year-old underfoot. Why had he fought to have custody of her all summer, Tracy asked herself, if he was only going to turn around and send her away?

He hadn't even bothered to drop her off at Camp Emerson himself. Instead he'd outsourced that task to Donna Romano, the girlfriend, still a first and last name to Tracy.

"It's a race day," her father said, when Tracy cornered him in the hallway, begged him to come. "Gotta drive down to Belmont. Second Thought's running at two."

Her father was a jockey's son who'd grown up too tall to follow in his footsteps. He'd become an exercise rider instead, and then a trainer, and then an owner, the circumstances of their lives changing with each job. When Tracy was born, the three of them lived in an RV in her mother's mother's driveway. Now they lived in a new large house with a silver front gate in Hempstead, New York. Well, Tracy and her mother did, anyway.

"What will we even *talk* about," she demanded, but he only shook his head, put two imploring hands on her shoulders. She noticed suddenly that she was eye level with him: her own father. She'd recently gone through a growth spurt that put her in the vicinity of five-eleven and made her slouch vigorously whenever she wasn't in motion.

"This place is supposed to be top-notch. I mean really hoity-toity," said her father—the same two embarrassing descriptors he'd used when first breaking the news. "I bet you'll end up loving it."

She turned toward a window. Through it, she could see Donna Romano adjusting her bra, inspecting her reflection in the window of the car. It was a new Stutz Blackhawk with shag carpeting on the floor and an engine whose roar reminded Tracy of her father's voice. "Top of the line," he had said, when he picked her up in Hempstead. It seemed to Tracy that everything in her father's life was new. Rental house, girlfriend, Pekingese puppy, car. Tracy was the only old thing in his orbit; and even she was being cast out.

As it turned out, Donna Romano was a chain-smoker. In between drags she asked Tracy questions about her life that she'd clearly been stockpiling for the very purpose of this trip. When she was not busy answering them, Tracy snuck glances at Donna Romano. She was extremely pretty. Normally, this would have gone far with Tracy. She loved pretty women. She loved the most popular girls at her middle school—though *revered* might have been a better word, since a large part of her actually despised them. Still, she was fascinated by them, perhaps due to the fact that, physically, they were her opposite, and thus seemed somehow like specimens she wished to examine, at length, under a microscope. Where most of her classmates had long, straight hair, parted in the middle, Tracy's hair was large, red, and indefatigable. Where some of her classmates' freckles were delicate, Tracy's were so pronounced that she had been nicknamed Connect the Dots, or CTD for short, by a group of sixth-grade boys. She was supposed to wear glasses; she owned a pair that she never wore, which resulted in her squinting frequently. Her father once told her casually that she was built like a plum on toothpicks, and the phrase was at once so cruel and so poetic that it clicked into place around her like a harness.

The roads turned from asphalt to gravel to dirt. Ramshackle homes appeared every few minutes, their front lawns repurposed as graveyards for rusted-out vehicles. It was eerie, this contrast between natural beauty and man-made decay, and Tracy began to wonder if they were going the right way.

And then, at last, a sign came into view. *Van Laar Preserve*, it said. Their mailed instructions had indicated this was the sign to follow.

"I wonder why they don't put the name of the camp on the sign," mused Donna Romano.

Maybe it was so perverts couldn't find it, thought Tracy. This, she knew, was what her father would have said. Against her will, she often heard his voice as a sort of narrative presence that underscored her life. That year—the first of the divorce—was the longest they had ever been apart.

The truth was that as a younger child she had been his shadow, had loved him unreservedly, following him everywhere, raising carrots, flat-handed, to the velvety muzzles of his favorite horses. Although she would have died before admitting it, Tracy missed him profoundly, and had spent the better part of her last school year anticipating a summer of being at his side.

The dirt driveway forked. An arrow to the right directed them to *Camp Emerson: Where Lifelong Friendships Are Made*. And then the trees broke open onto a lawn with several rustic wooden buildings in a row. In front of them was a lone counselor standing behind a folding table, from which hung a damp posterboard sign that said, unconvincingly, *Welcome*.

The counselor approached the Blackhawk with a folder, handed it to Donna through a window. Then he formally dispensed the Three Rules of Camp Emerson like a dutiful town crier—including the final one, the most important, a phrase that would echo in Tracy's head for days, for weeks. For the rest of her life.

When lost sit down and yell.

Tracy had difficulty imagining how lost she would have to be before the option felt correct. Her voice, it seemed, had been continuously decrescendoing since birth, so that by age twelve, she could scarcely be heard.

Very, she decided, at last. Profoundly, irreversibly, lost.

"You'll be in Balsam," said the boy, interrupting Tracy's thoughts. He extended a long arm to his right. Donna Romano tapped the gas, and the Blackhawk rolled forward.

Alice

June 1975

The last of the parents were leaving.

From the sunroom in the house at the top of the hill, Alice watched as their cars rolled by, wipers on, a slow parade.

Camp Emerson was a half mile away, but the Preserve's main house—Self-Reliance, they'd named it—had been built on a high ridge in the land, and from it she could see all around her: Lake Joan to the east; to the west, the long driveway that led to the main road into town; to the south, Camp Emerson; to the north, the wilderness. Hunt Mountain and its foothills.

She'd been standing there for two hours. Ninety-one cars had gone by so far. Inside all of them was a parent or parents, leaving a child or children behind.

This had been Alice's ritual for the twenty-three years she'd been married to Peter Van Laar. Each first-day-of-camp since she was eighteen she'd stood at this window at the front of Self-Reliance, watching, sometimes with a child in her arms, sometimes alone. She liked to imagine the families inside the cars. Liked to invent names for them, and problems.

The final car disappeared from sight. Alice straightened. She checked the clock behind her: 4:45. Her daily countdown was underway: at five o'clock, she was allowed one of the pills Dr. Lewis had prescribed her for her nerves. One was the recommendation—though two wouldn't hurt her "on very bad days." By this Dr. Lewis meant days when she was thinking too much about Bear.

Two, then.

A thud down the hall: the drop of the iron knocker against the front door. That would be T.J.

That morning, Alice had sent word down to the director's office, requesting a meeting.

Now, from her pocket, Alice fished out the little glass bottle. Chewed her two pills, fifteen minutes early.

Then she closed her eyes, rehearsing in her mind the words she would use.

It's Barbara, she'd say. *She'd like to join in on camp.*

It had been five years since T.J. Hewitt stepped in as director of Camp Emerson. She hadn't wanted to; her father Vic, she insisted, was perfectly capable of continuing in the role he had performed beautifully for decades.

But Vic's infirmity—first physical, then mental—became impossible to ignore during the summer of 1970, when he had frightened several campers by shouting at them nonsensically on the very first day of the session. In front of their parents, no less. The parents, incensed, stalked up to the main house to complain. And Peter had deposed Vic, then and there, assuring the parents that he would personally oversee that session, until a suitable replacement had been found.

They searched for one only briefly before Peter suggested T.J. take on her father's former roles. Alice had been against it. She was so young, and a woman. Who had ever heard of a woman groundskeeper? But Peter had insisted. They'd find a replacement eventually, he said.

So far, they hadn't. Not one who met with Peter's approval, anyway. And so, like her father before her, T.J. now occupied both roles: Preserve groundskeeper in the fall, winter, and spring; camp director in the summer. She still lived in the cottage she'd grown up in, which also served as the camp director's office, and now as Vic Hewitt's convalescent home, as well, for most of the year.

In the threshold of the sunroom, now, T.J. cleared her throat. She looked uncomfortable, unhappy—though to be fair, this was her expression anytime she was inside of a building. The woods were her domain.

"Hello, T.J.," said Alice, and T.J. nodded, avoiding a direct address. For as long as Alice had known her, T.J. had never once called her by name. There was a haughtiness about her that Alice had always found irritating. She wasn't like this with Peter, thought Alice—no, with Peter she was deferent.

"Have a seat," said Alice, and then watched as T.J. turned in a full circle, searching for whatever perch would convey the least commitment, the greatest sense of haste. She settled at last on an ottoman. Sat at its very edge. Elbows on knees. Head down.

Her hair was newly short, lopped into a bowl shape, so crooked and wrong-looking that Alice imagined T.J. must have done it herself. It was difficult to reconcile the woman sitting before her with the girl Alice met twenty-three years ago, when she'd first set foot on the grounds: three years old, always in motion, following her father from place to place. She'd been *Tessie Jo* at the time, a frilly name, a name for a doll or a cow or some sort of entertainer, all wrong for such a stoic child. By sixteen she'd adopted the more androgynous *T.J.* as her name, but she'd worn her hair in a thick braid for a decade longer. Until now.

"How are you?" Alice asked. She took a mint from the bowl beside her, which the staff kept well stocked. The pink ones were the best.

"Arigh'," said T.J., in that accent. That *accent*. Alice had been in the region more than two decades and still found it hard on the ears.

"Is your father well?"

"Well enough."

"Any problems with the facilities this year?"

"Naugh," said T.J. She swatted at something invisible at the back of her neck. Examined her hand.

"I'll get down to it," said Alice. "I imagine Mr. V has already spoken to you?" She paused, waiting for T.J.'s response—because in fact she had no idea whether Peter had talked to the girl. She'd had no word from him since Thursday, when he left for Albany. What she did know was that Barbara was still at home.

T.J. shook her head. No.

Alice exhaled. Of course, she thought—of course he hadn't. If nothing else, she could bank on the promise that he would shirk every one of his duties, that he would fail her—fail Barbara—time and time again, that he would be absent from their lives when their lives became difficult. Which meant that, these days—the way Barbara was acting— he was mainly gone, usually without announcing his departure. His returns were similarly quiet.

T.J. shifted, straightened her back.

"Well," Alice said to T.J., forcing herself to speak brightly, lightly.

"Then this will be news to you. We've decided—Barbara has decided—that she'd like to join in on camp this year."

She smiled a little, as if she were delivering good news.

She had known that T.J. wouldn't like it. It was one of the reasons she'd been putting it off. For generations, there'd been a strict divide between the Van Laar family—Albany bankers, outdoorsy but staid—and the camp they owned, which was always the province of the Hewitts. First Vic. Now his daughter. And, too, there was the fact that T.J. liked things done in a particular way, in a particular order. She'd be annoyed, Alice guessed, by the lateness of the request.

But for an instant, something passed over T.J.'s countenance that Alice couldn't categorize. Consternation? Anger? She wouldn't meet Alice's eyes. Since she'd entered the room, she'd been gazing steadfastly to the right of Alice's head.

T.J. shook her head a second time.

"Sorry," said T.J. "Can't do it."

Alice stared.

There was such confidence, such finality, in T.J. Hewitt's voice. As if she had a say over any of this, thought Alice. As if she were the employer of Alice, and not the other way around.

Alice breathed in. The mint in her mouth had dissolved completely. She took another from the dish and bit down before responding.

"It would mean a great deal to us," she said. "I know you're close with Barbara. I'm sure you've noticed that she's been having—difficulty. Acting out. We think it would benefit her to be around some new friends."

Well, Alice did, at least. Peter wasn't certain. But there were so many reasons it made sense to let her go—not least of them that she would be out of the house for the party. The first one they'd thrown in fourteen years. They were having a hundredth-anniversary celebration for the Preserve, bringing two dozen friends and relatives to the grounds for a week in August. The last time they had had dinner guests in Albany, Barbara had emerged only once from her room. She'd been wearing a sort of costume, really—her hair dyed some terrible color, her eyes lined heavily in black. Peter's cousin Garland had burst out laughing, and Barbara had retreated, slammed the door. She'd kept the hair color and the eyeliner ever since, despite Alice's exhortations.

They would have no such worries this time—if only Barbara could go.

T.J. looked down at the floor.

"Have you told her yet?" she said.

"About camp?" Alice said. "She's the one who asked to go."

"No," said T.J. "About what's happening in the fall."

Alice paused. Shook her head.

"I'll tell her at the end of the summer."

Then, in a moment of inspiration: "I'll tell her after the end of her session at camp."

"Session's underway," T.J. said, in that way of hers.

"Just barely."

"Cabins're full."

A slow incredulity was rising in Alice's chest, and yet she also felt muted by something, unable to access her deepest reserves of rage, the ones she relied on with Peter when she really needed to be heard.

The pills, she remembered. The pills had their hooks in her, were loosening the tight knots in her shoulders, sending a flood of relief down her front and back, a waterfall of warmth and calm. *Focus*, she instructed herself.

She took in the objects in the room around her: a trick Dr. Lewis had taught her. *Grandfather clock. Plants growing lushly. Stone-tiled sunroom floor.*

She spoke again, careful to articulate. Her tongue was a fat slug in her mouth.

"You know Barbara as well as anyone does," said Alice. Better than I do, she thought, against her will. "You know it will do her good."

But T.J. was standing now, preparing to walk out of the room. If she'd had a hat, she would have placed it on her head.

A whole summer, thought Alice. A whole summer without Barbara, her rages, her storms, the hours she spent weeping aloud, disturbing the staff. All of them pretending politely not to hear. But they did, every one of them, and Alice did too. How pleasant it would be to have these months all to herself, while just down the hill her daughter was removed, but safe. Occupied. Content.

"I'd better head back," said T.J.

Alice smiled. The pills were dissolving her guard. There were words in the back of her mouth that she'd normally trap with her teeth. She had been doing that for most of her life, with Peter, with everyone. Usually, she was gifted in the art of shutting up.

Not today.

"It's not really your choice," said Alice. "It's got to happen."

"Or what," said T.J. abruptly. Too loud, Alice thought. Why did everyone have to speak so loudly, all of the time.

Quiet: it was all that she wanted.

Alice opened her mouth. No words came out.

A minute passed, or maybe five. She felt sleep coming on. She knew she should have been embarrassed by her posture, the way her head was tilting to one side now—but that emotion, too, was inaccessible to her, abstract, something she understood conceptually but couldn't feel.

"It's Mr. Van Laar's idea," said Alice, at last. "It's what he wants."

It was a last resort. Embarrassing to have to use it. Embarrassing, she thought, that her own words were meaningless in this household.

T.J. looked at her. Deciding whether or not Alice could be believed. And then her expression changed into something resigned.

"Fine," said T.J. "We'll put a bunk in Balsam. She'll start tomorrow."

With no further questions, T.J. walked out of the room. Out of the house.

If Bear were here—

Alice stopped. She was not supposed to indulge these fantasies, said Dr. Lewis. Each time her mind drifted toward one, she was supposed to bring herself back to reality. And yet the vision came to her forcefully: if Bear were here, he would follow T.J. out the door. She closed her eyes, allowing herself—just for a moment—to remember her son, vibrant, delightful, trailing T.J. Hewitt all over the grounds. *Tessie, Tessie.* His high sweet voice, just on the other side of a thin curtain between her world and his. She could hear it easily.

On the chaise, Alice turned her head to watch through the windowed wall of the sunroom. T.J., departing, paused on the lawn, removed something from her pocket, put a hand to her mouth. Spat. Chaw, the men called it. A disgusting habit.

Alice watched the back of T.J. Hewitt until she was out of sight.

Her form was tall and thin and graceful, and Alice reflected, not for the first time, that she could have been pretty.

That was the real sin of it, thought Alice. The way she had ruined her looks.

The sound of footsteps caught her ear. Heavy, plodding ones: Barbara.

She'd be heading to the kitchen. Her favorite place, of late. Alice grimaced.

Yesterday, Alice had asked the new cook—whose name she couldn't remember—to stop feeding Barbara so often. To make excuses if she had to. But Barbara could be very manipulative, Alice knew, and she had little faith in the cook's ability to handle her.

She made her way to the threshold of the kitchen, and paused there, trying to be quiet.

There was Barbara, of course, regarding the contents of the pantry, her back to the room. She was wearing shorts and a T-shirt, and Alice noticed with a sort of disgust that her once-insubstantial bottom was round now, and her legs were the legs of a woman. Behind Barbara, the cook caught Alice's eye. Raised her hands, as if helpless.

Alice didn't enjoy assessing her daughter's body in this way. She understood conceptually that it was uncharitable; and yet she also believed that part of a mother's duty was to be her daughter's first, best critic; to fortify her during her childhood, so that in womanhood she could gracefully withstand any assault or insult launched in her direction. This was the method her own mother had used upon her. She hadn't liked it at the time, but now she understood it.

"Barbara," said Alice, and her daughter jumped, and then turned, a loaf of bread tucked under her arm. Just for a moment, Alice felt tender toward her. She had always been skittish, ever since she was a toddler—the only baby on earth who didn't like playing peekaboo or hide-and-seek, who cried when she was startled, even in fun.

"Dinner's at half past seven," said Alice.

Levelly, Barbara put the loaf down on the countertop and began sawing.

"Did you hear me?" said Alice.

Barbara nodded. Reached for the butter. Spread it over the bread. Kept her head lowered. A half inch of blond was visible now at her part; the rest of her hair was still that terrible dull black. Her face, at least, was pretty. No bad dye job could change that.

The cook looked on uselessly. She was a tiny little thing, perhaps twenty-five, married, judging by the plain ring on her finger.

Alice sighed. There was no point in saying anything—not today. Not when Barbara would be away for the whole rest of the summer. What harm, after all, in letting her indulge in one more helping of bread and butter and jam.

"I spoke to T.J. just now," said Alice, and finally the girl looked up. There was the version of Barbara she loved, at last. Some sign of animation in her face and eyes.

"And?" said Barbara.

"She says you can start camp tomorrow."

Triumph. Barbara looked down quickly, but Alice could see that she was working to keep her mouth straight, stopping a smile.

"I'll have someone pack for you," said Alice.

It was good, thought Alice. This would be good. To have a break from each other. Things would get better this way.

Tracy

June 1975

This, Tracy learned, was Camp Emerson:

Three buildings formed its northernmost edge, closest to the main house up the hill. One was the commissary, where they ate their meals; the next a building called the Great Hall, which contained a nurse's office, two small rooms that could be used for activities on rainy days, and a large community room that was mainly used for dances and performances that required a stage. The third building in this small cluster was the Director's Cabin. The only campers who had ever seen inside it were those who had gotten into trouble of one kind or another.

South of these buildings lay the rest of the campground. Near the lake at the eastern edge were a small beach and a boathouse. A long building called Staff Quarters sat at the southern border of the grounds—this was where kitchen workers and other seasonal staff resided. To the north of it were fourteen cabins—seven for boys, seven for girls—in two lines on opposite sides of a creek that could be crossed by small bridges here and there. Every one of these cabins was named after an Adirondack tree or flower.

Tracy's cabin, Balsam, was lit inside by warm yellow bulbs that hung, uncovered, from the ceiling. At night, these same lightbulbs summoned an army of insects through the tattered screens in the cabin's windows.

The cabin was furnished with eight twin beds, four and four against opposite sides. Small wooden trunks sat at the foot of each bed. The cabin's walls were made of unfinished wood, and so too was its ceiling, inscribed with names and dates and inscrutable references by generation after generation of campers.

Most surprisingly, against one wall of the cabin was a fireplace. Tracy was told, later that summer, that the cabins originally had been used year-round by friends of earlier generations of Van Laars on short hunting trips; but since the founding of Camp Emerson, the fireplaces had gone unused, except by bats that occasionally colonized the chimneys and then had to be relocated.

That first day, after the mothers—and Donna Romano—had disappeared, the counselor and counselor-in-training (CIT) sat the campers in a circle to begin icebreaking exercises.

It was during these exercises that it became clear to Tracy that all the other girls in her cabin had known each other for years. They tossed catchphrases and gestures back and forth as if playing ball, buckling with laughter from time to time for reasons she couldn't discern. *Inside jokes*, Tracy thought—a term that terrorized her with its implication that anyone who didn't understand them was, by definition, an outsider.

The other revelation that came out of these exercises was that there was a definite hierarchy among Tracy's cabinmates.

At the top, of course, were Louise and Annabel, the counselor and the CIT. Both were beautiful in different ways: Louise, at twenty-three, seemed to be a woman already. She was short, much shorter than Tracy, with long dark hair and dark eyebrows and the bearing of an athlete. She was also—a word Tracy had learned earlier that year—*stacked*. Annabel was seventeen, tall, willowy, fair, a ballet dancer who moved with all the assurance of someone whose family had never had to worry about paying a bill. Tracy loved them both immediately. She had the weird desire to miniaturize them, to take them out and play with them like dolls.

Next came Balsam's campers, who ranged in status from the two Melissas—the clear rulers, wiry blond gymnasts from Manhattan's Upper East Side—to a girl named Kim, who had the habit of speaking, at length, on topics no one else seemed to care about.

Last in the line came Tracy, whose size, she believed, was already drawing stares from the others. Upon being asked to introduce herself, she found that her voice had been completely taken from her. A slow resignation settled in: this was what her summer would be like. She'd keep to herself. She'd speak to no one. She'd go unnoticed, hiding behind books whenever possible. Staying out of it. Blending in.

She unpacked the last of her belongings. From her toiletry kit she removed the new glasses she had been prescribed that year; these she placed at the back of the single drawer she'd been assigned. It would be better, she thought, not to see anything too clearly this summer.

Suddenly she was blinking hard. To cry now would be catastrophic— and yet the disappointment of it all weighed heavily on her shoulders. Because there was always a part of her—despite her understanding, cultivated over years of such disappointments, of where she would fall in any social hierarchy—there was always a part of her that hoped that this time would be different. That some graceful, lissome boy or girl would have the patience and acuity to pick Tracy out of a crowd, take notice of one of the positive qualities that she infrequently allowed herself to number: her sense of humor, or her drawing ability, or her singing voice, or her loyalty, her devotion to anyone who showed her even a modicum of interest.

Tugging her ill-fitting uniform shirt down over her ill-fitting uniform shorts, Tracy exhaled, releasing entirely the hope she had had for the summer.

At the opening campfire that night, Tracy looked on as a series of strange songs and rituals were performed at the bottom of a natural amphitheater, a little hill that led down to a patch of grassless land. On the hill, large split logs had been set up as rough benches, with an aisle down the center. The dark lake was just visible beyond.

A certain energy was appreciable in the air: it was the energy of teenage hormones, of sidelong glances, a taking note of who had changed over the past year, and in what ways. It wasn't just the campers, but the counselors, too. All over, they were sidling toward one another, whispering in each other's ears, making gestures Tracy could not understand. Each one of them, she would learn, was a celebrity in his or her way; campers strove earnestly to learn facts about them, about their home lives and romantic prospects and heartbreaks; these facts were then traded eagerly as whispers in the dark.

In front of them, the presentations continued. Several counselors performed a ritual that involved the chopping of a log; announcements were made about new policies, facilities, events.

Then came skits. One—a dramatic enactment of the rule that had made such an impression on Tracy earlier—involved a large male

counselor affecting the voice and gait of a small child and walking
around and around the campfire to illustrate his confusion.

"I thought I knew where I was going," said the counselor, projecting
his voice with aplomb, "but it turns out I did not!"

And a female counselor strode forward to goad the crowd.

"What should Calvin do?" she asked mock-seriously. She placed her
hands on her cheeks.

When lost, yelled the crowd, in chorus, sit down and yell.

"Help!" said Calvin. "I need help!" He checked an invisible watch.
"One minute has gone by," he exclaimed, "so I guess I should yell
again!"

The reason for this was provided: an attempt to extract oneself from
the woods could lead to disorientation, could pull even an experienced
woodsman irretrievably into the Adirondack forest. The terrain was
dense, with thick underbrush; when the trail was no longer in sight,
it all looked the same.

"Sixty-five percent of people," said Calvin, "are less than twenty
feet from a trail when they first begin to feel disoriented."

Tracy listened, fascinated. She imagined the pull of the woods, the
cool, shadowy smell of them, the velvet of moss on rock—and then
the gradual realization that she'd lost her bearings. The slow horror
of accepting her predicament.

In between skits, the male counselors roughhoused with one another,
with their charges. Called out to girls across the semicircle. Kevin
thinks you're a fox!

Then a tall, thin woman strode right into the center of things. She
stood in front of the fire, silhouetted by the flames, looking something
like the way Tracy had always pictured Ichabod Crane.

Everyone fell silent.

"Welcome," said the woman. She introduced herself to newcomers:
she was the camp director, T.J., and everyone was invited to call her
that.

Her age was difficult to discern. At some angles, she looked very
young—in her twenties, maybe—but her voice bore a gravelly authority,
something Tracy wasn't used to hearing in women her age. Everyone
stopped and listened, even the loud male counselors, who otherwise
hadn't shut up.

The woman—T.J.—took out a piece of paper that seemed to have reminders on it.

She went through them, one by one.

She emphasized and elaborated upon the same rules from earlier. Dispensed a few others, as well: any camper caught outside his or her cabin after curfew would be given one warning and commissary duty for two nights. A second infraction would lead to dismissal from camp.

She paused then, looking up.

Above her, the pine branches were lit orange by the fire. Beyond them, the sky was as black as Tracy had ever seen it, and as full of stars.

"Another thing," said T.J. "Due to the concern of certain parents, this year's Survival Trip will look a little different."

A collective groan.

T.J. held up a hand. "Now listen," she said. "You'll still be on your own, in groups. You'll all be responsible for your own well-being. The only difference is, you'll have a counselor nearby for those three nights. But they'll stay about a hundred yards away, unless there's an emergency you can't resolve yourselves."

Silence. And then a solitary voice—male—booed loudly. The rest of the group laughed.

Tracy waited, breath held, to see what T.J. would do. She didn't look like someone who suffered fools gladly. But she grinned.

"I don't like it either," she said. "Trust me."

That night, after lights-out, Tracy lay in her bed, looking up into darkness, listening first to silence and then to the low sound of stories told in whispers and laughs.

She was alone. She would remain so. Her only job, she told herself, was to make it through the summer.

Louise

June 1975

In the dark, Louise held her breath, listening. On the other side of the partition: small wet sniffles. Somebody crying and trying to hide it. This happened every session, on night one.

Louise sat up in bed. Tiptoed past Annabel. Drew aside the curtain. Scanned the room, looking at every camper in turn.

Tracy.

There were Tracy's eyeballs, glinting in the moonlight, returning her gaze.

Outside, on the steps leading down from the porch, Tracy now sat next to Louise, trying to make herself small. She tucked the nightgown down over her knees. Wrapped her elbows around them, too. She looked, Louise thought, like a large six-year-old.

Again, she sniffed.

"Do you want to talk about it?" asked Louise. Her standard opening—one she'd devised over all four summers—one that left no room for insistence that everything was fine.

The girl shrugged. Embarrassed.

Earlier, at dinner, and then at the campfire that followed, Tracy had seated herself at the end of everything, and then hadn't said a word. She kept her gaze down. Upon returning to the cabin, she had read a book while the other girls talked, shrieked, ran chaotically about the room, bouncing off every surface like electrons. There was a particular brand of humor employed by twelve- and thirteen-year-old girls, especially when they weren't in the presence of boys: it was at once disgusting and innocent, bawdy and naive. When it wasn't being used for ill—when no one was its target—this type of humor delighted Louise. From the wall, she watched them quietly, fondly, recalling what it was like to be in this moment of life that was like a breath before speech, a last sweet pause before some great unveiling.

"Did someone say something to you?" Louise asked the girl gently.
"Are you upset?"

The girl shook her head. "I got scared," she said. Almost impercep-
tibly, she inched closer to Louise, who put her arm out, encircling the
girl as well as she could.

"What about?" said Louise.

"We were telling stories," said the girl. There was pathos in the
phrasing. *We*, thought Louise. Not *they*. A wistful bid for inclusion.

"What about?"

She paused. In the moonlight, Louise could make out only the outline
of the girl's face.

She said something then, so quietly that Louise couldn't make it
out. She angled her head sideways.

"*Slitter*," the girl whispered, and then looked around quickly. Afraid
of who else might have heard.

Of course it was Slitter.

Louise almost smiled in relief. This was one of a half-dozen stories
that passed down from one generation of campers to another, sometimes as a prank, sometimes as a warning. The extent to which each
camper believed in their veracity was often unclear. Some told them
with a smirk, happy to instill fear in others; some told them tremu-
lously, wanting to unburden themselves of the horrible knowledge they
had acquired. T.J. had actually addressed the issue at training that
year: the little ones, she said, get so scared. Let's head off the ghost
stories, please.

There were several that fit the description: Old Jones, the ghost of
an Adirondack guide who rattled the cabin windows at night; Scary
Mary, purportedly the jilted wife of a Van Laar ancestor from several
generations back.

But Slitter—or Jacob Sluiter, the actual spelling of his name—was
no ghost. He was a man, still alive, as far as Louise knew. Still haunting
the imaginations of her campers, year after year. The rumors about
him—and his rumored connection to the Van Laar Preserve—were the
most persistent of all of the stories she'd heard.

"You don't have to worry about him," said Louise. "He's in a jail
cell. About two hundred miles away."

But Tracy shook her head quickly.

"He's not," she said. "He escaped."

"I don't think so," said Louise.

"He did," said Tracy. "T.J. said so. She said it to one of the counselors from Spruce. And the counselor told the CIT, and the CIT told Caroline."

Louise paused, unconvinced. For one thing, T.J. would have told her, Louise, first, if this was true. Wouldn't she have? Unless she hadn't had a chance to.

Louise smiled at the girl. "Even if that's true," she said, "he'd have a pretty long way to travel before he reached this area. And I don't see why he'd want to."

"I heard them telling stories," Tracy said. She pulled her knees in closer. "The other girls."

"Those old stories have been around a long time," Louise said. "Doesn't mean they're true."

Tracy wouldn't hear it. She was shaking her head now, imploring Louise to listen. *They were talking about the boy,* she whispered.

Louise paused.

She knew what boy. There was no need to say his name.

Louise

L ouise is running.

On most days, this motion—legs pumping, arms pumping, head and neck erect—feels correct to her: her natural state. Her daily runs on the grounds of the Preserve constitute the only times in her life when she is fully at ease, when her worries are, just for a moment, stayed. She was a sprinter in high school, but she likes running distances better. On long runs she thinks of her body as somehow the mother of her brain—or the way a mother should be, anyway. The way other people's mothers are.

Today's run is different.

Today Louise runs frantically, unseeingly. She trips over the ground. Rights herself. She ignores a counselor who calls out to her from across the lawn. "Fine, forget you!" says the counselor—good-natured, oblivious. Louise doesn't look back.

Already, she has searched in the following places for Barbara: the latrines, the commissary, the community room, the beach. Already, she has checked the nurse's office and the boathouse. She has gone up to the main house, where a sympathetic maid prowled the corridors for ten minutes while Louise waited outside. But Barbara has not been in any of these places, and no one Louise has spoken with has seen her this morning.

When she reaches the Director's Cabin, she pounds on the door. Waits thirty seconds. Pounds again.

She's home, Louise knows. T.J. is a woman who strictly adheres to her routine, whose mornings are always the same. At 6:30, she plays reveille over the public address system, signaling to campers that the moment has come to wake up and get to the showers. And at 8:05 she emerges and walks to the commissary, catching the end of breakfast, inspecting the ranks.

Louise checks her watch: 6:40 a.m. In twenty minutes, the campers will be walking to the commissary for breakfast.

Still no answer. She places her palm on the door handle. Depresses the latch. Except for the bathroom stalls, there are no locks at Camp Emerson. Still, it feels wrong to enter the Director's Cabin (in which T.J. lives year-round—in which she grew up, no less) without an invitation to do so, despite the fact that Louise knows T.J. in a way that feels different from the other counselors. Shares a history with her that she keeps hidden from everyone else on the grounds.

At last, Louise swings open the door. She has to.

"Hello?" she calls. Steps into the wood-paneled living room, which doubles as the camp's main office. A desk faces a window in the front wall; two small chairs opposite hold a permanent place for campers in need of a talking-to.

Louise has spent hours and hours in this room. On one occasion, a whole cold January week.

Louise listens. The house smells like T.J.: the camphor and tar of her homemade blackfly repellent; beneath it, the iron and musk of her sweat.

From the back of the house, she can hear the shower running.

She puts a hand to her face, wiping sweat from her brow, from her upper lip. She doesn't know what to do next. To wait for T.J. to finish her shower feels incorrect. To pick up the phone and call anyone without T.J.'s guidance feels similarly wrong. Who would she call, anyway? The police? The volunteer fire department? God forbid—the Van Laars themselves? She can see the telephone across the room on T.J.'s desk—the only one on the camp's premises. The other one in the vicinity is in the main house. Self-Reliance.

Louise tiptoes down the hall toward the bathroom. The door is open. T.J.'s clothes are in a pile on the floor.

She pauses outside it. Should she call out more loudly?

Too late: one high metal squeak, the turning of a knob. The shower goes off. Abruptly, the curtain flies open—and there is T.J., and her short wet hair, and her lean torso, and her small breasts, and the farmer's tan she sports all summer.

Louise whirls on her heel, but it's too late. They've already locked eyes.

"I'm so sorry," says Louise, at the same time that T.J. lets out a holler.

"What'n the *hell*, Louise," says T.J., after she catches her breath.

"I'm so sorry," Louise says, again and again. She walks back down the hall, still saying it.

Behind her, she hears T.J. opening drawers.

"What are you doing in here?" calls T.J.

Louise clears her throat. "It's about Barbara Van Laar," she says.

"What about her?"

"She wasn't in her bunk this morning."

For what feels like a minute: silence.

Then T.J.'s footsteps in the hallway. She enters the office, clothed.

"She's got a bunkmate, right? Did she notice Barbara leaving?"

"She says she didn't hear anything. Slept through it."

There is a good chance, Louise knows, that T.J. will hold Louise accountable. Because a counselor's job is to hear things: the cruel words spoken by one camper to another. A clap of thunder in the distance: everyone out of the lake.

The screen door—most important. The screen door as it swings open in the night.

Louise waits for T.J. to say something. Anything. At last, she speaks.

"But you were in the cabin last night," says T.J. "You and Annabel. Right?"

If Louise hesitates, it is only to breathe in. She's been expecting this question. She's prepared.

"Yes," she says swiftly.

"You're sure," says T.J. "You and Annabel both."

"Both of us," says Louise.

She is not a habitual liar, but she is a practical one. It has been necessary for Louise to lie periodically throughout her life. A matter of survival. Still, it never feels good: especially when she's lying to someone she respects. Someone like T.J. Hewitt—to whom she has confessed, on several occasions, certain things that she has never told another soul. To lie to her now gives Louise a sick feeling in her stomach.

But if T.J. is onto her, she doesn't reveal that now. Instead, she shifts her attention away from Louise, and to the public address system that sits on and under her desk.

She strides across the room. Lifts the microphone. Turns on the system.

"All cabins," she says. "Please send one counselor to the Director's Office. CITs, you're in charge for the morning."

She switches the system off, turns her back to Louise for a moment. Without pivoting, she asks: "Have you seen him this week?"

John Paul, she means. Louise knows this without asking.

For a second time this morning, she lies to T.J.

"No."

Tracy

The arrival of Barbara Van Laar at Camp Emerson was met mainly with silence. There was silence as the Van Laars' black town car rolled slowly up the driveway and then across the lawn, conducted by a driver; silence as the girl herself, Barbara, traveled the half mile from the main house on foot, apparently having refused to ride alongside her own possessions.

She came into view at 8:05 a.m., just as breakfast in the commissary was letting out. She saluted unsmilingly as she passed the exiting campers, who bumped into one another as they strained to get a look. She was wearing clothing the likes of which many of them had never seen: cutoff jean shorts that barely covered her bottom, and beneath them black stockings with intentional-looking runs in them, and black army boots, and a T-shirt with a word on it that none of them could quite make out, but presumed to be something rude. Her hair was artificially black, and cut into a stringy bob that ended just below her jaw, and her lips were painted red, and her eyes were rimmed in charcoal. Most surprising were the silver spikes—more than one—that adorned each earlobe, along with what appeared to be a dog collar encircling her neck, and two black leather cuffs on her wrists.

Barbara's inaugural walk across the lawn would be discussed for months afterward: it was the first time any of the campers had seen her in the flesh, though she'd been talked about for years. Most of the conversation centered on her appearance and attire, which was, to most of Camp Emerson, a shock. The only campers who knew what to call her were the Manhattanites, who used a word that the rest of them had never heard.

Punk.

Any other camper who arrived in Barbara's clothing would have been immediately shuttled to the bottom of the social heap, met with incredulity or ignored entirely. But Barbara Van Laar was too interesting to ignore, her personal history too intriguing and complex. Though no one said it aloud, the goal of every camper on the grounds was to befriend her.

The next time they caught sight of Barbara, she was being led by Louise toward the little beach that bordered Lake Joan, where the residents of several cabins, including Tracy's, were waiting to take their swim tests. Out of the clothes she'd arrived in, Barbara looked younger.

A long metal dock, T-shaped and warmed by the sun, jutted out from the beach. The swimming instructor, a tall blond Atlas named Mitchell, led the first cabin out to the end of it.

"On my count," said Mitchell. And then, on three, the younger campers from Spruce plunged into the water, shrieking when they surfaced.

"Rule number one," said Mitchell. "No screaming unless you're in danger."

Tracy stood at the edge of the group, uncomfortable in her bathing suit, a towel wrapped tightly around her waist. She had been at camp less than twenty-four hours, but it had not escaped her that the other campers in Balsam—consciously or not—habitually placed some phys- ical distance between themselves and her.

Barbara and Louise, by that point, had reached the end of the dock.

"Mitch," said Louise, and then she said it again, louder. "Can I interrupt for a second?"

Everyone turned to look.

"This is Barbara," said Louise. "She'll be with us in Balsam this session."

Louise gestured in the direction of Tracy's group. "Those girls over there are your cabinmates. Wave, Balsam."

Dutifully, they did. Barbara held up a hand, and then wove her way through the campers, inserting herself precisely into the gap next to Tracy. She gazed straight ahead, then, toward the lake—pretending, apparently, that she was not the focal point of everyone nearby.

In her peripheral vision, Tracy could see Barbara wasn't *pretty*, exactly, but there was something appealing about her, something confident and mature. She stood with her hands on her hips, feet slightly apart, very still, her posture upright. She didn't fidget or slouch. It made Tracy straighten.

Before she could look away, Barbara turned her head sharply in Tracy's direction, meeting her gaze. But it wasn't annoyance that registered on her face, or disgust. No: in the split second they locked eyes, Barbara looked unmistakably amused.

"Balsam," said Mitchell. "You ready?"

Tracy removed the towel around her waist with reluctance.

On Mitchell's count, the group of them plunged in.

Their task was to swim to a buoy fifty yards away and then turn back. As they swam, Mitchell watched them, assessing their form and speed, making notes.

Tracy was a decent swimmer: years of lessons at the Y made her so. Had she pushed herself to her limit, she might have been toward the front. But she would not have been first. That title belonged to Barbara, who swam so gracefully and fast that she was out, and toweling off, before the second-place finisher touched the dock.

"Hey, speed racer," said Mitchell, impressed.

Barbara said nothing in response. She dried herself, all business. Slicked back the hair and bangs that clung to the sides of her face.

At lunch, Tracy placed herself at the end of the table, as she had done for each of the meals she had taken at Camp Emerson so far. And as usual, the rest of the girls clustered together, away from her. But a moment later, to Tracy's surprise, Barbara Van Laar deposited her tray directly across from her, and sat down. Immediately, the table's attention shifted.

Barbara was wearing her red lipstick again—either she'd smuggled it in, or special exceptions were being made for her already—and her bright mouth as she bit into and chewed her food functioned, to Tracy's eyes, something like a fishing lure.

"What?" asked Barbara—the first word Tracy had heard her speak. Her voice was low, quiet; behind it there was the same note of amusement Tracy had noticed in her earlier gaze.

"I like your—" Tracy said, and then she closed her mouth. Don't be weird, she instructed herself.

"My what?" asked Barbara.

Tracy hesitated.

"My lipstick? Borrow it," said Barbara.

"Are we allowed?"

"Are we not allowed?" said Barbara.

Tracy considered this. "I think we're only allowed to put it on for dances," she said. "That's what they told us at orientation."

Barbara shrugged. "I wasn't at orientation," she said. "If someone wants to say something to me, they can."

"Why did you miss it?" Tracy asked her.

"My parents," said Barbara. "They forgot to sign me up for camp."

Tracy nodded. This she could relate to: the feeling of being forgotten. To her right, she could sense the rest of Balsam leaning toward them, straining to catch what they were saying.

That—their second full day of camp—marked the start of what would become their normal routine.

Each day, they woke at 6:30, to the reveille played over the speakers. They showered.

At seven, they made their way to the commissary for breakfast; at 8:30 they gathered by the flagpole for flag-raising and opening assembly.

After that they had swim lessons, and first elective, and lunch, and second elective, and free period, and dinner, and, usually, some scheduled evening program.

Twice a week, in place of one of their electives, they had Survival Classes, led by T.J. Hewitt herself. In them they learned to build shelters, forage for food, and build spears with which to fish. They learned how to find or make potable water, and how to build traps for small animals, which they also learned to skin and cook.

These classes were the heart of Camp Emerson: the reason it had been founded in the first place, the campers were told. They were also important training for a tradition that occurred toward the end of each summer—the one for which Camp Emerson was most famous.

The original name of the tradition was the Solo Trip. In the earliest years of Camp Emerson, when Peter Van Laar I still reigned from the house at the top of the hill, all campers were sent into the woods alone for three nights with nothing but their wits to keep them alive. No camper had ever died, but stories of parched and emaciated children staggering out of the woods had been passed down through the decades. By the time of Tracy's tenure at Camp Emerson, the Solo Trip had become the Survival Trip. Thanks to the intervention of a new generation of concerned parents, campers were now sent off in small groups. And this year, as T.J. had explained, those small groups would be chaperoned by a counselor.

For these classes, campers were divided not by cabin but by Survival Group—each of which consisted of approximately twelve campers. Groups were carefully constructed to include no more than two campers from any cabin or age group, designed to allow older campers to mentor younger ones.

Tracy's Survival Group met, for the first time, on her fourth day at camp. They'd been told to meet at the flagpole, where T.J. Hewitt would be waiting for them. And there she was, when they arrived: silent and fierce-looking, uninclined to make small talk of any kind.

Tracy was pleasantly surprised to find that her group included Barbara Van Laar, who nodded to her when their eyes met, but otherwise stood as silently as their instructor.

The last person to arrive was a boy—fourteen, perhaps. One of the oldest campers on the grounds. Immediately, Tracy reddened. This, she thought, was the most beautiful person she had ever seen in her life.

He was tall, and wore a shell necklace around his neck, and his skin had, in early summer, already acquired the kind of tan that wouldn't ever be possible for Tracy to achieve. His hair was long—to his shoulders, almost—and on his feet he wore huaraches, though they'd gone out of fashion several summers before. Like the rest of the campers, he wore a uniform; but his accessories convinced Tracy that his regular attire was most likely bohemian, a style Tracy associated with the previous decade.

"Tracy?" someone was saying. T.J. Hewitt was looking down at her clipboard, taking attendance. "Is Tracy not here?" said T.J., her pencil poised to strike out Tracy's name.

"Here," said Tracy quickly—forcing her gaze away from the boy in question, who stood across from her in the little group around the flagpole.

In doing so, she caught the eye of Barbara Van Laar—who wiggled her eyebrows up and down. She burned.

"All right," said T.J. "That's everyone."

Then she set off abruptly in the direction of the woods, where they spent the next hour learning how to orient themselves. By the end of the hour, all of them understood the basics of navigation with a compass, or with the sun.

If both of those techniques failed, concluded T.J., the most important thing was not to panic.

For a bonus, she asked them: Who knew the origins of the word?

"Which word?" someone said.

"*Panic*," said T.J. But no one raised a hand.

She explained. It came from the Greek god Pan: the god of the woods. He liked to trick people, to confuse and disorient them until they lost their bearings, and their minds.

To panic, said T.J., was to make an enemy of the forest. To stay calm was to be its friend.

When the day's lesson was over, Tracy set off on a slow walk back to her cabin. She was moving in a languorous daze, bewitched by T.J.'s words, and also by Lowell Cargill—the name of the boy, she had learned. She was so distracted, in fact, that she didn't notice who was at her side until they were halfway to Balsam.

When she finally looked to her left, she saw that Barbara Van Laar was keeping pace with her, watching her, a sort of half smile playing on her face.

"What," said Tracy—ready to be teased.

Barbara shook her head. "Nothing."

Tracy looked straight ahead. She was interested in Barbara in the same way that everyone at Camp Emerson seemed to be. But she was certain she had nothing to offer her: no stories in her past, no social cachet. She had divorced parents, yes, but loads of the other girls did too. She couldn't imagine that Barbara would want to talk to her. And yet there she was, Barbara Van Laar, walking right alongside her, bouncing on her toes, clapping her hands every so often as she swung her arms ahead of her, as if keeping time to a song in her head.

"He's cute," said Barbara, after they had walked in silence for a while. "Don't you think?"

"Who is?" said Tracy.

Barbara laughed. Rolled her eyes. Tucked her hair behind her ears.

"Pretty sure you know," said Barbara. "But if you don't want to talk, that's fine."

I do, Tracy thought. But her words, as usual, failed her.

On her second night at Camp Emerson, she had heard—overheard—something she didn't quite understand. It was, she believed, about Barbara.

She'd been trailing two of her bunkmates back from the latrines.

"Isn't it awful," Caroline had whispered. "To be a—*replacement* for your older brother."

Tracy widened her eyes in the dark. What a truly terrible thing to say, she thought. And Amy must have agreed with her, because she replied, "*Caroline*," in a tone that bordered on shock.

"What?" said Caroline, growing bolder. "I'm only saying what I think."

"Do *you* think he's cute?" Tracy said now. It was the best question she could come up with. And Barbara shrugged.

"I guess so," she said. "If you like the artsy type."

"What type do you like?" Tracy asked.

"I don't know," said Barbara. "I don't really think about that stuff anymore."

Tracy nodded. She wasn't certain what Barbara meant, and she was too embarrassed to ask.

"I've got a boyfriend now," said Barbara. An explanation. Then there was no time to say anything further, for the two of them had reached the porch.

Louise

Two Months Later
August 1975

At 7:00 a.m., the search for Barbara begins.
While they wait for the counselors to arrive, following T.J.'s request over the intercom, T.J. sits in her living room, on a brown love seat so old that it's swaybacked in the middle. She keeps her head down. Imagining, no doubt, a particular scene: revealing to the Van Laars that their daughter has gone missing while in her care.

Louise stands awkwardly nearby—feeling somehow that it wouldn't be right to sit. That she doesn't deserve to.

"What's she been like this session?" T.J. asks. "Happy?"

"Oh," says Louise. "Yeah, I guess she was. Is. Everyone likes her. Admires her, I think."

"She never said anything that made you think she might run off?"

Louise shakes her head.

The truth is—and she doesn't know how to say it—Barbara has never actually seemed to need her, or to look up to her in the way the other girls have. She has always struck Louise almost as a peer. They like each other, but they are not close; over the last two months, Barbara has never made a confession to her, or sought her advice on a friendship or a crush—something that happens at least once a session, usually more, with all the other campers she's ever had.

"Who's she close with?" T.J. asks. Reading her mind.

"Her bunkmate. Tracy."

T.J. pauses for a moment, thinking. "They were paired for the Survival Trip. They shared a tent."

Louise nods.

"We should find Tracy. We need to talk to her too."

A knock at the door. The first counselors, arriving.

Through the front window, Louise can see groups of CITs and campers moving slowly past T.J.'s office toward the commissary for breakfast, dragging their feet as they strain to catch a glimpse of what's going on inside. Everyone must know that something's wrong.

There are fourteen cabins, fourteen counselors, fourteen CITs, meaning the room is crowded once everyone has arrived. T.J. stands up on the seat of the small sofa she's been sitting on to get a better view. She begins.

"Barbara Van Laar was not in her cabin this morning," says T.J. There is no need to say *A camper from Balsam* or *Louise's camper.* Everyone here knows who she is.

"In a moment," she continues, "I'm going to give each of you an assigned location. We'll spread out over the grounds and do a high-speed search for her. See if we can find her ourselves. No need to frighten the family unnecessarily. But first," says T.J., "is there anything I need to know?"

The counselors are silent. They shift a little, looking around to see if any of them will speak.

"Anything happen overnight?" says T.J.

This is the moment, Louise knows, when any of them might snitch— might say something about seeing Annabel in the woods last night, drunk; say something about Louise's nightly outings to be with other counselors. But no one does. Everyone, Louise knows, is hoping that this is all a misunderstanding with an easy fix.

T.J. tries a different tack. "Anyone aware of any—relationships Barbara might have formed while she was here?"

"One of my kids had a crush on her," says a counselor named Davey. He's a nice boy with glasses who once, embarrassingly, wrote a song called "Louise" and played it in front of a group at the Clearing when everyone was wasted. No one has mentioned it since.

"You think they were together?" said T.J.

Davey shakes his head. "No, I think he just liked her. He got ribbed for it. But I know he asked her to last night's dance. And she said no."

T.J. nods.

"I'll go talk to him after this," she says. "Anyone else?"

Silence.

"All right," she says. And gives them the plan.

*   *   *

T.J. herself, after speaking with Davey's camper, will walk up to the main house, Self-Reliance, to give it a thorough search—beyond what Louise did earlier. The rest of them are given assignments that cover the camp and its environs. Seven of the counselors have been given cabins and buildings; the other seven the nearby woods. All of them have been instructed to blow the whistles they keep around their necks all summer in a pattern of two threes—T.J. demonstrates on her whistle, quietly—if Barbara is located.

And if they learn something else, or see something else—a clue, or anything suspicious—they are to blow their whistles in four twos. And T.J. alone will come to them.

"Any questions?" T.J. asks.

A counselor called Sam raises his hand. He's new this summer. He's just finished high school and is heading off to college in the fall, making him one of the youngest counselors on the grounds.

"Was her brother a camper?" he asks. "The Van Laar boy?"

A shocked silence. Louise isn't entirely certain why, but there is a universal understanding at Camp Emerson that Bear Van Laar should be spoken of only in whispers. And certainly never mentioned to T.J., who knew him, who was said to be close with him.

Louise is probably the only counselor who remembers his disappearance well. She was nine, just a year older than Bear, when it happened. She'd never met him, but she remembers every single resident of Shattuck—her hometown, five miles from the Van Laar Preserve, and the source of all of its staff—participating in the search.

T.J.'s expression changes for a moment. Something passes over her face that Louise can't identify. She fears it's anger. Braces for impact. T.J. rarely raises her voice, but when she does she is frightening to behold.

Instead, she speaks gently. "No," she says. "No, Bear was never a camper here."

Some of the counselors are glaring openly at Sam, who looks confused. Uncertain what he's done.

"All right," says T.J. "Get going."

Louise has been assigned to the Staff Quarters.

On the way she passes the trail toward the lake. Decides, instinctively, to turn down it.

Here is Lake Joan: named, she has been told, for the wife of an English settler. She scans the opposite shore, watching for movement; and while she looks, she ranks her worries.

The most pressing one is Barbara Van Laar, and where she has gone, and whether she is safe.

Next comes the worry of John Paul, and his whereabouts at this moment, and how likely he is to come to her—Louise. To punish her in some way, as he has done in the past.

Then there is the worry of being let go from this job. The worry of where she will live, if that happens.

Back to Shattuck, she thinks. To the house she grew up in. Back with her mother—whose behavior has become, in recent years, something untenable—and her younger brother Jesse, eleven years old, whom Louise loves like her own child, whose sweet disposition cannot possibly withstand for much longer the constant parries of their mother at her worst. Lately, Jesse has shown worrying signs of an inability to learn anything at all in school, and this is her fourth worry. Louise dreams often of rescuing him, bringing him to live with her, raising him on her own: a goal she hopes to realize before another year goes by.

If she were to be let go from her job, she would have no option but to move home to Shattuck—despite the fact that her entire life, to this point, has consisted of one attempt after another to escape.

Growing up there, she tried to sideline herself, simply sit out the teenage politics that dominated life at the central high school. But she continually found herself entangled in tricky situations without meaning to be, and at last she resigned herself to the idea that in a place as small as Shattuck, no one was permitted to be invisible. Like everyone else in the township, she had certain marks in her favor and certain liabilities. She had the advantage of athleticism, and the disadvantage of extreme poorness. She had the advantage of intelligence, and the disadvantage of a mother who was constantly, notoriously drunk. But it was her unusual prettiness that set her apart, that shuttled her to a place of social notoriety without her consent, that caused a sort of unrest all around her that she generally wanted no part of.

If anyone bothered to ask her, back then, what she did want, she would have said: to listen to music, Zeppelin and the Dead most importantly, but also Procol Harum, and Joan Baez, and Joni Mitchell; to see George McGovern elected someday (now that Bobby Kennedy was dead and gone); to go into a line of work that would make a difference in the world; to meet a good man who took her seriously; to travel the country and the world. But nobody asked her, and so she kept these wishes quiet, writing them only in journals, summoning them to the forefront of her mind whenever a birthday or a well or a star presented her with a formal opportunity to make them known to the universe.

While she waited for these wishes to be realized, she focused on her studies. She was prized and uplifted by the central school, where she was the salutatorian of her graduating class. She got a full ride to Union College, with some help from a guidance counselor whose brother worked in admissions. But at Union she had struggled. Couldn't afford even her books. By the end of her first year, she'd dropped out.

The one lasting thing that came out of her education was a boyfriend—John Paul McLellan—one year above her, a philosophy major who'd grown up in Manhattan. He was different from any of the boys she'd grown up with, and although a lot of girls liked him, he was infatuated only with Louise, a fact he made known to others two weeks into her time on campus, as if staking a claim. His friends told her at a party, pointing across the room: *He's in love with you.* And there was John Paul, leaning against a wall with his arms crossed, laughing appreciatively at something someone was saying. Handsome in an understated way. He wore glasses, which Louise took as an outsized sign of responsibility and intelligence.

When she dropped out, he suggested that she take a job at the summer camp owned by his godparents.

"Camp Emerson," he had told her. "A couple hours up the Northway, on the Van Laar Preserve."

Louise had looked at him, startled. "I know it," she said.

That John Paul had never before mentioned his connection to the Preserve—despite the fact that Louise had spoken with some frequency about where she grew up—should not have surprised her. He never spoke much of his family; what she knew of them she had gleaned from casual remarks John Paul had made and from gossip she'd heard.

She knew he had a very Catholic father who came from money and had founded a law firm in Manhattan; she knew the McLellans were said to be close friends of the Bouvier family. Still, the fact that John Paul himself had not made the connection between Shattuck—just a few miles from the Preserve—and the summer home of his godparents was evidence to Louise that he listened very little to anything she said.

Because to Louise—to all the residents of Shattuck—the Van Laar Preserve occupied a place of importance in their lives that was simultaneously acknowledged and resented. Following the closure of Shattuck's paper mill, which had been for three generations the main employer in the town, the Preserve with its summer camp functioned as a sort of industry unto itself. It provided decent full- or part-time work to two dozen of the townspeople of Shattuck year-round; in the summer months, with the camp open, that number tripled.

It did not escape Louise that of this number none were counselors, a position seemingly reserved for wealthy alums of the camp, college students who wanted summer work that might also be a good time. All the Preserve employees Louise knew from Shattuck, meanwhile, occupied roles that required their hands, their bodies.

When John Paul suggested, therefore, that she apply for this particular job, Louise tried to express her concern in a way that made sense to him, that didn't provoke the annoyance he often displayed when she questioned his ideas, but—in typical fashion—he waved her off. He was practically *related* to the Van Laars, he reminded her. Mr. Van Laar was his godfather. Their fathers worked together: the Van Laars as the founders of the bank that had financed all of Albany and much of New York City, too; the McLellans as their legal representation. One day, John Paul said, he would take over the bank for both families. John Paul could easily get Louise a job at the camp, he said. All he had to do was ask.

That was four years ago. She has worked at Camp Emerson every summer since. She has never once met the Van Laars in person, despite John Paul's connection to them. They function as a distant presence on a hill to the north, frequently sighted local celebrities about whom the children and counselors of Camp Emerson speculate and gossip. The other three seasons of the year, she works at the Garnet Hill Lodge, a resort at the base of Gore Mountain, running programs for the children of guests who spend each day skiing or hiking, and most nights drinking in a smoky, upscale lounge. Throughout this period, she has somehow maintained a relationship with John Paul—who has finally finished his degree at Union, though it took him six years and two forgiving deans to do so. When they have seen each other, it has been in Schenectady during John Paul's semesters at college, or at the Garnet Hill Lodge, or—in summers—at the Van Laar Preserve, where he stays with his parents for a couple of weekends each season. During the first of these weekends she made the mistake of suggesting that he try to sneak her, Louise, inside of Self-Reliance, to sleep in a real bed for a night. In response, he looked at her as if she were stupid. "They're my hosts," he said. "I would never do something so rude." Instead, they had, and still have, uncomfortable sex in his car, in the parking area adjacent to Self-Reliance; or sometimes pressed up against a tree in the woods, or sometimes on a bed of pine needles on the forest floor. Louise is the one who remembers to bring the towel.

Sometimes, with a certain self-reproach, Louise asks herself why she has stayed with him all these years. What, after all, do they even have in common anymore? She feels more and more distant each year from the person she was when they met. Indeed, sometimes it shocks Louise to remember that she was ever a college student at all. Today, she thinks of her year at Union almost with embarrassment: another life, a youthful folly, a waste of time.

When she allows herself to be honest, the answer is queasily obvious: Louise has stayed with John Paul because he represents to her the possibility of a better life. For herself, yes; and also for her brother Jesse.

They're engaged, Louise reminds herself. They're getting a ring, even, as soon as John Paul gets a job. Someday, she tells herself, they'll have a house together. They'll have a comfortable bed. A big one, with too many pillows. They'll have two children. They'll have four bedrooms, and the extra one will be for Jesse, whom she will bring to live with them while he's still young enough for it to meaningfully alter the trajectory of his life, to prevent him from becoming angry, or depressed, or submerged in the beery haze that permanently afflicts most of the boys she grew up with.

For this future, she is prepared to wait. Because in the wake of John

Paul's graduation from Union, and before he joins the family business, the work he'll do "for the rest of his life"—a phrase he says with a sigh—John Paul has decided to take a year to travel, to visit friends in places as far-flung as Los Angeles and Vienna, and as close to Louise as the Van Laars' house at the top of the hill.

Indeed: for the past week John Paul has been staying with his family at Self-Reliance, for a long-planned celebration of the Preserve's one hundredth birthday. Embarrassingly, Louise allowed herself to look forward to his visit. Perhaps, she thought, the special occasion—and the length of his stay—meant that she'd at last be invited up to Self-Reliance, introduced to the elusive Van Laars, whom she'd otherwise only glimpsed in passing, as they drove by in their dark cars. Perhaps, on her one day off, she'd be asked up to the main house for cocktails, or dinner. Presented formally to the Van Laars and their guests as John Paul's fiancée.

But none of this has come to pass. As usual, Louise has seen him only twice: once on his first day on the premises, when he wandered down from a cocktail hour on the lawn, tipsy, and kissed Louise in front of her campers; and then once more last night, in the Clearing with Lee Towson, after she'd almost given up on seeing him at all.

She certainly hasn't seen John Paul's family, his mother and father and sister—who have introduced themselves anew, with polite detachment, each of the three times they have met Louise, and who seem to be operating under the assumption that John Paul will find someone more suitable to marry when the time is right. In the past, Louise has been able to reassure herself that John Paul has his own mind about things, almost to a fault; he has said to her repeatedly that one of the things he likes about her is that she's not like other girls he dated in the past. Girls his family has approved of.

But after last night, she sees the McLellans' assumption might prove to be correct. And a feeling of humiliation descends upon her. Four whole years sunk into a wish for a future that isn't meant to be.

On the bank of Lake Joan, a loon calls, sending chills down her spine. Louise, roused from her thoughts, sets off again.

According to her watch, it's 7:10 a.m. This, to Louise, is a relief: it means the Staff Quarters will be largely empty, since almost everyone who lives inside is a kitchen worker or a member of the grounds crew, and all of them are up and out before reveille every day. Louise is friends with many of them; she knows some of them from Shattuck.

But among them there is one person she doesn't want to see.

Lee Towson arrived at the start of the summer and immediately caused a stir. He was hired to work in the commissary as a prep chef and dishwasher. Traditionally, staff members don't mingle much with the counselors, but Lee was noticed straightaway. He is fine-looking and tall, with thickly lashed eyes and shoulder-length hair that he keeps tied in a low ponytail. He gives an impression of speed and lightness. Once, while waiting in line for her tray, Louise caught a glimpse of him juggling utensils at the rear of the kitchen. When he noticed her watching, he fumbled them. Pulled a face. Laughed at himself, with her.

She hasn't been the only one to take note of him, of course; all the counselors have, male and female alike. Early in the summer, he was issued an invitation—a command—to join the counselors at the Clearing, and ever since then he has been a regular presence. He is said to have grown up in Queensbury, not too far from the camp; another boy she knows from Shattuck has claimed him as a cousin. He is said to deal a little here and there. Other rumors about him include a stint as a roustabout for a traveling circus, a stint in jail for possession of controlled substances, and a habit of sleeping around. But Louise mistrusts gossip implicitly, having been the subject of many false rumors herself.

For the past two months, Lee and Louise have engaged in low-level flirtation at every turn. At the Clearing, jokes between them turn into hilarity quickly, Louise doubled over, unable to breathe. Small touches straddle the line between friendly and more. The warmth of his hand on her back, on her shoulder; once, briefly—after several beers—in a straight line downward, from where it had been on her shoulder to where it stopped, on her ribs, just beneath her right breast: a memory that sparks the kind of desire she has rarely felt in her life. She imagines his body beneath his clothes. She imagines him gazing upon her unclothed body, then reaching for it.

This desire, in truth, was what drove her out of her cabin last night.

Over and over again, Louise replays the events of the night in her mind: first her campers, all nine of them, heading in a line toward their cabin as Louise waved goodbye from the Great Hall. This would have been at eleven o'clock, or thereabouts. Annabel, too, turned and waved as she walked behind them.

Annabel, who was supposed to be in charge.

Next in Louise's memory: the warm night air, damp from an earlier storm; the walk to the Clearing, a small treeless patch just past the edge of the woods, a place that generations of counselors have outfitted with a stack of split logs and a firepit and turned into an after-curfew outdoor club; the pine branches, fat from rain, that doused her when she brushed against them; faint music from Lee Towson's guitar; faint smoke from a bonfire. Then the back of Lee's neck as he bent over the instrument, then the front of him as she rounded the fire, as he looked eagerly up at her, barefoot, his hair tucked behind his ears.

Where is everyone, said Louise, or Where'd everyone go, or something equally silly.

They both knew why they were there.

Louise settled onto a stump by the fire, several feet from where Lee was sitting. As she did so, she felt aware of where John Paul was in relation to them both: only a few hundred yards away, in one of the many guest rooms she had never seen at Self-Reliance. It was his last night on the property. After his first-day stroll down the hill to greet her, he had never returned. Each night, after her charges had gone to sleep, she had waited for him on the porch of Balsam. By the fourth night, she had grown angry. By the fifth, resigned. By last night—the sixth night that John Paul had been on the premises, the fifth he had not come to her—she had grown indifferent.

This was the night she had walked to the Clearing, where Lee Towson was waiting—apparently for her. And this was the night that John Paul had decided, at last, to go looking for Louise.

How he found the two of them in the Clearing, Louise still isn't certain. Perhaps he had heard Lee's guitar, or seen the small fire he'd built in the pit. Either way, at a certain moment Louise had spotted him standing between two trees, an apparition that startled her so much that she had yelped and clutched her chest, breathing hard.

"John Paul," said Louise. "You scared me."

She was prepared to make light of it, arranging her face in a smile, when Lee turned and John Paul lurched out of the woods in his direction. He was, Louise saw, drunk again. His face was arranged in an angry grin, and he swayed first to one side and then the other. Lee, light on his feet, rose quickly to face him.

For a moment, no one spoke.

And then they were on one another, John Paul the aggressor, but also the first to fall. In two quick swings Lee had him on the ground. He looked at Louise, almost in apology, as John Paul lay still beneath him. His glasses had been thrown from his face and now lay beside him on the ground. His eyes were open and unfocused. He blinked slowly.

"Boyfriend?" Lee said.

"Fiancé," said Louise, and immediately regretted it.

She had never once spoken of him to Lee, though she imagined he might have heard that she was dating someone.

"You need any help with him?" he asked.

"No," she said.

"I'll wait here," said Lee. "Make sure he's okay. You should go."

John Paul was making small hurt noises now, turning his head from side to side. He seemed at first to be laughing, and then Louise understood the sound was a cough. He sat up slowly, shook his head like a dog, sending blood from his nose in all directions. He felt for and then found his glasses, which looked bent. His right eye, too, was damaged in some way.

When he was fully upright, he pointed one finger in her direction.

"Whore," he said. The word was quiet, direct. She'd been called it before in her life. Once or twice by her own mother. Generally it did not faze her. But in front of Lee Towson, it stung.

"Yeah, sure," she said, or something like that. "Okay. Whatever you say." A half laugh, dismissive, a mutter, a roll of the eyes. The same things she's always said, and done, when called a hurtful name. She doesn't remember. Anything to show she doesn't care.

Last night, it worked. John Paul stared and then retreated, first walking then trotting. Back to Self-Reliance. Back to his mother and father and sister, who do not know Louise's name.

Next to her, Lee Towson shifted in place.

"Well," he said. "Guess I'd better get going."

She wanted to stop him, but her shame prevented her from speaking. Then she was alone.

The Staff Quarters are inside the only two-story building at Camp Emerson. It sits on the banks of Lake Joan, just south of the creek and the boys' cabins. Louise has never once been inside.

Now she ascends the steps to the interior. To her right, she's greeted with a long hallway and a line of doors, some standing open, others closed.

"Hello?" she calls.

Silence.

She begins to walk down the hallway. She stops at each open doorway, leaning in. She knocks at the closed doors; opens these too. Some rooms are neat, others chaotic. In all of them she detects the scent of men: their deodorant, their aftershave; beneath these trappings their sweat and shit and semen.

She's almost finished checking the second floor when she hears the creak of someone coming up the stairs.

She tenses. She feels fearful without knowing exactly why. She trusts everyone who works at this camp. Likes most of them, too, with the exception of a couple of counselors who seem more interested in partying than doing their jobs.

"Hello?" Louise says again, and at last the word is returned to her.

"Hello," says Lee Towson, emerging from the stairwell. "Hi."

He's bare-torsoed and tan. His golden hair is one-quarter damp. As always, she takes a moment to appreciate his physical form. He is the only man she's ever looked at in this way—the way she imagines she herself is appraised by others.

"What are you doing here?" says Louise. "Isn't it breakfast?"

"What are *you* doing here?"

"My camper's gone missing," says Louise. "We're searching the grounds."

"Which one? Not," says Lee, but he doesn't finish his sentence.

"Barbara."

"Shit."

Louise nods. And then, suddenly, without notice, her face crumples, her shoulders heave. She lets out a shuddering gasp.

"Oh no," says Lee, in genuine alarm. He comes to her, puts his arms around her. She turns her cheek, presses it into his bare chest. He is much taller than she is—most men are—and she feels engulfed by him in a way that normally makes her nervous. But this feels different: she feels safe here. Even through her tears she is aware of her body lighting up, pressing itself into him.

This is one of the few sheer pleasures Louise knows in life: the near-otherworldly feeling of touching another human's body with your own body in a way that, for the first time, transcends mere friendliness. These are the times in her life that Louise has felt most acutely the animal nature of her humanity, and therefore they have been the most comforting. To be a human is complex, and often painful; to be an animal is comfortingly simple and good.

After a moment they each step back.

"Where's your shirt?" says Louise, and he grins. "Maple syrup accident," he says. He extends an arm, showing her the balled-up cotton T-shirt he's been holding. Then he starts down the hallway, stops before a door.

"I have to keep searching," says Louise.

"I just need a new shirt," he says. "Then I'll help you."

"Don't they need you in the kitchen?"

"Breakfast is made," he says. "They'll be fine."

He opens the door to what must be his room. She follows. Lee nods toward the bed on the right—neatly made, Louise notices—and tells her to have a seat. He tosses his old shirt into a hamper. Pulls on a new one.

"How's your fiancé today?" says Lee, without looking in her direction. She can hear a certain emphasis on the word. Laughter underneath it.

"I don't know," says Louise. "Haven't talked to him."

Lee raises an eyebrow.

"Embarrassed, I guess," says Louise. "Probably has a shiner."

At this, Lee grins. Looks down at the ground, mock-penitent. "Sorry about that," he says.

"You shouldn't be. He had it coming."

Lee hesitates, deciding whether to say something. And then: "You know we know each other. Him and me, I mean."

Louise did not. Lee reads this on her face. Shrugs apologetically.

"How?" says Louise.

Lee clears his throat. Looks away. "I'm afraid," he says, "that I am unable to answer that question directly. On the grounds of client confidentiality."

She can read him. She wants to ask: *What was he buying from you?* A little grass would be fine. Psychedelics are out of the question—John Paul has no interest in those. It's cocaine she's afraid of. This is the drug John Paul likes best, and also—after a particularly bad episode between them—one he swore to her he would never use again.

But she won't ask Lee. It's too humiliating.

"You been together a long time?" he says.

"Four years," says Louise.

"You really gonna get married?"

This catches Louise off guard. "Maybe," she says.

"You know," says Lee, "you oughta mess around a little before you do. My advice."

He looks up at her slyly, his implication bare. She feels a low thud of want in her stomach.

"I have to go," she says—ashamed, suddenly, to be so distractible.

"You sure you don't want help? Finding Barbara?"

She hesitates. She does.

"I don't think T.J. would like it," says Louise. And somehow she knows that this is true.

He nods. "It'll be okay, Louise. She prob'ly just ran away," he says. "They'll find her soon. Or she'll come back. Don't you think?"

She considers this. It's what she wants to believe.

"You're probably right," says Louise.

Alice

A phone is sounding someplace in the house.

Alice opens an eye. Closes it. The sun is up; already, the house is growing warm.

"Someone get that," she says unconvincingly. Her throat is dry. Her skin, too. In her temples, a familiar throb begins.

Where is everyone? It's eight in the morning, according to the clock on the wall. Surely someone on staff should be here to answer. Alice closes her eyes.

A banging now—the door.

If their behavior last night was any indication, every guest on the grounds will be just as bad off as she is. Even Peter, who prides himself on his abstemiousness—who judges her, keeps a running count of every glass she has—even Peter was feeling his oats last night, telling long-winded stories in his odd formal way, tripping at one point over an upturned corner of carpet, cursing it in his wake.

The pounding on the door stops.

She turns her head to the window. And sees, striding down the lawn in the direction of the camp, T.J. Hewitt—the source of the urgent knocking, she imagines.

Barbara, she thinks. Barbara has no doubt done something wrong, something so egregious that even T.J.—her greatest ally—can no longer ignore it. From the time of Barbara's birth, T.J. has watched over the girl each summer like a guard dog, a faithful companion, always on duty, just out of sight. She should have been like family.

She wasn't.

Through the window, Alice watches until T.J. is out of sight, then closes her eyes again.

For a while, she falls into and out of a dream, feeling trapped inside her body on the bed. T.J., in the dream, is wearing a carrier she'd made one year out of rope and a curtain, something that she had fashioned to take then-baby Barbara on hikes. The two of them were a sight: teenage T.J., all sinew and frown; Barbara's round baby face beneath her chin, peering out at the world.

Where are you going? asks Alice, in the dream. *To find Bear*, says T.J.

Alice's eyes open abruptly.

Awake for the day, then. She rises.

Alice's bedroom is across the hall from the largest bedroom, which Peter, of course, sleeps in. She slept there too, at one time. Now she doesn't.

She shuffles past his door. It's standing slightly open, and she averts her eyes.

Down the hallway now, past the room presently occupied by Marnie McLellan, John Paul Sr. and Nancy's daughter. Past—*think it*—past Bear's room, once decorated in the trappings of young boyhood, everything blue, everything messy, wet bathing suits and towels forever in a pile on the floor. It's long since been done over. This week, it's occupied by the Southworths.

A short, windowed corridor connects the southern wing of the house, where the bedrooms are, with the great room at its center. As Alice passes through it, something outside catches her eye.

Two vehicles are approaching, moving slowly up the driveway, making a turn toward Camp Emerson. One is Shattuck Township's single fire truck, the property of the only volunteer fire department in a twenty-mile radius. The other is a yellow-and-blue Dodge: a statie.

Alice pauses, entranced, reminded of another day.

In the great room, the telephone begins again.

"Mrs. Van Laar?" the man says, on the phone. "Mrs. Van Laar?"

He is, he tells Alice, a sergeant from the state police.

"I've got some hard news to relay," he says.

Alice, receiver in hand, takes in her surroundings.

What do you see, Dr. Lewis would ask her, in moments like this one.

There's glass on the floor, she thinks. Damage from the party last night. There's a painting askew on the wall. There's glass on the floor, and a painting askew on the wall, and a bottle of wine on its side, and a large wine stain on the rug.

Alice breathes.

What else, Dr. Lewis would say. She can almost hear him saying it.

She looks out the window. It's sunny outside, she thinks. It's sunny outside, and there's light on the water, and a worker, in the garden, is pulling weeds.

"Mrs. Van Laar," says the man on the phone. In his voice is a note of fear. "Mrs. Van Laar, I regret to inform you that your daughter seems to be missing."

What do you smell, Dr. Lewis would ask her.

"Are you there," says the man on the phone. "Mrs. Van Laar, a squad is on its way. Are you there?"

I smell day-old alcohol, she thinks. I smell stale smoke from cigars and cigarettes. Underneath it all, a lemony smell—the wood polish used on the furniture.

"Are you there, Mrs. Van Laar?"

And hear? Dr. Lewis would ask her.

"Mrs. Van Laar?"

I hear a dial tone, Alice thinks. She places the receiver in its cradle. The sound goes away.

And now? Dr. Lewis would say.

Alice closes her eyes. If she tries very hard—if the wind blows right—she can sometimes hear the voices of children from Camp Emerson.

Sometimes, she can even hear Bear's.

What do you taste, Dr. Lewis would ask her.

I taste nothing.

Focus on your senses. Anchor yourself to the world. What do you taste?

Nothing, thinks Alice. I taste nothing.

Through the sliding glass doors that lead to the lakeside lawn, someone enters the great room. It's one of the two young cleaning girls they've hired from town, just for the week of the party. She pauses on the threshold, holding her mop and bucket in her hands, surveying the damage: the worst to date. She has not noticed Alice yet, and for this reason she allows herself to register on her face the disdain she clearly feels, to mutter something under her breath. *Disgusting*, perhaps, or *fucking. Fucking unbelievable.*

"Good morning," says Alice, and the girl snaps to attention, looking guilty.

"Morning, ma'am," she says, and sets her mop and bucket down, and begins a retreat to the north wing, presumably for more supplies.

"Did you not hear the phone, earlier?" Alice says. "Or the knocking?"

"No, ma'am," says the girl. "I was out the back, putting the laundry on the line."

Reluctantly, Alice jerks herself into action. She strides down the hallway, toward the bedroom where Peter is sleeping. She throws open the door, telling herself that she is unafraid of what—or whom—she'll see inside.

But it's only Peter in the bed, sleeping hard, one elbow crooked over his forehead, as if to block the light. She has not seen him in this way—asleep, or in a bed, or even supine—in a year. More.

She says his name aloud. Once, twice.

"What is it?" he mumbles, at last.

"It's Barbara," she says. "She's gone missing."

Alice

Following Barbara's departure for Camp Emerson, it had taken Alice nearly a week to notice the padlock on her daughter's bedroom door. Barbara's room was on the other wing of the house; Alice had no reason to pass it.

But after six days of sitting in the sunroom, or lying in her bed, she had begun at last to feel lonely. Peter was gone, too; to Manhattan, most likely, though she could never keep track. And in the absence of her daughter and husband, the house had gone quiet.

And so, that morning, propelled from her chair by sheer boredom, Alice had decided to take a walk.

Now she stood outside her daughter's room, holding the padlock in her hand, marveling at Barbara's boldness. Surely she must have understood how angry Peter would be when he returned from his trip to find the doorframe damaged by the screws that held the lock in place. More than the doorframe, he would be angered by the implication of the act: that Barbara had any right to privacy, after the way she had recently behaved.

The lock, Alice knew, would have to be removed. The doorframe would have to be carefully repaired: that much was certain. Peter noticed everything about the house.

One of the gardeners made quick work of the lock. Promised to relay a message to a skillful carpenter he knew who could probably fix or replace the damaged wood.

"Thank you," said Alice absently. But she was already willing him away.

She didn't want anyone watching her as she opened the door.

She smelled it before she saw it: fresh paint.

There, across one whole wall—the largest in the room—was some sort of—*mural*, Alice supposed, though she wouldn't have used such a dignified word to describe the terrible pictures that loomed over Barbara's bed.

The main motif was flags. A British one. An upside-down American. Then safety pins, axes, handcuffs, knives.

In one upper corner, a sun and a moon bearing human faces smiled and frowned at Alice.

So this, she thought, was what Barbara had been doing behind the door she'd kept closed for the better part of June. Blasting her terrible records and painting this terrible mural.

She had done this in Albany, too. She had painted her walls as a ten-year-old girl, but at least in that instance she had had the decency, the common sense, to ask Peter for permission. That mural was innocuous: a sun and clouds and mountains and what seemed to be Lake Joan.

This one was disturbing.

A surge of competing emotions rose inside Alice. One was fear: there would be hell to pay when Peter saw this. But some other emotion was present, too. And at last she realized, with a pang, that it was jealousy. Never once in Alice's life had she ever felt the freedom to do something like this. To simply decide—*I'm going to paint a mural today*—and then undertake the project.

In a little room off the wine cellar were all the supplies used to maintain the house. There, Alice searched through racks of paint for the color she had chosen, when Barbara was born, for the room that would be hers at Self-Reliance.

There it was: *Fawn Pink*.

A beautiful shade of light rose.

Returning to the scene of Barbara's crime with a roller and bucket in hand, Alice set to work.

By the time Peter returned from wherever he was, there would be no trace of the mural, or the lock.

Tracy

Their first week of Survival Classes had centered on orienting oneself in the woods. Their second week would center on keeping warm and sheltered.

T.J. Hewitt had led them to a quiet place in the forest. Now she stood still, hands on hips, one foot up on a root.

"What do you see?" she said.

Silence.

Then a younger girl raised her hand. "Trees?" she said.

Quiet laughter from the group; the girl reddened. She had not meant the answer to be funny.

But T.J. pressed on. "Very good," she said. "What else?"

Rocks, they said. *A boulder. Leaves. Pine needles. Dirt. Branches.*

T.J. nodded. "All of these can be used in an emergency to keep you warm. The woods can be dangerous, but the woods are also generous in that way."

She turned abruptly and walked ten feet in the direction of one of the shorter trees in her vicinity.

"This," said T.J., "is a balsam fir. It's one of the denser trees nearby, with nice thick foliage, and also one of the younger ones. See how it's shorter than its neighbors? This means that its lower branches will form a nice shelter for you in the rain or snow, or even the cold."

T.J. demonstrated: she angled her long body beneath the lowest branches of the tree, lying in a C shape around the trunk.

"I could stay here for the length of a passing storm," said T.J. "But if I wanted to stay for longer than that, I'd have to get creative."

And she continued, discussing how to build makeshift walls, sending the campers off in different directions to locate fallen conifer branches.

Tracy was paying only partial attention. The blackflies were at their peak, and all the people nearby were waving at their faces with increasing desperation. Aside from that, two extremely distracting figures were tugging at her gaze: Barbara Van Laar, on her left; and Lowell Cargill, standing opposite her.

Lowell was swaying to his right and left, arms crossed around his middle, listening intently and respectfully to T.J.'s every word, seemingly impervious to flies and heat and boredom.

It made him even more attractive.

That evening, Tracy sat on her bed with her journal in her hands, writing. This was how she spent her time on nights when they had no other scheduled activity.

Most of her cabinmates had chosen a different pursuit. Until lights-out at ten o'clock, they were permitted to roam from cabin to cabin, so long as they remained on the porches. Usually, they found their way to the porch of Pine, the cabin on the other side of the stream, where the oldest boys were housed.

The only other camper who had also stayed behind was Barbara—who, on several occasions over the past week, had tried to strike up conversations with Tracy. But each time, Tracy had stumbled, tongue-tied, unable to produce appropriate responses.

Now—the night after their first lesson on finding shelter in the woods—Tracy was writing sentences and questions in her journal. Something she could read aloud to Barbara: this felt more possible than unscripted speech.

"Barbara," said Tracy.

From the bunk above, a stirring.

"Yes?" said Barbara.

"I was wondering how you're liking camp."

A pause. "Oh," said Barbara. "It's all right, I guess."

"What's your favorite part about it?" Tracy asked.

"The food," said Barbara unswervingly. "I like being able to eat as much as I want."

The next line in her script read: *That's interesting. Mine is being in nature.* But Barbara's reply was so heartfelt, and mirrored her own emotions so precisely, that Tracy said, "Me too."

Before she could continue, Barbara's head popped down from the upper bunk and into the space between. Tracy slammed her journal shut—too late.

"Are you interviewing me?" asked Barbara, grinning.

"No," said Tracy. She shook her head vigorously. "I was just writing something else."

Barbara looked at her thoughtfully for a moment. "Can I come down?"

Tracy nodded, shifted to her right, while Barbara lowered herself from the top bunk with agility, rejecting the ladder in favor of a reverse pull-up. She managed to do this while holding in her hand a magazine that Tracy didn't recognize. After Barbara had settled herself on the bed next to her, Tracy snuck a glance at its cover: *Creem*, it said, in red balloon letters. And below the word was a picture of a woman dressed something like Barbara had been dressed when she first arrived at camp.

Now, with all the swimming they daily undertook, the black of Barbara's hair had faded. In the absence of hair dye and red lipstick, she looked younger.

"What's that about?" Tracy asked. She gestured to the magazine.

Barbara looked down at it. "Music," she said, speaking the word with real reverence.

Then she looked up at Tracy.

"You know," said Barbara, "I've been here a week, and I think this is the first time you've talked."

"That's not true."

"No, I mean, you *talk*," said Barbara. "But only when someone else talks to you first. You're really shy, aren't you?"

Tracy considered this. She wasn't always, in every context; with her mother and her mother's friends, she could be reckless and loud. Aside from that, she had a secret talent: she could sing. She was a showy alto belter, a shower singer; in the car she harmonized with her mother, who complimented Tracy frequently on the timbre of her voice.

"A young Patsy Cline," said her mom, whose taste—cultivated in a former life as a barrel-horse rider at third-tier New England rodeos—ran toward country music.

But this facet of Tracy's personality—the way she was with the grown women she loved and trusted—was too difficult to explain, and so instead she said nothing.

"You shouldn't be," continued Barbara. "You're more interesting than everyone at this camp. I can tell that about you. I bet you've got secrets."

Did she? Not really. But once again, this misapprehension seemed to be working in her favor, and so she said, "Maybe I do."

"See, I knew that about you," said Barbara. "I could tell it right off the bat."

The two of them fell silent. And then, from outside: the sound of distant guitar chords. Barbara looked up, enchanted.

"Come on," she said.

"Where?"

"Let's go. We're always the only ones in here. Let's go outside."

A moment later, she was trotting to keep up as Barbara walked swiftly in the direction of the music, growing louder now.

Rounding a corner, they came face-to-face with a little crowd that had assembled on the porch of Pine. All of their cabinmates were there, alongside two dozen other campers. And in the middle of the crowd—the guitar player himself—was Lowell Cargill.

Tracy took a step backward, her face reddening. He was singing a song she knew—one her mother liked. "You Were on My Mind," by Ian & Sylvia. She knew all the words. She froze her face, so that she did not mouth them.

And through the crowd—was she imagining it?—she caught the gaze of Lowell Cargill, and forced herself to *hold it, hold it*, to not look away until he did.

They stayed for the whole concert. Past sunset and into darkness. When, finally, the announcement was made that all campers should return to their cabins, Barbara and Tracy walked side by side, silent, both under the spell of the music, the cool night air, the fireflies.

"I missed that," said Barbara.

"What?"

"Music."

Barbara paused in her walking then, and Tracy stopped beside her.

"I have a favor to ask," said Barbara.

"Okay," said Tracy.

"I'm going to leave the cabin some nights," said Barbara. "After everyone's asleep."

Tracy waited. She was confused. The natural question to ask would have been *Why*, and yet the tone of Barbara's voice told her the inquiry would not have been welcome.

"Just sometimes. Not always," she said. "Anyway. Do you think you could keep it between us?"

Tracy nodded, slowly.

"Also," said Barbara. "Would you mind if I took the bottom bunk? It'll be easier if I don't have to use the ladder every time."

This gave Tracy pause. Would the upper bunk support her weight? But she couldn't bring herself to raise the issue, and so she said it would be fine.

"I'll just say I'm afraid of heights or something," said Barbara, smiling. "If anyone asks why we switched."

For the next two weeks, it became clear that Barbara had been lying about one thing: her nocturnal excursions did, in fact, take place every single night. At 10 p.m., all the girls in the cabin would climb into bed, and Louise or Annabel would turn off the overhead lights. For thirty seconds afterward, Tracy could see nothing at all; and then the dimmest shapes would begin to appear—furniture and windows and the bodies of her fellow campers—illuminated, she realized, only by the bright stars above the cleared land of Camp Emerson.

At a certain point, when no movement could be heard throughout the cabin, she'd feel the bed shift, ever so slightly, and Barbara's breathing would change, and then she would hear her footsteps, soft as a cat's, and then she would open the screen door, holding her breath, and close it behind her, equally quietly. The faintest creak of the hinge, and she was gone.

Tracy was never once awake for her return, so she didn't know how long she was gone on those nights. She remarked aloud, once, that Barbara must be very tired. In response Barbara insisted that she was a person who needed almost no sleep, and her energetic demeanor each day proved to Tracy that she was telling the truth.

If anyone else in the cabin knew about this routine, they didn't say. No one asked questions, and Barbara volunteered nothing—at first.

Jacob

The idea had come to him in a dream. *Limp Jacob*, a voice had said, and he'd woken up in his cell with the phrase repeating itself over and over. *Limp Jacob. Limp Jacob.* Was it taunting him? It bore a passing resemblance to his father's voice, and it sounded like something he might have said.

It wasn't until lunchtime that—watching a man he didn't know drag the dead weight of his leg across the prison's cafeteria floor—Jacob understood with a jolt the meaning of the phrase.

"Comma," he said aloud. "Comma."

And Harold Debicki, next to him, had asked what he was on about.

Limp, Jacob, he thought. But he didn't say it aloud.

The next morning, when the guard came to do his morning rounds, Jacob lay in his bed, unmoving. He'd go one step further than limping. He'd be paralyzed.

"Get up, Sluiter," said the guard.

"Can't," said Jacob. "Can't move my legs."

He said this calmly; to overact, he thought, would raise suspicion. Instead he said the same phrase in the same calm voice to everyone he met that day, and every day thereafter: *Can't move my legs.*

It took some practice, but after a time he really began to believe it. To move from place to place, he dragged himself across floors, even when he did not believe himself to be watched.

He'd never been liked at Dannemora, but after several weeks of this even his cruelest tormentors were advocating for him to the guards.

It isn't right, was the general consensus. He needed to be seen by a doctor.

The only time he allowed himself to move his legs was in his bed, at night. There, careful to wait until he heard the soft snores of his bunkmate, he cycled his legs, lifted them one after another, conditioning them back to strength.

Within several weeks he'd been transferred to Fishkill, the lower-security prison four hours south.

Within several months, he'd escaped.

Since that time he'd been moving north, following the Hudson in a straight line.

In terms of destination, he had only one idea: his ancestral land, the Sluiter tract, the place his grandfather used to take him camping. A little series of natural caves formed an easy shelter; inside one, the two of them slept side by side, and his grandfather, a natural storyteller, the only adult who had ever been kind to him, gave Jacob the history of their people.

The caves were close to a populated area, and therefore Jacob knew they would be dangerous to visit. But he couldn't predict how much longer he'd be loose, or alive—and so sentiment or folly drove him forward.

He traveled by moonlight or streetlight, along back roads. Most nights, he found one house to enter in a gentle way: a window open, a door easily picked. Most of them were the homes of the wealthy, summer cottages with water views. Inside, he took only what he needed, very quietly, trying not to rouse anyone at home. Only once had he come close to having a problem, and that was when the mistress of a particular house went walking past the kitchen in her bathrobe, moving so quietly he had not heard her approach.

For one whole minute he held his breath while she did her business. He did not hide; he stood still in the middle of the linoleum floor, arms straight, legs at ease. He was holding a knife he'd purloined from an earlier house. If she came out and saw him there in the dark, he would hold up a finger to his lips. He would tell her that to scream would put the rest of her family in danger. He'd have to kill her, that much was certain, a matter of necessity; but the rest of them, assuming there were others, would be spared.

The woman flushed. She washed her hands. She opened the bathroom door, and turned the light off. She walked out of the bathroom, and went down the hallway, most likely to her room.

She never looked his way.

*　　*　　*

During the day, behind the tree line, Jacob slept on the softest ground he could find.

It was summertime. There'd been little rain. The one night it poured, he had stayed inside the house he'd entered, sitting at the kitchen table, listening with all his senses for any motion in the house. When the rain stopped, he walked out into the fresh new air.

His father, who was not proud of him for anything, might have been proud of him for this one thing: his resourcefulness, his ability to make do with what nature and the rich provided.

He came from a long line of resourceful men. His great-great-grandfather and great-great-great-uncles had been loggers whose work was first threatened by Verplanck Colvin's grumblings about logging in the Adirondack Mountains. Sensing danger, they sold their land—and they were wise to do so. Within two decades, Governor Roswell Flower had founded the Adirondack Preserve. *Forever wild* was the sentimental term that prevented any further logging on the land—even their own property. In an instant, the Sluiter tract—those acres and acres that Jacob's ancestors had purchased at a bargain, dreaming of good fortune and financial security for generations to come—was stripped by the government of its profitability.

So his ancestors had pivoted to other work: tourism for some, guiding wealthy visitors from the city; factory work for others, manufacturing shirts and paper in towns like Corinth and Troy. A few—including his grandfather and his father—became builders and handymen. And the funny thing was that they always had work. The state was all right with it when the wealthy decided to clear the land for their colossal homes. It was only regular people—people like the Sluiters—who were barred from their former work, who were tasked only with keeping the land pristine for the enjoyment of the Roosevelts and Rockefellers of the world.

Therefore, when Jacob entered these homes each night—purloined food from their stocked pantries and refrigerators, purloined clothing—it was with a certain amount of enjoyment. Once or twice, in truly empty homes, he had even taken a shower.

He wasn't sure how many days it had been since his escape. He did know, from a front-page story on a newspaper on a kitchen table, that he was being tracked.

He also knew that the northern territory he was moving into was more remote.

This meant two things: that he'd be harder to find.

That he'd have to be more resourceful.

II

Bear

Alice

1950s • 1961 • Winter 1973
June 1975 • July 1975 • August 1975

Alice Ward, seventeen and a half years old, kept her eyes closed tightly on the way to Grand Central. It was a nervous habit: one she had had for as long as she could remember. It soothed her, allowed her to pretend, if just for an instant, that she was alone in the world. She did it only when she believed that no one was watching. In this case, she was wrong.

"Alice," said her sister, Delphine, the elder of the two. "Are you sleeping?"

Alice opened her eyes.

Three weeks earlier, in the ballroom of the Waldorf-Astoria, she had made her debut. Her military escort was a West Point junior whose name she had already forgotten. Her civilian escort was supposed to have been Stuart Parker, an unpleasant boy she had known since birth, until—miracle of miracles—he had come down with measles the day before the event. Delphine had been the one to come up with a last-minute replacement: a college friend of her husband George. Someone who happened to be staying with the two of them while in Manhattan to meet with a client.

His name, said Delphine, was Peter Van Laar. And yes: he had a tuxedo.

Alice's mother had been enthusiastic. Her father less so.

"Van Laar," he had said. "Do we know the Van Laars?"

They did, her mother assured him. The Van Laars of Albany. (In her tone was a note of concession: Yes, Albany. Still.) Bankers, thought Mrs. Ward. Conservationists. A Roosevelt had been very *lié* with the grandfather.

"How old is he?" Alice had asked.

"Oh, George's age," Delphine had said, waving a hand in the air, as if something so trivial as *age* did not matter at all in a man.

The answer, Alice learned later, was twenty-nine.

*　*　*

After a week, an envelope arrived in the mail. It was addressed to *Miss Ward and Chaperone*, and inside it was an invitation to Peter Van Laar's summer home in the Adirondack Mountains—the one he had spoken of, with surprising tenderness, while seated next to Alice at dinner.

I very much hope that you'll come, Peter had written, in a steady hand. *I so enjoyed meeting you.*

Now here they were, Alice and Delphine, awaiting a platform announcement at Grand Central. It was odd, actually, to be standing side by side like this; they had not spent so much time together since they were very small.

Delphine was five years older and five inches taller than Alice. She played the piano brilliantly. She never seemed shy. She had an intellectual air about her and an interest in politics, two traits that made her stand out from the rest of the Ward family, whose main topics of conversation at the dinner table tended toward gossip. At one point, Delphine had posed to her parents the question of applying to Barnard or Radcliffe, an idea at which her father had scoffed, even though, at Brearley, she had been first in her class.

Alice, meanwhile, had barely graduated.

Now Delphine was twenty-two and married to George Barlow. It was a love match, one that almost did not happen, due to their father's belief that George, despite his indisputable pedigree, was an *eccentric*. Soon she'd no doubt be expecting a baby. Alice could see Delphine's future laid out ahead of them clearly; it was her own she couldn't imagine. When she tried, she saw something hazy and indistinct. It gave her a knot in her stomach.

At North Creek they were met by an unusual car driven by a small ruddy man wearing corduroy clothes, *Miss Ward* on a card in an ungloved hand.

The driver, uncomfortably chatty, had asked questions of them that horrified Alice with their intimacy. Where had they come from, he wanted to know. Were they married? Did they work? She looked sideways at Delphine, waiting to see whether she would say anything, but Delphine was placid. Amused, even. She answered all his questions; asked him some in return.

"Who'll be hosting you at the Preserve?" asked the driver, and Alice waited for Delphine to respond, but instead she said: "Go on, Alice."

"Peter Van Laar," said Alice.

"Father or son?" asked the driver.

And without waiting for a reply, he expounded, at length, on the son's reputation in the town—not terrific, as it turned out—*coldness* being the primary criticism, which didn't bother Alice so much. She liked the cold. Got along best with people who were tempered in their movements and speech. In fact—though she had been nervous to meet him at the Junior Assembly, afraid that the difference in their ages would leave her with nothing to say—what she noticed and appreciated straightaway about Peter Van Laar was his stillness. His height and his steady blue eyes. The impression he gave of control.

They had danced together three times. Four, if you counted a half-finished turn about the floor at the end, just before she was pulled away by a relative saying good night.

With each rotation he had held her closer. He was very handsome. He had smelled, Alice recalled, like the woods.

"There's a story about the house," the driver was saying.

The roads were turning serpentine, and her stomach was beginning to churn. She leaned her head against a window.

"Are there ghosts in it?" said Delphine gaily, but the driver shook his head.

"Nothing like that. It was brought over from Switzerland. The whole house, is what I'm saying. *Chalet*, they call it." And he gave a little sound that was something like a laugh.

"Fascinating," said Delphine.

"Every part of it. The family shipped it over. Built it up again over here. This was near eighty years ago. You can imagine the manpower that took. Built a skid road just for the lumber. Dozen horses pulled every load. It's still told about in the town. Every man and boy in Shattuck over nine years old was hired by the Van Laars to put it all back together."

"Can you imagine, Alice?" said Delphine, and Alice pinched the back of one hand with the fingers of the other, willing the contents of her stomach to remain in place.

"Guess what they named the place," said the driver.

He waited.

"The house, I mean. Guess what that old family named the house," he said.

"Give me a minute. I'm thinking," said Delphine seriously. And then she said: "Manderley."

"No," said the driver. "Self-Reliance. *Self-Reliance!*" He slapped his knee once.

Neither of them responded; Alice because she didn't know what was funny, and Delphine, presumably, because she was processing the joke.

"Wasn't the Van Laars moved that lumber," said the driver helpfully.

"That *is* funny," said Delphine, though Alice could discern that even she, at last, felt uncomfortable. They were, after all, guests of the Van Laars.

"You all right, miss?" the driver asked Alice—noticing in the rear-view mirror, perhaps, the green hue of her face.

She was, she told him. Fine.

"Look straight ahead out the front window. Try rolling your window down some," said the driver. But she hadn't brought a headscarf, and her hair flew wildly about her face the moment she did.

She rolled the window back up.

Alice kept her eyes closed until she felt the car slow, heard the road beneath them shift from pavement to dirt. She opened them to find they had reached a long private drive. To her left was a series of working farm buildings: a dairy barn, a granary, a slaughterhouse. A woman and child stood out front of them, staring, not waving.

And then, at last, the Preserve: stands of tall pines that threw the earth into shadow, sloping lawn where others had been felled. At the top of the lawn was, she surmised, the house the driver had described.

Self-Reliance, said a little sign that they passed as they approached. The building itself was colossal. Its central structure was three stories tall, built of rough logs. Delicate wooden carvings descended from its overhanging roof and garlanded the shutters that framed its large windows. Two wings sprouted from its sides; a portico covered the drive. Gardens abounded, brimming with cultivated flowers designed to look wild. Scattered around it were smaller outbuildings, one a sort of miniature version of the house itself.

"My word," said Delphine.

The most shocking thing about it, thought Alice, was how far it was from anything else. How much work it would have taken to build such a compound in the middle of the woods. The Van Laars had placed the house atop a rise in the land, so that everything near Self-Reliance was also beneath it. Like Olympus, thought Alice, to whom such references did not normally occur.

The driver inched forward until the car met the grass and then rolled to a stop. It was only then that she noticed Peter, standing still as a buck in the shadow cast by the house. Waiting for them.

He stepped forward. He was even taller than she had remembered. Older-looking too. A hint of silver was in his hair, lit up brilliantly by sun as he strode across the lawn.

The driver hopped out. They waited a beat, until they realized he would not be opening their doors.

Peter was close now, and the knot inside Alice exploded into riotous pulsing nerves that threatened to chatter her teeth.

What would they say to one another, she wondered. What on earth was there to say to a grown man? Throughout her school years, she'd been surrounded only by girls. She reminded herself that dancing with Peter had been all right; the ballroom of the Waldorf had been dark and loud and there'd been little need for conversation. But here, in the broad light of day—everything was different.

Delphine rescued her.

"What a journey," she said to him happily, stepping out of the car. "I thought we might never make it."

All around them, the smell of sap in sun. Beyond that, fresh water: the lake.

Peter smiled, hands in pockets, his gaze at their shoes.

"I'm glad you're here," he said. And he held out two hands for their suitcases, which the driver gladly relinquished.

It was Delphine he walked alongside as they approached the house. Delphine he addressed when inquiring about the weather in the city, activities they liked. Alice trailed behind them, feeling more and more childish.

"Have you been to these mountains before?" he asked, and Delphine said that they had, once, when they were very small.

"Do you remember, Bunny?" she asked Alice—who reddened at the name.

Peter turned slightly, waiting for her reply. The truth was that she didn't, but admitting this would make her seem even younger in comparison to her sister. And so she said she did.

"You're familiar with the flies, then," said Peter.

"What, these?" said Delphine, waving a hand in the air, parting the small swarm that had gathered around their heads.

"Yes," said Peter. "Blackflies. They're usually gone by now, but June was cold this year. I guess they wanted to make your acquaintance," he said, and at last he looked right at Alice and smiled. His teeth were bright. A small thump of excitement descended from her throat to her abdomen.

She smiled back at him: an act of bravery.

It was then that an arrow sailed by, three inches from her nose, coming to a halt in the bark of a nearby tree.

Alice froze.

Peter blanched.

Delphine, unaware of what had just transpired, turned back to them, smiling pleasantly.

For a moment, no one spoke. Then a small child came running toward them, shrieking his apologies, very close to tears.

"Oh no, oh no," the boy was saying. "Is anyone gotten?"

It was a camper, Peter explained, after comforting the boy, admonishing him, sending him on his way.

"A camper—at what camp?" said Delphine.

Peter inhaled, as if preparing to begin a very long story. And then, thinking better of it, he said he would tell them at dinner.

"Remind me if I forget," said Peter.

All the windows in the house were open. Fans rotated slowly in each room. The whole place smelled of cut lumber, like something newly built. They were shown to their rooms by a person named Hewitt, who seemed to serve as butler, but whose roughness and attire gave him the air of a cowboy. He wore his hat indoors. He was silent, wiry, forty or so. Every age above twenty-five seemed interchangeable to Alice at that time. She had wondered—was still wondering—who else would be at the house. She had speculated with Delphine on the train.

"Peter's parents?" she said, and Delphine had shrugged. Maybe.

"Does he—live with them, do you think? In Albany?"

Delphine considered. "George had an apartment," she said. "Before we got married, I mean. But it was really his father's."

"Did you ever see it?"

Delphine smiled. "Yes," she said. Only afterward did Alice understand her implication.

Her room was large and lake-facing, with a four-poster bed and a patchwork bedspread. It had a full-length standing mirror in which she inspected herself, putting two hands on her cheeks and pressing them in (she believed, in those days, that her face was too full), imagining what she looked like to Peter. She was often told she was pretty—prettier than Delphine, in fact, her one triumph over her sister. But she thought of herself as stupid, and was fairly certain others did too. And unfunny, unwitty. Being humorless, she thought, was even worse than being dumb.

A knock at the door startled her so much that she yelped.

She opened it, still breathing hard.

It was Hewitt, the butler—the *helper*, Alice corrected herself. In those clothes, he was nothing like the Wards' butler in the city. "Family's having cocktails on the lawn," he said. "You can join if you like."

"Thank you," said Alice—and only then did she notice, peering out from behind Hewitt's leg, a tiny bright-eyed girl with a thin braid.

"Well, who's this?" said Alice, and it was the first time Hewitt smiled.

"This is Tessie Jo," he said.

The girl grinned. Buried her face into the fabric of Hewitt's pant leg.

The front of the house was, in fact, the back of it: the lake side. The water looked cold and comfortable all at once, the sort of water that contained warm pockets, hidden springs.

Four adults in high-backed chairs sat on a small beach, facing away from her. Alice didn't, at first, know who they were; and then she heard her sister's laugh, charming and warm, a laugh that was often commented upon by others. Delphine had put on a hat that Alice had never seen before, and was sitting next to Peter. From the back the group looked like two couples; only the empty fifth chair said otherwise. In front of them, the little girl—Tessie Jo—ran back and forth across the beach, stopping from time to time to make piles of wet sand.

Peter caught sight of Alice before anyone else and rose from his chair with formality.

"Miss Ward," he said.

She approached, trying to look carefree. But again she felt ill with pretending.

One of the other members of the party stood, too, and Alice recognized him as Peter's father. He had to be: he was a white-haired version of the son, similarly thin, groomed, similarly severe.

"Miss Ward," said the elder. "We're happy to make your acquaintance."

Alice had reached the group by then, and she turned her back to the lake, facing the house and all of them, standing awkwardly in the middle of the little arc of chairs, as if she were about to break into song. What, she wondered, could Peter possibly have said about her? Peter, who had known her for all of one night?

Peter's mother—she assumed—had remained sitting, as had Delphine. The mother looked younger than the father, but dowdier, carrying thirty extra pounds, wearing a dress that—Alice thought it before she could stop herself—did nothing for her figure. She smiled abstractedly in Alice's direction.

Peter stepped forward. "Did you find your accommodations comfortable?" he said.

Alice was struck, suddenly, by the stiff way he spoke, as if he were from another time. Their friends in the city were loose-lipped, irreverent, delighted by scandal. Politeness, they believed, was only to be directed at those who ranked lower than you, who served you in some way.

"Very comfortable," said Alice. "Thank you."

Dinner went better. The wine was helping Alice, who had only been tipsy twice before in her life. She did not like the taste of alcohol or the way it made her body feel. But she did enjoy the way it gave the room a warm, comforting shine. Delphine carried the conversation, and for once she was grateful for her sister's vivacity, even as it emphasized Alice's lack thereof.

The talk moved from the history of the Adirondack Mountains to the daily operation of the farm down the road: a special passion of the elder Van Laars. Then the flies—always the flies—and finally gentle inquiries into their life in the city, their education, their pursuits.

"And how is old George Barlow?" asked Mr. Van Laar Sr. in between bites. "Haven't seen him since Peter's college days. I always found him funny."

In his voice was a certain dismissiveness, and Alice looked to Delphine to see if she would be offended. But instead, she smiled.

"He's still funny," she said.

"Liking his work?"

"His studies, you mean," said Delphine, and Mr. Van Laar raised an eyebrow.

"Surely not. At his age?"

"Oh yes," said Delphine conspiratorially. "He's dropped out of the family business to pursue a degree in ornithology at Columbia."

There was a twinkle in her eye as she delivered the news—which had been the gossip of last season in Manhattan, delivered over and over around the city as the punch line to a joke. *Ornithology!* If there was one thing Alice respected about her sister, it was that she had made a bold choice when selecting the man who would become her husband. George Barlow—though he came from wealth—was in no other way an obvious match for Delphine. He was not even very handsome; he was thin and slight, with an overbite, with dark eyebrows that were constantly furrowed. And yet her sister loved him: this much was plain to Alice.

"I'm sure you knew that, Dad," said Peter. "It caused quite a stir." But in his voice, too, Alice detected humor.

"I should say so," said Mr. Van Laar. He took a bite, and chewed it pensively. "You know, I thought Cornell was the place to study birds."

"It is," said Delphine. "But we couldn't leave Manhattan, so Columbia had to do."

"Is he earning good marks?"

"Top of his class," said Delphine.

This was when the conversation flagged. The sound of cutlery on plates could be heard throughout the room.

Delphine said: "May we hear about the summer camp?"

Peter and his father exchanged glances. Then Peter began.

In the 1870s, when the Adirondacks were still a nascent vacation destination for New Englanders, the original Peter Van Laar visited from Massachusetts and fell in love with the land.

He returned several times to conduct land surveys. At last—with the help of a skillful local guide—he selected the plot on which Self-Reliance would be built.

The Van Laars' version of the story, Alice couldn't help but notice, was different from the driver's. The people of Shattuck weren't mentioned much. In their version, Peter I—pronounced, in the Van Laars' lexicon, *Peter One*—carried lumber in bundles by hand, climbed tall ladders, personally oversaw the arrival of every part of the original structure from Switzerland, and made certain it was reassembled correctly. Just down the road from the house, a working farm was built to ensure that no guest would ever go without the comforts of home.

Peter I was known as unconventional. "The last Van Laar," said Peter III, "who could possibly be described as such." He smiled tightly. Continued: he was impish, playful, childishly exuberant until his dying day, beloved and reviled in equal measure by business associates. The subject of gossip columns. The possessor of dozens of mistresses.

When Peter I announced his idea for a summer camp, therefore, it was met with no surprise—but with a great deal of amusement, even ridicule, from his social peers.

Still, Peter I persevered. He dedicated to this cause a group of buildings he had originally constructed as hunting cabins. In his eighties already, no longer able to participate in physical activity with as much vigor as he had previously done, he commissioned a group of locals from Shattuck to build the rest of the necessary structures on the grounds. His dream was to indoctrinate generations of children in the importance of conservation, of responsible stewardship of the land. He named the camp after his favorite writer and thinker, another great advocate for the outdoors. The man who, incidentally, had also written the essay after which the main house was named. Camp Emerson ran for one eight-week session each summer, said Peter III. At first, its charges were few in number. But after several successful seasons— operating at a loss—the camp's reputation grew. Within a decade, Camp Emerson became a sought-after destination for the children of well-to-do New Englanders and Manhattanites. Today, most of the participants were the children of friends and acquaintances of the Van Laars.

Delphine clapped her hands together, delighted. "Oh, I love the sound of him," she said. "The first Peter. I love the whole story. Don't you, Alice?"

"Yes," Alice said.

"Did you ever attend yourself?" asked Delphine, and Peter shook his head quickly.

"Camp Emerson? Heavens, no," he said, as if she had asked something strange.

Across the table from Alice, Mrs. Van Laar had little to say. She sat pleasantly and quietly in her blousy, unfashionable dress, with her lipstick slightly askew. She smiled every so often at Alice, and she ate her dinner with real pleasure, closing her eyes as she chewed.

At a certain point Alice realized neither she nor Mrs. Van Laar had said a word for the better part of an hour, and no one else seemed to notice or mind, and she had the sudden realization that she was a consumable good being evaluated for purchase by the two men at the table, with Delphine as auctioneer. That the less she said, the better. The notion that some decision had been made already on her behalf began to settle onto her shoulders toward the end of the meal.

It wasn't unpleasant.

It let her return, in fact, to her preferred state of being: dreamy unavailability, a cultivated air of mystery that she hoped might mask the lack of intellect that she accepted as a fact about herself.

Every so often she saw Peter Van Laar gazing at her. More and more she allowed herself to meet his eye. Her pulse increased. She was a child.

She asked herself three questions: Could she live away from the city?

Could she live here, in this wilderness, for part of every year? Could she marry a man like Peter?

Her mother had known her father since childhood, but not well; she'd been eighteen on her wedding day, which took place soon after their first date.

Her sister and George Barlow had known each other for two months before they got engaged.

She looked out the window, toward the lake. There was something hypnotizing about it—something charmed. It was eight in the evening now, but it was July, and the last light of day shone powerfully off the water. Tall eastward-facing windows let in the warm calm breeze. The pines outside them stood still, watching her, awaiting her response.

Yes, and yes, and yes, she thought. Every answer would be yes, if he were to ask her these questions.

He did. In September of that same year, after two more visits to the city—the second time with his parents—Peter Van Laar had sought her hand in marriage, with the approval of her father.

He had selected a ring from his ancestral cache.

He had gone with her mother to have it resized, and bought a second one as well, something new from Van Cleef & Arpels, and a tennis bracelet to match.

She had accepted, grateful to have something about her life decided, uncertain what else she would do.

Her wedding gown had been duchesse satin with a full skirt and a sweetheart neckline. She was married at Saint John the Divine, two days after her eighteenth birthday, with a reception at the Pierre.

She had no bridesmaids. She had never had close friends. And in those days, having a matron of honor—as Delphine would have been—wasn't considered correct.

There was no honeymoon. Only a departure for Albany, to a home she had never before seen, an echoing city manse with cold marble floors and windows that rattled in winter.

Nine months later—and one month early—Peter IV was born. Bear, he was called, because his Christian name was in so much use among the Van Laars already, and because he was plump, and because of the down on his head that reminded everyone who touched it of the pelt of some baby animal.

How many hours did she spend watching him? The silk of his hair. The weight of him on her chest, as she dozed in the bedroom of the Albany house, or the sunroom of Self-Reliance. The warm fragile weight of her son. She pictured his bones inside him, suspending the rest of him with their careful architecture; the miniature lungs that lifted and lowered the back; the small limbs that twitched as he settled into deep sleep; the whole infant body somehow an impossibility in its scale, in its smell, in its composition, in the way it induced a sort of calm in her that—the conviction landed on her one day like an anvil—she would never again feel in her life.

Alice

1950s • 1961 • Winter 1973
June 1975 • July 1975 • August 1975

When Alice tried to be objective, she could acknowledge that
there were one or two very good years at the start.

Before and after Bear's birth, she was treated by Peter as the child
she was. This meant of course that he laughed at her; but his eyes
were warm as he did, and he sometimes laid an affectionate hand on
her head when she displayed what he termed her *lack of common
sense*, and sighed, as if contemplating the magnitude of all that he
would have to teach her. She didn't mind; she felt protected, which
at that time—was what she believed she needed.

But at some point, Peter's reaction to her mistakes began to morph
from amusement to annoyance. When she was eighteen, and learning
how to host a dinner party, Peter had smiled as he gently corrected
misspellings on the place cards, or vetoed calla lilies on the table; five
years later, he scowled, and sometimes yelled.

The one thing they agreed upon, always, was the value of their son,
whom Alice loved immediately and intensely. Peter, she knew, loved
him too—but his love sometimes felt to her like an investment, something to be given on the condition that there would be a return for
him later.

They would have no more children, Peter said; one boy was enough.
The implication, Alice understood, was that to have more than one
boy would complicate matters when it came to passing on the bank.
For four generations in a row, there had been only one boy. Only one
Peter Van Laar. Sometimes Alice had the feeling that her prompt
production of a boy—and such a fine one, at that—was the only thing
she had ever done that pleased her husband.

The summer months at Self-Reliance were when the three of them
were most often together. There, Peter taught his son to sail and ride
and play chess and shoot clay pigeons out of the sky. He was a good

teacher—patient, even—a quality he altogether lacked in other areas of his life. From a distance, Alice watched, contented, feeling something like pure love for her husband for the first time in her marriage.

It helped that Bear was good at everything he put his hand or mind to. He was quick with numbers; he was early to read. He was a big tall boy like his father—a relief to Alice, who had feared he might inherit her short stature.

Despite these gifts, there was no arrogance about him; he had none of the contempt that his father showed from time to time. Instead, he greeted everyone he met with a smile, learned the names of everyone who worked the house and the grounds, no matter their station. In this way he reminded her of somebody she could not name, until she realized with a jolt one day that it was her own sister. Delphine.

Tessie Jo, the groundskeeper's daughter, held him in a special thrall; four years older than he was, she treated him kindly, doted on him. In return he followed her everyplace she went, calling out for her, *Tessie, Tessie*. It was a joke between Peter and Alice: that Bear was in love with the girl. One of the few jokes they had together.

During the other three seasons of the year, Peter was hard at work, often staying at the office until eight or nine o'clock. Often in Manhattan for meetings with prospective clients.

In Albany, Alice would have been lonely, if not for her son. She had no friends to speak of. She was a bad conversationalist.

About this last point, Peter agreed. He said this frequently, matter-of-factly, the way he said everything, as if he were in possession of no opinions, only facts.

"The thing is, Alice," he said, "you're boring at parties. A drink or two will help you be more fun."

She had been twenty the first time he said this. She had been holding two-year-old Bear in her arms. She opened her mouth to respond, but no words came out. Peter frequently offered her criticisms, always couched as advice. And the thing was: usually she agreed with him. She *was* boring at parties. She knew nothing of current affairs. She was not well traveled, and she had no hobbies. She was not brilliant and witty like her sister. She had unkind thoughts about others, at times, but she had never mastered the art of expressing them in a clever mischievous way: in other words, she was not skillful even when it came to gossip. What she thought about most in the world in those days was Bear, and her all-consuming love for him. She sometimes felt that becoming a parent had revealed to her the existence of another dimension or another sense.

"And put that boy down," said Peter. "He's becoming a barnacle." He reached out for Bear, who refused him, burying his head in Alice's shoulder, clinging ever more tightly to her.

Generally, when Peter gave her any sort of advice, she took it. And, she discovered, he had thoughts about most facets of her appearance and personality. She should wear dresses that covered her shoulders, because her shoulders weren't her best feature. She should wear the highest heels she could, due to their difference in height. She should not shake hands with men when she met them, but incline her head in their direction. He felt to her as much like a coach as a husband: always seeking to teach her, better her, bring her up to his level. She did not fault him for it; prior to Peter, she had had little direction. She told herself to think of him as a mentor, in a way.

And so, before client dinners, Alice began to drink a glass of brandy at home. She did so in sight of Peter, who did not partake. And for a time it worked: she felt instantly more mature, more sophisticated, better able to return the conversational serves produced by the wives across the table from her, who were generally a decade or two older than she was, and looked at her with an expression that hovered between pity and contempt.

For several years, drinking was like this: a task she undertook when required to. She did not drink when off duty, when there was nothing social on her program.

At a certain point—she wasn't sure when, or how—it began to evolve. And a new routine was established: one glass of wine at home in the evenings. Sometimes two. More than that when she went out. Martinis, Manhattans when they went out—or gimlets.

There, that was it, she thought; wine at home, cocktails out. Her favorite moment of each day was a glass of wine with her son close by: her love for him never felt more urgent.

This amount of drinking, she decided, she could live with. This felt reasonable and responsible. She'd rely on Peter to tell her when she had crossed a line.

She could have carried on with this amount of drinking, and everything would have been fine. It was George Barlow, in the end, who changed things.

Carl

1950s • **1961** • Winter 1973
June 1975 • July 1975 • August 1975

It was seven in the evening already when the phone rang in the fire hall, jolting Carl Stoddard awake. He had fallen asleep on a cot after a long day in the sun. On ring two, he rose and blinked. By the third ring, he was in action, lifting the receiver with the same trepidation he always felt when answering. He disliked speaking in general; speaking into a telephone was worse.

"Carl Stoddard?" said a voice on the other end. This was Marcy Thibault, the local operator, whose years of experience had given her the uncanny ability to recognize voices.

"What's the bad news," said Carl—his standard response. A scripted line.

"I've got someone on the line for you from the Van Laar Preserve," said Marcy.

"Oh?" said Carl.

This was strange. Never in his life had Carl—a gardener at the Preserve—been contacted directly by his employers.

Maybe he'd left something there. Or maybe he'd done something wrong. Peter Van Laar was a man of strong opinions, and the landscaping was a special concern of his. Every year, the Van Laars threw a weeklong fling in July—the Blackfly Good-by, they called it, in celebration of the seasonal change that saw the pest's departure from the area—and Mr. V wanted everything just so.

"How'd they find me at the hall?" asked Carl. His heartbeat was quickening. He was a tall, blond-bearded, burly person, forty years old that summer, a football player in his youth—but he was timid, sensitive to changes in the weather and to the emotions of others, and he disliked conflict. Always had. Gardening was a vocation that suited him well.

"They didn't," said Marcy. "They don't know it's you there."

* * *

There were four of them that year in Shattuck Township's volunteer fire brigade. Aside from Carl, there was Dick Shattuck, the grocer; Bob Alcott, a history teacher at the central school nearby; and Bob Lewis, largely unemployed.

Together, a decade prior, they'd built the team from scratch, learning their trade from firefighting enterprises in neighboring towns, raising money for equipment at donation stands they set up at Christmastime and the Fourth of July. Once they got fire boots, they collected money in those.

They rented out an old garage and converted it to a fire hall with a bed and kitchen on-site. They had Dick's wife Georgette, whose artistic talent annually gilded the grocery store's front windows, paint a sign.

It took them four years to get a proper vehicle—but by July of 1961, they had the whole operation up and running. A truck and hoses and, in town, four hydrants a stone's throw from Shattuck's only intersection with a stoplight. The volunteers were well trained. Each one of them, except Bob Lewis, was considered to have a positive attitude.

The night of July 10, 1961, it was no coincidence that Carl was on duty: he liked it at the fire hall. Signed up for night shifts as frequently as he could. It was the only place, aside from his car, where Carl ever felt truly alone. Here at the hall, he had nothing to do but read, or daydream, or sometimes fall asleep, and only very occasionally answer calls.

It took several seconds for Marcy Thibault to transfer him. And when a voice came through the wires, it wasn't a member of the staff, but Peter Van Laar himself—to whom Carl nodded each time they crossed paths at the Preserve, but to whom he had actually spoken maybe twice in his life. Van Laar was known by his employees and business associates as a stern, intolerant man, quieter than his wife but more vicious. He seemed to have no interest in conversation with anyone who worked for him, except at the highest levels; even to those at the top of the staff's hierarchy—groundskeeper, housekeeper—he spoke only briskly. He had a wolfish look about him, a leanness that signified hunger.

"Hello? Fire department?" said Van Laar, after being connected. The tone of his voice made Carl sit up straight, place his hand on the table.

"Yes," said Carl, "this is Carl Stoddard of the Shattuck Volunteer Fire Brigade." For a moment, he considered reminding Mr. V of the connection between the two of them. But the quiet urgency in the man's voice dissuaded him.

There was silence on the line. Then came a clicking that Carl determined, after a moment, to be the sound of Van Laar swallowing repeatedly.

"Mr. Van Laar?" said Carl. "Is everything all right there?"

"It seems my son is missing," said Van Laar, at last.

"Bear?" said Carl reflexively. He closed his eyes. Raised a fist to his forehead. It was too complicated to explain how and why he knew the nickname of the Van Laar boy. But he did; they all did, everyone who worked on the grounds. They'd known him since he was a tiny thing. Each May he returned to the Preserve taller, more talkative. He was eight years old that summer: always smiling, always whistling, patrolling the grounds like a watchman, friendly with the staff, the opposite of his stormy father. A good little woodsman, interested in the same things Carl had been interested in as a boy. Bushcraft, survival, that sort of thing. That summer, especially, they had been close: it was only last week that Carl had taught the kid how to recognize which wood was good for a fire. *Loose and light and dry*, Carl had said. *Floppy, almost.* And he demonstrated what he meant, slipping a small knife down the length of a cedar plank. Sticking his thumbnail into it.

Just before Carl had left for the day, in fact, he'd seen Bear: he was tying his shoes at the base of the front door to Self-Reliance. He'd stood up and waved as Carl passed him in his pickup, and Carl had returned the gesture.

If Van Laar was curious about how Carl knew his son, he didn't ask. Instead, to Carl's dismay, he let out a wail, unguarded and wild, and in it Carl—a parent himself, a father of three who had once been a father of four—recognized a feeling he had the misfortune to know well.

"Don't worry," said Carl. "Don't worry, Mr. V. We'll find him."

Within five minutes, he had the other three volunteers on the line.

Within twenty, they were in the truck, speeding through the gathering darkness, making their way to the Preserve.

Carl

1950s • **1961** • Winter 1973
June 1975 • July 1975 • August 1975

It was nearly dark when the four volunteers arrived. Their vehicle—an International Harvester brush fire truck that they'd gotten cheap, just before Schenectady retired it—was having an issue that month with its muffler, and it roared as they came up the drive.

Before they'd departed, Carl had filled the others in on what he knew—which was limited, actually. The conversation with Mr. Van Laar had been brief.

"The Van Laar boy's missing," Carl told them. "This afternoon he left for a hike up the mountain with his grandfather. Turned back around on the path to the trailhead, because he forgot his pocketknife in his room. Never rejoined the old man."

"How far from the house was he when he turned around?" said Bob Lewis.

"Don't know," said Carl.

"How long did Van Laar wait there," asked Bob Alcott, "before he went looking?"

"Don't know."

"What'd the kid want with his pocketknife?" asked Dick Shattuck.

"Don't know," said Carl limply. "I guess we'll hear more when we get there."

It was then that a memory sprang forcefully to the front of his mind: something the boy had said once about his grandfather, in passing, that Carl had brushed aside.

The truck came to a stop at the top of the drive. Dick Shattuck killed the engine.

Then there was silence. All over the Preserve: a great quiet.

Carl, who was riding in the back, didn't know what he had expected to hear—footsteps, maybe, or hollers, or crying; the pet name of the boy, *Bear*, called over and over—but it wasn't this.

He hoisted himself painfully onto his feet. Jumped down from the truck bed with a thud. He'd gained sixty pounds in the past several years, and it slowed him down. His wife was concerned.

Behind him, his three companions were descending from the cab.

Ahead of them, a shape on the lawn shifted. It was a human, Carl saw; he saw next that it was Vic Hewitt, the groundskeeper. Carl's boss.

Vic was silhouetted by the low light cast out from the inside. He was tall and broad and had the odd habit of standing with his arms straight down at his sides, strangely formal, a soldier at attention.

He was waiting for them.

Carl had been inside the main house exactly once, upon his hiring five years earlier. That day, he had entered through the kitchen door; inside, the housekeeper had set out lemonade and cookies while he talked with his future boss.

"It's hard work," Hewitt had said. "I won't lie to you. Lotta land, not much staff. Runs all year, too, not just in summer."

Carl had nodded, but he couldn't focus. It was his good luck that he'd even heard about the job from a cousin who knew the last gardener—and that the last gardener had finally retired. Carl had only a small amount of experience with gardening, but he had a library card. He would have taken any job that was offered to him. He had a sick kid, and no money. He'd worked at the paper mill in town until recently, when the plant closed down, releasing sixty-odd men from their longtime employment.

"I like to work," said Carl. He was hungry: he thought about taking one of the cookies, a lacy brown thing that looked more decorative than nourishing. At last, he decided against it. Hewitt hadn't taken one.

"Do you know about flowers and that?" said Hewitt.

"Oh, yeah," said Carl. "I grew up on a farm."

"But flowers," said Hewitt doubtfully.

Again, Carl nodded. "My mother grew them. Won contests at the county fair." The last was an embellishment: his mother, still alive, had *entered* contests annually, and annually complained about her failure to place.

"Taught me everything she knew," said Carl. His tone, he understood, was bordering on desperate.

"You're Joe Stoddard's cousin, are you?" said Hewitt.

Carl nodded.

Hewitt rapped the tabletop with his knuckle, at last, and told him the job was his if he wanted it.

He did.

He found out later that his cousin Joe had told Hewitt he had a kid in the hospital in Albany, a fact that neither he nor Vic Hewitt ever acknowledged. By 1961 Carl had been working there half a decade, five years of fast learning that had only this year produced the desired results. It was a miracle, frankly, that he hadn't been fired by Hewitt or by Mr. Van Laar himself—though he had the suspicion that the former had at times fallen on the sword when the latter complained.

It was Vic Hewitt, now, who greeted the four of them as they walked up the lawn in his direction.

He lifted one of his hands wordlessly into the air. Let it drop again at his side.

"You heard, I guess," he said to them, when they were in earshot.

He nodded to Carl. Shook hands with the others.

Carl glanced sideways at Dick Shattuck, who normally spoke for them. But Dick was only returning his gaze.

It occurred to Carl then that his employment here meant that he was expected to take the lead, and the realization unnerved him. He'd never liked leading anything or anyone. Not even back in high school: he'd rejected his coach's offer to make him captain of the football team.

"What's the latest?" said Carl, after a pause, because he could think of nothing else to say.

"No news," said Hewitt. "Boy's still gone. Been out looking in those woods going on five hours now."

He hunched his shoulders. Looked down at the ground.

Vic was a stoic man, a skillful guide. By the outside world, he was perceived to be tough to the point of ferocity. Visual evidence of this came in the form of a missing right earlobe, rumored to have been the work of a black bear that Vic had subsequently wrestled to the ground.

But he was a father too, Carl knew. Had a girl, Tessie Jo, twelve or thirteen, a tomboy who'd been raised by her dad and was now his near-twin, working side by side with him whenever she wasn't at school. Carl could tell he was thinking of her—just as Carl was thinking of his own children. Imagining them lost, overnight, in the underbrush, now damp from an earlier storm. Remembering Scotty as he drew in breath after ragged breath on the white-sheeted hospital bed.

Vic Hewitt turned and looked over his own shoulder, past the house, toward the edge of the woods.

"Now, look," he said. "It's a sad scene in there. Mrs. V's beside herself. Whole family is, and all the guests. Tread carefully, is what I mean. No need to worry them further."

With that, he led them wordlessly toward the house, toward the large front door—through which Carl had never once, in all his years of employment, passed.

Alice

1950s • 1961 • Winter 1973
June 1975 • July 1975 • August 1975

In the Van Laar family, planning for the weeklong affair of the Blackfly Good-by began in late May.

The first order of business was determining whom to invite. The main house, with its ten bedrooms, could comfortably accommodate sixteen. The outbuildings could house eighteen more. Some of the decisions were simple: the regular attendees included the McLellans, the Van Laar family's closest friends and business associates across two generations; and the Barlows—Peter's friend George and Alice's sister Delphine. Alice's parents, too, were invited—although Peter made it very clear that the Wards' inclusion was a favor he was doing for his wife. Then there were more of Peter's college friends, and then came the business owners Peter was seeking to woo as clients of the bank; these varied every year, and generally got dropped from the list as soon as a commitment had been made. Finally, there were the minor celebrities he had met somehow downstate, and invited mainly for entertainment. These "extra" guests were limited mainly to pretty and harmless women, or very funny men, all of whom came solo and slept in the outbuildings.

After the guests were selected, and the rooms assigned, the other business was attended to. Flowers were ordered. A local fiddle-and-dulcimer ensemble was booked, along with a caller for the square dance that happened midweek. The Preserve, which had once contained its own working farm—before cars and trucks were quotidian—now relied on local producers to supply a week's worth of food for the thirty or so guests who descended on the house.

In general, each of these weeklong parties went off without a hitch, buoyed by Peter's careful planning, and by Alice's adherence to his instructions.

But the year of Bear's fifth birthday brought with it a challenge: George Barlow, Alice's brother-in-law and Peter's good friend, had died unexpectedly in June—a heart attack—leaving her sister Delphine bereft, and also leaving open the question of whether or not to invite Delphine.

Alice was conflicted. The truth was that she had not been as attentive to her sister as she could have been in the wake of her husband's death. They lived four hours apart. Alice had a child; Delphine did not. For years, their only prolonged visits had taken place at the Blackfly Good-by itself; but now Alice panicked slightly at the thought that their first correspondence since the funeral would be an invitation to a cheerful weeklong fling.

Peter scoffed when she voiced this concern.

"Nonsense," he said. "It will do Delphine good. Give her a bit of distraction. Besides," he said, "she's an intelligent person. I'm certain she's capable of deciding for herself whether to accept."

In his choice of words, Alice sensed a slight. *Intelligence* was a quality that Peter valued highly: one, she was certain, he would not ascribe to his own wife.

As it turned out, Delphine accepted the invitation. "With pleasure," she wrote in her reply.

Alice was relieved. Perhaps, she thought, this would be a chance to reconnect with her sister. To apologize for her years of absence. To start anew with Delphine, whom she had looked up to so much as a child that she might have been a celebrity. Now that they were both adult women, thought Alice, perhaps they could be friends.

On Friday, the day the first guests were due to arrive, Alice dressed carefully. Then she walked down the hall to the sunroom, where she stood before the window, steeling herself for her duties as hostess.

She turned to a small bar table, ready to perform her ritual. She lifted a tumbler. Poured herself a glass of brandy—really a type of wine, she reasoned.

She lifted it to her lips.

Behind her, a quick movement caught her eye, and she saw Vic Hewitt leaving the room.

"Vic?" she said, and he turned, embarrassed, his fisherman's hat in his hands.

"I didn't know you were in here," said Alice.

He nodded. He was the only person on the grounds who spoke less than she did. Peter described him as simple, but unmatched when it came to caring for the land. He wore a beard. He was the last in a long line of Adirondack guides, the most famous of whom had been mentioned by name in the guidebook that had launched the tourism industry in the entire Adirondack Park. The original Peter Van Laar had hired Vic when he was only a kid, sixteen or so. At first it was to lead their summer hunting expeditions, and then to keep the grounds, and finally, when the idea of Camp Emerson arose in Peter I's mind, to run that, too. Like everyone else who worked for the Van Laars, Vic Hewitt played many roles, and he did so without complaint.

Now, though, Vic looked nervous.

"Are you all right?" asked Alice—who was navigating the mild embarrassment of having been caught drinking alone.

Vic nodded. "Just going over all the plans, I guess," he said. "Making sure I got everything all set."

And Alice suddenly understood. The Blackfly Good-by was the week of each summer when he was brought away from directing the camp. For the party, he was tasked with leading multiple hunting and fishing expeditions, making conversation with groups of outsiders. Vic, she guessed, was like her. Preferred to keep to himself, or to be with his child, Tessie Jo.

Alice turned back to the bar table. Poured a second glass.

"Here," she said. "This will help."

He smiled. Bowed his head. Took the drink into his hands.

From outside came the sudden sound of tires on gravel.

The Blackfly Good-by began.

Delphine came up on Saturday, one day after the rest of the guests. Her arrival, in the early afternoon, was met with a funereal hush. The other guests murmured their condolences a second and third time, asking after her well-being. Within an hour, though, the crowd had resumed the day's activity: Vic Hewitt had set up targets on the beach, and the guests—men and women alike—were shooting arrows in the direction of the southern tree line.

The strange thing, the awkward thing, was what to do with a single woman who was not there to be beautiful or to entertain. The balle-rinas and actresses were there for either their looks or their outrageousness, the frisson of sex they lent to the party. Strangely, Alice had never felt insecure in their presence. She did not believe that anyone ever slept with them; she believed that they slept with one another, the young men and women who came to Self-Reliance each year, and a secret part of her applauded them for it. She wondered, sometimes, what it would be like to experience someone other than her husband—the only man she'd ever known.

Delphine, it turned out, was mainly ignored, except by her own parents, next to whom she sat at meals.

When George Barlow had been alive, they had occupied one another. They were the happiest couple Alice had ever known; they had the same sense of humor, and the same eccentricities. After marrying George, Delphine had stopped attending much to her appearance, preferring comfort to elegance. She wore pants, most of the time—unflattering ones at that. But George lavished praise on her appearance—not only to Delphine, but to those around her. Alice often caught them exchanging glances over meals, either in tenderness or in amusement.

Now that George was gone, however, Delphine's quirks quickly lost whatever charm they might have had. Furthermore, in George's absence, she had lost the target toward which her observations and conversation had once been directed; and she had seemingly also lost the ability to filter her thoughts.

For example: when asked after her well-being in the wake of her husband's death, Delphine was frank. "It's been awful," she said. "I don't sleep."

What, wondered Alice, could one do with this sort of candor? What reply could one possibly give?

Widowed so young—and without children—Delphine had somehow become like a child herself. This feeling was heightened by the fact that she could often be found spending time with the actual children on the property: with her nephew Bear, but also with the McLellan children, and with Tessie Jo Hewitt—nine that summer—whom Delphine seemed to especially enjoy. She taught them cards; she taught them to gamble with toothpicks. She brought them on walks, and taught them the names of birds; she carried George's binoculars around her neck, always, and passed them to the children to spy on a warbler or chickadee or hawk; and sometimes, when she thought no one was watching, she cradled the binoculars tenderly in her folded arms, as if they were her late husband himself.

Once or twice, Alice tried to approach her, to make small talk, but always Delphine demurred, waving Alice off.

"I know you're busy," said Delphine. "Go help Peter. It's really all right, Bunny."

And Alice complied, leaving her sister behind, experiencing as she did so a sense of guilty relief.

It was true, anyway, that their days were structured precisely: a fact about which Peter's oldest friends teased him. Frank McLellan and Howie Southworth and Merrill Williams and—formerly—George Barlow. They, Alice knew, were the only people who were allowed to, and she relished this part of the annual gatherings, relished hearing others articulate in a cutting funny way what made her husband so difficult. "How *do* you manage, Alice," she was often asked, and she laughed along with them, giddy and relieved, reassured that the parts of Peter that sometimes even scared her—well, they weren't so bad after all.

The first meal of the day was at half past ten. Peter preferred to eat much earlier, priding himself on needing very little sleep, but years of experience had taught him that guests who had stayed up until three in the morning drinking had little hope of showing up for seven o'clock breakfast.

After breakfast, rain or shine, there was an organized outdoor activity, each one a competition of some kind. Hikes were races; fishing trips were derbies. At the end of the week the pair with the highest score between them would be awarded, with great pomp and circumstance, a trophy, which they were instructed to bring back with them the following year. The McLellans, sporty Catholic Manhattanites, were the toughest couple to beat, and they had won ten times, to Peter's chagrin.

To Alice, the whole thing felt like one more way to let her husband down. She was decently athletic, but in any competition the pressure made her flounder, and Peter's frustrated gaze upon her caused her hands to fumble anything in her grasp.

It came as a relief to her, therefore, when the daily activity was over and a snack was brought out, after which people retired to their rooms for a rest and a change of clothes before cocktail hour on the lawn, which began—precisely—at five.

From there each evening grew increasingly raucous. Dinner at seven; then parlor games around a fire, either inside or out, depending on rain.

With the parlor games came further competition, more opportunity to earn points. And these games, thought Alice, were even worse than the outdoor ones. Once or twice—at charades, for example—she could feel herself on the verge of hot tears as Peter shouted guesses at her, and then commands: *Christ, Alice, try something different!*

The worst was a terrible game called Dictionary that involved a colossal 1930s edition of the *OED*. The premise was that the leader of a given round had to find a word so obscure that he discerned, via spoken poll, that nobody knew it. *Wadmiltilt* had been one. *Absquatulate. Opsimath.* The leader, on a scrap of paper, would write down the true definition; everyone else would write down an invented definition; and then every scrap of paper would be passed back to the leader of the round, who would shuffle the scraps and read the definitions aloud, and then everyone would vote on which one he thought was right, with the winner being the participant whose entry received the most guesses.

Alice was terrible at this game in every way.

She had, she thought, no creativity, and therefore her definitions were always the same: *a bird of South America* was one of her favorites, or *to laugh merrily*, if she suspected she had a verb on her hands. Worse than that: when it was her turn to be the leader, she could never find a word unknown to all. All around her she sensed disbelief when she proposed a word like *melee*, which she also mispronounced, and which—when she heard the correct pronunciation from an annoyed, embarrassed Peter—she realized that she knew.

On the opposite end of the spectrum from Alice was Delphine, who—despite having been denied the chance even to apply to college— seemed to know both the meaning of every single word and its etymology, which she explained unselfconsciously to her unreceptive audience. Over and over again she vetoed words, confessing happily that she knew them. The fifth time this happened, there were grumbles. The tenth time, polite silence. And finally, Delphine's expression changed: at last, she understood the social error she had been making.

They were in the middle of another round before anyone noticed she had quietly taken herself to bed.

"Where's Delphine?" asked Katherine Southworth, and Howie Southworth said, "She absquatulated," and everyone laughed loudly and for a long time.

"Good riddance," said Merrill Williams, who was the drunkest of everyone, and then, upon being shushed, he said it louder, cupping his hands about his mouth as he did so.

"Good! Riddance!" he shouted.

Some of the guests gasped. And then there was more laughter, hushed this time.

"Williams," said Peter lowly. "That's enough." Merrill rolled his eyes, stood from his chair, and tottered out the door, toward the lawn.

At last, the game broke up.

For a moment, Alice considered going after her sister. But this moment, when all the games were over and everyone did what they wanted, was always Alice's favorite of the day. It was the only time when she felt herself to be out from under the weight of Peter's judgment. Sufficiently inebriated, she felt charitable and warm, and she could look around at the beautiful house they owned, and through its windows at the beautiful land they owned, and she could sneak down the quiet hallway and into the quiet room where her beautiful son was sleeping, and give him a kiss, and she could feel, really feel, how lucky she was to have this lot in life. Her blessings were never more evident to her than they were in those small hours of the morning, when all the guests were free to do as they pleased.

Instead of going to her sister now, as she knew she should have done, she set off in the direction of her son's room, tiptoeing past several guests who were sleeping, full-out, on the sofa; dodging others—the *artists-in-residence* was Peter's silly name for them—who were running down to the beach in the dark to strip off and go for a swim.

But on her way down the hallway, she was stopped by the sound of someone crying quietly. She froze, listening. The noises, she realized, were coming from Delphine's room.

She was drunk enough to feel brave, and so she lay down on the floor of the hallway and peered underneath the crack in the door, and there she saw her sister, sitting on the edge of her bed, head lowered. She was shuddering with sobs, trying to quiet them with her hands.

Alice stood, horrified. Delphine must have heard their laughter, surmised correctly who its target was. Delphine was ashamed, too, thought Alice; for the opposite reason that Alice was. For knowing too much, rather than too little. For a woman, neither was an acceptable way to be. In a moment of bravery, Alice knocked gently at the door, and when no answer came, she turned the knob.

Delphine looked up, startled. She was wearing a long white nightgown, and her dark hair was falling about her face; it gave her a ghostly aspect.

"Are you all right?" asked Alice.

Delphine stared at her a moment longer, and then wiped her face with her sleeve, and then patted the bed next to her.

"Come here," she said, when Alice hesitated. And then she complied, walking slowly to the bed, sitting down next to her sister. She had not been so close to her, alone, since they were teenagers.

"I'm sorry, Delphine," said Alice, and then—shamefully—she hiccuped.

"For what, dear?" said Delphine.

"They weren't being very nice," said Alice.

"Oh, *that*," said Delphine. "I don't care a groat about that." She waved her hand as if shooing a fly. "People like them will seek a collective target almost automatically. People of our class, I mean. We were bred to do it. We've been doing it since birth."

She paused.

"Well, some of us have, anyway," she said.

Delphine reached for a glass of water on her nightstand. Drank from it. And then, as if reading Alice's mind, she passed it to Alice, who took it into her hands and gratefully drained it.

"What were you crying about?" Alice said, when she'd finished.

"George," said Delphine. "I'm always crying about George. He's why I accepted this invitation. I thought being in this place would help me feel close to him."

Alice nodded. Again, she hiccuped.

"Give me that," said Delphine, and Alice handed her the glass, and Delphine stood and disappeared from the room for a moment, and then returned with more water.

"Drink it," she said. "You'll thank yourself in the morning."

Alice did as she was instructed. She sometimes felt that her entire life was either following orders from those above her in station, or giving them to those below her. Only with her son did she have a connection that existed outside any hierarchy of authority. She loved him plainly, without condition or complexity. And she believed he loved her the same way.

"Is it working?" she said to Delphine, when she'd finished.

"Is what working?"

"Does being here make you feel closer to George?"

"No," said Delphine, and laughed once. "Not really."

Then she looked at Alice more intently than she'd ever been looked at in her life.

"Are you happy here, Bunny?"

Alice shifted. "Of course," she said.

"I mean really happy. I know you love Bear, and he's darling. Of course you would. But Peter? Does he treat you well?"

Alice nodded, silently. "Of course," she said—more quietly this time.

Delphine sighed. "I've always felt guilty, you know," she said. "In a way I feel I set you up with him. But I've worried since then that you'd be in over your head. George and I both thought he'd take care of you. Now, I'm not certain you're a match."

At this, Alice bristled. "What do you mean?"

"Only that he can be very inflexible, Bunny. And you're such a dear. I hope you stand up to him, once in a while. I hope you're getting what you want from this life, too."

Don't cry, Alice thought. To cry would be to fail some test her older sister was giving her. *Don't cry.*

It was useless. Tears came to her eyes and spilled over.

"Oh, Alice," said Delphine. She tried to take one of Alice's hands in hers, but Alice snatched it away. She wanted to leave. She wanted to stand up and walk out of the room. She'd been wrong to feel sorry for Delphine—she remembered only now that her sister could be direct to the point of cruelty.

"Listen," said Delphine. "The best part of being married to George Barlow for a decade was learning that it's all right not to do everything that's expected of you all of the time. This is a notion that has been positively liberating for me. The way we were raised—the way our parents raised us, I mean—it trained us to think it's our job to be absolutely *correct* in everything that we do. But it isn't, Bunny. Do you see? We can have our own thoughts, our own inner lives. We can do as we please, if we only learn not to care so much about what people think."

Alice's discomfort was increasing. A light had gone on in her sister's eyes; she looked, to Alice, a tiny bit mad.

Still, her sister continued.

"The interesting thing about George," she said, "was that he woke up to this fact long ago—the idea that one is free to do what one wishes in life, expectations be damned—and yet he never let this rupture his friendship with his old group. The people in there, I mean." She tilted her head in the direction of the main room. "Since he died," she said, "I've been trying to be more like him in that one regard: to be open to all kinds. Even *them*."

More distant peals of laughter. Alice drank from her glass.

"Sometimes," Delphine said, "I find myself sort of studying them, instead of engaging with them as a friend would. As George always did. It's a terrible tendency I have. Do you know," she continued, "that I've enrolled in the anthropology program at Barnard in the fall? It's the only thing that's keeping me alive. Thinking about finally getting my degree."

Then Delphine turned to her. "Alice, do you ever think about going to college?"

"Oh," said Alice. "No. No, I have Bear to take care of."

"How old is he, though? Five? Won't he be going to school in the fall?"

"Yes," said Alice reluctantly. "But then I'll have—the house to attend to."

"You should think it over," said Delphine. "You're smarter than anyone gives you credit for. You were always good with sums, I remember."

Alice sat with these words for a moment, uncertain what to do with them. She tried to remember if she had ever been given a compliment in her life that was unrelated to her appearance or her attire.

"May I ask you something?" said Delphine. And before Alice could respond, she ventured forth: "Do you ever worry that being born into money has stunted us?"

Alice blanched.

"I don't mean anything by it," said Delphine. "It's just—lately I've been wondering whether having all of our material needs met from birth has been a positive aspect of our lives. It seems to me it may have resulted in some absence of yearning or striving in us. The *quest*, I like to call it. When one's parents or grandparents have already quested and conquered, what is there for subsequent generations to do?"

She paused here, gazing off into some distance, thinking. "This," she said, "is the expectation I most want to defy."

Alice was frozen. She had no idea what she could possibly say. To talk about money ran contrary to every instruction she had ever been given in her life. It felt practically sinful. A long silence followed, until Delphine finally broke it.

"Think it over, anyway, Bunny," she said. "The college question, I mean. George has—had—a very good friend who teaches at Vassar. How far is Vassar from Albany?"

But Alice was shaking her head. "Peter wouldn't like it," she said. The truth was: she wouldn't like it either. But she felt suddenly that she did not want to let Delphine down, to deflate the impression she had of Alice, in this moment.

Delphine paused. "Why not, do you think?"

"Well, he has a lot of ideas about what I should do each day," said Alice. "He probably wouldn't believe I had time to do that too."

Delphine nodded. "And if you insisted?" she said.

Alice almost laughed. The idea of insisting on anything, when it came to Peter, was unimaginable to her. She wasn't—frightened of him, exactly, though there had been one or two incidents that caused alarm. It was more that she had come to see herself nearly exclusively through his eyes, and therefore being in his good graces was the easiest way to achieve a sense of well-being.

"I wouldn't insist," she said simply.

"You know," said Delphine, "Peter has always struck me as someone with more bark than bite."

Delphine smiled.

"But you're an adult," said Delphine. "And you know him better than I do."

When Alice emerged from Delphine's room, it was close to three in the morning, and sounds of snoring were echoing throughout the house. She felt sober now. She walked on the balls of her feet, avoiding floorboards she knew to make noise. Passing Bear's room, she opened the door to gaze, at last, upon his sleeping form; and then she continued to the room she shared with Peter.

Inside, she found her husband awake.

He was lying on his back, his hands behind his head, his fine thin torso bare, and just visible in the moonlight.

He turned his head slowly in her direction, but said nothing.

Alice undressed, awkwardly, before him, feeling his appraising gaze, despite the dark. Already, she could feel the food and drink from the weeklong party making itself visible in her waistline, and she made a note to herself to eat nothing all day tomorrow—not until dinner, at least.

She pulled her nightgown over her head and lowered herself into bed next to Peter.

"Where have you been?" he asked her.

"In Bear's room," she said automatically. "He was restless." She wasn't certain why, but it felt dangerous to tell him the truth.

For a long moment, Peter was silent, and she thought perhaps he had gone back to sleep.

But then he turned over, and the expression on his face was cold.

"You're lying," said Peter. "I checked in Bear's room. I looked all over the grounds for you."

He raised himself up on one elbow, suddenly. Alice tensed.

"Where were you?" he asked again. In his voice she recognized danger.

"I did go to Bear's room," she said. "Twice. But I also went to Delphine's room."

Peter paused, seemingly caught off guard. She knew this wasn't the answer he was anticipating. When they were first married, she had made a terrible mistake at one of these parties, when she was too drunk to understand what was happening. Her mistake, she understood, had been drinking so much. The rest was someone else's fault. A former friend of Peter's, who was no longer invited to their parties.

"Why on earth were you in Delphine's room?" he said.

"To check on her," said Alice. "I heard her crying. And Merrill had said that horrible thing."

Peter was silent for a moment. And then came off his elbow and lay back down, the conversation finished.

Alice closed her eyes. She pictured Delphine's kind face, her dark hair, her upright posture. The well-being and confidence that emanated from her person, despite her recent loss.

Peter spoke again.

"I know she's your sister, Alice," he said. "And I'm sorry to say this. But I'd stay away from Delphine. She's always seemed manipulative to me."

The words landed heavily in the empty room.

"All of us worried that George would change when they married," said Peter. "And do you know something? He did."

After that, the two of them were silent.

Carl

1950s • **1961** • Winter 1973
June 1975 • July 1975 • August 1975

In the large main room of Self-Reliance, Vic Hewitt was tending to a blaze in the stone fireplace that centered the space. A dozen people stood or sat around it; nobody spoke. They ranged in age from twenty to eighty. Aside from the Van Laars themselves, the only two Carl recognized definitively were the younger Mrs. Van Laar's parents, come up from the city. Their daughter—Bear's mother—was absent. Taken to bed, perhaps. Crying in some other room. Carl's wife had been that way for Scotty's final weeks. For the whole year after.

Everyone in the room appeared to have recently returned from spending hours in the woods. Their faces were dazed and drawn and streaked with dirt; their clothing was stiff, newly dried by the fire after the rain that had fallen earlier.

A queasy stillness pervaded the room. Reality settling in. He could imagine them at the start of their search, early in the afternoon, in the daylight: nervous, tipsy laughter as they scoured the grounds, sure they'd find the child, shouting for him in the rain, hopeful that he was pulling a prank, hopeful that by cocktail hour they'd be recounting the tale of their search over drinks.

He could imagine their mood as it shifted.

They should have called earlier, Carl was thinking. This had been the truth unspoken by all four volunteers as they drove toward the Preserve. Vic Hewitt, at least, should have known better. All four of the volunteers had basic tracking skills, and Dick's brother Ronald had a hound, Jennie, with a good nose on her. But Ronald had been unreachable, so they'd left without a dog. Between the rainstorm and the general trampling the ground had taken by then, both tracks and scents would be more difficult to pick up tomorrow. Why hadn't Hewitt called?

*　*　*

None of the central room's dozen occupants had risen upon their arrival. It was only when Vic Hewitt spoke that anyone seemed to take notice of them at all.

"The folks from the local fire department are here," he said— addressing the younger Mr. Van Laar. "In case you'd like a word."

In the kitchen, away from the crowd, the elder and younger Mr. Van Laar faced the volunteers. It was then that Carl remembered his hat, a floppy felt thing his wife had given him several birthdays ago. He snatched it from his head, pawed at his hair and beard, smoothing them.

When no one else spoke, he did.

"Well," said Carl. He looked down at the floor as he spoke, unable to meet anyone's gaze. "So. When's the last time you saw the boy?"

"Three o'clock," said the elder Van Laar.

"And he was—hiking?"

"You know this already," said the younger Van Laar. "We spoke on the telephone." There was impatience in his voice as he said it. It occurred to Carl that he might believe they were going to set out into the woods this very night. They wouldn't get far, doing that; they had one flashlight and one headlamp between them, and the latter was out of batteries, if Carl remembered right. There might be more equipment lying around the estate, but still—the state police, with their taxpayer dollars, would have to be called to make any progress at all.

"Would you mind repeating the information for the others, sir?" Carl asked. "In case I missed anything when I told them."

"The two of us were hiking, yes," said the elder Van Laar. "Bear had been begging to go for a hike. We left the house around three o'clock. We walked through the woods—there's a shortcut, about a quarter mile long, that connects our house to the trailhead at the base of Hunt. But as soon as we reached the trailhead, Bear said he'd forgotten his pocketknife. He wanted to turn back for it."

"How come?" asked Dick Shattuck—unable to keep quiet any longer, it seemed. Carl was relieved.

"He said he wanted to show me something," said the elder. "I don't know what it was."

For a moment, Carl felt dizzy. Firewood, he thought. *Loose and light and floppy*. He wanted to show you how to figure out what wood was good for starting a fire, thought Carl. And then he thought, I taught him that. He had, in fact, taught Bear many things: How to whistle with an acorn cap. How to whittle an owl and a bear and a fox's head. How to tell when rain was coming. The same things he had taught his own Scotty.

"And you said all right," said Shattuck, prompting Mr. Van Laar.

"Yes," said Mr. Van Laar. "I was impatient. But I said yes."

"You watched him head back toward the house," said Shattuck.

"Yes."

"When did you lose sight of him?"

The elder considered. "Almost immediately," he said. "There's a turn that the path takes"—here Van Laar demonstrated with his hand—"about a hundred feet from the trailhead, back in the direction of the house. I watched Bear until he reached that point, and then he turned left, and was gone."

"What's the trailhead like?" asked Shattuck.

Carl knew. He'd been there himself a handful of times with Bear, who'd been given permission from his parents to go as far as the base of the mountain whenever he liked, but no farther than that. The trailhead was a turnaround at the end of a dirt road that led to Route 29, the main paved road into town. Hunt Mountain, by virtue of its small size, wasn't among the most popular peaks in the Adirondacks, but when the weather was good there were usually a half-dozen cars parked here and there in the lot.

"What do you mean," asked the elder.

"I mean—is it a busy place? Active?"

"Not usually," said the elder.

"And today? Were there other people on the mountain, do you think?"

"I wouldn't know about that," said the elder. "There were no cars in the lot, but I never got as far as the mountain. I stood at the trailhead, waiting for Bear, until it began to rain."

There was silence then. Uncomfortable.

Carl watched Bob Lewis. Of the four of them, he was the cynic, the pessimist. He had a paranoid streak that sometimes caused him to leap to conclusions about bad actors and questionable motives.

Twice, he had made the case for arson when a fire's cause couldn't easily be explained. (So far, there had been no actual cases of arson in Shattuck Township—not on their watch, anyway.)

On cue, Bob L. spoke up.

"Why were you going for a hike in a storm?" he asked the elder Van Laar.

The question was abrupt. Lewis tempered himself. "If you don't mind my asking, sir."

"The storm was sudden," said Mr. Van Laar. "It came from nowhere. The sky was clear when we left the house. The sun was out. Not a hint of moisture in the air. And then," he said. But he didn't continue.

Dick Shattuck cleared his throat. "Mr. V," he said, "how long would you say you waited for Bear at the trailhead, after he turned back?"

"Difficult to say," said the elder Van Laar. "Fifteen minutes, maybe. Twenty. I didn't check my pocket watch when he left, but I did when the rain began. That was at three thirty-five. That's when I lost patience and headed back myself. The path through the woods is short. As I said. It shouldn't have taken him so long."

The conversation continued, but Carl stayed silent. Calculating. Mr. Van Laar had said Bear had set off on a hike with his grandfather at 3 p.m. Carl had left work early that day, at half past three. That was when he saw the boy bent down in front of the house, tying a shoe, about to set off someplace.

If he was doing his math correctly, it was possible that he, Carl Stoddard, was the last person to see the boy before he disappeared.

He thought of speaking up about it. Decided against it, for now.

Both Van Laars simultaneously leaned their weight against the countertop behind them, suddenly exhausted. In general, they moved as a pair. Same height, same eyes, same steady fluid movements. There was an athleticism to them that Carl didn't generally associate with rich people. He had once seen Peter III playing an impromptu game of baseball on the lawn during a different year's Blackfly Good-by. He had knocked a ball completely out of sight and then run around the improvised bases in a casual lope that concealed what Carl, from his football days, immediately understood to be an impressive reserve of speed.

"Did anyone see him after that? Anyone aside from you, I mean," said Shattuck.

"No one that I know of," said the elder.

"Do you think he ever reached the house?"

"Unclear," said the younger. Bear's father. "No one saw him there, but many of the guests were resting at that time. Or outside, I suppose."

Carl swallowed hard. He wanted to speak up. To say, *I saw him. He was tying his shoes. It was half past three.* But he understood what would change the moment he revealed it.

Shattuck continued, and the moment passed.

"Who do you believe was inside the house?"

The younger Van Laar nodded. "I was," he said. "My wife was. Certain guests, as I said. Certain members of the staff."

"And when did you start searching for Bear?"

The two Van Laars glanced at one another.

Then the younger spoke. "Dad found me at the house," he said. "Around a quarter to four. I'd been resting in my bedroom. He told me he couldn't find Bear."

On saying the name, his voice rose.

Carl looked away, afraid suddenly that he would cry.

"And then," said Shattuck, more gently.

"We went out, the two of us, into the rain," said the elder. "We didn't want to alarm anyone just yet. We began—calling for him. For Bear. And I suppose people heard us. And slowly a group formed. We fanned out. We all wandered in the woods for a while. We split into smaller parties. One group went all the way up Hunt, all the way to the top of the mountain. Another went down to the beach to walk along the waterline. Another searched Camp Emerson, all the cabins, every building. There were twenty of us searching, or thereabouts. We spent about three hours searching, all told. Got thoroughly soaked in the process."

The four volunteers nodded collectively.

"When did you let the boy's mother know?" asked Bob Lewis. Again, the question felt wrong, too abrupt, the subject too tender.

It was the younger Van Laar who answered. "She heard us calling," he said. "She came outside." His voice was tight.

Carl had stopped looking in the Van Laars' direction altogether. If he cried now—

At last he allowed himself to bring forth, queasily, the memory that had been threatening to surface for hours. It was of Bear last summer, little and strong, sitting on a stump beside Carl as he planted flowers in the earth. The boy had been whittling contentedly, something of his own creation. Then, hearing a low male voice calling for him, he had paused in his efforts, and stiffened.

Carl had glanced up at him. Watched him for a moment, waiting for him to respond.

He hadn't.

"That your dad calling?" Carl prompted him gently. Again came the voice: "*Bear Van Laar! Peter Four!*"

Bear shook his head. "That's my grandfather," he said. And then, so quietly that he almost couldn't be heard: "I don't like him much."

At that he collapsed his little knife, sighed heavily, and put it into his pocket. He stood, shoulders hunched, and walked in the direction of Self-Reliance.

It was 8:45 p.m. now. The sun was down. They walked back through the somber main room, which had emptied a bit since they'd entered. Then out through the front door and onto the lawn, plump with groundwater, squelching with each step. There was a very full moon that night, so bright that it cast faint shadows in their wake. The four of them and Vic Hewitt walked north, in the direction of the path through the woods that the boy and his grandfather had taken together earlier in the day.

"Do you know what he was wearing?" Bob Alcott asked Hewitt.

"Short pants, as I recall," said Hewitt. "And a red shirt, I think. Short-sleeved. Least that's what he was wearing when I saw him this morning."

"Long pants," said Carl reflexively. He remembered this well. The boy had cuffed them in order to tie his shoes.

A pause.

"Oh?" said Hewitt.

"I think so."

"How come?"

"I think I—saw him. Out front of the main house. Right before I left."

Vic Hewitt looked at him hard. "What time would that have been?"

"Three thirty or so."

All of them looked off toward the woods.

"Carl," said Vic. "Any reason you wouldn't have told us that earlier?"

Carl thought. "It just came to me," he said. "Just now."

Shattuck, bearing the single flashlight they'd found in the truck, swung it back and forth across the tree line at the edge of the lawn. With every sweep of light, the forest's density was underscored. Parts of it looked positively thicket-like. Impenetrable. The only clearing was the entrance to the path in question. The last place Bear was known to have been.

"Should we shout for him?" said Carl.

Hewitt hesitated. "Don't think so," he said finally. "Got no response all day. Hate to agitate the family further. Let them rest awhile."

Shattuck nodded. He aimed the flashlight in the direction of the path, again, and then shone it back toward the house before speaking. When he did, his voice was measured.

"Look," he said. "The four of us could head into those woods and swing our one flashlight around awhile. See if we find any tracks. Or we could go back to the house, dig up some more flashlights, or some torches. Have everyone fan out again. But with the number of folks you already had out here tramping around, I think we'd be better off bringing a hound in before the boy's scent is gone completely. Don't you?"

Vic Hewitt nodded. He wasn't meeting their eyes. He was looking in the direction of the woods.

"Ask me," said Shattuck, "I think we'd be wise to call the staties in. Only if you're asking." It was what Carl had been thinking, too. What all of them were thinking, no doubt.

Hewitt gave no response. He was listening.

"Vic?" said Shattuck. "You all right?"

A sudden rush of movement in the woods. The frantic rustling of a trapped animal. From the cleared path toward the mountain emerged a small figure, running flat-out.

For a moment, everyone was hopeful.

But it wasn't Bear. It was a girl, Carl saw. Shattuck swung the light in her direction. Her face was white and panicked, her mouth open in a sort of silent wail. Her clothes were damp; her hair matted to her head, her long braid a sodden rope that hung heavily over one shoulder and down the front of her.

"What'n the hell," said Hewitt lowly, and only then did Carl realize who it was.

Hewitt strode quickly in the direction of his daughter, Tessie Jo.

The rest of them remained in place.

Carl

1950s • **1961** • Winter 1973
June 1975 • July 1975 • August 1975

Tessie Jo was taken—mouth open, eyes closed—into her father's arms, and then into the great room, and then down the hall, where a bath was run for her by one of the maids while, in a nearby room, her father calmed her down.

The few remaining guests scattered. The volunteers—Carl in the lead—excused themselves, and returned to the front lawn, where they stood, hands in pockets, wondering what to do.

Bob L. spoke first. "You think she saw something?"

Dick Shattuck: "Let's hope so."

But Carl had a different idea. "They were friends," he said. "Good friends. Bear followed her everywhere. Looked up to her. Had a crush, maybe."

The other three looked at him.

"Maybe she's just upset he's gone," said Carl.

And this, indeed, was the word handed down by Vic Hewitt, when he came striding down the hallway again: the girl was in shock. She was tired and cold and starved, out in the woods with no food or drink since afternoon, when Bear was first reported missing. She was terrified of losing her friend—one of the only friends she had, said Vic—adding that she'd never gotten along well with the kids at her small school. For now, Tessie Jo had been fed soup by Darla McCray and put to bed, still shivering. The hope was that she wouldn't get sick.

All four men received this information, nodding. And then Vic told them that they should go home, get some sleep. He'd take it upon himself to keep watch overnight. Tomorrow, the five of them, and the state police, would start over. With hounds, this time.

As the truck pulled out of the driveway, they saw Vic in the dim light cast forth by Self-Reliance. He was walking toward the wood-shed. He would build a campfire for his solitary watch, thought Carl;

maybe the blaze, or the smoke, would draw the boy back toward the house.

To that point, Carl had resisted allowing entry to a feeling that had been hovering on the outskirts of his consciousness. But from the back of the pickup truck, he watched as the lights of Self-Reliance turned off one by one, and he at last allowed himself to think it: if that were *his* boy, lost in the cold woods overnight—down with an injury, perhaps—well, he would still be out there searching. Calling Bear's name until his own body gave out.

At home, Maryanne was still awake. She was sitting up at the kitchen table, laying out a hand of solitaire. She'd played almost every night since Scotty died; said it helped to empty her mind before sleep.

"Any luck?" she asked Carl, without turning. She was straight-backed, tense.

"No," said Carl. "Search'll broaden tomorrow. We'll bring Ron Shattuck's hound." And then he paused, considering.

He had told nobody, yet, what Bear had said about his grandfather. The way Bear's posture had changed upon hearing his name called in that stern voice. For a moment he considered telling Maryanne. But he could never predict her reactions to what he said, these days. Any wrong thing might drive her to anger—the emotion she most readily expressed, lately, as if all of her sadness since Scotty's passing required replacement with *something*. But she spoke first.

"I'll come too," said Maryanne calmly.

"To the Preserve?" said Carl.

"Yes."

Carl paused. His deference to the Van Laars was so ingrained that his first reaction was to wonder whether she would even be welcome on the grounds. Then he came to his senses; surely the Van Laars would want as many hands as possible. "Are you certain?" he asked.

Maryanne nodded. Placed a seven atop an eight. "Mother will watch the girls. I've asked already."

"All right," said Carl. Still tentative. He settled at last on the one subject he generally knew to be safe: "How were they?"

Maryanne smiled, waved a hand. "Oh, all right. Jeannie's upset about a grade. Margaret's upset about a boy. Antonia's upset about a friend." She turned to him, at last, and for a moment he saw a glimpse of humor in her eyes. "I'd be more worried if everyone was fine."

A surge of warmth arose in him. He had the instinct to go to her, his straight-backed, pretty wife, and place his hands on her arms, and stand there for a while. They so rarely touched one another these days. They had not made love in a year; the last time it happened Maryanne had wept so violently afterward that he promised himself he would not ever approach her again. Not until some invitation was issued, at least, and so far there had been none. So that night, also, he did not go to her, but cleared his throat instead, and walked up the stairs to the bathroom, where he washed before going to bed. One or two hours would pass, he knew, and then Maryanne would enter the room quietly, already dressed in her nightclothes, and she would lie down beside him, and no part of their bodies would meet.

In the early morning, he woke to the smell of breakfast.

His mother-in-law was seated at the table already, coffee in hand. But for her boots, Maryanne had dressed herself in her church clothes, her Sunday school teacher outfit—blue dress, cloche hat—which normally would have been odd for a day's work in the woods. But these were the Van Laars' woods, and these clothes, in Maryanne's mind, were a sign of respect.

At six in the morning, Carl phoned the fire hall to let Bob L. know he'd be driving separately, due to Maryanne's decision to come.

"Well, that's fine," said Bob L. "Turns out everyone else's wife is coming too." A note of complaint was in his voice.

The wives' decision to come may have served as a harbinger, but the full scope of the volunteer effort only became apparent upon Carl's arrival at the Preserve.

There on the lawn stood what appeared to be most of Shattuck's adult citizens: several hundred bodies, waiting for instruction. Ron Shattuck was there with his hound, Jennie; another several dogs were on-site too, held by men Carl did not recognize.

Up near the house were four patrol cars with open windows.

And at the very top of the hill, standing before the front door of Self-Reliance, were the elder and younger Van Laar men. To their right was Vic Hewitt, conferring with the staties.

Carl, taking in this scene with Maryanne beside him, faltered

momentarily. Last night, the four members of the volunteer fire department had seemed to be in charge; today they had been deposed. He
scanned the crowd until he saw Dick Shattuck, looking similarly uncertain, for once in his life. His wife, too, was beside him—a thin woman
named Georgette whom Maryanne had been calling stuck-up since all
of them were in grade school together. Maryanne was making small
throat-clearing noises now, and he took this to mean she wanted him,
Carl, to take charge in some way.

So Carl strode, Maryanne on his heel, toward what he perceived to
be the action. On the way he caught the eyes of the Bobs and Dick
Shattuck; they followed behind.

When they reached the group of men standing out front of Self-
Reliance, no one turned.

With some trepidation, Carl spoke up.

"Morning," said Carl, drawing raised eyebrows from several troopers,
and a pause from Vic.

"Men, this is Carl Stoddard," said Hewitt. "He's a groundskeeper
here and a volunteer firefighter nearby. Carl, these men are from the
state police. They'll be helping us search."

"Anything happen overnight?" said Carl, and Vic shook his head.

"I built a fire best I could," said Hewitt. "Despite the damp. Sat up
all night. I guess I dozed a little, on and off."

"No sign," said Carl uselessly.

Hewitt shook his head. "I was saying," he continued, "most important thing is not to disturb any tracks that might be left. Or scents.
More than they've already been disturbed, I mean. We'll let the men
with dogs head out first, get a good head start. While they're searching,
I'll divide the rest of the crowd up and teach them how to move. What
to look for."

The troopers nodded, listening. It was interesting, Carl thought,
that none of them asserted any authority here; to a one, they all seemed
to recognize their place, as subordinates to the family running the
operation, and to Vic. It was true, too, that the Hewitts had been
known for generations as the best guides in the region, and Vic was
thought to have a special gift. A few of the troopers were local boys
who no doubt knew his reputation.

Abruptly, then, Vic Hewitt turned and strode away, leaving Carl and the others alone with the troopers, who closed in on themselves to form a tight circle.

Bob L., never shy about complaining, was the first to say it. "It's like we're not here."

The men with dogs went first, as planned.

Ten minutes after the hounds, the rest of the crowd departed, some in vehicles, to the locations assigned to them by Vic Hewitt. The four firefighters and their wives had been given the task of searching a square mile of woods on the opposite side of Route 29; they drove to the site in question and pulled over in a line at the edge of the woods.

The goal, Vic had said—raising his voice as well as he could to address the entire crowd—was to form a line of humans, evenly spaced, and march forward as a collective. Keep your eyes on the ground, said Vic. Sweep them left to right. Watch for unusual colors, unusual depressions in the undergrowth. Every thirty seconds or so, call out for the boy.

This, it turned out, was the most difficult part for Carl. For all the men.

They were unaccustomed to raising their voices in this way, to calling out one person's name repeatedly.

As it turned out, the women were more willing to do so; and so it was their voices that echoed throughout the woods. All of them were mothers. All of them regularly set aside their innate sense of propriety to holler with abandon for their children.

Around the Preserve, they could hear others doing the same, the boy's name resounding like an echo.

An hour went by. Two, three. The day wasn't hot, but Carl found himself sweating nonetheless. Something about Bear's name being called tugged at his conscience, made his heartbeat increase, triggered the same memory that had been bobbing at the outside of his mind since yesterday afternoon.

"*Bear Van Laar*," the boy's grandfather had called out. And Bear had jumped, startled, unhappy to leave Carl's side.

One foot in front of the other now. The crunch of the pine-needled forest floor. If Carl had been by himself, he would have taken off his shirt. He worked to focus on the ground, as he'd been told to do—as he knew to do. But the landscape was beginning to blur before him. He took a sip from the canteen of water that hung from his neck.

Maryanne generally noticed such things, quickly observed when he or one of the children was ill or nervous or otherwise out of spirits. But today she was focused on the task at hand. Early on she had tied her dress up into a knot at her knees. Now she was stepping high with her booted feet, calling out for the boy.

Suddenly Carl stumbled, and fell to the ground. The whole chain stopped.

He was feeling a sort of pain in his stomach and chest, something viselike and twisting. He could say no words.

The name they had been calling changed now. *Carl*, they were saying. *Carl. Carl.*

It was the last thing he heard before losing consciousness.

III

When Lost

Tracy

1950s • 1961 • Winter 1973
June 1975 • **July 1975** • August 1975

She was afraid to use the word, to even think it, but sometimes Tracy felt like she was falling in love with Barbara Van Laar.

She was fascinated by the details of Barbara's face and body, her eyes—long-lashed and perennially sleepy—and the shape of her strong legs, and the nails she bit down to nothing, and the very light hair of her forearms and thighs, which looked like spun gold in the sunlight, and which emphasized the artificial black of her hair. If she caught Tracy staring—which she must have—she said nothing, only smiled vaguely in her direction, as if accustomed to being the recipient of such gazes.

More important: Barbara was the first friend she'd ever had who seemed to like Tracy as much as Tracy liked her. She told Tracy she was funny, for one thing: she laughed loudly and often at things that Tracy said, drawing interested gazes from those around them. She told Tracy she was smart. She harbored a disdain for the mainstream without disdaining the people who partook in it. Indeed, she was the least judgmental person Tracy had ever met.

Barbara's position at Camp Emerson was an interesting one: she had the glamour of an outsider, that summer being her first at camp, and yet she was also an insider in ways the rest of them could never be. She had frequented the grounds in the off-season; she had seen into closets and back rooms and kitchens that were off-limits to other campers.

Most intriguingly, she was apparently quite close with T.J. Hewitt, the camp director, who was essentially a mystery to every other camper on-site. Yes, she led them all in outdoorsmanship lessons; but even then she was serious and standoffish. The only things Tracy knew about her personal life centered on her history on the grounds. She was the daughter of the former longtime director of the camp, Vic Hewitt, a legend whose likeness hung in a place of prominence in the commissary. Said to be ill in some way. Other than this fact, they knew nothing at all about T.J.; the counselors revered her, never gossiped about her. She seemed more like a mascot than a living person: someone to be greatly respected, but never spoken to directly.

The first time, therefore, that Tracy passed T.J. while walking with Barbara, she was surprised to hear her new friend call out the director's name brightly.

"What's happening?" Barbara said.

Unlike everyone else on the premises, T.J. did not wear a uniform. Instead she wore cutoffs—corduroy or jean—and a T-shirt or a plaid flannel, and high socks, and brown Danner hiking boots laced tightly to the top. On her head was a hairstyle so laughably askew that on anyone else it would have been ridiculed. But on T.J., the cut seemed simply to indicate a lack of concern for earthly matters. It functioned, like a monk's tonsure, to separate her from the laypeople at the camp.

She'd been kneeling before one of the small bridges that spanned the creek separating the boys' cabins from the girls'. She was hammering a row of nails with frightening speed. Now she looked up and frowned.

"Where're you supposed to be?" she said.

"Can't remember!" said Barbara. Teasing. She turned to Tracy. "Can you, Tracy?"

"Lunch," Tracy said quickly. "We're walking to lunch right now."

"Ah, that's right. Sorry, T.J., I'm new here." Barbara grinned. T.J. didn't. But it was clear she was fighting a smile.

"Get out of my hair," she said, and, raising her hammer in the air again, turned back to her work.

They continued on their way. At a certain point Barbara noticed Tracy's expression: wide-eyed, waiting for an explanation.

"What?" she said.

Tracy glanced back over her shoulder.

"Oh, T.J.?" said Barbara. "She's harmless. I don't know why everyone's so intimidated by her."

"What does she do the rest of the year?" asked Tracy.

"Takes care of her dad. Takes care of the grounds. Comes to stay with me in Albany when my parents have to go someplace."

Tracy looked at her. "She—*babysits* you?" She couldn't imagine it. The long silences, she thought, would be unbearable.

Barbara laughed. "I wouldn't call it that. She just stays with me, makes sure I stay out of trouble. The Hewitts are like family."

Tracy shrugged. "If you say so," she said.

When Tracy was not with Barbara, she was making attempts to learn about her. For one thing, she was becoming increasingly curious about her history. If her bunkmates knew the full story of Barbara's brother's disappearance, the arrival of Barbara herself had precipitated a sort of respectful silence on the matter.

Only once was Tracy privy to anything of substance.

Halfway through the summer, she was walking back from the washroom on a break when she came across Lowell Cargill, the other object of her affection, seated at a picnic table. His face was obscured by a newspaper.

Above the fold, the date: *July 13, 1975*. Below the date, a man's face gazed toward the viewer: bespectacled, balding, unsmiling. This, she ascertained from the caption, was Jacob Sluiter—known to the campers as *Slitter*. She had heard whispers in the dark about him, knew there to be some rumored connection between Slitter and Bear Van Laar; but the details to that point had eluded Tracy.

As nonchalantly as possible, she sat at a different table, facing the paper. She squinted in the article's direction, attempting to make out details. In moments like these, she regretted not wearing her glasses. *SIGHTING REPORTED*, said the headline. And beneath it, large words like *dangerous* and *armed*.

"Nervous?"

Tracy flinched.

Lowell Cargill was regarding her over the top of the paper in his hands.

"Says here he might be making his way northward, toward his old hunting grounds," said Lowell casually.

He folded the paper. Crossed one leg over the other, ankle to knee.

Then, seeing Tracy's face, he added: "Don't be scared. He was all the way down at Fishkill when he got out. If he's walking, he wouldn't be in this area yet. And I bet they find him before he gets here."

He paused.

"Unless he hitchhiked," he added uncertainly. "But who would pick him up?"

"Where did you get that paper?" Tracy asked.

"From the canteen," said Lowell. "They sell papers there every day. Most people just don't want 'em."

I do, thought Tracy. At home, she liked reading the daily paper with her mother. And she saw it as further evidence of her compatibility with Lowell Cargill that he, too, read the newspaper: a quality she considered unusual in a boy his age.

Abruptly, Lowell stood up and stretched his arms into the air, revealing a slice of midriff that thrilled her.

"You can have this if you want," said Lowell. "I'm done with it."

She took it into her hands—knowing without a doubt that she would keep it in her trunk for the rest of the session, a sort of holy relic, sanctified by Lowell Cargill's touch.

The PA system crackled to life then, announcing the end of free hour, and Lowell turned away.

Then, as if remembering something, he turned. "Hey," he said. "Barbara said you're a good singer. Do you want to sing with me sometime?"

Tracy felt all the blood in her body leave her head.

Lowell furrowed his brow. "It's okay if you don't," he said. "I was just wondering. I'm trying to learn how to harmonize."

He began walking.

Tracy watched the back of him, cursing herself for her cowardice. And then, when he was ten strides away, she willed herself to speak. "I will," she said. And then again, louder.

"Right on," said Lowell. "I'll find you."

On her top bunk, after dinner and before lights-out, Tracy folded the front page of *The Saratogian* into a small square, and read the article.

From it, she learned the full story of Jacob Sluiter. He was, she read, a notorious killer who had haunted the Adirondack Park just over a decade prior. Sluiter was accused of and prosecuted for eleven murders, all of which took place between 1960 and 1964, the year in which he was finally apprehended. Most of these killings took place at campgrounds or remote cabins. The victims—couples, sometimes single women—were bound and stabbed; no firearms were used. What allowed Sluiter to elude capture for so long was his deep knowledge of woodcraft, forged over the course of a childhood spent in rural poverty. He could trap and fish with great skill. During each of the four winters he was on the lam, Sluiter moved from unoccupied cabin to unoccupied cabin, stealing canned goods and other provisions left behind by summer people; from May to September, when the region became more populated and owners returned to their cabins, he camped out in the wilderness. He might have gone on this way forever if not for a stroke of bad luck: a cottage he assumed to be empty for winter was, in fact, the site of its owners' annual Christmas celebration. Pulling into the driveway, the owner spotted a fire in the fireplace. Before Sluiter could get to his gun, the owner was inside, on top of him.

Jacob Sluiter was tied to a chair while the authorities were called. On December 23, 1964, he was captured at last.

He confessed to nothing. He maintained his innocence, despite the evidence that damned him irreversibly: possessions from victims among his belongings; his fingerprints at all the crime scenes; testimony from two siblings about sadistic tendencies; and, at last, a positive visual identification from one survivor of an attempted homicide. Still, Sluiter denied it. His lack of transparency, wrote the reporter, led to speculation that Sluiter may have been responsible for even more homicides than those he was accused of. Certain cases involving persons who'd gone missing while out hiking—who were formerly considered to have simply gotten lost—were reopened.

Including Bear Van Laar's? Tracy wondered. This was the frightening rumor she'd heard her first night at camp.

The article went on: ten years after Jacob Sluiter's capture and sentencing—life in prison, without parole—he feigned illness to oblige a transfer to a lower-security prison. And three weeks ago, Jacob Sluiter escaped that prison, over two hundred miles south of Camp Emerson. The issue of *The Saratogian* she held was published in his fourth week of being on the lam; the headline reported a possible sighting near Schoharie, New York.

To the side of the article there was a diagram, a sort of map that displayed the location of Sluiter's known killings, and also of his previous apprehension. And Tracy couldn't help but notice two of the several reference points the artist had included on the map. One was the town of Shattuck, five miles from Camp Emerson. And the other was the Van Laar Preserve itself. Tracy used her finger, and the key, to judge the distance from where they were to where Sluiter's arrest had been. Twenty miles, or thirty at the most. She traced a path from Camp Emerson, to the arrest, to the closest killing, also twenty or thirty miles away, and in the process produced a neat isosceles triangle, an eastward-pointing arrow with Camp Emerson as its tip.

Tracy

1950s • 1961 • Winter 1973
June 1975 • **July 1975** • August 1975

Lowell Cargill, it turned out, was more than just talk. An excruciating week went by, and then he arrived on Balsam's porch—guitar case in hand—and knocked on the door. One of the Melissas answered, confused. When he asked for Tracy, her mouth fell open further.

Lowell's suggestion was that they go to the amphitheater to practice, and this was how Tracy found herself following him silently across the grounds of the camp. She tried and failed to think of something to say to him. But Lowell seemed comfortable not talking—until they arrived at their destination. Then he sat down on a stump, opened his guitar case.

One thing Tracy had noticed, the first time she heard Lowell sing, was that he evinced no self-consciousness at all—but really *sang*, his eyes closing sometimes, as if blocking out the rest of the world.

Today was no different. He began the same Ian & Sylvia song he had sung before—the one that Tracy knew.

Facing Lowell now, Tracy was conflicted: a large part of her was struggling not to burst into hysterical giggles, and she began to dig her fingernails into her own palm to prevent them. But another part of her found Lowell's passion inspiring, even attractive. His earnest face, beautifully sculpted, moving in agitated ways: it was perhaps the most erotic thing that Tracy, at twelve, had ever witnessed.

"Okay," said Lowell, when he had sung the song through one time. "Now I'll teach it to you."

"I know it already," Tracy said.

For an hour, they rehearsed—Tracy teaching him, this time, how to hold his note while she held hers. She suddenly found herself missing her mother—a track rat, an exercise rider, tomboyish and forthright, tall, with red hair and freckles like Tracy. She ate her food messily, hunched over her plate, and laughed loudly, and walked with her knees and elbows out, loose-limbed, jangling as she went, her gait reminding Tracy somehow of a marionette's. Her only moments of gracefulness were on horseback. In the year following her parents' divorce, most of Tracy's anger had been directed at her mother—whose vicinity made her an easier target. But now, in her mind, Tracy thanked her for this one thing: teaching her daughter to harmonize.

That night, Tracy floated back to her cabin like a ghost. Upon entering, she was met with the inquisitive gaze of Barbara, who must have heard where Tracy had been.

She sat down next to Barbara on the lower bunk and gazed at the floor.

"What happened?" she whispered.

Quietly, Tracy told her.

It was the first time in her life that she felt she had a really good story to tell. One in which she—Tracy Jewell—was the protagonist, the ingenue. Barbara, next to her, was nodding sagely as she spoke.

"Did he say he wanted to meet again?" asked Barbara.

"Yes," said Tracy.

Barbara thought. "Well, he likes you," she said. "That much is obvious."

It was strange, but Tracy knew that she was correct. There was no doubt about it: Lowell Cargill liked her.

"What happens next?" Tracy asked her.

She shrugged. "Depends how experienced he is," said Barbara. "Maybe he'll ask you to the dance. Or maybe, next time you play together, he'll try it with you."

Try *what*, Tracy wondered—though a part of her knew.

"You're not scared, are you?" Barbara asked.

"No," Tracy said. "I'm not scared."

She was petrified.

A long silence ensued.

"Do you ever listen to music?" Barbara asked.

She did—but not any music she'd confess to Barbara. She listened to her mother's music, or to bands and boys who could be found on the cover of *Tiger Beat*.

Barbara continued without waiting. "Kissing someone—someone

you want to kiss, I mean—is like living inside the best song you ever heard. It's the same feeling."

Later, atop her bunk, Tracy took out her journal and enumerated everything she knew about sex.

What parts of the anatomy it involved: this was at the top of the list.

What actually happened between those parts: she knew the technicalities, but couldn't quite grasp the mechanics.

She turned her face to the window: the moon was nearly full.

That's the last thing she remembered seeing before they were woken, in the morning, by the sound of an air horn.

"*Survival Trip*," whispered one of the Melissas. All around Tracy, the campers of Balsam sprang into motion.

Barbara, on the bottom bunk, was the first one dressed and out the door.

Tracy

1950s • 1961 • Winter 1973
June 1975 • July 1975 • **August 1975**

Tracy has known for one hour that Barbara is missing. So far, she has not had to lie.

She's been asked the following two questions, several times: *Do you know where she is? Did you hear her leave?* To both of them, Tracy can safely answer, *No.*

Now, with the counselors pulled away to search, the CITs have been tasked with keeping everyone to their routine. On the walk to the commissary, Tracy forms a plan. She lets herself lag at the back of the group, then ducks behind a building. Waits, breathing, until her cabinmates are out of sight.

She needs to go someplace. She thinks it will be a quick trip, just a lark—to see if she can rule out the place she believes Barbara might have gone. She makes a promise to herself: if she doesn't find Barbara there, she'll confess to the authorities everything she knows.

It's not a decision she makes lightly. Because Barbara swore Tracy to secrecy. And the fact that she entrusted Tracy—Tracy!—with such an important secret makes her loath to break Barbara's confidence so readily.

She knows where it is that Barbara goes each night.

Although Barbara will tell Tracy nothing about her boyfriend, she did tell her once about their meeting place: an observer's cabin at the peak of Hunt Mountain, something formerly occupied by a string of men whose job it was to keep watch for wildfires in the surrounding area. Next to it is a fire tower that affords an even better view. Both structures have gone unoccupied lately due to staffing shortages. But both are convenient as shelters from bad weather. Or as places to meet in secret.

"At *night?*" Tracy whispered incredulously. And Barbara laughed.

"Do you know how many times I've climbed that hill?" she said. "I could do it in my sleep."

"But how long does it take you to get there? And how do you *see*?" said Tracy.

"Half an hour. I run it. And I bring this." Barbara glanced around. Then she plunged a hand between the top of her mattress and the bed frame. She produced a flashlight—her own, apparently, separate from the one they were to use on bathroom visits overnight.

Tracy's theory, today, is that Barbara perhaps fell asleep there; and she wants to rule out this possibility. She believes she can climb up and down Hunt Mountain in an hour and a half. She'll be back in time for her morning activity—hopefully with news of Barbara, or maybe even with Barbara herself. She'll get in trouble, she knows, but she doesn't care. Barbara is the only reason she likes camp, anyway.

From behind the Staff Quarters she sets off, with purpose, toward the closest woods: the thicker forest that stands between Camp Emerson and Route 29, hoping to remain unseen on her way.

No such luck: within twenty seconds she spies Lee Towson, one of the cooks. Very handsome. Said to be friends with Louise.

He's carrying two bags of garbage, and as he walks he rocks his feet from heel to toe so carefully that he makes no noise at all. Tracy jumps, startled, when she sees him, and the movement draws his eye.

For a moment, they stand and stare at one another. Then Tracy holds up one finger to her lips, a pleading expression on her face, and Lee nods and continues on his way.

August in the Adirondacks does not feel like August to Tracy. On Long Island, she imagines, it's swelteringly hot. Here, in the woods, it's pleasant. It feels impossible to become thirsty: the air itself feels full of cool water, velvety on the skin. Tracy walks, invigorated, careful to stay just inside the tree line. She tries to keep the buildings of Camp Emerson visible to her right.

Five minutes go by in this way, and then she stops short. There ahead of her is the driveway that stretches from Route 29 to Self-Reliance. She'll have to cross it to continue, but she can't: a slow line of police cars is moving past her. She stands in the dim forest, waiting.

Four cars drive by, then five.

Tentatively, she peers out from behind a tree until it's safe to cross the road. Then she enters the woods to the north.

Now, there is no edge to follow.

On her right, a long tract of forest stretches toward Self-Reliance; on her left, another one stretches toward Route 29. She can see the peak of Hunt Mountain through the top of some nearby trees. If she walks in a straight line, she'll reach it in ten minutes.

Time passes. The ground descends into a little valley, and she loses sight of the mountain; but she tells herself that if she keeps the sun on her right, she'll be fine. The problem is that it's becoming difficult to tell. The woods themselves are becoming thicker, closing in. The undergrowth, sparse near the driveway, has become nearly impassable in places. Already, she has cuts on her shins and calves.

Up ahead, Tracy can see that the land will rise again, and this reassures her: it makes sense to her that there would be an incline on the approach to Hunt Mountain. Soon, surely, she'll catch sight of the peak again.

She doesn't even have a watch. Later, she will understand how foolish she was, how clearly disrespectful of those woods—to think she could enter them so cavalierly, without a watch or compass, without long pants or even water, disregarding every single thing that T.J. Hewitt has painstakingly taught them over the course of the summer so far. But at nearly thirteen, Tracy swings wildly between self-abasement and overconfidence. There is no middle ground.

Tracy begins counting in her head to determine how much time has passed. *One-Mississippi*, et cetera, until at least ten minutes have gone by with no sight of Hunt Mountain, and no sight of the sun.

Only then does Tracy let herself acknowledge what she's done. The great mistake she's made.

She sits down—too late now. She's covered too much ground. Truly, she's been lost for half a mile.

She sits down regardless, hearing in her mind the voice of that counselor, the greeter, the first person who ever spoke to her on this land.

She yells.

Judyta

1950s • 1961 • Winter 1973
June 1975 • July 1975 • August 1975: **Day One**

Judyta Luptack, born and raised in Schenectady, was for many years never the first at anything. In her own family, she was third, behind two brothers, ahead of another. Academically, she was generally in the middle of the pack. When, in gym class, she was asked to run a race, she was usually toward the front. But she never won.

Therefore, when the *Times Union* published that article, she was met with an unfamiliar feeling. Was it pride? Not exactly. More like surprise.

"Nation's First Class of Female State Troopers Graduates at Albany," read the headline. And there below was a picture of the four of them: Cindy and Linda and Niecy and her—*Judyta Luptack, 21*, said the caption.

Her father turned to her mother. "Well, if one of them had to make the papers," he said, "I'm glad it was for this." And that was all that anyone said about it after that, except her brother Leonard, who began referring to her as *The Nation's First*, instead of by her given name.

Five years have passed since that time, and Judy—now twenty-six—has done well. Each year, she has exceeded the benchmarks set for her. She makes good clear reports; good arrests. She is a go-getter, not a slug. (According to her former sergeant, all troopers fall into one of these two categories.) And last year, after some particularly impressive work, she was recommended for promotion to the New York State Bureau of Criminal Investigation, making her the first female investigator in the state.

Now The Nation's First, having recently completed her requisite months of training with the BCI, rides alongside a senior investigator on the New York State Thruway. His name is Denny Hayes, and he seems—without ever directly mentioning it—to have appointed himself Judy's mentor. As such, he has accompanied her each workday for the past two weeks. It does not escape her that she's not the only new investigator in the BCI. But all the others are, of course, men.

In the passenger's seat, Judy crosses and then uncrosses her legs, uncertain which better demonstrates a completely asexual nature. (She is not, in fact, asexual; but she understands that to be thought of as such would be convenient in her line of work.) At least, in plain clothes, she can wear pants now.

Next to her, Denny Hayes is whistling. He whistles a great deal. She recognizes his type: early forties, a father, a former athlete, someone well-liked in high school.

"The Van Laar Preserve," says Denny, in between whistled tunes. "This'll be interesting."

This morning, they were on their way to conduct interviews relating to a larceny case in Long Lake when a call came over the radio: a missing thirteen-year-old girl at a remote compound in the mountains near the small town of Shattuck. Their car was the closest to Shattuck, so they'll be the first BCI investigators to respond.

"You familiar with the Van Laar family?" Denny asks.

She's heard the name, she says. (She hasn't.)

"Remember a news story about a boy who disappeared in the mountains? Twelve or fourteen years ago, this was," says Hayes.

Judy would have been a child. But reminding people of her youth seems sometimes to offend them, and so she says, "Yes, I think so."

"Well, the interesting thing there is," says Hayes, "they caught the guy who killed that little boy. Sick fellow. But he's dead now. So, another kid goes missing from the same place. Who dunnit this time?" He looks at Judy and winks, as if telling a joke.

The land they pass becomes more and more rural. With her appointment to the BCI, Judy has been transferred to Troop B, headquartered in the Adirondacks at Ray Brook. This would be fine—preferable, even—but for the fact that Judy, two weeks into her new position, is still living with her parents in Schenectady; and this means a daily commute that borders on the impossible.

It's two hours from her house to Ray Brook. But the transfer was the only way she could break in as an investigator, she has explained—repeatedly—to her parents. One day soon, she'll convince them that she should find her own place, closer to work; but none of Judy's siblings have ever moved out prior to marriage, and so for now Judy thinks it best not to rock the boat. For fourteen days, instead, she has set her alarm for 4 a.m., and dealt with the howls of her brothers when the beeping begins at that time.

"Here we are," says Hayes.

They pull down a long driveway. On the left is a group of old farm buildings, seemingly no longer in use. A sloping lawn breaks into view, and suddenly they're facing a house that looks like something out of one of her history textbooks in school.

She can feel Hayes's sideways gaze on her as they pull in. Reading her.

What Hayes doesn't know is that Judy is used to being around rich people. Starting at twelve years old, she worked—first off the books and then on—at the Iroquois Golf Club, where her father is still head of the janitorial staff. She washed dishes and then bused tables and then waited tables. Even today she sometimes gets a call from Chick Janowicz, the general manager, to cover a shift when someone is out sick. And every December she works the elaborate Christmas party for cash. Everyone in the Luptack family does: even her mother.

Hayes parks the car at an odd angle on the lawn. A few local troopers are already on-site. Four EnCon vehicles are present too, unoccupied: forest rangers, probably already out in the woods, conducting an initial search.

Hayes regards them for a beat. Then asks: "What's your guess?"

Judy looks at him.

"Take a guess. About what happened to the girl."

"Oh," says Judy. "I'm not sure."

"Runaway's my guess," says Hayes. "Girl this age goes missing it's almost always a runaway."

Judy is silent.

"She's prob'ly got her thumb out on a back road as we speak. Just hope we find her before a bad guy does," says Hayes.

Then, without waiting for Judy, he gets out and sets off in the direction of the nearest trooper, a portly man with sandy eyebrows, and reaches for a handshake.

*   *   *

Judy hesitates. She gets out, turns in a slow circle, taking in the house, the lake on its far side, the woods all around. To the south is some sort of organization, a children's school or camp: she can hear high-pitched shrieks and laughter coming from that direction.

When Denny Hayes returns, he gives her the facts of the case.

It's the Van Laars' daughter who's missing, he says. Thirteen-year-old girl from the same family whose son went missing over a decade before.

Her name, says Hayes, is Barbara Van Laar; she was attending the camp on the grounds; she was last seen asleep in a bunk in her cabin the night before.

The brief statements the troopers have gotten have yielded no theories or leads. Everyone seems surprised by her disappearance. No one has any idea where she might have gone.

Complicating everything, he says, is the fact that *another* camper is now missing: Barbara's bunkmate, a girl named Tracy Jewell, who has no connection to the family. This one was last seen just a couple of hours prior, on a walk from the cabin to the commissary for breakfast. Her parents have been alerted; they're driving this way.

In light of these two disappearances, all the campers are now gathered in the Great Hall, with two troopers assigned to that post. Their parents are being called, one set after another, and instructed to come and retrieve their children. But with ninety-one families and only two landlines, the process is taking a good deal of time. In the meantime, no one is allowed into or out of the Great Hall without showing ID. If necessary, any campers whose parents can't reach Camp Emerson today will sleep there, all together, overnight.

"You know the family's against it?" says Hayes.

"Against what?"

"Having the parents come to pick the campers up. Two kids gone missing, two separate incidents. Including their own daughter. And they're talking about finishing the session. Not wanting to cause any unnecessary alarm."

Judy thought she'd be shadowing Hayes for the day, but she ascertains quickly that his plan is to split up, get statements separately. Cover more territory that way.

"You can bring people into the car to conduct interviews," he says. "For privacy." Then he points down toward the camp. "See that building in the far distance? Long flat building? Trooper I spoke to says there's a good place for interviews in there. Says the Van Laar parents are already down there. That's where I'll be, if you need me."

He turns back to her. Winks.

"But you won't need me. Right?"

"Sure," says Judy. Hayes pats her once on the back. Already she is growing very weary of the casual touch of the men around her, even when—as in Hayes's case—it seems more paternal than lascivious. He inclines his head toward her.

"Listen, honey," he says, in a whisper. "I'll handle the tough stuff. The Van Laar girl's friends and counselors. The parents—if there's anyone to watch, it's them. You're in charge of the folks up here at the house. The minor players, you know what I mean? Don't be nervous."

She wants, badly, to step sideways. To move far away from him. Instead she nods.

"You remember what to do? You remember your training?"

Judy nods.

"Good luck," says Hayes, and strides down the hill toward the summer camp.

Outside the house called Self-Reliance, Judy Luptack contemplates the iron knocker, in the shape of a fly. Three times, she lifts and drops its thorax, feeling oddly squeamish about touching it.

After a moment a woman comes to the door. A maid, perhaps.

The woman takes her in for a beat before speaking. "May I help you?"

Judy speaks aloud, for the first time, the words she has been trained to say: "I'm Investigator Judyta Luptack. I'm here to assist in the search for Barbara Van Laar."

Inside the main room, a dozen people stand and sit in small groups. They aren't like the rich people she knew from her work at the golf club—those were generally older men and women who dressed in stiff formal clothes and sat up very straight in their chairs.

The people here, on the other hand, are sprawled out in pajamas and robes. Judy gets the feeling that they're in no hurry to change. Two of the women wear silk nightgowns, and through them she can distinctly see the outline of their breasts. Two young girls—more hired help—move quietly about, picking up the remnants of a party.

Judy looks down at her notepad, busying herself, steeling herself for her first approach.

She's already decided who it will be: an older man who comes closest to reminding her of one of the members at the Iroquois Golf Club. He's white-haired and tall and seated on a low bench near the front door, tying up a sturdy pair of hiking boots. Next to him is a woman who might be his wife.

Judy walks toward them, stands before them, clears her throat. The room feels very quiet to her. Conversations have stopped.

The couple doesn't hear her, or they don't care.

"Excuse me, sir?" says Judy—and feels suddenly transported back to her work at the club.

Slowly, the man looks up.

"May I ask you a few questions?" she says.

Jacob

1950s • 1961 • Winter 1973
June 1975 • July 1975 • August 1975: **Day One**

At dawn, walking just inside the tree line that borders the Northway, he had reached a stream and felt the inexplicable urge to follow it to its beginning. Some memory awoke in him that felt almost ancestral: he *knew* this stream, though he didn't know how.

Jacob does not believe in any god except himself. He's superstitious, though, inclined to subscribe to the idea that coincidence does not exist, that when one encounters the unexpected or uncanny it's important to spend a few extra minutes considering the *why*.

Why, he wondered, had he come across this stream in the middle of his journey north? Why did it look so familiar to him? In the near-light, he considered options: it was time to bed down for the day, but the stream drew him forcefully into the woods. What harm, he thought, in following for a while?

Some hours commenced then of walking and wading and sinking slightly, at times, into the marshy ground. His shoes became muddy, soaked through; he'd have to swap them out for a stranger's as soon as he could.

The woods were growing thinner: through the last remaining trees before him, he could see a county road crossing his path. The stream he'd been following disappeared into a culvert.

He waited awhile, and then—seeing no cars—he darted across the road, found the culvert on the other side, and continued.

There, just beyond him: a series of small cabins, one after another, moving away from him in two lines that framed the little stream. Here and there, small bridges crossed it. To his left were larger buildings; beyond them, a hill.

In an instant, he understood why he was drawn to the water, and why he had followed it this far.

He'd been to this place before.

Judyta

1950s • 1961 • Winter 1973
June 1975 • July 1975 • August 1975: **Day One**

Judy Luptack, having asked the gentleman before her for a few minutes of his time, is waiting for a response.

She begins again. "My name is Investigator Luptack. I'm here to help locate Barbara. May I—"

"I'm afraid not," the man says. And he turns his back to her. Looks out the window, toward the trees.

For a moment, she stands frozen, uncertain what to do. Old instincts instruct her to defer to him—this man she could have served at the golf club. New ones say to be direct.

"Sir?" she says. "It will only take a moment. Just a few questions."

"I'll wait for your sergeant," says the man. "I don't like repeating myself."

"There's no—" Judy begins. *Sergeant* is not the word for the person above her in the BCI: it's *senior investigator*. But she doesn't feel like telling Denny Hayes, who occupies that role, that she's failing already.

Instead she says, simply, "Please."

Upon hearing the word—the abasement in her voice—the man's shoulders drop slightly. He regards her.

"Very well," he says. "Briefly."

"We can go to my car."

"We can go to the kitchen," says the man.

The kitchen is enormous. The elderly couple sit across from her at a large table. The husband, arms and legs crossed, leans back in his chair.

Judy clutches the pad in her hands. She doesn't want to put it on the table; she doesn't want either of them to read it upside down.

"Name?" she begins.

"Peter Wallingford Van Laar the Second," says the man.

"Date of birth?" says Judy.

The man raises an eyebrow.

"February twenty-third, 1898."

Judy notes these facts in the lined pad. And adds to them: *Demeanor: tense.*

"What's your relation to the victim?" Judy asks.

"Victim?"

"To Miss Van Laar," says Judy.

"I would appreciate it if you'd refrain from referring to my granddaughter as a victim," says the man.

Judy flushes. He's correct.

"There's your answer, anyway," says Mr. Van Laar. "I'm her grandfather. This is her grandmother," he says, inclining his head toward his wife. "Mrs. Helen Van Laar. Date of birth May the third, 1898."

These facts, Judy dutifully notes as well.

Then she pauses, waiting for her training to kick in.

"Can you both tell me about your day today? What time you woke up, what you did after that?"

The man sighs heavily. He's the sort of person from whom disapproval radiates nearly autonomically. He folds his hands on the table.

"Miss . . ." he says.

"Luptack."

Investigator Luptack, thinks Judy.

"Miss Luptack, you look very young," says Mr. Van Laar. His wife glances at him swiftly. "You might be—twenty years old? Twenty-two?"

He waits. *Twenty-six*, thinks Judy. She doesn't say it.

"My guess is you have not been doing this work very long," says Mr. Van Laar. "Allow me to assist you."

"Peter," says his wife—the first word she has spoken—but her husband holds one hand out in her direction, and she doesn't continue.

"Our granddaughter has run away," he says. "The reason I know this is because she has threatened to run away nearly every day for two years. Increasingly, 'appeasing Barbara,' 'not upsetting Barbara,' has become nearly the only topic of conversation in my son's household. She's a thirteen-year-old girl acting the way that most thirteen-year-old girls act. Only worse."

He pauses. Coughs.

"Our whereabouts this morning are not important pieces of the puzzle you're trying to solve. What you and your people need to be doing is sending a large search party into those woods. Because they're the only danger to Barbara in this moment, aside from Barbara herself."

He stands up abruptly, then looks down at his wife, waiting for her to follow suit. More tentatively, she does.

"Now," says Mr. Van Laar. "That's where I'm heading, with some dogs. That's where I was heading when you detained me. Jot that down in your notebook. In case any of your superiors are looking for me."

He walks out of the room. His wife looks at Judy for a moment before following, her expression inscrutable.

"Sir," says Judy. The word comes out before she knows what she'll say next.

He waits. "What is it?"

"It's just—in light of your grandson's disappearance," says Judy. "It seems as if we should treat Barbara's with the same care."

The man's expression changes completely. He has been annoyed with the conversation; now he's enraged. He opens his mouth to speak, and Judy is reminded of an animal baring its teeth.

"Don't talk about my grandson," says Mr. Van Laar. "Don't even speak his name."

He leaves. His wife follows.

Judy sits for a moment, alone in the large kitchen. It looks as if a party took place the night before. Containers of food are open on the counter, things that should have been refrigerated. Cold salads, chocolaty desserts.

Judy looks down at her notepad. She crosses out the word *tense*. *Demeanor: hostile*, she writes.

A stack of flatware in the sink, precariously arranged, shifts suddenly, and the noise bounces sharply off the walls.

Judy doesn't flinch. The noise of kitchens generally comforts her.

She's thinking about Mr. Van Laar's disproportionate reaction to her mention of his grandson. The hate in his eyes, the flash of his yellowing teeth. She'd seen that same expression on someone else.

Now it returns to her: Mrs. Charles Hanover, she thinks. At a Christmas party at the golf club several years ago, she had rounded a quiet corner to find Mrs. Hanover methodically going through the pockets of furs in the coatroom. Now and then she produced something, examined it, and put it into her own purse. Judy watched, stunned, until Mrs. Hanover turned and caught her eye. Then she smiled, found her own coat, put it on, and walked out.

Judy had rushed to the kitchen to find Chick Janowicz, the GM, who raked his hands over his cheeks and stood looking at the floor for a few beats. Then he nodded, departed, resigned to his fate.

From the kitchen, Judy had heard the howls of indignation all the way down the hall. Then the swinging door flew open and there were the Hanovers, the wife in the lead, an angry finger pointing in Judy's direction, the expression on her face exactly the same as Mr. Van Laar's had been at the mention of his grandson.

"You have no idea what the hell you saw," Mrs. Hanover was saying to Judy. "You little—"

"Paulette," her husband said warningly.

Mr. Janowicz had to threaten to call the police before Mrs. Hanover finally turned out the contents of her purse. Inside it were five wallets and two cigarette cases. Though the Hanovers were banished from the club, Paulette Hanover was never reported to the law.

Rich people, thought Judy—she thought this then, and she thinks it now—generally become most enraged when they sense they're about to be held accountable for their wrongs.

Tracy

1950s • 1961 • Winter 1973
June 1975 • July 1975 • August 1975: **Day One**

She learns, that day, the answer to the question she has had since the start of camp.

What are they actually supposed to yell when lost? Their instructions stopped short of the answer.

As it turns out, Tracy yells: I'M LOST.

She yells this continuously, in a kind of hysterical chant; and then, remembering that she is supposed to conserve her voice, she pauses for longer intervals.

At first, shouting this ridiculous phrase, she seethes with self-loathing and embarrassment, certain that she's only a stone's throw from the edge of the woods, certain that some ten-year-old camper will at any moment come wandering over in his uniform, looking scornful, pointing in the direction of the camp. Still, she continues to shout it, resigned to her fate. Better to get it over with, she thinks.

She's been thirsty for a while. Now she's growing hungry. This alone convinces her that perhaps too much time has passed. And is the light around her growing dimmer? Impossible, she thinks. It was early morning when she struck out. But in the woods, time seems to move strangely. She's entered a different reality from the one she knew.

"I'm lost," Tracy yells, again and again.

The world around her is blurry and green. She curses herself for her vanity, for being too proud to wear the glasses she was prescribed this year.

This is no longer an adventure. Real fear has settled in, finally, and she screams without words. Now, she does not say "I'm lost" or "Help"; instead she simply hollers, guttural primal howls that are punctuated, every so often, with *"Mom, Dad"*—a surprise to her. Tracy thinks of herself as independent, even at her age. But here she is, thirsty, hungry, crying, screaming for her parents, who don't even speak to one another anymore.

After a while of carrying on like this, Tracy freezes in the middle of a howl to listen with her whole body. She holds her breath. Hears what sounds like footsteps.

She waits for a bit.

"Hello?" she says.

For a moment, nothing; and then she hears the noise again.

"Hello?"

Tracy stands up from her spot on the ground. She turns slowly. Notices, at last, a face peering back at her from behind a tree.

Then someone steps into view.

Louise

1950s • 1961 • Winter 1973
June 1975 • July 1975 • August 1975: **Day One**

Behind the stage in the Great Hall are three makeshift dressing rooms, a wardrobe, and a doorway to the outside. For the time being, the state troopers who arrived first on the scene have made the whole hall their command post, with the backstage area apparently serving as interrogation rooms.

Inside the first dressing room—the smallest—Louise sits alone in a vinyl chair.

One hour ago, her CIT—having abruptly noticed the absence of yet another camper of theirs—tore wild-eyed through the grounds of the camp, hollering for Louise, finding her on her walk back to the Director's Cabin from Staff Quarters.

"Tracy's missing too!" Annabel said, breathless—and a nearby trooper said, "Who?"

In short order, the two of them were being walked by a phalanx of policemen toward the Great Hall.

Over and over again, on that walk, Louise had tried to catch Annabel's eye. *Remember*, she wanted to tell her, with her gaze. *Remember your promise.*

But Annabel wouldn't meet her gaze.

Now Annabel is in the dressing room next to Louise's. Through the thin wall that separates them, Louise can hear muffled sounds she thinks might be sobs.

She can also hear the angry voice of a different woman, and a man: Mr. and Mrs. Southworth, she surmises. Annabel's parents. Guests, this week, of the Van Laars.

A light tap on Louise's door, and then it swings open before she can respond.

A man walks in, fortyish, balding. He stops and stares at her a moment, as if realizing something. He's not in uniform: instead he wears a yellow Oxford, short-sleeved, with a red tie. He carries his brown suit coat over his elbow.

"Louise Donnadieu?"

She nods.

The man smiles. He's thin, unmuscled.

"Remember me?" he says.

Only then does Louise look closely at his face, which, she realizes, does ring a bell.

"Denny Hayes," he says. "Used to live in Shattuck. I know your mom."

"Oh," she says. "Mr. Hayes."

He holds up a hand, shaking his head. "Please," he says. "Call me Denny. You're a grown woman now, right?"

The words shock her, though she supposes they're technically true.

"How is she?" asks Denny Hayes.

"Who?"

"Your mother."

Louise pauses. "All right, I guess. We don't talk much."

He nods once. As ready as she is to change the subject.

If she remembers correctly, Denny Hayes was one of several men who used to float around their house just after her father left town. She glances at his hand. Notices the wedding ring there. If he was married back then, she didn't know it—but she wouldn't have been surprised.

Nothing her mother did, or does, surprises her anymore. Not even when she got pregnant with Jesse when Louise was eleven. Not even when she confessed to being uncertain about who the father was.

God, thinks Louise—please don't let this man be Jesse's dad.

"How 'bout you?" Denny asks. "You married or anything? Got kids or anything?"

"No," says Louise. "Just working."

"I've got two," says Denny. "Boy and a girl. Third on the way. Moved away from Shattuck seven years ago, when I got promoted. I live in North Elba now. Close to work."

Louise nods.

"Mind if I sit?" says Denny.

The dressing room is tiny and bright, the only two chairs in it side by side. The two of them angle their knees awkwardly toward one another. Too close for Louise's liking. In the mirror, she watches him fumble in his breast pocket for a notepad and pen.

"So," says Denny. "You're her counselor. The Van Laar girl?"

Louise nods.

"Any idea where she might have got to?"

"I don't," says Louise. Quietly.

Denny glances at her. "Lady out there," he says, checking his notes, "T.J.? Lady with the short hair?"

"The director," says Louise.

"Right. She said you were the one who first reported her missing. That true?"

Louise nods.

Denny regards her for a while. Deciding whether to say something. "You didn't notice?" he says. "Didn't hear the door or nothing?"

Louise feels a tightness in her throat—though she cannot possibly be about to cry, she thinks. She can't remember the last time she cried.

"Were you in the cabin overnight?" says Denny.

Louise opens her mouth to produce a response, but no sound emerges.

Denny puts the notepad down then. Lays the pen gently on top of it.

"Look," says Denny. "I'm really not supposed to give out any kind of guidance here. But for an old friend, I will."

He leans toward her, lowers his voice.

"You don't wanna get yourself in trouble here," he says. "Don't wanna say anything you can't take back. Because if you lie," he says, "that'll be a problem for you later."

Louise looks up at him. He's a foot from her face. His mustache looks damp.

"There's a girl the next room over," he says. "She works with you, I think. I'm gonna talk to her next. If it turns out you two have different stories," says Denny, "well, that looks bad. That raises questions."

"I understand," says Louise.

"You were a nice kid when I knew you," says Denny. "I always liked you. I heard some people gave you a hard time when you got older, said things about you and all. I never believed 'em."

Louise waits. "Thank you," she says at last. She hates him in this moment. Hates his implication. Because most of what was said about Louise related to invented trysts with other students. And once, a teacher.

"That's why I'm gonna give you some advice," he says.

He stands up, tucks the pad and pen away.

"Ask for a lawyer," he says. "And don't say I'm the one who told you."

Louise speaks without thinking.

"I have one already," she says.

It feels good to say it, to watch his expression waver for a moment.

"Well, good," he says. "Won't have to find you a PD, then. Should the need arise."

She looks at him blankly.

"You know what a PD is, don't you?"

Silence.

"A public defender," says Denny. "A free lawyer. Sounds like you won't need one of those."

Only then does Louise realize what she's done.

Alice

1950s • 1961 • Winter 1973
June 1975 • July 1975 • August 1975: **Day One**

A nice ranger has placed a towel around Alice's shoulders; after a while, he retrieves another one and places that around her, too. At one o'clock in the afternoon, she sits in an Adirondack chair in a patch of sunlight, shivering so badly that her teeth clack. She remembers this from Bear's disappearance. It's shock, someone told her then.

"Don't worry, ma'am," says the ranger, crouching down, placing a hand on her knee. "We'll find her, okay? That's what all our training helps with."

Alice nods once. She wants him to stay with her.

Several other rangers with bloodhounds are pacing the camp, looking for scents. Earlier, she was asked to produce a pair of Barbara's used underwear to help the dogs. She had looked at the ranger requesting it, horrified, until he apologized.

"It's really the most useful garment for the hounds," he said.

She couldn't do it herself. Instead she asked them to find a counselor. They could go through Barbara's belongings on their own.

Now, Peter is in one of the camp buildings with some detective. He's told her not to talk to anyone until Captain LaRochelle arrives from Albany. The same captain who oversaw Bear's case.

Peter trusts him.

More to the point, he doesn't trust anyone else.

Alice looks out at the lake. The truth is: she has no idea where Barbara could be. Everyone seems to be implying that she's most likely run away, but Alice is worried that it might be something else.

Barbara has always been difficult.

As a toddler, she threw such terrible tantrums that Alice was concerned about what their Albany neighbors would think. At six, she showed no sign of stopping; no amount of yelling, or bribing, or spanking, or even slapping—Peter had tried this, a quick strike across the face when things got really out of hand—would quell them. Instead, Barbara would shriek ever louder, terrible screams that made it impossible to think.

Bear was never like that.

These episodes of Barbara's were in the end the determining factor in their decision to send her away for school as early as they did. At seven years old, she was enrolled as a boarder at Emily Grange, where by all accounts she caused no problems—at first.

But lately they had been hearing something new.

In the middle of the last school year, there was a telephone call from the head of school, Susan Yoder. She was a formidable woman—a lesbian, thought Alice—who was said to be progressive. She was the first person Alice had ever met who requested the honorific *Ms.* She had invited Alice and Peter to campus to have a meeting with her in person: something they had never before been asked to do.

Peter was incensed. "For the amount we pay them," he said, "one would think this person might understand what an imposition it is to ask a man to take time out of his workday."

Ms. Yoder began her conversation with a note about "compassion"—a word she used frequently—a word Alice had never once heard used aloud in conversation, prior to that day.

And then she went on to describe what she referred to as Barbara's "inappropriate" behavior on the school grounds.

"Most recently," said Ms. Yoder, "she was—discovered—with a boy from town in her room."

Next to her, Peter tightened his grip on the arm of the chair.

"In what state," he said.

"Excuse me?"

"What was the state of my daughter," he said, "when she was found?"

"Oh," said Ms. Yoder, reddening. "Clothed and all that."

"But," said Peter.

"But—well, the reality is we can't be certain what they had been doing prior to Mrs. Burke's entry into the room. Having an unmonitored boy in a girl's bedroom is—certainly not ideal."

She smiled slightly. Attempting to dispel some of the tension in the room. *Kids!* Ms. Yoder seemed to be saying, with the shape of her mouth.

But Peter was still as a stone. Alice could tell some decision was forming in his mind.

"Mr. Van Laar, let me assure you that we aren't too concerned. This behavior is quite normal for a girl of Barbara's age," said Ms. Yoder. "We only want to be certain—"

Peter interrupted.

"And who is responsible for the oversight?"

Ms. Yoder frowned, confused. "Which—"

"Who is responsible for allowing the boy into the dormitory?"

"Well, Barbara is," said Ms. Yoder.

For a moment, Alice was frightened. Peter was capable—not often, but capable—of outbursts. But Peter simply let Ms. Yoder's words sit in the air.

"Who was the boy?" he said at last.

"I'm not sure of his name," said Ms. Yoder. Her expression was changing, slightly. She was taking on a defiant aspect. Could she, too, have a temper? Alice wondered. She was usually so preoccupied by Peter's that it rarely occurred to her to worry about anyone else's.

"How old was he?" asked Peter.

"I'm not sure," said Ms. Yoder. "But Mrs. Burke in West House didn't seem concerned, if that's what you're asking."

Peter wasn't finished. "Please describe him," he said.

Ms. Yoder sighed. "I was not there to see him," she said. "But Mrs. Burke in West House described him as thin and dark-haired." She had only seen the back of him, Ms. Yoder continued, as he escaped through the window—Barbara's room was on the first floor—and ran into the woods that bordered the school.

"What was he wearing?" Peter had said.

"I'm afraid I don't know."

"Did he say anything?"

"Mrs. Burke didn't mention."

"And Barbara?"

"She said he was a friend from town."

Peter scoffed. A long silence ensued.

Alice focused on the objects in the room. A small marble statue of Lady Justice, blindfolded. On the bookshelves, a collection of books in neat rows, stripped of their jackets, organized by height. On the wall, a framed photo of a girls' field hockey team from long ago. Ms. Yoder's team when she was young, thought Alice.

She didn't notice that Peter had risen from his chair. "Thank you, Miss Yoder," he said. Emphasizing the first part of the name.

The woman furrowed her brow.

"I'm afraid there's more to discuss," she said. "In situations like these, we generally take some sort of disciplinary action."

"Whatever you think best," said Peter. "Come, Alice."

She rose. But before they left the room, Ms. Yoder spoke again.

"Mrs. Van Laar," she said, looking directly at Alice. Making a point. "May I answer any questions for you?"

If she did have questions, they would not come to her. And so she shook her head, and followed her husband silently from the room.

On the way to the car, Alice asked him if he might like to wait for Barbara, to talk to her directly. He shook his head.

"She'll only lie," said Peter. "I can't abide it."

In the car on the way back to Albany, he was silent while Alice, next to him, struggled to find something to say.

She had noticed recently that she was adopting the habits of Peter's mother, who on most occasions sat off to one side, smiling pleasantly, largely letting her husband run the show. When Alice had first met her, she had wondered about her intelligence. But on the rare occasions the two of them were alone, Mrs. Van Laar had demonstrated a capacity for conversation that went beyond anything she displayed to her own husband. She was even witty, in her way.

"Early for the leaves to be changing," said Alice finally. And Peter affirmed that it was.

That night, he came to Alice to tell her that a decision had been made. The Emily Grange School couldn't handle Barbara, he said. She'd have to go someplace else.

After consulting on the phone with a friend later that evening, Peter had emerged from his room with an announcement. Barbara would be enrolled next year at Élan, a school in Maine for children with discipline issues. He described it as a "behavior modification program."

They'd have the summer together at the Preserve, he told her; and then she would go.

"Tell Barbara, would you?" he said casually. Alice flinched.

"She'll hate it," said Alice.

"That," said Peter, "is neither here nor there. What's important is setting her on a right path. Preventing her from making some irreversible mistake. Can you imagine," he said—but he stopped himself.

Alice understood. A boy in Barbara's room at Emily Grange meant the possibility of sex—if not now, soon. And sex meant the possibility of a pregnancy.

Prior to marrying into the Van Laars, Alice had never met a family so obsessed with its own reputation. Peter had explained it to her once, concisely, when they were younger, when Bear was four or five.

"Banking is an industry that relies on trust," he said. "If we wish for customers to trust us to make decisions about their money, then they must trust our judgment in all things." This, said Peter, was one of the reasons that Peter I had founded the Preserve and Camp Emerson; their interest in conservation was genuine, but also shrewd, designed to augment their reputation in the region. The friendships they'd curated with well-connected people over time were just the same: Shrewd. Chary. The Van Laars were meticulous about anyone they brought into their life, and ruthless about those they excised.

The thing was: Alice still hadn't told Barbara about their plans in the fall. She was stopped, always, when she considered the commotion that would ensue: Barbara raging, making a scene. There was something so violent about Barbara, something inherently aggressive that Alice had noticed since her birth. Even beyond the tantrums she had had as a younger child, the teenage Barbara now seemed permanently stormy, always one misapprehension away from throwing a vicious punch.

When Barbara asked to spend the summer at Camp Emerson, therefore, it became in Alice's mind another excuse to defer the announcement.

Her latest decision was to tell Barbara at the end of the summer.

That would be best, thought Alice. One swift single blow, and then up to Élan. Perhaps she could even tell her after she was in the car, packed for Emily Grange. After they were safely in the car, with a driver at the wheel.

She had planned it all out.

Barbara, she would say—speaking quietly. There's been a change in plans.

Suddenly, Alice is roused from her thoughts by a sound someplace far in the distance.

It sounds like a young girl, crying out.

"Does anyone else hear that?" she says.

She turns to look over her shoulder, but the ranger assigned to attend to her is gone.

Judyta

1950s • 1961 • Winter 1973
June 1975 • July 1975 • August 1975: **Day One**

Through the kitchen window, Judy watches as the elder Mr. and Mrs. Van Laar move across the lawn in the direction of the woods. He walks with a quick aggressive stride; she hustles along behind, trotting every few steps to keep up. These men never seem to really like their wives, Judy thinks. Not the ones at the club, and not the ones here. Her own father—as strict as he is with his children—not only defers to her mother but practically worships her. Once, on their twenty-fifth wedding anniversary, he read to her a god-awful poem of his own creation, paper rattling in shaking hands, Judy and her siblings willing themselves not to laugh.

Judy gathers her strength once more before turning back in the direction of the large main room with the fireplace. Gathered around it, still, are young men and women who aren't so much older than she is. She isn't certain how they fit into this picture, but she understands it will be her job to find out. All of them, she thinks, look inappropriately casual, their demeanor almost offensively relaxed.

She hovers for a moment, looking down at her pad as if noticing something important on it.

"Officer," someone says. In her tone is irony, derision.

Investigator, she thinks, before turning. A young woman, reclined on a sofa with her feet draped over its back, is looking in her direction. Her head is resting in the lap of a young man. She looks familiar—an actress? A singer? Judy feels as if she's seen her on TV.

"What's the working theory?" says the girl.

The young man she's resting on puts a hand over his mouth, as if suppressing a laugh.

Judy ignores her. Looks down at her pad again.

"Who's the prime suspect?" the girl tries, sitting up now.

"Shut up, Polly," says another girl across the room, curly-haired, rubbing sleep out of her eyes.

Polly looks to the young man next to her. "What are you laughing at?"

"The way you said that," he tells her. "It's just so—*earnest!*" And he allows the laugh he's been hiding to burst forth.

"I'm sorry," he says, looking at Judy. "I know this is serious. I'm hungover."

"I'm interested," says Polly. "I want to know."

Judy detests these people. And then remembers her training; feels guilty about her quick leap to hatred.

Unswervingly, surprising even herself, Judy walks straight through the main room, ignoring them all, and heads down a hallway on the other side. She'll gather her thoughts before interviewing any of them.

A part of her acknowledges that she is moving in this direction, away from the crowd she is supposed to interview, out of personal curiosity— she has always wondered about the homes of the members she serves at the golf club, and this one, she is certain, is even grander—and yet she assures herself that if she is caught by a colleague, she's within her rights to tell him she's simply looking for more people to interview.

Some of the doors along the hallway are open, and some are closed. She limits herself to the open ones. Into these, she pokes her head, knocking softly.

Most are untidy. Beds unmade, suitcases open, contents spilled out.

In one, she finds a man still asleep, snoring loudly, apparently unaware of, or uninterested in, the commotion on the grounds.

She goes on her way. The next door is closed but not latched.

She puts a finger to it and pushes. Inside, there is the vague smell of fresh paint. The walls are a light pink that makes Judy wrinkle her nose.

Someone's suitcase is open on the floor in front of her.

Judy steps forward tentatively, her weight on her heels.

Inside are feminine things that someone has not taken care of: dresses and slips and high heels and a bikini, bright orange, still wet from a swim. Judy—herself very neat—suppresses the urge to hang it up someplace.

Inside the room, it becomes clear that the walls have been hastily painted. A quick effort on the part of the hosts to make things look nice before the start of the party, Judy guesses. Her own mother might have done the same.

Her thoughts are interrupted by a rapid knocking on the front door. The voices in the great room quiet.

Judy goes to investigate.

Louise

1950s • 1961 • Winter 1973
June 1975 • July 1975 • August 1975: **Day One**

Annabel, as it turns out, does have a different story.

Alone in her dressing room—Denny Hayes has excused himself, has told her to wait there—Louise can no longer hear the anguished indiscernible outbursts that punctuated the first thirty minutes that went by. Instead, she hears Annabel's laugh, on occasion. She's calm now. Off the hook. Denny Hayes is joking with her mom and dad.

The crybaby, thinks Louise. The canary.

There is no doubt in Louise's mind that Annabel talked.

Finally, a knock.

Denny Hayes enters without waiting for a response. In his hands he is holding something Louise recognizes.

He says nothing. Sets the brown paper garbage bag on the vanity to the left of Louise. Then sits down opposite Louise, regarding her, silent.

Louise brushes some nail shards off her lap.

The smell of Annabel's vomit, still inside the potato chip bag, reaches her, and she retches. Hides it.

Why on earth, she asks herself, did she assign Annabel the task of disposing of this evidence? Why did she not deal with it herself?

Denny clears his throat.

"Found your bag," he says.

Louise half laughs. "Annabel's bag."

"Not what she says."

It takes Louise a moment to process this. She expected Annabel to cave—to confess that both of them were absent overnight, that Annabel was out partying when she should have been watching the girls. That Annabel was drunk, high. That she was sick the next morning. This wouldn't have surprised Louise. Annabels always cave.

What she didn't expect was an outright lie.

"Annabel told us about your night," says Denny.

"*My* night?" says Louise. "Did Annabel tell you about *her* night?"

Denny stands and steps toward the vanity, opens the bag. Again, Louise gags. Denny, on the other hand, betrays nothing. If the smell affects him, he doesn't show it.

From the bag he extracts the beer bottle, the end of a joint, and a smaller bag: this one contains white powder. A substantial amount of it.

"What the hell is that?" says Louise. Though she knows; of course she knows what it is. She's been dating John Paul for four years. The substance has been a point of contention between them for nearly that long.

"Did you get this here," says Denny, "or back in Shattuck?"

"That's not mine," says Louise. "If that was in there, Annabel added it."

Annabel, Louise is beginning to understand, is not the innocent kid she pegged her for.

"I've never done coke in my life," says Louise.

Denny pauses. "But you know what it looks like?"

Louise says nothing.

"The lawyer you mentioned," he says. "Can you reach him?"

Louise, accompanied by Denny Hayes, walks slowly up the hill toward the main house. Her feeling of breathlessness is unfamiliar: years of long runs up steep inclines have caused her resting heart rate to be low, her demeanor to be generally calm. But now she breathes quickly, nostrils flaring, armpits damp.

John Paul, she reminds herself, owes her this.

Four years of togetherness. Four whole years of her life. Their relationship has meaning, she tells herself. She is right to do this. It is not unusual to ask one's fiancé for help in an emergency.

This is what Louise intends to do: at the top of the hill, she will knock on the great double doors of Self-Reliance and ask to speak to John Paul McLellan.

John Paul, whose father is a lawyer.

When Denny asked where they're heading, she left out specifics. All she said, instead, was that she had a family friend up at the main house.

"You do?" said Denny. Skeptical.

In front of the house now, a small group of young women Louise's age are gathered, talking in low tones. They eye her. Her counselor uniform.

It's Denny who lifts the iron door knocker, forged in the shape of a blackfly. He batters the door three times with it.

Louise stands behind him, heart racing, rehearsing the words she will say first.

After a moment, a young woman opens the door, clad in a kind of silk nightgown. She's shockingly beautiful, and Louise blinks, trying to decide if she's famous.

Denny, too, looks dumbfounded. For a moment he stands there, mouth open.

"Need something?" the young woman asks.

Denny steps back theatrically, makes a sweeping gesture with one hand, indicating to Louise that this is her show, not his.

"Is John Paul here?" says Louise. "John Paul McLellan?"

The young woman takes her in. Louise shifts a bit. Tugs at the uniform shorts that ride up on her legs.

"Father or son?" the young woman asks. In her voice, Louise can hear an accent. Italian, perhaps.

"Son," says Louise.

The young woman nods, and disappears down a hallway. Louise closes her eyes, imagines what this person will say—"There's a *counselor* for you, John Paul"—some sort of smirk on her beautiful face—and experiences one moment of reflexive jealousy. Despite everything.

Denny Hayes, she notices, has moved a respectful distance away.

She can't remember much about him from the year or years he was dating her mother, but if she thinks about it, she does remember a certain kindness in him. Or at least a lack of cruelty.

She wonders if he, like her, feels small in this moment, standing before the grand facade of a house in which they are not welcome.

She can hear footsteps now: the young woman returning with John Paul. She wonders how much he'll remember about last night. On other occasions, following a fight, he has been remorseful, conciliatory, swearing off drinking for a time before returning to it with fervor the moment he reunites with friends from school.

She hopes that this morning is no different. She hopes he'll feel guilty about last night, rather than enraged.

But when the footsteps down the hallway crescendo and then stop, she sees it is not John Paul Jr. who has returned.

It's John Paul's father instead.

Mr. McLellan looks worried, pale, much different from how he was the last time she saw him, over a year ago now: then he had been tipsy, pink-faced, swilling strong drinks at a restaurant John Paul had chosen. It had been clear to Louise, upon their arrival, that the McLellans had not been expecting her. She had believed that the purpose of the dinner was to announce the news of their engagement, but it had not come up at all, and they had fought about it on the way home. The father had been all right on that occasion—nicer than the wife and sister, at least. She recalls that the McLellans had talked the whole time about politics—something Louise knows something about, actually. Something she even has strong opinions about. But no one had asked.

Today, standing before her, Mr. McLellan shows no recognition on his face. His expression is entirely blank.

"Mr. McLellan," Louise begins. And fumbles for words.

"Go on," says John Paul's father distractedly. "May I help you?"

"I'm not sure if you remember me," says Louise. "I'm—I know John Paul."

Mr. McLellan looks at her, head tilted slightly. Trying and failing to place her. And then, after a moment, his expression changes.

"Oh, Christ," says Mr. McLellan. Lowly enough so that only she can hear him. "Are you the reason he's gone?"

Louise blinks. "*Gone?*" she says. But Mr. McLellan ignores her.

"Were you with him?" he asks.

At this she hesitates—not out of fear so much as uncertainty.

"Sort of. Briefly."

Mr. McLellan looks impatient.

"Here's what I know," he says. "He looked like hell when he came through the door in the middle of the night. The rest of us were sitting up talking in the great room when he came in: face beaten within an inch of his life. He was bleeding from his lip. He said something about a girl—that's you, I presume—and stumbled down the hallway. Drunk as hell."

Mr. McLellan shakes his head, disgusted. "In front of all our *friends*, this happened. Then this morning, he was gone. No sign of him or his car."

Mr. McLellan looks at her as if waiting for an apology. When none is issued, he continues.

"Is there anything I should know about last night? If there is, you need to tell me. Quickly."

"No," says Louise. "I mean, not really. We had an argument. He—"

She pauses, choosing her words. *Threatened me*, she wants to say. "He was angry with me. My friend had to—step in. That's how John Paul got hurt."

"Your friend," says Mr. McLellan. Regarding her.

"I don't know where John Paul went," says Louise. "I came here to find him. To talk to him. I had no idea he was gone."

Mr. McLellan nods slowly. His eyes, Louise notices, are much like John Paul's: a very light green, beautiful in sunlight. But Mr. McLellan's, that morning, are shot through with red veins that seem to be increasing in number as their conversation goes on.

"Do you know what this looks like," he says to Louise. His voice is low and vicious. "That he's gone now. Do you understand what this looks like, with Barbara gone too?"

She does. For Louise has been thinking it also.

Denny is clearing his throat loudly now, ready to go.

Mr. McLellan moves as if to turn back inside, but stops.

"Are they taking you in for something?" he says.

"Yes," says Louise.

"What is it?"

"Drugs," says Louise. "But they weren't mine."

For an instant, the fleeting hope that Mr. McLellan might offer her some counsel crosses her mind.

But Mr. McLellan only takes a step backward, into the shadows of the house, as if being pulled inside by an invisible force.

"Best of luck," he says, and turns, and lets the door swing closed behind him.

Tracy

1950s • 1961 • Winter 1973
June 1975 • July 1975 • August 1975: **Day One**

The stranger doesn't speak. The stranger stands thirty feet away. Without Tracy's glasses, everything beyond twenty is a blur.

"Hello?" Tracy says.

But the figure before her says nothing. Instead, it holds a finger up to its lips, and then gestures once—a beckoning wave—and then begins to walk silently in the direction from which it apparently came.

Its silver hair glints in the scant light that filters through the trees above. The way it moves is ghostlike, and for a moment Tracy is reminded of Scary Mary—one of the legendary ghosts on the Preserve—who is always described in this way. A gray-haired lady, standing still in the woods. Campers report seeing her only from a distance; then she moves on.

The problem with this theory is that this stranger walks, in Tracy's mind, more like a man than a woman.

The stranger turns and waits. For a moment, Tracy considers staying in place. But her hunger and thirst make the decision for her. She moves instead in the stranger's direction.

They walk for perhaps twenty minutes, Tracy trailing behind. Whether the figure ahead of her is leading her to safety or danger, she doesn't know.

And then she sees a clearing through the trees, and suddenly she is oriented again.

The stranger points silently in the direction of Self-Reliance, and then recedes into the wild again.

There, ahead of Tracy: a swarm of activity on the lawn. All of the police cruisers that crossed her path as she was setting out that morning are parked now at odd angles on the lawn, along with four pickup trucks, an ambulance. Tracy wonders if there's any chance that—in the hubbub surrounding Barbara's disappearance—her own absence has gone unnoticed. With this in mind, she turns south and begins to walk in the direction of Camp Emerson. She keeps her head down, picks up her pace.

She's almost at the ridge that drops down toward camp when she hears a woman shouting: "There she is!"

There's something familiar about the voice.

"Barbara?" someone calls.

"No," the woman shouts. "Tracy! Tracy's back."

And suddenly, her back still turned to Self-Reliance, Tracy realizes why the voice sounds familiar: it belongs to Donna Romano.

Judyta

For five minutes, Judy has been standing in one corner of the main room, watching as a middle-aged man speaks quietly in the threshold of the front door to a young woman on the other side. The young woman is beautiful and small, with long dark hair parted in the middle. She wears a Camp Emerson polo and looks up at the tall man before her with an expression that hovers on desperation. Judy can't hear what they're saying.

The girl retreats, the man retreats, the front door closes. A moment later, Denny Hayes enters. Catches her eye, beckons her toward him.

"Listen, honey," says Hayes, when she reaches him. "I got Barbara Van Laar's counselor with me. I'm gonna transport her to the Wells station. See if I can get any more out of her. I'll be back in an hour or two."

She frowns. This seems odd.

"Don't worry," he says. "You won't be alone for long. We've got a dozen more BCI guys heading this way. Captain's even coming up from Albany."

He raises his eyebrows. "Family's connected. You know."

She nods.

"Who was that man?" she asks. "The one in the doorway?"

Denny looks down at his pad, searching for the name. "John Paul McLellan Sr.," he says. "The Van Laars' lawyer. That girl back there said he was a family friend."

Denny and Judy look at each other for a moment, each registering the improbability of this statement.

"What did the parents say?"

"The parents?" says Hayes. Caught off guard.

"The Van Laars," says Judy. The last thing he told her when they parted ways this morning was that he'd handle the interviews with the parents, at the Great Hall down the hill.

"Oh," he says—looking flustered. "They went back to the house. Wanted to wait for Captain LaRochelle. I guess they know him."

He recovers himself, then continues. "If you get hungry, EnCon brought sandwiches. They're on the lawn."

She's not hungry. But she does have to pee. After several cups of coffee at the station that morning, she's had to for most of the time they've been here.

She's not certain what procedure is. Nowhere in her training did she come across this exact scenario: What do you do if you're in someone's private home for hours and hours with no access to the outside world? Rich people especially. She doesn't want to ask these people for anything. If she were a man, she'd piss in the woods.

She's heading in that direction when she hears a voice.

"Excuse me?"

She turns. It's a young woman in a silk nightgown. Judy had noticed her earlier, when she first walked in.

"Do you have a moment?" she says, and in her voice Judy notices an accent.

Judy nods. Takes her notebook out.

"I want to tell you something," says the woman. She glances over her shoulder.

"Go ahead," she says.

"Very early this morning," says the woman, "a man came back through the house after being out most of the night. And he looked like he'd been fighting. His face looked—terrible. He was bleeding."

Judy writes down phrases.

"Now he's gone," says the young woman. "When the counselor and the other policeman came looking for him, I was the one who opened the door. They asked me to get him, but I couldn't find him. I went all over the house." She raises her eyebrows, puts her hands forward, palms up, in a gesture that Judy interprets as—*Do you see what I mean?*

"Do you know his name?"

"John Paul McLellan," says the woman. "There are two of them. I mean the younger one. The son. I found his father and sister instead," says the woman. "They told me he'd left early. His father went to talk to the counselor instead."

Judy nods. This lines up with what Denny told her.

"Do you know how the counselor knew them? The McLellans?"

"No."

"Any idea how the son's face got like that?"

"No. No one's talking about it. I think that's strange. Don't you?" The woman leans in closer. "His father is said to be a close friend of the family. I think he works for the bank."

Judy looks at her, trying to determine how trustworthy she seems.

"Did Barbara's parents see his face like that? Mr. and Mrs. Van Laar?"

"No," says the woman. "They were asleep already."

She hesitates for a second, and then says: "I believe that you'd have this information by now if they did."

Judy writes this down.

"Well, thank you," she says. "Is there anything else to add?"

"He seemed drunk. When he came through the house, he smelled like liquor. But all these people drink too much," says the woman, waving a hand in the air, indicating every guest in the house.

"Also," she says, "he drives a blue Trans Am."

Judy looks up, startled by the specificity of the observation. She had not pegged this woman for someone who would notice cars.

"Why do you know that?" she asks.

The woman looks at her levelly. "I've been inside it," she says.

Judy flushes. Then looks down, scribbling.

"And your name is?" she says.

"I'd prefer not to give it," says the woman. "If that's all right." She looks down. Looks up again at Judy.

"I don't know these people well," she says. "A friend of mine told me to come. Some girl I met in New York City while I was auditioning for a play. I thought it sounded fun. The land here is beautiful, but the people are—terrible. I can't wait to go back to Los Angeles."

Judy nods.

"Or Rome," says the woman. "Maybe I should just go back to Rome. I had steady work there. Here, not so much."

And then, as if catching herself, she smiles at Judy, and Judy—against her will—blushes.

"What's your name, darling?"

"Judyta," says Judy. Not *Investigator Luptack*. Not *Judy*. Not *Joo-DEE-tah*, as most Americans say when forced to pronounce her given name. Instead she pronounces it just as her mother does—*Yoo-DIT-ah*—and the Italian woman sighs, as if hearing a poem, and tells her it's beautiful.

Louise

1950s • 1961 • Winter 1973
June 1975 • July 1975 • August 1975: **Day One**

There's a state police satellite station in Wells, New York, and this is where Louise is driven by Denny Hayes, who on the way regales her with the story of his life, describes the two children he's had with a woman he loves. He tells her their hobbies, describes the minor trouble they've caused as of late—nothing serious.

He waits, perhaps expecting a response. An acknowledgment, at least. Louise gives none, and at last he goes quiet.

The Wells station is tiny and austere, a concrete building whose only ornament is a pay phone on the wall.

There's one trooper sitting at one desk. Otherwise, the building seems completely unoccupied.

"Got a nickel?" Denny asks her. When she shakes her head, he fumbles in his own pocket and produces one for her, then gestures to the phone.

"Go ahead," he says, and then he retreats to a different corner, respectfully lowers his head, pretending that doing so will prevent him from overhearing everything she says.

She puts a finger to the dial. Hesitates. She does not want to call her mother, but she has no one else to call.

At last, reluctantly, she dials the number to her childhood home, closing her eyes against the memories that the act invokes: being forgotten one too many times at a friend's house; calling home from the nurse's office, sweaty with fever, knowing that no one would answer the phone. Now, like then, it rings many times in a row; but then there comes a little voice on the other end that catches Louise off guard.

"Hello?"

"Jesse?" says Louise. "Jesse?"

He doesn't ever answer the phone. He's timid to the point of incapacity: a trait bemoaned by their mother at every opportunity.

"Jesse, are you all right?"

"Louise," says Jesse. "Mom's sick."

"What kind of sick?" Louise asks.

"She's in bed."

"Is she awake?" Louise says. "Is she breathing? Jesse?"

Across the room, Denny Hayes raises his head.

"She's okay," says Jesse. "Just hasn't left her room for a while."

Louise closes her eyes.

"Have you eaten today?" she asks him quietly. She wishes for privacy. Angles her back toward Denny.

On the other end of the line, she hears a quick shuddering intake of breath: this is Jesse trying not to cry. She pictures him, the corners of his mouth tucked down.

"Listen," Louise says. "Listen. Go to Shattuck's. Get a few things and put it on my account. Not Mom's," she says. "Mine."

"Aw, Lou," says Jesse, and she can almost hear his face reddening at the thought. To interact with any adult outside the family is almost unthinkable to Jesse.

"Do it," says Louise. "Jesse, I need you to try to do it. You can't go hungry."

Jesse hesitates. Behind her, Louise can hear Denny clearing his throat.

"What should I get?" Jesse says at last.

Suddenly, a different voice: the operator, requesting more change. Louise has none.

"Cheap stuff that'll fill you up," says Louise, with urgency. "Bread and cheese. The kind of cheese that comes in a jar. Get whatever cooked meat you can find on sale. Whatever they've got."

"Okay," says Jesse tearfully. "I'll try."

A moment passes in silence. And then he speaks again: "Louise? Why did you call?"

But there is a click on the line—time's up—and the operator ends their conversation abruptly.

She stands there with the phone in her hand for some time, gathering the strength to turn back toward Denny—who has clearly heard everything. Who remembers her mother, who no doubt witnessed her mother at her worst. He might pity her, thinks Louise. If there is anything Louise despises, it's the feeling of being pitied—especially by someone like Denny Hayes, who is himself pitiable in ways too numerous to count.

And sure enough, when she hangs up the phone and steels herself to face him, he is looking at her with a somber expression on his face, his lips a straight line of compassion, feigned or real. Louise stares back at him defiantly.

"What?" she says.

"You all right?" he says. He's holding something in his hands. It's a paper cup of coffee. He holds it out to her. She doesn't take it.

"Sure," says Louise. "Except I'm under arrest for something I didn't do. That's the only thing wrong with me."

Denny's expression hardens.

"Come on," he says, and walks her into one of two back rooms, and places her at a table there, and puts the coffee down roughly. A little splashes out, scalds her hand. He tells her that a different investigator will be by to speak with her shortly. He has to return to the Preserve.

Then he closes and locks the door between them.

Alice

1950s • 1961 • Winter 1973 • June 1975
July 1975 • August 1975: **Day One**

Alice sits up very straight, listening for that sound again. It was a girl's voice, crying out. She couldn't make out the words, but the tone of the voice made it clear that the girl was distressed.

It wasn't Barbara. She'd recognize both of her children's voices anywhere.

She makes no move. Closes her eyes, which sometimes helps her hear things better. She sits in her Adirondack chair, listening for the voice again.

"Alice."

She's been expecting the young ranger who's been assigned to watch over her. But it isn't the ranger who stands before her. It's her husband, regarding her with something like disgust.

"Why do you look like that?"

"I heard a girl crying out," says Alice. "I was listening."

Peter looks at her, skeptical. "Barbara?"

"No. Not Barbara."

"They did find another girl," Peter concedes. "Barbara's cabinmate. Apparently, she went looking for Barbara."

Alice nods. Satisfied.

"Has anyone asked to interview you since the last time we spoke?"

"No."

"Good."

Unsteadily, Alice stands up from the chair. The depth of its seat makes her rock several times before she rises. Peter makes no move to help her. Watches her impassively instead.

"Captain LaRochelle is on his way from Albany," he says. "Father personally requested him. We'll be communicating only with him when he arrives."

"Will he want to speak with me?" says Alice.

"No," says Peter. "You're too upset."

"What do you mean?"

"You're too upset. You've taken to your bed again."

She says nothing. She wishes for a pill.

"Go on," he says. "I'll help you up to the house."

Two pills. Dr. Lewis's words echo in her ears, as always: *on very bad days.*

What is today, if not one of those?

She'll take two, she thinks, when she reaches Self-Reliance.

IV

Visitors

Carl

1950s • **1961** • Winter 1973 • June 1975
July 1975 • August 1975

When Carl Stoddard regained consciousness, he was laid out flat in the back of Dick Shattuck's pickup truck, looking up at the sky. Beneath him, the truck bed was rumbling; above him, the world was racing. Overhanging tree branches blurred into a steady green. He blinked slowly, trying to imagine how it was that he had gotten to be here. Then he heard Maryanne's voice.

"Thank God," she was saying. "Thank God."

She peered over him, her face upside-down, her head swaying each time there was a bump in the road.

Dr. Treadwell, pressing a gentle stethoscope to his bare chest, said it was an arrhythmia. His was a regional clinic, not equipped for much more than first-aid care and the occasional delivery of a baby whose mother couldn't make it to Glens Falls. Dr. Treadwell, eighty now, knew his limitations, and they precluded a more formal diagnosis than that.

"You'll have to go to the hospital, I'm afraid," he said.

Carl glanced at Maryanne. Both of them, he knew, were thinking the same thing: the emergency room was a much more expensive proposition than a local doctor. They were still working to pay off the mountain of bills that resulted from Scotty's care.

"Is it really an emergency?" said Carl. "Couldn't I—couldn't I call and make an appointment with someone? I'm not in any pain."

He was, in fact, in a bit of pain—though only when he exerted himself.

"Carl," said Maryanne.

Dr. Treadwell cleared his throat. He sat down. "Professionally, I can't recommend you wait," he said. "But if you *were* to, I would move as little as possible, rest in bed, drink plenty of water. I'd avoid cigarettes, coffee, and . . ." He looked at Maryanne. "Any activity at all that elevates the heart rate."

At home, Maryanne walked him up the stairs to their bedroom. Turned on a light. Kept one hand on his back as he maneuvered into bed, still aware of some dull pain in his chest.

When he was settled, she sat down on the edge of the mattress. As always, he had the feeling she was reading his mind.

"It's all right," she said. "Carl Stoddard's presence on those grounds won't mean the difference between finding the boy and leaving him unfound."

He broke their gaze. Looked up at the ceiling.

"I know the land," he said.

"You know who else knows the land well? Better than you, even?"

Carl nodded.

"Vic Hewitt," said Maryanne.

"What if you go back?" Carl asked. "I'm sure they still need extra hands."

Maryanne scrutinized him. "Who'll look after you?"

"I'm fine," said Carl. "Dr. Treadwell said so. I'll rest. Jeannie will help."

"*Our* Jeannie?" said Maryanne. "Or another one?"

He smiled. Most of the humor between them, now, could be found in the gentle deriding of their remaining children. It was something mundane; something that reminded them of before, when the fragility of their children's bodies wasn't so heavy on their minds. Maryanne had once confessed to him, in the wake of Scotty's death, the fear that she would be unable to let the girls out of her sight. To make fun of them, ever so slightly, was a reminder to be light with them as well.

Maryanne placed a hand on his cheek. It was the most generous touch she'd given him in a year. She stroked his hair back from his forehead. He blinked rapidly to prevent himself from crying.

"You're a good soul," she said.

He put his hand over hers. Brought it to his mouth. Kissed it.

"All right," said Maryanne. "I'll go."

*　　*　　*

He woke up some time later to the sound of Maryanne's footsteps. They were different from the footsteps of his daughters, who had been traipsing around the house with abandon since their mother's departure.

Now he sat up first on his elbow, measuring how that felt, and then, when no light-headedness threatened to fell him, he swung his legs over the edge of the bed, and then rose slowly until he was on his feet.

"Maryanne?" he called tentatively.

Upon receiving no response, he shuffled toward the threshold of his bedroom. The house—their house—had been in Maryanne's family for 150 years. It was close-walled, low-ceilinged, built to accommodate only the insubstantial height of her ancestors. Across the upstairs hallway was the dormer bedroom that all three girls shared; Scotty had slept downstairs, on a former sleeping porch that Carl had imperfectly winterized. Now the Stoddards rarely ventured onto it, despite the small size of the house.

It was a surprise, therefore, to descend the staircase and find Maryanne standing quite still in the threshold of that room. For a moment he gazed upon her rigid back, inside her Sunday dress, both hands pressing upon the doorframe as if bracing against a storm.

He spoke her name quietly so as not to startle her, but still she jumped.

"What are you doing out of bed," she said to him. "You should be in bed."

"I feel better," said Carl—a half-truth. In fact, the walk down the stairs had made him dizzy.

He approached her, and together they gazed out onto the closed porch. A twin bed still sat at the edge of the space, but the rest of the room was bare, every artifact boxed up and placed in the basement: Maryanne's work. She had been asking him to do something to it, to make use of the space in some way, an instinct that Carl understood to be self-protective rather than cold.

"Maybe we can open it up again," Carl said now—imagining this to be the thought on Maryanne's mind. "Put the screens back on. It'd be nice to eat out here in summer."

But Maryanne said nothing.

Carl was beginning to feel like he should sit down. He shifted his weight from one leg to another.

"How was the rest of the day?" he asked. "Did they find anything?"

Maryanne nodded.

"What was it?"

"Carl," said Maryanne. "How well do you know that boy?"

He frowned. "Oh, a little," he said. "He liked the outdoors. He used to come around asking about the plants we were putting in. Once I taught him how to build a fire."

"Carl," said Maryanne, "why are you talking about him like he's dead?"

He paused. "How do you mean?"

"You said *liked*," said Maryanne. "You said he *liked* the outdoors."

"I don't know."

"They did find something," said Maryanne. "A few feet off the path to the trailhead, buried in some underbrush. Ron Shattuck's hound sniffed out a little carving of a brown bear. Just like the ones you know how to make."

"All right," said Carl.

"That's strange," said Maryanne. "Don't you think it's strange?"

"Not so much," said Carl. "I taught him how to whittle once. Taught Bear, I mean. I probably taught him how to make a couple things. Maybe that was one."

"Does anyone else know that?"

"I'm not certain. I think Vic Hewitt probably does. The boy hung around Vic, too."

And then, catching himself: "Hangs."

"I overheard them talking," said Maryanne. "They're curious about it. They'd like to find the person who carved it. The police were saying this, and the news spread. It was all we came up with at the end of a full day's search. The hounds are useless because of the rain. There's nothing. They'll keep searching, but."

She trailed off. And then, abruptly, she turned from the threshold of Scotty's room and walked to the kitchen, began to open cabinets. Searching them for some kind of dinner.

"Want help?" Carl asked.

"No," said Maryanne. "You go back to bed. Shouldn't be down here to begin with."

She thought for a moment, and then: "Why do you think he had it with him?"

"Not sure," said Carl. "Must have liked it."

"And why do you think he dropped it?"

"Not sure."

Carl took the stairs one at a time, resting for several seconds in between. In his peripheral vision he noticed his girls regarding him silently from the dining room table, where they were meant to be studying. He waved at them. *Back to your schoolwork.*

On the upstairs landing, he allowed himself to acknowledge why he'd used the past tense when speaking about Bear Van Laar. The truth was: he'd been thinking of Scotty. The two boys were becoming closer in his mind.

Carl

1950s • **1961** • Winter 1973 • June 1975
July 1975 • August 1975

Maryanne went back to search the next day, and the next. Each evening she reported on the day's events: as word spread, there were more and more people in the field. A hundred the second day. Five hundred the third. The whole town of Shattuck had paused in its daily operations to contribute to the cause: every adult older than school age, and some children as well. For two whole days, the grocery store was closed while the Shattucks and their employees searched for Bear, meaning that anyone who'd run out of milk or bread or toilet paper had to drive half an hour to get some.

Vic Hewitt, said Maryanne, had been in charge of operations so far; each day he sent small groups farther and farther afield in every direction. Still, there was no sign of Bear.

What Vic shouted at the group each morning was formal and hopeful, meant as much for the ears of the parents as for the searchers themselves.

What Maryanne learned in whispers from the other wives was less so.

The hounds, they said, had lost the boy's scent quickly on the first day. Ron Shattuck's Jennie had been the one to sniff out the carving of the bear, halfway between the house and the trailhead; after that she had not pointed for the rest of the day.

The problem had been the downpour on the day of the boy's disappearance. *If not for the rain*, they said—but no one would finish the sentence.

"Vic's losing hope," said Maryanne, the evening of the third day. "You can tell. His posture's different."

Carl nodded. It was difficult to imagine a boy of Bear's age surviving in the wilderness much beyond this point. Even one with his know-how.

"Are people speculating?" Carl asked.

Maryanne hesitated for a moment before responding.

"They are," she said carefully. "There's a lot of folks who think the boy just wandered off. Out of curiosity or anger, no one's sure. No telling how far a boy his age and size could have gotten before realizing he was lost. After that," she said, "well, if he were down with an injury, he might have succumbed to the cold overnight."

Carl nodded. This was his theory too—the main one, anyway. He hated to say it, to even think it, but this sounded like the most probable theory. Except—

Maryanne continued. "But Carl," she said, "people have another thought too."

He knew what it was before she said it.

"The carving," he said.

"No," she said. "Not that."

"Then what?" Carl said.

Maryanne hesitated. "There's a rumor," she said. "It's that you were the last person to see Bear alive."

Carl paused. Nodded.

"That's true. I saw him just as I was leaving. He was sitting on the front steps of Self-Reliance. Tying his shoes."

She looked at him, blinking. "Why on earth did you not tell me that?"

"I have to tell you something else," said Carl.

Maryanne put her face in her hands.

"No, Maryanne," said Carl. "Nothing like that. My God."

He reached for one of her hands and took it.

"Bear was afraid of his grandfather," he said.

"How do you know?"

He described the change in the boy's expression when he heard his name called; he described what he had said. *That's my grandfather. I don't like him much.* He did not say outright what he was thinking, but Maryanne did.

Then she began to cry.

"What's wrong, Maryanne?"

"Nothing," she said.

"Please."

She swiped at her nose. "All right," she said. "I'm crying because I think you're probably right."

Her shoulders were hunched and miserable. Her head was down.

"And because I think no one will believe you," said Maryanne.

Neither of them could sleep. Maryanne tossed and turned. Carl lay still, looking up at the dark ceiling, feeling the ache of his heart as it thudded inside him. He had managed to find an appointment with a doctor at Glens Falls for Monday morning. Until then, his only job was to keep calm: an increasingly impossible task.

At some point they heard a knock at the front door. Maryanne sat up, listening; it came again louder. Carl didn't know what time it was. Midnight or one, maybe.

"I should get that," said Carl. But again, when he tried to sit up, he found his vision dimming at its edges.

"You stay here," said Maryanne. She moved to the closet and retrieved from the top shelf a shotgun that had been her father's. She loaded it. Headed for the door.

"Maryanne," whispered Carl, feeling useless. "Whoever that is can come back in the morning."

But she ignored him.

He listened hard. The front door opened. He heard the voices of men, low and murmuring. He propped himself up, straining to hear more.

A pause, then, followed by footsteps on the stairs—lots of them— which meant Maryanne was not returning alone.

Carl ran his hands over his face, around his mouth. Three days of stubble had made his chin rough. He was wearing a white undershirt, yellowed at the neck and armpits.

Then into the room came Maryanne, followed by Dick Shattuck, Bob Lewis, and Bob Alcott.

The three big men overtook the little low-ceilinged room. Carl, looking up at them from his bed, felt like a child.

"Carl, these men have something to tell you," said Maryanne.

The police would be coming for him in the morning. His friends wanted to alert him before they did.

"We don't believe you had anything to do with the boy's disappearance," said Dick Shattuck. "Want you to know that. That's the reason we're here, I guess."

Carl put a hand to his chest.

"What should I do?"

He heard that it sounded pathetic.

"Run for the hills," said Bob L. "These yahoos'll hang you."

"Bob," said Shattuck admonishingly.

"Sorry, Maryanne."

"I don't know, Carl," said Shattuck, head lowered. "I wish there was something we could do."

For a moment, there was silence in the room.

"They have no evidence," said Bob Alcott. It was the first he'd spoken. He was a quiet man, a history teacher at the central school. "All their evidence is circumstantial. That won't cut it in a court of law."

Carl wasn't certain what that meant, but it was the first thing he'd heard that brought him comfort.

They had a brief conversation, after the men had left, about whether he should, in fact, disappear. Maryanne was for it. Carl against. His chest was hurting more than ever; he had to consciously remind himself not to put his hand to it, because each time he did, Maryanne looked like she was going to cry.

Finally, at three in the morning, Maryanne put her arms around him, holding him like a child, and they both fell asleep that way.

At seven in the morning, the second knock came.

Alice

1950s • **1962** • Winter 1973 • June 1975
July 1975 • August 1975

S he wanted to love the new baby.
Over the course of a nearly unbearable labor, Alice chanted these words like a prayer: *I will love the new baby. I will love the new baby.*

Peter, of course, was nowhere. Other fathers waited in the waiting room, reading newspapers—but not her husband, who had a meeting he couldn't miss. When the baby was born, he'd be driven over from the bank. The baby would be handed to him. And then he'd go back to work, and the baby would be taken to the nursery, and then, at last, Alice could sleep.

She pictured only this as she labored: the moment of rest.

I will love the new baby, thought Alice.

It hadn't been like this with Bear. She knew she would love him from the moment she felt his first kick. She'd been eighteen years old then, married only a few months. She had nothing to do inside her new house, with Peter gone all day. The first fluttering motions of her baby felt to her like gifts.

After nearly ten months of carrying her son inside her like a pearl, she delivered him into the world, and he was no longer hers alone. As soon as Alice brought her son home, people began to take him from her.

First there was her own mother, who lifted the babe from her arms as soon as she walked in the door to the Albany house. Ordered Alice upstairs to wash her hair.

Next came the Van Laars, mainly Peter's father, who inspected Bear as if inspecting livestock. He made pronouncements about the size of his head, the length of his legs. Both were deemed respectable. The baby was handed back.

Last came the two nurses—Peter's idea. One for the day. One for the night.

Peter interviewed them in private, so she only met each of them on their first day of work. The day nurse, Francine, was a matron, gray-haired and thin, who worked with quiet efficiency and smiled frequently and tended as much to Alice as she did to Bear, especially in the months just after his birth. Alice liked her very much, actually, and told Peter so.

But the night nurse, Sharon, was different. She was red-haired, stout, not much older than Alice. Catholic, Alice thought: she lived at home with her parents still. She spoke often of being the oldest of ten, with a kind of pride in her voice that often turned to authority when Alice questioned anything she did.

The worst part was that Peter generally took her side.

"He's cold," said Alice, hearing Bear cry in the night. "She has him in those light pajamas. The house is so drafty."

And Peter would say—"A lowered body temperature induces sleep."

"He's hungry," said Alice. "He didn't eat a good dinner."

"If he starts eating at night, he'll only want more."

Sharon stayed with them for several years at the start of Bear's life, impervious to Alice's disapproval of nearly every choice she made. She hummed cheerfully to herself as she took him up to bed, and Alice watched her go, longing to hold the soft small body of her son, clad in cotton; longing to feel that weight in her arms.

"Maybe," she said once to Peter, "maybe I could put Bear to bed each night, and then Sharon could be the one to wake up with him, if he's restless."

Peter, who'd been reading, looked up in annoyance. "Honestly, Alice," he said. "What are we paying her for? To sleep here? Sharon should be paying us," he said. "Rent."

The best parts of Alice's day were the two hours between Sharon's departure in the morning and Francine's arrival, and the two hours at the end of the day, when they switched. During these four hours, with no one to watch or correct her, she played with him, or read to him, or lay with him on her bed, observing him. He was smart, Alice thought—most importantly, he was smart. He spoke early and he made observations about the world that shocked her with their clarity. He counted early. He sang in a sweet voice all the songs she taught him— Alice liked to sing—and repeated them sometimes for Peter, at Alice's urging. Even Peter smiled, on these occasions.

When he cried, he was easy to console, said Sharon. Alice heard him overnight—she always did—but his cries were over quickly.

When Bear was two, though, and saying words, he suddenly began to cry for Alice in the night. *Mamma*, he began to say.

The first night he did this, Alice sat up straight in bed.

"What is it?" said Peter sleepily.

Down the hall, Bear called again. *Mamma*.

"He's never done that before," said Alice. Peter shrugged. Turned over.

"Sharon's in the room with him," said Peter. "She'll tell us if anything's wrong."

The cries stopped quickly, but Alice couldn't sleep for an hour. What if he had been calling for her because of something Sharon was doing? What if she was hurting him in some way?

The next night, the same thing happened, and the next. Until one night, she heard him say, clearly and plaintively—*Mamma, you hear me?*

The first time he called out this way, Alice bolted out of bed with an urgency she had never felt before. Her whole body was on fire with the need to go to her son. Peter, behind her, called after her, but she didn't stop.

She threw open the door to Bear's nursery, and light from the hallway spilled in. Sharon was still prone on the twin bed in her corner of the room, awake but unmoving. When she saw Alice she sat up. Her nightgown was bunched up around her knees. She wore curlers in her hair.

"Mrs. Van Laar, what are you doing?" said Sharon, but Alice was already at Bear's crib. There he was, her son, soft in his cotton pajamas, his arms outstretched to her, grinning now with glee at the novelty of seeing his mother overnight. She lifted him out and he wrapped his limbs around her tightly and her body rewarded her, flooded her with the same calm that came whenever she was reunited with her son.

"Mrs. Van Laar," said Sharon, and Bear said, "Mamma!" Delighted. He put both hands on her cheeks. She put her forehead to his.

Then, from the doorway, she heard a different voice. Peter's. Angry.

"Alice," he said. "What are you thinking?"

She turned to him, the boy still in her arms. "He called out for me," she said.

Peter held a hand out, palm up, in Sharon's direction. "He has his nurse right here," he said. Sharon nodded once, firmly, victoriously.

"Give him to Sharon," said Peter. "Alice."

Her son held her more tightly.

"Alice," said Peter. And he went to her, and took the boy gently from her—immediately, Bear began to wail—and handed him to Sharon, in her curlers, in her nightgown, and then he took Alice by the elbow and led her from the room.

Bear's cries continued. For ten minutes, he cried forcefully, screaming for Alice.

It was torture: a sort of physical distress that surpassed almost every pain she'd ever known. Alice cried too. "He needs me," she said. "Peter, he's calling for me."

"Put some beeswax in your ears," said Peter. "Tie yourself to a mast."

She didn't know what he was talking about. He often spoke in riddles, or used references to literature or history that she didn't understand. She felt he got some pleasure out of doing so—out of flaunting his education, when she didn't have one. Not like his, anyway. During the day, the long hours in between her mornings and evenings with Bear, she sometimes tried to make herself read the books in Peter's library that he had kept from college. But generally she got bored of them, and went for walks instead, or read smutty novels she'd found in bins outside the public library in town.

Mamma? Bear called down the hall—one more time, a certain defeat in his voice—one more question unanswered, and finally he was silent.

"I can't do this," whispered Alice. She was certain Peter was asleep. He hadn't moved in minutes.

But he spoke to her. "You can," he said.

You will, he meant.

Now, in labor with her second child, Alice was fighting the urge to push.

If she could just keep the child inside her, she thought—if she could just protect him or her from the world for one minute longer.

But the urge was becoming unbearable, and at last a balding doctor was brought in holding a mask, which he placed over her face without warning. She remembered this from Bear's birth. This is very rude, Alice thought, and then suddenly she had no more words.

That was when she heard her own name being called—not *Alice*, but *Mamma*, a distressed cry that she recognized at once as her son's.

Bear was there.

He was standing in a corner, eight years old, wearing an expression she had rarely ever seen on his beautiful face. Over the nurse's shoulder, she saw him, and she cried out.

"He's there," she said—"he's right there."

Why did nobody notice him? "He's come back," said Alice. The search was over.

She tried to point but the nurse restrained her.

"Please," said Alice. "Please bring him to me. I don't want him to leave again."

Bear was flickering now, candle-like.

"Go to him," Alice said. "Please, please. He's leaving."

She had to get off the bed. She had to get to him. If she didn't get to him quickly he would be gone. She rocked left and right.

"Mrs. Van Laar," the doctor said, "Mrs. Van Laar, you need to keep still."

With all of her strength she wrested her ankles from the doctor's grip and rose off the table. She was trying to get her legs to the floor.

In the corner, Bear raised his arms to her as if he were a toddler who wanted to be held. It was unbearable—unbearable—to be kept from him.

The doctor shouted something she could not understand. She was weeping, and she could not see well, but she was almost to the corner where Bear was. He stretched his hands toward her, and she lunged for him. She could almost touch him. She could almost feel his skin. Her hands and his hands grasped for one another.

Someone took hold of her. She was forced backward, onto the bed. Her limbs were held down by hands and then cords.

She was wailing now, openly, great yells that shook her whole body, and the nurse put a hand on her forehead, telling her it would be all right, that her baby was coming soon.

My baby is there, thought Alice. In the corner. Right there.

Over and over again she wailed his name. *Bear. Bear.* And the name itself became a chant or incantation, assumed all of its many meanings at once. *Abide. Endure. Sustain. Accept. Convey. Bring forth. Give birth to.*

If she said it enough, she thought, perhaps the word would summon him in her direction.

But it was too late: he flickered out of sight, and was gone.

He had left her again. The place in the corner where he had been was empty.

The mask was placed abruptly over her mouth, this time for longer. Then she slept.

"It's a girl, Mrs. Van Laar," said the doctor.

She opened her eyes. Closed them. The light overhead was too bright. *Bear*, she thought, and she sat up as well as she could, but still he was gone.

"My son," she said—but the words came out in a croak.

"Your daughter," said the doctor, bringing the baby to her. She was wrapped in a blanket. He held her out to Alice expectantly, but her arms were heavy at her sides.

"Mrs. Van Laar," said the doctor. He was young, despite his hairline, and he sounded frightened. "Are you all right?"

There was a window in the room and it faced a courtyard. Through the glass, Alice could see a very green tree waving its branches. Beyond the tree was another building, and then sky.

"Mrs. Van Laar?"

A nurse came and grasped her arm.

"This will clear your milk up," said the nurse. And she gave her a shot before Alice could respond. She had not nursed Bear. She had a half-formed thought that she would have liked to try it, once, with this child.

In the hallway, murmuring. Peter's voice: he'd arrived from work.

After a moment he came into the room, holding the new baby in his arms. He sat down on the bed with her. Two nurses hovered behind him and he turned to them, speaking sharply.

"A little privacy, please," he said, and they scattered.

Then he turned back to Alice.

"Peter," said Alice urgently. "I saw Bear. He was right there." She pointed to the corner. She could picture him: tall for his age and handsome, in need of a haircut, wearing his favorite blue shirt. His fingernails with dirt beneath them from love of the woods. One baby tooth missing.

"We have to find him," she said. "He's alive, Peter. He was here."

But Peter was shaking his head. "It was the gas they gave you."

"It wasn't," said Alice. Her voice rose, and she knew she would cry. "I saw him."

Peter was shaking his head.

"I think it was a sign," said Alice. "Even if he wasn't here. I think it was a sign that he's alive."

She lowered her face into her hands, hiding. Peter hated crying.

Inside the dark of her hands she heard him sigh. Next would come shouting.

But instead she felt his hand on the side of her face. She grasped it.

"Look at me," said Peter, with surprising gentleness. "Look at me. He's gone."

"You don't know that," said Alice.

Peter paused. "We have to live our lives as if he is, Alice." He looked down at the baby in his arms, who stretched a tiny hand suddenly upward and then let it down.

"Barbara," said Peter. He pronounced it in three syllables. *Bar-ba-rah*. "I'd like to name her Barbara."

Alice was caught off guard. Twice, in the past month, she had tried to broach the subject of names with him. She liked *Darien* for a boy— she had known a boy with that name in her youth, and had always found it beautiful—and *Charlotte* for a girl. But each time she asked, Peter had brushed her off, saying he was busy.

Now here he was, next to her, suggesting a name she had never considered at all. *Barbara*. She knew several people with the name—all of them Peter's age. It was a name she associated more with his generation than the baby's.

"If that's all right with you," added Peter finally.

"Why Barbara?" asked Alice.

"It's just a name I've always liked," said Peter. "I think it has a nice ring to it. *Bar-ba-rah Van Laar.*"

And he gazed down at his daughter with such sudden tenderness that Alice said she liked it too. It was important, she had heard, to let one's husband feel invested in the children. Any interest he expressed should be rewarded.

It was only later, when they were back in the Albany house after a week in the hospital, that Alice found the book of names she had bought from a bookstore. This was when she was expecting with Bear—whose Christian name, too, had been chosen without her input.

She turned to the section on girls' names, and then to the page on *Barbara.*

From the Greek word "barbaros," said the book, *meaning "foreign," "wild," or "strange."*

Alice looked up with a jolt. How terrible, she thought—how absolutely terrible to name a baby *strange.*

The book went on. *"Barbarian" derives from the same root,* it said cheerfully.

Alice shuddered. Did everyone know this about *Barbara?* She often had trouble discerning what sort of knowledge was common, and what facts were considered obscure.

She closed the book sharply, resigned. She wouldn't bring it up with Peter—she couldn't. The name was fixed, the birth certificate issued. She'd just live with it, she thought. There were lots of famous Barbaras, after all.

Alice

1950s • **1962** • Winter 1973 • June 1975
July 1975 • August 1975

For two months after Barbara came home, things seemed better. A newborn in the house distracted her from her grief—which to that point had felt all-consuming.

She hadn't wanted to get pregnant so quickly after Bear. It was Peter who insisted they try. *We aren't getting younger*, he said.

Besides, he said, *it will give you something to do.*

But something changed in the middle of Barbara's third month, when, in the early hours of the morning, Alice woke to the sound of a child calling for her.

Conceptually, she understood that an infant of Barbara's age could not produce her mother-name, the name Bear gave her. *Mamma.*

She sat up in bed. Held still. Listened.

There it was again.

Mamma.

The nursery was dark and quiet. She tiptoed into it. The new nurse, Lorraine, was asleep on one side. Barbara was asleep on the other. For two minutes, Alice listened, standing in her nightgown in the center of the room. But there was only silence.

She tiptoed out again, and as she was closing the door behind her, there it came: *Mamma.*

She pivoted. Drifted back toward the nursery that used to be Bear's. Put a hand on the doorknob.

"Alice."

She jumped.

At the end of the hallway was Peter, frowning.

"Go back to bed," he said.

* * *

It kept happening. She heard the voice each night. Sometimes, it seemed to be coming from outside her window. Sometimes, from a lower floor. Often, from the nursery.

Despite the night nurse, she slept very little.

Peter, noticing this, brought in the family doctor—the same elderly physician who'd been treating the Van Laars since Peter's father was in his twenties.

Dr. Lewis was his name, and the first pill he ever prescribed to Alice was meant to help her sleep.

But the word broke through the pills, inflecting her dreams with dark and anxious images. *Mamma. Mamma*, came the call.

She couldn't talk to Peter. She couldn't talk to her own family. Everyone in her life encouraged her to move on, to move forward on the assumption that Bear would not ever be found.

But this, for Alice, was an impossible task.

Until she had proof to the contrary, she allowed herself to imagine that her son might still exist in the world, someplace just out of sight, an actor in the wings who might at any moment walk onstage.

Alice would wonder, later, whether this notion was what prevented her from fully embracing Barbara. Some part of her feared that Bear— wherever he was, in this world or the next—would sense some division in her motherly heart, would vanish or perish because of it.

And so each night, before she fell under the spell of Dr. Lewis's pills, she did not pray that the voice she heard would stop, but that it would come to her, again and again. That Bear, in any form possible, would continue to visit her for the rest of her life.

The problem began when Bear's visits got longer.

Alice

1950s • **1962** • Winter 1973 • June 1975
July 1975 • August 1975

It was a nice place, and very discreet. These were the two words that everyone used when describing it.

Her parents were the ones to take her, presumably at the request of her husband and father-in-law. They were silent, all of them, for the three-hour drive. Not even the radio played.

When imagining the hospital, Alice had pictured something historic—something not dissimilar in appearance, in fact, from Self-Reliance. Set in nature, perhaps. A beautiful old building where she'd be given time to rest. Instead, the building—on the North Shore of Long Island—was brand-new, Brutalist in style, made of yellowy concrete that darkened in the rain. The grounds were treeless and barren. On benches here and there, uniformed employees sat with charges who looked half asleep.

Perhaps they had the wrong place, thought Alice. But no, there was the sign: *The Dunwitty Institute*. Founded by a friend of Dr. Lewis, who had recommended it.

In the front seat, her father turned his head toward her mother, trying unsuccessfully to catch her eye. Surely they, too, saw what she saw; certainly they'd understand that some mistake had been made. But her mother got out of the car without a word, and her father, after a beat, followed suit. Then he opened the back door for Alice.

She had no roommate. At least there was that. She was granted this privilege, said a nurse, by virtue of her family connection to Dr. Dunwitty. The nurse—a thin frowning woman in her late middle age—had revealed this disapprovingly, clearing her throat after speaking the words as if ridding her mouth of their taste.

No books were allowed. No television.

The only permitted activities were puzzles of various kinds: jigsaw, crossword, acrostic. There was some theory behind this, no doubt; idly, Alice wondered what it might be.

What she hated most was that Bear didn't visit her here. The first night, she prayed that he would: some company would have been nice.

Instead, she was visited only by nightmares in which she returned to those terrible first days of searching, in which she was thwarted over and over again by forces or people she couldn't control. When they were children, Delphine had called them *can't-get-there* dreams: visions of missed trains and exams, traffic that stopped the car just before the boat departed. They'd happened to Alice all her life, but none of them compared to the ones she had at the Dunwitty Institute.

For one month, she had no visitors, and she was permitted no telephone calls.

On the thirty-first day she was there, a nurse came into her room and retrieved her. Alice followed her, puzzled, down a long hallway she'd never seen before. At its end was a pay phone. The nurse handed Alice a coin.

Alice looked at it.

"Well?" said the nurse. "Go ahead."

But there was no one, she realized, that she wanted to call.

She fed the coin into the pay phone. Dialed a number she remembered from childhood. On the other end, a woman's voice.

"Is Geraldine home?" Alice asked. The name of a friend from Brearley, to whom she had not spoken since she'd married Peter.

A pause. "May I ask who's speaking?"

"This is Alice, Mrs. DeWitt. Alice Ward."

"Oh, Alice," said Mrs. DeWitt. "Alice, I was so sorry to hear—"

Swiftly, she hung up the phone.

A week after that, she was told she had a visitor.

If she had known who it would be, she wouldn't have emerged from her room. But she didn't ask, and this was how she came to find herself face-to-face, across a table set for checkers, with her sister, Delphine.

Alice turned to the nurse. "I want to leave," she said. "I don't want to be here. I'd like to go back to my room, please."

But the nurse said: "Come now, that's your sister, and she's driven such a long way."

Delphine smiled tightly, first at the nurse and then at Alice. "I won't keep her long, Nurse," said Delphine, using her grandest and airiest voice. And the nurse, obedient, practically bowed her way out of the room.

For some minutes, they sat in silence. The only way to survive this, thought Alice, was to imagine herself into a different world. And so, just as she had done in childhood, she closed her eyes, sitting quite upright, and left the earthly world.

You're outside Bear's room, she thought. *He'll wake up shortly. He'll call for you.*

"Alice," said her sister.

Mamma, thought Alice.

"Alice. Can you hear me?"

Mamma.

"I'm sorry," said Delphine.

v

Found

Judyta

1950s • 1961 • Winter 1973 • June 1975
July 1975 • August 1975: **Day One**

Judy stands outside, hands on hips, considering the cars in the parking area next to the house. Stately Cadillacs and Oldsmobiles and Lincolns, mostly. She tries to picture a blue Trans Am among them. It would have stood out.

She turns in a full circle. Two dark angry ruts in the dirt driveway indicate a car backing out with vigor, then pulling off toward Route 29.

She knows that the information she now has on John Paul McLellan Jr. is important. His late reentry into the house; his battered face; his disappearance this morning: all together, they make him at minimum a person of interest. But as a junior investigator, she isn't authorized to do anything without her superior's approval.

She checks her watch, wondering when Denny Hayes will return.

After a few minutes, she walks back into the house. While she waits for Hayes, she knows she should continue to isolate and interview everyone else she can find.

The lanky young people sprawled out on all the furniture in the great room are the people she is least eager to speak to. They look somehow like they should be feeding one another grapes; like young gods—in their own minds, at least. Still, she approaches them, one after another, asks them politely if they'll speak with her, and then brings them into an empty sunroom she found while walking the house.

There, she asks them her standard questions: name, age, occupation, primary place of residence—to which every one of them replies *Manhattan* or *Los Angeles*.

The last person she interviews is a thin, severe-looking twenty-three-year-old. The only one who tells Judy she has been staying in the main house itself, as opposed to an outbuilding.

Her name, she says, is Marnie McLellan.

Upon hearing the girl's last name, Judy pauses, goes still for a moment.

"Occupation?" she says.

"Gallerist."

Judy doesn't know the word. She writes it down; tells herself she'll look it up later.

"Relationship to the Van Laars?" she says.

"Goddaughter."

"Are you close?"

Marnie McLellan lifts her chin. "Extremely."

Judy holds her pen over her notepad. She must, she knows, tread carefully here.

She asks the girl the same set of questions she's asked everyone else, and gets similar answers—she was at the party, she stayed up late, there was a good deal of noise, a good deal of drinking. She went to bed at four in the morning. She knows Barbara well—the families have spent a good deal of time together, have vacationed together, too; but she has no theories about where the girl might be now.

"How would you describe Barbara?"

"Oh, miserable," says the girl. "Just a really unhappy person."

Judy nods. In her notepad, she writes: *Dislikes B.*

"How so?" she says.

"Well, she's always given her family a really hard time. I know she's gotten into trouble at school. She's supposed to be kind of fast for her age. And she wears clothes and makeup that are—" Marnie pauses here, summoning up the words to describe them. "They're terrible. All black everything. Dark rings around her eyes. Spikes in her earlobes. Really upsetting, if you ask me. The product of a disturbed mind."

Judy hasn't heard this before, about Barbara.

She writes: *B. dressed oddly.*

At last, Judy works around to the questions she's been waiting to ask.

"Are the other members of your family staying on the grounds as well?"

"Yes."

"Can you tell me their full names?"

"Why?"

"Just trying to put together a list of all the guests. To make sure I've covered all my bases before my boss gets back," Judy adds. Smiling, deferential.

Marnie is very still.

"My father," she says, "is John Paul McLellan Sr. My mother is Nancy McLellan."

Judy looks at her. "Occupations?"

"My mother's a homemaker," says Marnie. "My father is a business partner of the Van Laars."

"A banker?" says Judy.

"An attorney. He represents the family, and the bank."

Judy nods, writing. Then asks, with forced calm: "Do you have any siblings?"

"My brother is John Paul McLellan Jr."

"Occupation?"

Marnie scoffs, then recovers herself.

"Not much," she says. "He graduated from college last year. He'll take over the bank one day. If he ever gets his act together."

Judy considers this. "What makes you think that?"

Marnie looks at her as if she's dumb. "The Van Laars don't have a boy. Not anymore, anyway. But we do."

"I see," says Judy. Writing this down. "And do you know where I might find them?"

"Who?"

"The other members of your family. Your parents and brother."

"I have no idea," says Marnie, after a pause.

"Have you seen them this morning?"

Marnie hesitates for a moment. "I've only seen my father," she says. "But I don't know where he is now."

Five minutes later, Judy walks back out through the main entrance to the house, the one with the blackfly knocker. She looks down the hill toward the camp. The mounting evidence against John Paul McLellan Jr. has become too much to ignore.

A lone state trooper stands on the lawn.

"Excuse me," she says. "Has Captain LaRochelle arrived yet?"

He looks at her blankly.

"I'm Investigator Luptack," she says. "I was told the captain would be arriving soon? To speak to the family?"

He shakes his head. "Nope. There's a couple more BCI guys down there, but no captain yet."

Judy thanks him. Then, with purpose, she walks back into the kitchen of Self-Reliance, where she has seen a telephone on the wall. Glancing over each shoulder, she lifts the receiver, dials into the station, and requests a BOLO: all officers in the region will be informed, over their radios, that they should be on the lookout for a blue Trans Am.

This is too important to wait for Denny Hayes's return. If she's made a wrong assessment, she'll deal with the consequences later.

Having interviewed everyone she can find at the house, Judy walks back out to the front and perches for a moment on the edge of an Adirondack chair, scribbling frantically in her notebook. She wants to capture all the exact words and phrases she can remember.

From some distance away, she hears someone calling: "Ma'am?"

She doesn't look up.

"Ma'am?" the voice says again, closer this time. She hears footsteps. Turns.

Approaching her is an EnCon ranger, fifty something, bearded; a few steps behind him, a giant girl, wearing a towel around her shoulders. She looks taller than Judy by a head. Taller even than the EnCon ranger, who himself is not a small man.

Behind the two of them, a couple follows: a man in his fifties and a woman who looks about Judy's age. Is she the girl's sister?

"I'm looking for someone from the BCI," the ranger asks.

Judy looks down at herself. At her suit, which clearly separates her from the troopers, the rangers, the guests.

"That's me," says Judy finally. "Investigator Luptack."

The girl with him looks shaky. Reaching the line of Adirondack chairs at the front of the house, she sits down hard in one. Puts her elbows on her knees.

"This is Tracy Jewell," he says. "She was Barbara Van Laar's bunkmate. She's got a few things she'd like to share with you."

Tracy

1950s • 1961 • Winter 1973 • June 1975
July 1975 • August 1975: **Day One**

Tracy sits in a chair on the lawn, drinking a glass of water, eating a sandwich someone has brought to her. Next to her is a woman police officer—the first one Tracy has ever met, or even seen.

At least, she *thinks* this woman is a police officer. She wears no uniform, only a suit. She looks young, but her notepad and pen give her an air of authority.

She's waiting silently for Tracy to speak.

"What did you say?" Tracy asks.

"The person you met in the woods. Can you give us any details?"

"Oh," says Tracy. "Not really."

"Do you know if it was a man or a woman?"

"I think it was a man," says Tracy. "But I'm not sure. I should wear glasses, but I don't."

She thinks. "It had gray hair," she adds.

"Did the person say anything to you?"

Tracy shakes her head. "It didn't talk. It just waved at me. Led me out of the woods."

The woman nods. Scribbles quickly on her notepad.

"Are they trying to find the person now?" says Tracy. "The rangers?"

"I think they probably are," says the woman.

"It was trying to help me," says Tracy. "Whoever it was."

"I'm sure you're right," says the woman. "We'll just want to have a conversation with the person. See if they've seen anything we should know about."

She pauses. "Tracy," she says. "Why did you go into the woods to begin with?"

Tracy is silent.

"Would you like to share that with me?"

Tracy takes a bite. Chews. Drinks water. She pulls the towel she's wearing more tightly around herself.

Then—breaking a promise to Barbara, keeping a promise to herself—she tells Investigator Luptack why it was that Barbara went into the woods.

"Every night?" Investigator Luptack says, holding her gaze. "Barbara left every night?"

"Almost," says Tracy. "Except once, when she was injured."

"And always to the observer's cabin?"

"That's what she said."

"But she never said who her boyfriend was."

Tracy shakes her head. "No."

Investigator Luptack nods. "Thank you, Tracy," she says. "That's very helpful. Is there anything else you think might be helpful? Did she ever mention anything about her relationship with her family?"

Tracy hesitates.

"Did she get along with her parents?"

Tracy shakes her head. "No," she says softly.

"Any idea why?"

"I guess—they were strict with her. Her father was, anyway. Her mother wasn't very involved."

Investigator Luptack nods. "And do you know if anything happened recently that might have frightened Barbara, or made her upset, or made her angry?"

Tracy thinks. She's about to say no—Barbara has never been specific in her complaints about her family—but then she remembers something.

"Yes," she says. "They painted her walls."

Investigator Luptack's expression changes.

"Here at this house?"

"Yes. Her mother had them painted pink."

"And why did that upset her?"

"I don't know," says Tracy. "Maybe she didn't like the color."

Judyta

1950s • 1961 • Winter 1973 • June 1975
July 1975 • August 1975: **Day One**

Twenty minutes later—after the girl has been released into the care of the couple Judy has determined to be her father and his girlfriend—Judy stands in the main house, in the hallway outside the pink room, considering its door. She could open it, she thinks. No one's inside. But she isn't certain what the consequences of this action would be, and so she hovers there for a while, waiting.

She hears footsteps at the end of the hallway.

A side door opens, and through it walk a man and a woman. The man is tall, elegant, his dark hair streaked with silver. The woman, who comes second, is so incredibly thin that she looks ill.

The man pauses, stares at Judy for a moment. He is ten yards away. Then he shakes his head a bit, inscrutably, and ushers the woman into one of the bedrooms off the hall.

Are these the parents? Mr. and Mrs. Van Laar?

When the man comes out, he is alone, and he leaves through the same door without glancing in her direction.

"Judy," someone says, and she jumps.

It's Denny Hayes.

"C'mon," says Hayes. "I've been looking for you. Captain just got here. He's about to start a briefing down at the camp. You can fill me in on your morning while we walk."

He takes off. Judy follows, trotting slightly to keep up.

She leads with the most important facts: that Barbara's bunkmate said she had a boyfriend; that she was sneaking out each night to see him at the observer's cabin at the top of Hunt Mountain.

She tells him about the painted bedroom walls—and that Barbara was upset over them.

Next, she tells him what she's learned about John Paul McLellan: the bloody face, the late return, the disappearance of him and his blue Trans Am.

She saves for last the fact that she's already put out a BOLO for the car.

For a moment, Denny stops and turns toward her, and Judy is afraid that he'll chastise her for not seeking permission from a higher-up. But instead he says, "Judy. You're actually doing really good work here."

Judy frowns. The *actually*, she thinks, was unnecessary—but she'll take it.

"Speak up in the captain's briefing, okay?" says Denny Hayes. Then, without waiting for a response, he keeps walking.

The Command Post, Judy learns, has been moved from the backstage area of the Great Hall to the Director's Cabin, on LaRochelle's orders: they'll need near-constant access to a telephone.

This means that T.J. Hewitt—the director, who lives there—has been displaced to an empty room in the Staff Quarters.

At five in the evening, inside the Director's Cabin, Captain LaRochelle now stands at attention in front of the longest wall. He is an imposing man. Military haircut, very upright posture.

Around him, a dozen investigators sit or stand. Half are from B-tour, staying late; the other are C-tour investigators, just arriving for their shift. Judy and Hayes arrive last, as LaRochelle, consulting his notes, begins to speak.

"Persons of interest so far," he says. And with his fingers he ticks them off.

"John Paul McLellan Jr. Godson of the Van Laar family. Came home last night with a bloody face, nowhere to be found this morning. Still at large. BOLO's been issued."

Judy is startled. She is still figuring out how information gets transmitted from person to person in the BCI. She isn't sure how Captain LaRochelle knows this already.

He continues. "Louise Donnadieu. Barbara's counselor. Currently in custody on an unrelated charge, but not sure how long we can keep her there. I've got"—he checks his notes—"Investigator Lowry working that lead."

He pauses.

"Unknown person seems to be roaming the woods near the estate," he says, "according to a girl named Tracy Jewell, Barbara's bunkmate. We have no description on this person other than that he's tall, because Tracy wasn't wearing her glasses. But we haven't spotted anybody yet. Nor have we spotted any sign of Barbara herself in the nearby woods. The hounds did pick up a scent on her, but it seems they may have been trailing a path she took on a different organized outing, several days ago."

He looks up. "So basically, we've gotten nowhere near where we need to be, nine hours into this search."

Another investigator speaks up. "Sir, have the parents said anything notable?"

"Not really," says LaRochelle. "I spoke to Mr. Van Laar at length just now. He described Barbara as unhappy and troubled. His suspicion is that she's a runaway. But he didn't have any idea where she might have gone."

"Any reason to suspect him?"

"Not that I'm aware of at this juncture," says LaRochelle. "But obviously we'll be watching him closely."

He points to one of the investigators who's just arrived for C-tour. "That means you," he says. "You're in charge of keeping an eye on the parents overnight."

A beat of silence. Then the same investigator who asked about the parents speaks again. "Sir," he says. "Do you find it suspicious at all that the father wouldn't speak to any of us? That he wanted to wait for you?"

LaRochelle considers this. "I wouldn't say suspicious, necessarily," he says. "I worked with them closely on their son's case. Could just be there's a level of trust there."

To Judy, this sounds dubious. But as the newest investigator in the room, she has no intention of saying so.

"What else do you have for me?" says LaRochelle, and Hayes elbows her gently.

Judy clears her throat. Raises her hand.

Then she tells LaRochelle about what Tracy Jewell said: the

boyfriend, the overnight meetings at the observer's cabin, the painted walls.

LaRochelle raises his eyebrows. "Anyone else heard anything about a boyfriend?"

Around the room, heads shake.

He points to one investigator. "You. Find a ranger. Ask them if they've been to the observer's cabin yet. If not, get them moving."

He pauses. "Do we know where Barbara Van Laar was in school?"

An investigator raises his hand. "Emily Grange. Down near Latham."

"You," says LaRochelle to the investigator. "Head there. Get numbers from them for Barbara's friends. Ask about a boyfriend."

"You," says LaRochelle, pointing to an investigator coming onto C-tour who has half a sandwich hanging from his mouth. "Head for the Van Laars' house in Albany. Check Barbara's room there for anything relevant. Bring back Polaroids, if you can."

He pauses.

"Questions?"

A moment of stillness, and then one hand goes up, from the edge of the room. It's an investigator Judy hadn't noticed, until now, perhaps the oldest person in the room.

"Is it worth considering Jacob Sluiter?"

A general shift in the atmosphere of the room. For a moment there is a standoff; LaRochelle seems to be waiting for the investigator to explain himself, to offer excuses or some rationale.

He doesn't.

LaRochelle folds his arms. "It's possible, I guess," he says. "Him being on the loose. But to me that seems less likely than other explanations," says LaRochelle.

The investigator nods, though his expression signifies that he is not completely satisfied.

"Could he have been the unknown person in the woods? The one who led the Jewell girl toward the house?"

LaRochelle frowns. "Now let's think about that," he says. "Convicted sexual offender and murderer sees a girl, alone and lost, in the woods. Is he going to lead her to safety? Or is he going to seize upon the opportunity to do what he's done in the past?"

The old investigator says nothing. The two men regard each other, as if sending silent messages to one another that the rest of the room can't read.

"I'm not saying it's out of the question," says LaRochelle. "I'm just saying—when you hear hoofbeats, don't look for a zebra."

Judyta

1950s • 1961 • Winter 1973 • June 1975
July 1975 • August 1975: **Day One**

It's almost six o'clock at the end of their first day on the Preserve. To Judy, this math doesn't compute. She feels as if she's been there for a year.

Hayes is driving north to BCI headquarters at Ray Brook. After that, she'll start the long drive to Schenectady. The thought makes her want to cry.

"Tired?" says Hayes.

"A little."

"Get ready," says Hayes. "Case like this, you'll be working around the clock."

He rolls down the window. Shakes a pack of cigarettes in his hand, offering one to Judy, who declines.

"Don't smoke?"

"No."

"That's good," says Hayes. "My old man died from it, I think. He didn't call it cancer, but he sure died coughing."

He pulls from it. Blows a plume of smoke sideways out the open window. "I only smoke in the car. That's my compromise with myself."

Judy gives a weak laugh. Just enough to demonstrate that she's been listening.

"Can I ask you something?" says Hayes, and Judy tenses, expecting something personal. It will be a very long time before Judy feels at ease enough around her colleagues to divulge anything at all about her family or her history. But when Hayes continues, it's benign: "Why'd you get into police work?"

She considers her options. *I wanted to help people* sounds trite. *I thought it sounded interesting*—too vague.

At last, surprising herself, she tells the truth.

"*The Mod Squad*," says Judy.

"The—" says Hayes, as if he hasn't heard.

"*The Mod Squad*," says Judy. "It was my favorite show."

Hayes starts laughing. Keeps laughing until he coughs, flicks his cigarette out the window. "I'll be damned," he says. "First time I ever heard that one."

Judy grins.

"*The Mod Squad*," says Hayes, laughing and laughing until at last easy silence descends on the car.

Which is when the radio crackles to life.

John Paul McLellan, in his blue Trans Am, has been spotted and detained. He's on the side of the thruway, ten miles south.

Denny Hayes glances at her. Glances at his watch. "Six o'clock," he says. "We're off. We could go home."

He looks at her. "Do you want to?"

Judy shakes her head.

Hayes radios back, pops his magnetic light onto the roof, careens over the grassy median, and reverses direction.

When they arrive, the state trooper who pulled him over has John Paul McLellan handcuffed. He's sitting on the grass near his car. He's been punched. Several times, from the look of his swollen lips, his black eye.

The trooper fills them in: McLellan is obviously drunk, he says. In fact, that was the first thing he noticed. He would have pulled him over anyway, even without the BOLO. He failed his field sobriety test resoundingly.

"He's all yours," says the trooper.

"I've been at a restaurant," says McLellan, from the ground.

Presumably, "restaurant" means bar. The smell of the liquor on his breath is evident from several feet away. As is the smell of marijuana.

Hayes opens the passenger door. Begins a search.

"You can't do that," says McLellan. "I haven't authorized a search."

"Unfortunately for you," says Hayes—voice strained and muffled as he bends low into the car—"by virtue of the fact that the scent of an illegal substance is discernible from within your vehicle, I do have the right to search it."

In quick succession, Hayes finds a roach clip, two crushed cans of Genesee, and what appears to be residue from cocaine on the center console. And he hasn't even gotten to the trunk.

Based on this evidence, along with McLellan's clear intoxication, he has placed McLellan under arrest.

Judy, meanwhile, takes his license and registration back to the unmarked car, and radios both over to Ray Brook.

From the driver's seat, while waiting for the operator to come through, she watches McLellan steadily. He's sniffing, his mouth and face moving in strange ways. At first she attributes this to the coke; she's never done it herself, but she saw people in high school do it, boys mainly, other jocks. But as McLellan turns his face upward, toward the sun, she realizes he is crying.

Hayes has moved to the trunk now. He's opening it.

Hayes's back is to her. With gloved hands, he's removing an improbable number of objects from the small trunk, placing each one carefully on the ground. Golf club. Golf club. Duffel bag. Satchel. Book. Shoe. Book. Shoe.

Last, Hayes removes a paper bag.

McLellan isn't looking up, Judy sees. He's staring hard at the ground.

The color of the bag, which Hayes is handling carefully, looks strange. Not like most paper bags Judy has seen before.

And then she realizes: the bottom of it is darker than it should be.

Judy, keeping a close eye on McLellan to ensure he's still sitting, gets out of the car and walks toward Hayes, who's now squatting on the ground, looking inside the bag. As she approaches, he begins lifting each object out in turn, using two gloved fingers to do so.

Underwear, shorts, a T-shirt. Small, white, blue.

It's a uniform. Covered, by the looks of it, in blood.

Judy looks at McLellan. His head is still lowered.

She looks at Denny Hayes, who's saying something Judy can't hear. *Shit. Shit.*

His face looks drained of color. For all his bravado, he seems unprepared for this. He's a father, Judy remembers: all other things aside, he has his own children.

*　*　*

All three of them are silent on the ride to the station, until Denny talks.

"Did you kill her?" he says, and the noise of the question is like a gun going off. Judy can hear the air moving around the car in its wake.

She glances at McLellan in the rearview. He's looking out the window, his expression inscrutable. For a time, she thinks he won't speak at all—until he does.

"I invoke my right against self-incrimination," he says.

Spoken, she thinks, like the son of a lawyer.

At Ray Brook, they process him quickly and put him in a holding cell. He's given one phone call. Judy has no doubt who'll be on the other end.

Sure enough: from his mouth comes a quavering *"Dad?"*

And then the hand goes up, over the brow, hiding what Judy knows will be self-pitying tears.

Nothing he says is surprising: he got in trouble, he needs help. He needs his father to come to him.

Hayes enters the room. Says, "Judy, go home."

It's eight o'clock now. She won't reach Schenectady until after ten.

Louise

1950s • 1961 • Winter 1973 • June 1975
July 1975 • August 1975: **Day One**

It's nearly midnight. Louise has been in a holding cell for ten hours. She's been given water, but nothing to eat.

She feels light-headed, ill. She wishes for outside air.

She eyes a cup of now-cold coffee—which she normally doesn't drink—and takes a sip.

Finally there is a brusque knock at the door. Someone opens it without waiting for a response.

It's a man, fifty, wearing thick glasses and a sweater vest over his brown tie. He looks like an English professor, thinks Louise. He's carrying a Coke in his hand. The only sign that he works in law enforcement comes in the form of a badge. He sits down opposite Louise, crosses one leg over the other.

She braces herself. She will simply tell him the truth, she's decided: she was out overnight last night. But so was Annabel. The drugs in the bag are Annabel's, not hers.

The man does not introduce himself, but takes a sip of his Coke and begins.

Something about his aspect and outfit makes her expect kindness from him, but his tone is stern.

"What's your relation to John Paul McLellan?" he says. He looks directly at her. He has no notepad in which to record her answers.

The question throws her off: this wasn't what she was expecting to discuss.

"I'm his fiancée," says Louise automatically. "We're engaged. We've been together four years."

"Huh," says the man.

She waits, guarded, for more. Willing herself into silence.

"That's not what he said about you," the man says.

Louise moves a little in her chair. Don't ask, she tells herself; Louise, don't ask. But she can't help herself.

"What do you mean?"

The man excavates a speck of dirt from beneath a thumbnail. He sniffs, and his thick-rimmed glasses slide slightly down his nose.

"He said you two used to sleep together," the man says. "You know, a while ago. It's over now, he says, but you're still hung up on him."

"That's horseshit," says Louise, without thinking.

"Where's your ring?"

Louise flushes. This has always been a point of contention between her and John Paul. He says he wants to get her a nice one, something beautiful—and that he can't until he has a real job.

"I'm not wearing it today," says Louise. "I don't wear it at camp. It's too nice."

"Look, I don't know what's true," says the man. "That's just what he said. Just telling you."

Louise looks at him sideways. "What's your name," she says.

The investigator blinks.

"You know mine," she says. "What's yours?"

"Lowry."

"I'm not supposed to be talking to you, Lowry," she says.

"Who gave you that advice?"

Silent, Louise reminds herself. Say nothing.

For a minute, the two of them sit without speaking. The man leans back in his chair, hands behind his head. Comfortable. He looks up and out the one high window in the room.

The professorial attire, thinks Louise, is a ruse. A trick designed to disarm suspects. This man is like every other cop she's ever met.

Suddenly Louise's stomach grumbles so loudly that the sound fills the room.

"Hungry," says the man. A statement, not a question.

He stands, walks into the other room. Returns with an apple and a little knife. He pares the apple from its skin, and then slices it, and then hands her pieces one at a time, which she doesn't decline.

"Why are you asking me about John Paul?" she says, after the apple is nearly gone.

"You can't figure it out?"

Louise says nothing.

"You know why you're here, right?" the man says. Trying again. But again, Louise says nothing.

"You're being held right now for a minor crime. We're getting a bail hearing scheduled as we speak. That'll happen tomorrow, probably, at the earliest. But you're here for another reason, too."

Silence. She waits. The man watches her, measured. She does not like his expression: he believes her to be impressionable, credulous, a local who never left home. If he only knew, she thinks; if he only knew the restaurants she's gone to with John Paul, the movies she's seen. The books she's read, on John Paul's recommendation and on account of her own curiosity. I'm different from what you think, she wants to tell him. But Denny's warning—*don't talk without a lawyer*—remains at the front of her mind.

The man leans forward.

"We know," he says, "that you know what happened to Barbara Van Laar."

It catches her off guard.

"I don't," says Louise, before she can stop herself. But for some reason, even to her, the words sound false: high-pitched, a note of complaint in their intonation.

"That's different too," says the man.

"Than what?"

"Than what your boyfriend said."

Alice

1950s • 1961 • Winter 1973 • June 1975
July 1975 • **August 1975**

This, thought Alice, was what Self-Reliance had been built for. At ten in the morning, she stood in the center of the great room and turned in a slow circle as, all around her, the house was resurrected. They had not held a party—the Blackfly Good-by, or any other—since Bear's disappearance. But the house's one hundredth anniversary seemed to Peter to be an auspicious occasion to restart the tradition. "Good for business," he said. He had several potential clients he wanted to invite.

The obstacle was the amount of work that had to be done. Most of Self-Reliance's bedrooms had been closed for longer than Barbara had been alive. Now they were being unsealed, the dust coverings pulled from the furniture, the windows opened. Cut flowers were driven up from the florist they used in Albany. Wildflowers, at Peter's command: bunches of wood sorrel and dewdrops and jack-in-the-pulpits, in vases all over the house, on nightstands in every bedroom. Peter had had the sofa and chairs in the great room reupholstered, and had bought new furniture, too: three dozen Adirondack chairs, locally made, now stood at attention in a neat semicircle on the lawn leading down to Lake Joan. The old ones, splintered and ancient, had been scrapped for firewood by someone on staff.

It wasn't only the house that had been remade. For the past weeks, ever since Barbara's departure for camp, Alice had been attending to herself, her physical person, for the first time in years. It was a welcome turn. This party and its planning had reignited some fundamental part of herself, her character. Certainly she had never let herself go, not all the way—but she had also not been quite as careful with her clothing, her skin, her nails. She used to wear her hair in a sort of voluminous bob that ended at the nape of her neck. Very chic, she had always been told. But after Bear's disappearance she had stopped going to her normal hairdresser, not wanting to answer questions again and again. Her hair had grown long, shamefully so. To hide its length, she pinned it into a low twist.

A week after Barbara's departure for Camp Emerson, she had asked one of the staff to drive her down to Albany for a hair appointment. She returned with her hair in a long straight sheet down her back, freshly dyed to conceal the gray at her temples. In her hand was a bag from Whitney's, and inside it were seven new outfits, including two miniskirts and a bikini. The salesgirl, impossibly young, had egged her on: "You've got the figure, after all," she said.

Now it was Saturday morning—the day the party was set to begin— and Alice stood before her closet, deciding which new outfit to choose.

"Mrs. Van Laar," someone said.

She turned. It was a young man she did not, at first, recognize. One of the temporary staff Peter had hired, she guessed. He was wearing a uniform, anyway.

"What is it?"

"Someone's at the front door," the boy said.

"A guest?" Alice asked—horrified. Surely not yet, she thought. It was only eleven in the morning. The guests were not due until late afternoon.

"I'm not sure," said the boy. "It's a couple. They're—" he hedged.

And just then, Alice heard her mother's voice, familiar and terrifying at once, impatient and out of sorts.

Alice blinked, frozen. She was in no way ready for their arrival.

"Thank you," she said to the boy, who retreated. And then, with reluctance, Alice pulled from her closet a mock turtleneck and a corduroy miniskirt, and put them both on.

"Good heavens, Alice," said her mother, in the great room. She took Alice in with a sweep of her eyes, from top to bottom: her flat-ironed hair, her short skirt, her bare legs and feet. And then she pronounced: "You're *gaunt*."

It was and was not an insult.

"Mother," said Alice. "You're early."

"Well, I thought you'd need the help," said her mother, casting her gaze around the room, her implication clear.

At times, Alice was impressed by the creativity of her mother's criticisms, the poetry of the language she used to describe all that she found lacking in the world around her. A different sort of daughter would have distanced herself from her mother long ago, or at least made the decision to laugh about it all. But at more than forty years old, Alice still—embarrassingly, she realized—strove to successfully anticipate and ward off the complaints that emanated from her, a deluge of observations designed to sound neutral, each more cutting than the last.

"You go off and get ready," said Mrs. Ward. "I'll direct the others."

Alice froze. Ordered herself to say it: *I am ready.*

"Thank you, Mother," she said instead. She avoided meeting her father's gaze. If she did, she might have cried, for she knew he would be looking at her with something like pity. Why did she let it all bother her? At this point in life? Peter had been telling her for years—well, never mind what he said. He was part of the problem.

Alice retreated down the hallway, self-conscious now about her body, her bare legs. She could feel her mother's gaze, still, burning into her.

In the bedroom, she opened her closet door and stood there for too long, staring at but not processing the visual field before her. Colors were there, and textures, and garments of various lengths.

And then, above the clothing rack, another swath of fabric drew her attention, and she reached for it.

During Alice's time away—the only term that was ever used to describe her stay at the Dunwitty Institute—Dr. Lewis had urged the rest of the Van Laars to remove all hints of Bear from their Albany house and from Self-Reliance, too. And so his two rooms had been stripped to the studs. The walls—once covered, to Bear's delight, in wallpaper designed to look like maps of the world—had been painted white. His clothing, gone. His toys and books. This, Dr. Lewis said, was the way to let Alice heal; and in the Van Laar household, the advice of Dr. Lewis—a friend of Peter II's from his Yale days—was taken.

But there was one possession of Bear's that they had not seen.

When Bear was born, someone had given her a blanket for him, blue with a silk ribbon trim in a moon-and-star pattern. As he grew, he was rarely without it. But when, at four, he was still trailing it about the house, Peter had issued a command that it be taken from him. And Alice had complied, had kept it hidden from him here on this shelf of her closet, though the boy had wept pitifully for it each bedtime for a week.

When Alice returned from her time away to find all of Bear's artifacts removed from the house, she had known enough to mask her dismay. (She would rather be there, in a Bear-less home, than in that other place again.) As soon as she was unmonitored, she had retired to her room and thrown open the door to the closet. And there it was: the blanket she had hidden from him so long ago.

Now, Alice held the blanket to her face, trailed over her cheek its frayed edges, which Bear had a habit of tapping lightly with his fingers.

She wouldn't change her outfit, she decided. She would say nothing to her mother. She simply wouldn't change.

She draped the blanket over her face. She lay on her bed like that for a time. She had had none of Dr. Lewis's pills since her trip to Albany. She had been distracted by preparations for the festivities. Something to *do* for once, thought Alice. It had not occurred to her, during all of that planning, to have a very bad day.

Someplace else in the house, she heard her mother issuing commands. *There*, she was saying. *There. No. Yes. No.*

Mechanically, Alice's right hand went to her bedside table, and pulled open its drawer, and she felt the comforting curve of the bottle inside, and heard the comforting rattle of the pills, and into her mouth she took one of them, and then two of them, and then three, and then four. She bit down on them and chewed. Then she put Bear's blanket back over her face. *A shroud*, she thought, *a pall*, and then laughed a bit to herself.

When she opened her eyes, she heard voices on the lawn. Many of them. She tried to sit up but could not. There was darkness above and around her. As a child, she had avoided naps: for waking from them caused in her a sort of supernatural despair. Bear, too, had been like this: the only time he was bleary was after his afternoon rest.

She felt it now. Despite the heat of the afternoon, she pulled the covers around herself.

After a minute, or an hour, she rose.

Then the nightstand, then the drawer, then the pills. Two more. Three.

She walked with a hand on the wall. She felt her way down the hallway and into the kitchen, where she fumbled in the cabinet for a glass, and then ran water from the sink. It came from a well, and tasted sweetly of the earth.

A small trickle of liquid escaped the side of her mouth, and she ran a hand below her chin to catch it. And then she noticed movement: in her peripheral vision, a hesitant human form. She turned. The new cook. The girl from town. The nameless one.

"What," said Alice.

"Nothing."

"Nothing, *ma'am*," said Alice, but the girl only blinked at her.

The cabinets. The wall. The two steps up into the great room. Careful, careful. The back of the sofa. The side of the central fireplace, pleasingly rough.

She stopped short at the glass door that led to the lawn. There before her were her guests—hers too, she thought—not just Peter's.

Now they had begun without her. No one had thought to rouse her—not even her own husband. Outside, in the sun, all of them were tipping their glasses back, tipping their heads back in merriment.

She scanned the crowd for Peter and spotted him speaking with the McLellans: husband, wife, daughter, son, each one, thought Alice, terrible in a different way.

She moved as if to place a hand on the sliding glass door, but found it was open instead. And so she tipped forward through it, which caused a woman ten feet in front of her to shriek her name gladly—"Alice!"—and then pause.

The crowd, having heard this greeting, turned—and then hushed.

Alice was realizing something: there were too many pills inside her. After a week of not taking any, especially. After a day of not eating. She put a hand to her hair and found it out of order, great strands of it hanging down in front of her ears. She put a hand to her outfit, her short skirt, and found it up too high around her waist.

Her eyes swam toward Peter's. He was too far from her. He was saying something to the McLellans, something about her: she could see him moving his mouth. The McLellan boy, John Paul Jr., had become a man. He'd take over the business, it was said, and she could see it: he already had the air that all these men had. The feeling he was owed something. Everything.

Through the haze of her intoxication, she had a sense of déjà vu: a feeling of living a particular series of scenes for the second time in her life.

She put a hand to her face to make certain she was intact.

Then she retreated.

Back into the house, into its shade, back down the hallway toward Bear's room, unstoppably, where she lay on the bed that was no longer her son's, where she curled into another tight arrangement of bones and flesh, where, several hours later, two guests would find her deeply asleep.

Outside, she heard again the voices of her guests, rising slowly into mirth once more.

The party would go on without her.

Louise

1950s • 1961 • Winter 1973 • June 1975
July 1975 • August 1975: **Day One**

L ouise feels ill.
"I don't believe you," she says, over and over.
"That's up to you," says the detective. Lowry. She has the feeling she has already said things to him that she shouldn't have said. But if there's one thing that sets her off, it's being lied on. All her life, people have been telling lies about her. Today it's happened twice already: first Annabel, now this. Her face is hot with fury, with the injustice of it all. She's rankled. She can't shut up.

"You're lying," she says, her heart racing.

"Nope," says Lowry, with a sort of calm assurance that makes her want to reach across the table and—

"When did it start?" says Lowry.

"Fuck you," says Louise.

"All right," says Lowry. "You can sit a while longer. I got no other place to be."

John Paul, said Lowry, has been found with a bag of Barbara's clothing. Bloody, he added—holding Louise's gaze as he said the word.

He had no idea what was in the bag, said the detective.

But he said Louise had asked him to get rid of it for her.

"You know what that reminds me of?" said the detective. "The other bag you asked someone to get rid of for you, earlier today."

Now, Louise looks back at him steadily, her face flushed with anger. She tries and fails to keep her voice level.

"Listen to me," she says. "I had nothing to do with either one of those bags. I knew about Annabel's. But that was *her* stuff in it. Not mine."

Lowry assesses her.

"I get it," he says. "Barbara looked a lot older than thirteen."

Louise's stomach turns. She used to hear this sentiment expressed a lot: about herself.

"No, she does not," she says. Careful to use the present tense, to dodge what she assumes is the grammatical trap the detective has laid for her. "She looks like a thirteen-year-old who wears black eyeliner. She looks like a kid."

Lowry nods. "I guess I could see that too," he says. "That makes sense, actually."

She doesn't take the bait.

He tries again. "How long have you known Lee Towson?"

She's silent. She pictures Lee in his apron, grinning at her from the commissary kitchen. Wonders where he is right now.

"It was his idea, right?" says Lowry. "He asked you to bring her to him?"

The absurdity of the accusation riles her, but she understands, in a new way, that Denny Hayes was correct when he told her to ask for a lawyer. That nothing she says now will serve her.

"What do you have me here for," says Louise, finally. Her hunger has become nausea.

Lowry looks at her, surprised.

"You can't keep me here, can you?" says Louise. "Can't I leave?"

"Nope," says Lowry, shaking his head. "Technically, you're being charged with possession of a controlled substance," he says.

"That's a lie too," says Louise.

"Well, we don't know that yet. All we know is that's the charge that's been laid on you. So until bail is set for that charge and you pay it, you're with us."

"But that's not really why you're keeping me here," says Louise. "You already told me that."

Lowry smiles. "Did I?" he says.

Louise says nothing.

"Louise," says Lowry. "If you're done talking to us, that's fine. That's your right. But hear me out. I'm gonna tell you something that I think might help you."

He pauses, sips his Coke. From the inner pocket of his jacket he produces a plastic-wrapped oatmeal raisin cookie, softened in the heat, which he slowly removes from its packaging, dips into his coffee, and begins to eat.

"Maximum sentence for possession of a controlled substance is five years," he says, chewing.

Louise blanches. In five years, her brother Jesse will be sixteen. Practically grown. In five years, it will be too late.

"But if you have information on the whereabouts of Barbara Van Laar—anything that will help us—we'll be in a better position to help you too."

Louise is looking at the table. If she looks up, she's afraid the tears she's been fighting off will be loosed. She'd rather be dead or jailed than let this man see her cry.

"Anyway, I can put a call in now," says Lowry. "See about setting a bail hearing. But."

He checks his wristwatch theatrically.

"It's late in the day now. Magistrate might not be available till tomorrow."

He walks out of the room.

Louise is alone.

For a time, she's quiet, letting this disaster descend onto her shoulders. Her first emotion is horror: that John Paul could have done something as evil as this. Her second is fear. That they'll believe him over her.

One thing that's true: he's always had a mean, vindictive streak. She has seen this side of him, mainly with others, mainly with other boys at parties, when all of them were drunk and high.

Only once has he ever turned that side on her.

Louise

1950s • 1961 • **Winter 1973** • June 1975
July 1975 • August 1975

It was her second winter at Garnet Hill Lodge. It was a Monday, a slow day anyway, and terrifically cold, which frightened off so many reservations that Louise's boss let her off early. So Louise, bored and lonely, took the opportunity to borrow a staff car and drive down to Union College.

John Paul lived that year in a group house with several other boys—one of whom opened the door at the sound of Louise's knock.

"John Paul's out," he said, after taking a few beats to register her face.

"Oh," said Louise. From behind the boy, she heard the noise of what sounded like a party. A low droning note was sounding over and over—a record skipping. A girl laughed merrily. The record was fixed. A boy roared.

She recognized the roar.

"Steven," she said. "I think he's home."

Inside, a dozen people stood or sat in small groups while Zeppelin played in the background.

Most of them were girls she didn't know. Young: freshmen, probably. They were dressed up, wearing going-out clothes, their hair washed and blow-dried. Where are they going on such a cold night? thought Louise—and then realized that this house was their destination, its residents their motive for taking such care with their appearance. Louise, in her parka and hat, felt like a friendly snowman.

Across the room, John Paul swayed slightly, a sort of drunk that made Louise's chest tighten. He had a beer in one hand and wore no shirt, despite the cold. The skin of his shoulders and chest was flushed pink. He had a beautiful thin build and a nice head of hair and very white teeth, and normally Louise thought him handsome. But the quickest way to make an attractive man ugly was to give him too much to drink. Drunk men frightened her. She had learned young how to coddle them, how to laugh just enough at their bad jokes to prevent them from feeling insulted, but not so much that her laughter egged them on. Coiled just below a surface of good humor lay their strength and their meanness, two guns waiting to go off.

"Louiiiiiiiise," said John Paul, when he spotted her. He lurched across the room, put his arms around her shoulders, leaned so heavily on her that the two of them almost toppled.

"*Who are these people?*" she whispered.

"New friends," he said. Slurring. "You'll like 'em. C'mon."

But still there was no introduction, and so for a long time Louise sat on a sofa with no drink in her hand, wearing a polo shirt with a *Garnet Hill Lodge* insignia, her goddamn work-issued uniform, and watched as the people around her grew drunker, as the music got louder, as the atmosphere of potential sex got thicker and more obvious.

The girls reminded her of something, or someone, many someones, and with a jolt she realized finally that it was her campers at Camp Emerson. Not just in their richness and carriage, but also in their youth; the youngest looked sixteen or seventeen years old. Two of them began dancing with one another in a wobbly slither, and she watched John Paul watching them, and it was at that point that she took herself up to his bedroom, without saying goodnight.

She rarely smoked cigarettes, but she saw John Paul's on the bedside table and a silver lighter beside the pack, *JPM* monographed on its side, and she lit one and smoked it. She liked the warmth of it in her lungs.

She put the lighter into her pocket. She wanted to take something of his.

She put out the cigarette and lay there for a long time. There was a window next to the bed, and she looked out and saw that the moon was almost full. From below she heard the music quiet, change to something calm. She didn't know what time it was.

Louise woke up to the sound of the door slamming open. She sat straight up, clutching her heart. There was John Paul, a shadow in the doorway.

Downstairs, people were still talking.

"Where'd you go," he said. His voice was low. She couldn't tell if he was more sober or more drunk than he'd been when she left.

"To bed," she said.

"Don't talk to me like I'm dumb," he said—one of his go-to phrases in any fight. He wasn't dumb. He needed everyone to know this. "Why didn't you say you were going?"

Louise felt her anger rise up in her throat. Normally she thought carefully about everything she said to John Paul before she said it, but tonight she dropped her guard.

"Didn't want to get in your way," she said.

"What did you say?"

"Thought you'd have more fun without me."

John Paul closed the door behind him, throwing the room back into darkness. Suddenly she couldn't see him. Something in Louise woke up enough to be scared.

"John Paul," she said, and then his hands were on her, feeling for her roughly, pulling her up out of the bed by her clothing.

"Who'd you fuck," he said. His voice was too loud. She cringed. The voices downstairs stopped—they were listening.

"*Shhhh*," she said—remembering too late that being shushed was one of John Paul's triggers, that telling him to lower his voice was worse than slapping him in the face. He had told her this in these words.

"Don't shush me," he said. He shouted. "I asked you a question. Who. Did. You. Fuck."

A tiny giggle from downstairs.

"No one, no one," whispered Louise urgently. John Paul's grip on her collar was tightening.

"You sure?" he said. "Because I know you've got that in you. I've seen it."

Once, thought Louise. One time. The first week they were together. Her second month at Union. So drunk that she barely remembered. So drunk that it wasn't right.

"John Paul," Louise said. "I went to bed. I was tired."

He held her there a few more seconds, breathing into her face. Then, slowly, he loosened his grip. He let his arms drop and took one stumbling step backward.

Louise's eyes were adjusting. John Paul's glasses glinted in the streetlight coming in from outside. He put his hands on his waist, hung his head briefly. Then he pushed past her and collapsed into his bed, diagonally, taking up too much space. There was no room for her.

Louise looked at him. She didn't want to wake him. Didn't want to raise his ire a second time. She could sleep on the floor. Or she could go back out into the cold, get into her staff car, hope it started, hope a gas station was open at that time of night. She could make the drive back to the Garnet Hill Lodge. She could leave him behind forever.

A small flame of rage was burning in her belly.

"I hope you die," she said to John Paul, before she could stop herself.

He was on her. His left hand grabbed her shirt. His right hand punched her, twice, while she flailed with her arms, trying to protect her face. She kicked at him. She fell to the ground. Curled into a ball there, protecting her head, trying to protect her stomach. He kicked her once, hard, in the back.

Don't cry out, she told herself. *Don't cry.*

It was a sick instinct, one designed to sacrifice her body in the service of her pride. She could not bear the thought of those girls downstairs, in their going-out clothes, hearing her beaten.

John Paul, above her, was panting.

"Say it again," he said.

She was silent.

She waited just long enough. In her mind, she went through a checklist: her car keys were on the table just inside the front door. Her purse was on the floor next to the bed, but she'd leave it. It was too hard to find in the dark.

"Say *I hope you die, John Paul*," said John Paul. "Say it."

She let a few more moments of silence go by and then tackled him around the knees with all her strength. She was smaller than he was but she had the dual advantages of sobriety and gravity. She tackled him and he hit the ground, hard, and she jumped up—the pain in her face and her back unabating—and ran down the stairs. As she grabbed the keys on the table she heard him thundering after her, down the stairs.

She sensed faces watching her from the living room. She did not turn. She flung open the front door and almost died slipping on the icy stairs, but she righted herself. She got into the staff car and tried to start it, once, twice, three times. It was very bad at starting in the cold.

John Paul came out of the house and launched himself down the stairs and it was the ice that saved her. Unlike Louise, he went down, hard, and stayed there. That's when the car started; that's when she backed out fast into the dark and empty street and then threw the car into first, second, third, fourth.

Her heart was still pounding. The gas gauge was at a quarter tank, maybe a little less. It would not be enough to get her back to the Garnet Hill Lodge; this much she knew. And her purse was back beside John Paul's bed.

Both eyes were swelling, but the left one was worse. She rolled down her window and broke free from the top of the side mirror a small piece of the ice that had formed there. She held it against one eye, then the other.

She had an eighth of a tank as she approached the exit for Shattuck. The Garnet Hill Lodge was another half hour up the thruway from there, and forty-five minutes of local roads after that. She could go home, could sneak into her house and sneak out again in the early morning and hope that Jesse and her mother would not see her and her mangled face. But if they did, she thought: if Jesse did.

She took the exit. She had no choice.

And then, waiting at the light at the bottom of the off-ramp, she had an idea.

She'd never been to the Van Laar Preserve in winter. She had no idea how plowed it would be. In the Adirondacks, snow accumulated fast and rarely melted, so that by March you could find yourself hip-deep in places that weren't plowed by private service. But the family spent Christmas there, she had heard, and there had been no big snowfall since then.

Sure enough, when she arrived at two in the morning, the entrance was clear. At the end of the driveway, the huge dark house sat dormant. She cut her headlights, waited until her eyes adjusted. No sign of anyone on the grounds. The moon was bright that night and the snow reflected it broadly. It was easy to see, even at that hour. She got out of the car.

She could not feel her feet by the time she entered Balsam.

She felt, just inside the door, for the flashlight that sat on a ledge there all summer, and was glad when her fingers touched it.

On her way past the commissary, she'd taken from the woodpile on its porch as many split logs as she could carry, as much kindling. Now she moved to the disused fireplace along one of Balsam's walls—one of the few remainders of its history as a hunting cabin.

She shone the flashlight up into the flue, which looked clean enough; and so she built a roaring fire, using the lighter she had stolen from John Paul, praying that the kindling would catch.

She dragged one of the cots as close to the fire as she could get without singeing herself. She took off her boots, her sodden socks, and placed them in front of it, and then put her feet there too, allowing them to roast. She lifted another thin and floppy mattress off another cot and put it on top of herself.

She fell asleep there.

For the second time that night, she was roused from sleep.

"Get up," said a voice.

Louise was disoriented. In the warmth of the fire, her eyes had swollen closed almost completely, and she could make out only a figure holding one object in each hand. One of them looked pistol-shaped; an outstretched arm was raising it in her direction.

"Get up," said the voice, a second time.

The pain in her back and ribs made Louise move slowly, but at last she stood.

The figure lowered its arm.

"Louise Donnadieu?" it said, after a pause.

Then, with the object in its other hand—a fire extinguisher, it turned out—it leveled a spray of foam at the flames for what felt like a very long time, until cold and dark had seeped back into the cabin, and Louise began shivering again.

At some point during that minute spent in silence, Louise understood that this was T.J. Hewitt.

"Thought you'd be smarter than to put a fire up a chimney this old," said T.J. "Could have burned the cabin down."

"I didn't know you lived here all year," said Louise.

"Where else would I live?" said T.J.

"I guess I thought you lived in town," she said.

"What town would that be?"

Louise was silent. Shame was beginning to creep in, and regret. Already, this was her favorite of all the jobs she'd ever had, and now she'd surely lose it.

"Who did that to your face," said T.J.

Louise said nothing. She stood up, turned to face her boss, barely visible now in the absence of the fire.

"Do you have any gasoline?" she said.

In the Director's Cabin—T.J.'s actual house, Louise now understood— T.J. lit a proper fire. Its light and shadows flickered against the walls around it. T.J. had applied a cold steak to half her face, saying it would help the swelling. With her other eye, the open one, Louise now saw the cabin's history: the books on the bookshelves, novels and how-to guides; the pictures on the wood-paneled walls, fading prints of bears and birds and tranquil mornings on still lakes. On one wall, a map of the entire Adirondack Park. On another, a poster of animal tracks.

T.J. went to the small kitchen off the main room and stood before the stove, stirring a pot. Louise watched the back of her. She had a long braid that year that hung straight down her back. The rest of her was barely wider than the braid, but she was strong: no doubt about that. The muscles of her legs and arms were sharply on view all summer, above her socks, below her T-shirt sleeves. Louise had seen her casually carrying a long wooden canoe above her head: a feat of strength that would have been difficult even for a man.

She did have gasoline, T.J. had said; but it was way up past the main house, and frankly she was tired. She'd give Louise a place to sleep that night. They'd fix the car in the morning.

Now she returned holding a bowl of soup in one hand and a glass of water in the other. She placed both on a low table in front of Louise. Reached for the steak on Louise's face. She held it absent-mindedly in two hands, the juice of it dripping, and regarded Louise as she began to eat and drink.

"What," said Louise, who didn't ever like to be looked at closely, and certainly not with her face in this state.

"Just thinking about whether you need to see a doctor."

"I don't," said Louise.

"Are your insides busted up? Did he kick you?"

Louise paused, recognizing the trap. She could dodge it. *Did who kick me?* But, certain that she was out of a job anyway, that she'd never see T.J. again after this, she nodded.

"He did," she said. "But I don't think anything's busted inside me. My face hurts worse."

T.J. nodded. Returned to the kitchen to put the steak away. She approved of honesty, Louise knew. It was one of the subjects on which she expounded each summer, at the start of session: *Honesty. Integrity. Vigilance.*

"Was it your boyfriend?" T.J. called over her shoulder.

"It was," said Louise.

"Want me to kill him?" said T.J., and Louise grinned, and then flinched in pain.

Abruptly, T.J. walked down the hallway, and Louise wondered whether she was going to bed. But a moment later she returned, holding something out to her. A large photograph, unframed.

Louise had to hold her eye open with two fingers to inspect it. It was a photo of a group of people, standing on the lake side of Self-Reliance, organized in three rows. In the front row, sitting, were children of various ages; behind them were adults. Their expressions were joyful. The photographer had captured them in various stages of talking and laughing and turning. Only some of them were grinning at the camera.

Louise turned the photograph over. On the back, written in black ink: *Blackfly Good-by. 1961.*

She looked up at T.J., uncertain.

T.J. sat down next to her on the couch. Regarded the photo alongside her. She pointed to a tall slim girl, twelve or thirteen, standing at the edge of the second row.

"That's me," said T.J. "I was about the age your campers are now."

She pointed to the tall man next to her, who had a hand on her shoulder. "That's my dad," she said.

"He looks nice," said Louise.

"*Nice* isn't the right word," said T.J. "But he's good."

Then she moved her finger down on the photograph, to a boy of ten or so, sitting cross-legged on the ground in the front row. He was blond, and grinning impishly, one shoulder angled lower than the other.

"Recognize him?" she said.

Louise did, vaguely, but she didn't know why.

"That's your boyfriend," said T.J.

Louise inclined her head. Spread open the swollen eyelid. Her eye was tearing now. She was trying to find an angle that would let her see more clearly.

Sure enough: that was John Paul. She'd seen a picture of him at that age, on the desk of his room at Union College. In the picture he'd been standing with another boy. She had only asked him about it once, and he'd brushed it off. "An old friend," he'd said.

"John Paul McLellan," said T.J. now. Pondering something, it sounded like. Remembering something—unpleasant.

"How did you know he was my boyfriend?" Louise asked.

"How do you think you got this job?" T.J. said.

That quieted her for a bit. She didn't like to think of herself as someone with connections. Everything she'd ever gotten, she'd earned for herself—until she met John Paul.

"I always hated him," said T.J. "Wasn't my choice to hire you. It was the family's."

Then she stood up abruptly and walked again down the hallway. Only this time she did not return.

Louise set the picture on the low table in front of her. Thought for a bit.

A moment later she picked it up again.

1961, said the writing on the back: that would have been the year the Van Laars' son went missing.

She inspected the picture more carefully. There were twelve people in the back row; fourteen in the middle row, including T.J. and her father standing off to one side; and ten in the front row of children seated on the ground. On one side of John Paul was a girl who was most likely his sister, Marnie, a frown on her face, annoyed by something—the same expression she'd worn when Louise came to dinner.

But on the other side of John Paul was something more interesting: a little boy was there, just a bit younger than John Paul. Eight or so. He was smiling broadly, had both arms in the air. A woman in the row behind him—his mother, Louise assumed—was clutching his hands and smiling down at him, her head lowered in his direction.

She recognized him, suddenly, in two separate ways.

This was the boy in the picture on John Paul's desk. *An old friend*, he had said. He wouldn't tell her more.

This was Bear Van Laar, the family's missing son, the subject of so many whispered stories at Camp Emerson. She had never seen a picture of him.

The fire behind her cracked loudly, and she jumped.

In the morning, she woke to find the photo gone, and her host holding out the telephone to her.

"What time is it?" Louise asked.

"Ten thirty. You slept well."

"Shit," said Louise. "Shit."

She was due back at the Garnet Hill Lodge by noon. She still had the staff car—which had no gas in it.

Louise jumped up, wincing. She began feeling for her boots.

"Louise," said T.J. calmly. "Think a minute."

"I gotta go," said Louise. "I gotta work."

"What are you gonna tell them when they see your face looking like that?"

Louise paused. "I was night skiing. And I ran into a tree."

"Well, they're not gonna let you work like that," said T.J. "And you shouldn't be driving with your eye swollen shut. So you might as well call in with that excuse instead of delivering it live."

Louise had never called out of work in her life. It was a point of pride to her. It was one of the things T.J. sensed about her, she thought; one of the reasons T.J. liked her.

"Go on," said T.J. "I give you permission."

They were interrupted by a sudden coughing from down the hallway: loud enough to make Louise jump.

"Oh," said T.J. "That's Dad. I should have told you he was here."

"He lives with you?" said Louise. Last summer, she had learned that the former director was still living, if deposed; but she had never once spotted him on the grounds.

"He does," says T.J.

Louise considered. "If I stay here, and you go out," she said, "will he need anything from me?"

"No," said T.J. "We've got a pretty good system. I come back in once or twice a day to tend to him. He's fine on his own, otherwise. Doesn't need much."

Louise said nothing.

"You look scared," said T.J., grinning. "He's shy, but he doesn't bite."

Louise stayed at T.J.'s for a week. Because T.J. tended to her father only in his room—bringing him soft food on a tea tray, and then returning twenty minutes later with an empty bowl—Louise intersected with Vic Hewitt only twice: the first time, she came out of the bathroom after a shower to find T.J. emerging with her father from his room. Walking behind the old man, she supported him carefully: arms beneath armpits, hands clasped tightly at his front.

Louise gasped, before she could stop herself, and then said, "I'm sorry, I'm sorry."

There was something so intimate about the moment that Louise felt guilty for even seeing it. She put her head down.

"You're all right," said T.J., "but get out of the way so I can bring him in there."

And Louise backed into the other bedroom, allowing them to pass. She had barely seen his face.

The first time had been accidental; the second time was intentional. After T.J. went out one morning, Louise watched at the window until she was a hundred yards away, a dark figure in the snow. And then she went still: from down the hallway, she thought she could hear low voices coming from Vic Hewitt's room.

She walked down the hallway, holding her breath, making each footfall lighter than the last. Mr. Hewitt's door was closed, but not latched; she could see the tiniest crack in it, and she put her face to it, and then nudged the door open, little by little, until she could see inside.

Vic Hewitt lay on top of all the blankets, clad in corduroy pants and a sweater, his long feet bare. He was thin to the point of pain— very different from the tall, broad figure T.J. had pointed to in the black-and-white photograph from early in the last decade. He looked up at the ceiling, blinking.

The voices she had heard, Louise realized, were emanating from a large radio just to the right of his head. An announcer gave a call sign she recognized immediately: *WNBZ, out of Saranac Lake.* It was the only radio station that reached the town of Shattuck.

She nudged the door open an inch further, straining to hear the news, when suddenly Mr. Hewitt spoke.

"Hello," he said to her, though he didn't turn his head.

Louise had not thought he'd heard her.

"Hello," she said.

"Who are you?"

"Louise," she said.

Silence.

"Do you need anything?" Louise asked. But he said nothing more, and at last Louise retreated.

While T.J. was out each day, Louise read the books on her shelves, many of which were how-to manuals and guides, but a number of which were classics of American and British literature, the kinds of books Louise had been assigned during her only year in college. She read *Walden* out of sheer boredom and found herself annoyed by Thoreau: his self-regard, his tone of superiority, the way he doled out advice so obvious as to be insulting. Here was a rich person playing, thought Louise. There were poor people far more resourceful and self-sufficient than he was; they just had the grace and self-awareness not to brag about it.

"Have you read this?" she asked T.J., upon her return, and when T.J. nodded, she shared these feelings aloud.

T.J. was opening cabinets in the kitchen, reaching for pots and pans.

"Oh," said T.J. "He wasn't as bad as all that, was he?" But she was smiling, and Louise was convinced that she agreed.

In the evenings, they played cards—Rummy 500, mainly—almost always in silence, until Louise got comfortable and restless enough to begin asking questions about T.J.'s life. Some of these T.J. answered readily; others she dodged. Things T.J. would not talk about included: the Van Laars, the Van Laars' children, the guests who came to visit the Van Laars. Things T.J. was happy to talk about included: the operation of Camp Emerson, her passion for hunting and fishing, building repair and maintenance, planting schedules, and—most of all—her father. About Vic Hewitt, T.J. was happy to speak at length. She regaled Louise with stories of his smarts, his skillfulness, his quiet humor.

Of all the stories she told, the ones about her father brushed closest to revelations about the Van Laars themselves, because they often involved Vic correcting or preventing some act of mismanagement of the estate itself. But she never used their names, Louise noticed; in fact, T.J. seemed to prefer to pretend that they did not exist.

Every evening, T.J. had exactly one quarter-tumbler of rye whiskey. She always offered some to Louise. The first three nights, she declined, still feeling too raw. But the fourth night, she accepted.

One thing she admired about T.J. was her moderation, when it came to drinking. Always the one small glass, and no more.

She made a note to adopt this habit of T.J.'s. In the future, when she had her own home, when and if she became a mother: if she drank at all, this is how she would drink.

The night Louise took a glass of whiskey into her hands, it loosened her tongue, and she spoke freely, veering into territory she had so far avoided.

"Do you have a boyfriend?" she asked T.J., who laughed into her glass as she said no.

"You're smart," said Louise. "Don't ever get one."

"I won't," said T.J. "Promise." With one finger, she drew a little X across her chest. Louise could tell T.J. thought she was funny— intentionally or not. It brought out in Louise the desire to clown a little, to be egged on—a part of her that was close to extinguished. With John Paul, she always had to be the straight man.

"Where do you want to be," said Louise, "ten years from now?"

"Are you interviewing me?" T.J. leaned back in her chair, knees wide, chin lowered, cards pointing at the floor.

"Yeah," said Louise. And repeated the question, this time holding an invisible microphone in her hands, which she then swung in T.J.'s direction.

"Aright," said T.J. She put her hand of cards facedown on the table. "I'd like to be up north. I'd like to be living off the land. I think I'd like to try that for a while."

"By yourself?" said Louise, into her invisible microphone.

T.J. nodded.

"In a house? A tent? A cave?"

T.J. was laughing now. "Put your microphone away," she said.

Louise shook her head. "I'm afraid I can't, ma'am," she said. "My producers won't allow it."

"Who are your producers?"

"Mike and—Chuck." Louise picked up the nearly empty glass of whiskey in her unoccupied hand and finished it off. She wanted more. Something was happening in her belly that she recognized as desire. It startled her. She had never wanted a woman before, not really, but T.J. was registering to her as something different from a man or a woman, something altogether separate from those terms. She had an interesting face, high cheekbones, and full lips and a strong jaw. She had broad shoulders and a thin, tall build. How old was she? Based on the picture she'd produced, and some math—late twenties, most likely. Maybe five or six years older than she was. Older, too, than John Paul.

"Aright," said T.J. "I'll talk. But this is off the record."

She stood abruptly and walked toward the kitchen, speaking as she went.

"I've got a cabin on a lake up north. Inside the park," said T.J.

She opened and closed a cabinet. Returned to the living room with the bottle of whiskey, which she poured for herself. It was the first night she had had any more to drink than her quarter-glass, but it did not alarm Louise: instead it enlivened her, sent a little shiver of energy up her spine. She held her own glass out for more.

"My people built it a long time ago. Been in the family since," said T.J. She walked to the wall, where the map of the Adirondack

Park had been hung. She pointed to a little lake fifty miles to the north; a tack marked the spot. Then she returned and sat down in her place across from Louise. Left the whiskey on the table between them.

"We used to go up there twice a year for hunting. Me and my dad. It's not much to speak of, but it's got four walls and a roof and a stove for winter. You can only get to it by canoe, and first you've got to portage the canoe through a mile-long trail that's gotten pretty over-grown by now."

"It's on an island?" said Louise.

T.J. nodded.

"Why'd they build it on an island?"

"Good fishing," said T.J. "And a good vantage point."

"Against the Indians?" Louise had heard stories most of her life about the Algonquins and Iroquois who came through the region for hunting. None of them had permanently settled and farmed the Adirondacks; Europeans had been the fools who were first to do so, lured there by overcrowding in New England and a government lie about plentiful arable land.

"No," said T.J., looking at her strangely. "For hunting."

Louise tried to imagine what edible animals there would be on an island.

"There's a deer population that goes back and forth," said T.J.—reading her mind. "They're strong swimmers. And there's waterfowl. Squirrels, if we get hungry enough. But mostly we just fish."

"Who's *we*?" asked Louise, and—seeing T.J.'s expression shift—immediately regretted it. She'd been thinking of her dad. Remembering the trips she once took with him, before his stroke.

T.J. sipped her whiskey. She never grimaced, Louise noticed; she held the liquid in her mouth awhile before quietly swallowing it down.

"Well," T.J. said. "I guess I better get to bed."

"No," said Louise.

T.J. raised her eyebrows.

"Will you stay up a little longer?" said Louise. "I've still got a full glass."

T.J. nodded. Her eyes stayed on Louise's for a moment until she stood up, breaking their gaze. She strode to the kitchen, ran the tap.

Added water to her whiskey. Then she turned and leaned against the kitchen counter, far from Louise but in sight of her.

On the rare occasions that Louise got drunk, or even tipsy, she became aware of her own appearance in a way that was exciting or unsettling, depending on her company. Her body and face were sometimes assets and sometimes liabilities. That night, she was glad for them, despite the black eye. Or because of it. She liked the feeling of T.J.'s gaze on her, over the rim of her cup. Louise was behaving irresponsibly, she knew. But that night she had an urge to do what she was not supposed to do.

Louise stood and stretched, allowing her shirt to rise up on her waist, and walked into the kitchen.

T.J. was right next to the sink and she did not move when Louise approached.

"I should get some too," said Louise. She let cool water run into her cup, then let it run over. Her side was next to T.J.'s side. She turned and leaned against the counter also, too close to T.J. to pretend their proximity was accidental. Their flanks and arms were touching.

"Louise," said T.J. She shook her head, looking down at the floor. "What?"

Between them was an electrical current, a buzzing sensation making its way back and forth between their bodies. Louise could feel it. She was certain without knowing why that T.J. could feel it too. They were animals, Louise thought—and it almost made her laugh. Humans were animals. They had the same instincts, the same ability to communicate beneath and apart from language.

Louise turned her body so she was looking at T.J.'s profile. She put one hand very gently on the small of her back. It was the first gesture she made that left no room for doubt.

"I employ you," said T.J. "I am your employer."

Louise said nothing.

Abruptly, T.J. moved away from the counter and walked down the hallway. She poked her head into her father's room, checking on him, and then she continued, and closed the door to her own bedroom. The lights went off.

*   *   *

Louise lay on the sofa, watching the last flames of the fire die out. She closed her eyes tightly. She was trying not to cry. If she was lucky, T.J. would let her forget how foolish she had been.

There were only embers left behind the grate now.

Soon the room would be full dark. Then it would be morning.

Louise

1950s • 1961 • **Winter 1973** • June 1975
July 1975 • August 1975

T.J. never spoke of that night again.

They spent the rest of the week together, letting Louise's face heal, and then Louise returned to the Garnet Hill Lodge. In midspring she would get a phone call from T.J., requesting confirmation of her participation in that summer's camp session, which she was happy to provide. The only difference from then on would be that T.J. would invite her in for talks in the Director's Cabin, from time to time.

Whatever crush Louise had on her diminished in some ways and in others grew stronger. In T.J., she sensed two dueling forces: anger, and the power to control it. Against her better judgment, she found them equally attractive.

When she was not vigilant, her mind drifted at times toward the thought of a life with T.J. Running the camp alongside her. Caring, when asked to, for her dad. There were two women in Shattuck like this, Louise thought: two former professors from downstate who'd set up a home just outside the town. One wore her hair in two long gray braids; Louise saw her sometimes at the grocery store. No one asked them many questions. No one talked about them either.

But any fantasies Louise had about this life were short-lived.

Because coming in from dinner one day at the lodge, two weeks after the incident with John Paul, Louise was handed an envelope by the man who staffed the reception desk.

She waited until she was back in her little room to open it. There, she sat on her hard twin bed and read through a letter she'd known was from John Paul the moment she'd seen it.

In it, he begged her forgiveness.

I haven't had a drink since that night, he said. *I can't believe what I did. My mother would be so ashamed of me. I want to do better.*

He ended by asking if he could see her to apologize in person. He understood if she never wanted to speak to him again. But he had to ask the question, at least, he said.

At the bottom of the page, he'd drawn an arrow. She turned the letter over. *P.S.*, he wrote. *Don't worry—I didn't tell anyone anything.*

Louise put the letter down on the bed.

She wouldn't respond. Hopefully that would be the end of it.

One evening later that week, someone knocked at her door. She found one of the ski instructors on the other side. A little smirk was on her face.

"You've got a visitor," she said. "He's waiting in the staff lounge for you."

John Paul was alone when she entered. He was sitting at the round table next to the coffee percolator. He was bent forward, elbows on knees, one leg vibrating with nerves. When Louise entered, he sat straight up.

He looked terrible. Worse than she did. Two weeks after the incident, her face had mostly healed. Her ribs and back no longer hurt, though one large bruise still lingered on her flank, light purple now. John Paul, on the other hand, had dark circles under his eyes. His hair was a mess.

"Oh, God," he said, upon seeing her. He put his face in his hands. The action reminded her of her brother Jesse, when he was trying not to cry. And sure enough: when John Paul removed his hands, tears were running openly down his cheeks. He took his glasses off. Wiped his face.

He stood up and Louise flinched, positioned herself behind a chair. She had left the door open intentionally. She glanced back over her shoulder, wondering how loud she'd have to yell to get anyone to come running.

But John Paul, perhaps sensing her fear, sat back down slowly.

"Can we go somewhere private?" he asked.

"No," said Louise.

"Can we sit down, at least?"

Reluctantly, she pulled out the opposite chair.

Mainly, he said what he'd already said in the letter. He added that he'd gone to a meeting—a program called *Alcoholics Anonymous*, something she'd vaguely heard of, though she couldn't remember where.

He went on: She was the best part of his life. He respected her more than anyone else he knew. More than his own family. He liked her self-sufficiency, her enterprising nature. He thought she was smarter than any girl he knew.

He wanted her to give him another chance. He was begging for it. They'd start slow, he said; but he was serious about her. His plan was to marry her. Together, he said, they could have the sort of life that would have meaning and value. They could have children together. A nice house.

Her brother, Jesse, he said, could come live with them.

She wondered for the first time if he'd ever read her journals. His articulation of her secret hopes was so precise that it startled her.

"You don't have to answer me now," said John Paul. "All I'm asking is that you think it over."

Louise was silent.

"We could have a good life together," he said, at last.

Then he stood, shoulders and head low, and lifted two paper bags from their place on the floor beside him. "Here," he said. "I brought you groceries."

He closed the door gently behind him on the way out.

Goddammit, thought Louise.

The problem was: the groceries were too complicated. They were beautiful and expensive, the sorts of things that John Paul's mother had probably bought for her family when he was small. There was a T-bone steak in there, and broccoli, and shrimp, and three beautiful oranges. There was a loaf of bread, and butter packaged in a way she'd never seen before, and a tall container of milk. And there was a cake—a whole Bundt cake—in a white box.

She was hungry. She pulled off a piece of the Bundt cake and sat there chewing it.

She looked sideways at the sink and two hot plates that constituted their shared kitchen. She could make a feast for the other staffers at the lodge. But she was off that night, and she had a better idea.

Her mother's house was a white rectangle: small upstairs, small downstairs, stacked one on top of the other around a steep central staircase.

It was quiet and dark when she arrived at half past six. Through one first-floor window she saw the blue flicker of the TV. Through one second-floor window she saw a small lamp turned on. Jesse's room.

Inside, she put the groceries on the kitchen table. Ten minutes prior, she'd had to stop short at an intersection and in doing so had sent the shrimp scattering out of their wax paper and onto the salty floorboard of her car. She'd thrown it into park and scooped them up, knowing she'd still cook them.

Jesse had never had shrimp in his life.

Now, she ran water into a large bowl and put the shrimp in there to soak.

As she worked, she realized that she smelled something.

She followed the scent around the central stairs—passing her mother on the way, asleep in her recliner—and then ascended.

Please not that, she thought.

She opened Jesse's door without knocking.

He had heard the front door. He had opened a window and hastily put away whatever he'd been smoking, but he was looking at her, guilty, his eyes stripped of their usual curiosity, narrowed instead by the chemicals now swimming in his bloodstream.

"Where is it," said Louise.

"What?" said Jesse.

"Don't lie to me," said Louise. "Don't ever lie to me. I'm not Mom. I'm on your side."

He said nothing. He was sitting on his bed, his arms hugging his knees.

Louise looked in the little trash bin next to his desk and found it immediately: a poorly rolled joint, hastily extinguished, still warm to the touch. Still capable of setting the contents of the bin on fire.

"Idiot," said Louise—a word she regretted immediately—because when she looked back at her brother he was crying.

"Oh God, Jesse," said Louise, and she rushed to him, sat down next to him, clasped him to her. "Jesse, where'd you get that?"

He shrugged. She pushed him away from her, held him by the shoulders. His face was red. He held out one hand and placed the back of two fingers to her left eye, the hurt one, still faintly bruised and swollen. It was only then that she remembered that she, too, had something to explain.

"Come on," said Louise. "She's sleeping."

Downstairs, she sat him at the table and gave him a tall glass of water.

"Drink that," she said.

Then she began to cook. She put a pot of water on to boil the broccoli. She salted and peppered the steak and put it in one pan to sear in a pat of butter. She put the cleaned shrimp in another.

"You ever had shrimp, Jesse?" she said proudly, and he said, "Yeah."

"Who gave you shrimp?"

"Howie's mom."

Howie: a friend from school whose parents no longer let him play with Jesse.

"Won't be as good as mine," said Louise—though even as she said it she knew it wasn't true.

She turned and saw Jesse's glass was empty, and she filled it again.

The only good thing about a nine-year-old boy being stoned was the pleasure he took in eating the food she'd made for him. Jesse closed his eyes and tipped his head back as he chewed, making small satisfied noises in between bites. He'd gotten even skinnier since the last time she saw him, and the quick inventory she'd taken of the kitchen told her why.

"How long have you been smoking dope?" said Louise.

"Not long," said Jesse. "Month or two."

"Where'd you get it?"

"Kid at school."

"Do I know him?"

"No."

"How old is he?"

"Not sure. Eighth grader."

"Do I know his parents?"

"No. He's from Minerva."

Louise chewed. The steak was delicious. She was glad not to have ruined it.

"Jesse," she said. "How did you afford it?"

He was silent.

"You're not selling, are you?" she asked.

"No," said Jesse. "No, Louise. I swear."

She believed him, for now. Jesse was shy to the point of incapacitation. She couldn't imagine him in sales of any kind. But the thought of an eighth-grade boy giving him anything for free—that didn't sit right with her either.

There was a noise in the hallway then and they both looked up. Their mother: one hand on each wall, supporting herself. Her hair was unwashed, her eyes blinking against the light that hung on a chain over the kitchen table. Face pallid, mouth downturned. She came toward them slowly, propping herself up with the countertops now, and then veered toward the cabinets, which she opened one after another, looking for something to eat.

She pulled down a box of old crackers and put a few in her mouth. She went to the sink and ran the tap, bringing a cupped hand to her mouth for water.

Then, without a word to either of her children, she moved slowly back in the direction of the recliner in the living room, her home for most of each day.

Louise looked at Jesse. He was coming back to himself now. The food had helped, the water. His face was less flushed. His eyes were opening. He wouldn't meet her gaze; he looked to the wall, and then down at the table.

"Jesse," she said. "Stop talking to that boy. Stop smoking the grass he gives you, too."

"Why," he said. He picked at something on the tablecloth.

"Because I'm gonna bring you to live with me," she said. "And I can't do that if you're incarcerated."

"When?" said Jesse.

"Pretty soon."

"How," said Jesse. Incredulous.

There was a long pause while Louise considered saying it. She couldn't take it back, if she did. She had always tried her best to never give her brother false hope. To keep every promise she made, unlike the rest of the adults in his life.

She lifted a shrimp from her plate. She took its tail off, prodded at its translucent skin, deveining it. John Paul, at a restaurant, had been the one to tell her what the vein really was.

She chewed.

"I'm engaged," she said.

Jesse looked at her.

"To John Paul?" he said.

"Who else would I be engaged to?"

Jesse would not meet her eye.

"Jesse?" said Louise.

Jesse stood. Brought his plate to the sink.

"Well, aren't you going to say congratulations?"

"Congratulations," said Jesse. And then he walked out of the kitchen, leaving Louise alone.

"Promise me, Jesse," said Louise, calling after him. "No more pot." But she could tell that any authority she had once had with him was diminished, or lost entirely.

VI

Survival

Judyta

1950s • 1961 • Winter 1973 • June 1975
July 1975 • August 1975: **Day Two**

Her alarm is sounding.

Judy opens her eyes, then closes them again. Just for a moment, she thinks.

"FOR CHRISSAKE, JUDY!" comes the cry from the other room. Her brother, incensed. "IT'S FOUR THIRTY IN THE MORNING!"

Her day begins.

She needs to move out. She knows this. She has the funds; she just needs the guts to tell her parents she'll be breaking an unspoken rule. Among the Polish families of Schenectady, New York, a girl who moves out of the home before marriage is odd at best; a scandal at worst.

Last year, with her own money, she purchased a green VW Super Beetle with a sunroof. It was expensive—and impractical, her father said—but it gives her a feeling of independence. And it has a nice radio, an upgrade she's now glad she insisted on; it keeps her awake for the two hours of her commute to the Preserve.

At seven, when she arrives, she finds that she's beaten Denny Hayes to work. Technically, B-tour starts at 8 a.m., which means she has an hour to prepare for the day.

A trooper dozes lightly in a folding chair outside the Director's Cabin, now the Command Post.

Judy puts her hand on the wrought-iron handle, depresses it, and opens the door before the trooper opens his eyes.

"Morning," Judy says.

"Oh," says the trooper, rousing himself. "Badge?"

Overnight, the Command Post has been better established. The existing furniture has been cleared to the sides of the room, or pushed into the kitchen; a few folding tables and chairs have been brought in in their place.

A large chalkboard on wheels is pressed against one wall.

On it, someone has drawn a chalk line down the middle. On the left of the line, at the top, is written *Bear Van Laar*. On the right of the line: *Barbara*.

For a while, Judy stands in the center of the place, turning.

The walls are decorated with small prints of dogs undertaking various humanlike pursuits: playing poker and hunting and courting one another. The pictures have wrinkled and withered from their long battle with the dampness of the lake-adjacent air. The whole house looks as if it was decorated carefully and thoughtfully thirty years before, and then never once touched. A time capsule from the Second World War.

The only framed image that isn't dog-related is a map of the Adirondack Park. In it, someone has inserted a tack right where Self-Reliance sits, on the bank of Lake Joan, close to Hunt Mountain.

A filing cabinet—brought in by the BCI, she guesses—sits in a corner, next to a few crates of folders, paper, pens—and bankers boxes. Five of them. Labeled with words she can't read from across the room.

Judy, alone in the Command Post, walks in that direction. Bends down.

Peter "Bear" Van Laar IV, reads the lettering on the box.

She lifts the lid. For the next hour, she reads the documents inside.

At the bottom are dozens of photographs. Several are of Bear from what must have been the year before his disappearance. Here, he grins from ear to ear, holding up a fish he's caught; here, he looks off pensively into the distance, hand in hand with a woman Judy recognizes as his mother.

Against her will, Judy finds herself fighting tears, swallowing the tight knot forming in her throat. Something in Mrs. Van Laar's expression reminds her of her own mother, who loves her children so fiercely that it sometimes feels like a weight.

At 7:50, Judy places the material back in order, puts the lid on the box, just before Captain LaRochelle enters the Command Post.

The first thing he does at morning briefing is point to the chalkboard—where both children's names have been written.

"Who did this?" he says.

All of them glance at each other. No one owns up.

"Might have been one of the A-tour guys," someone says.

Captain LaRochelle frowns. "Whoever did it," he says, "don't do it again."

He picks up an eraser. Goes to work on the chalkboard. "We're searching for Barbara Van Laar," he says. "Bear Van Laar's case is closed."

Against her will, Judy's eyes drift to the corner, where the bankers boxes full of evidence are resting.

On the now-clear chalkboard, LaRochelle begins to write.

Their prime suspect—still John Paul McLellan, at this point—is out on bail, awaiting his hearing for driving under the influence and felony possession of a controlled substance. Recognizing his status as a suspect in another crime, the judge in his case agreed to include a clause in his bail terms that prevents him leaving the county; he's holed up at a local hotel until his next hearing.

Louise Donnadieu—whom John Paul claims was the one to ask him to dispose of the bag of clothing—is still in a holding cell in Wells, New York. Her bail hearing will be today. He'll ask the magistrate in her case, as well, to consider when setting her bail the fact that she's being looked at for Barbara Van Laar's disappearance.

Lee Towson, the other person named by John Paul, has still not been located; a BOLO has been issued for his car in the states of New York and Colorado, where he is rumored to have gone.

The rangers haven't yet located the unknown figure in the woods, the one reported by the camper named Tracy Jewell.

"Could have been a hiker, even," says LaRochelle. "The girl wasn't far from Hunt Mountain when the unknown person provided assistance. But we'll keep trying to track him down."

Judy listens, trying to be attentive. But her late night and early morning are catching up with her, and she puts her fist under her chin to prop it up. Denny Hayes, across the room, looks her way, and she sits up straight.

Next, LaRochelle details the results of the work that C-tour and A-tour did overnight. They've got another clue to the puzzle of who Barbara's boyfriend might have been, he says: A Susan Yoder, the director of the Emily Grange School, said Barbara had a male visitor in her room. Got in trouble for it. A witness thought it was a boy from town, but Barbara wouldn't say. The C-tour investigator who learned of this will pursue the lead.

"Next," LaRochelle goes on, "who was it gave me the clue about the paint on the walls?"

Judy, mildly embarrassed, raises her hand.

"That was brilliant," says LaRochelle. "Look at this." He walks to a table where gloves and a box are laid out. Puts on the gloves, lifts from the box an object retrieved from the Albany house. It's a sketch-book, he says. Most of what's in it seems meaningless: doodles of hearts and music notes and moons and stars. But toward the end of it, there's something interesting.

He lifts the sketchbook into the air, so they can see it.

There on the page is a surprisingly skillful rendering of a room with several pieces of furniture in it. A bed, a dresser, a nightstand. Behind the bed is a wall; on the wall is what looks to be a design for a mural.

Judy frowns, trying to remember why the drawing looks familiar. And then it comes to her: this is Barbara's room, at Self-Reliance.

The room with the freshly painted walls.

Captain LaRochelle confirms this to the rest of the investigators. Then he says: "We haven't noticed anything suspicious on the page I'm showing you. It's difficult to discern what some of the pictures are, on this small scale. But our hope is that removing the pink paint in Barbara's room will uncover something of interest."

They've found a conservator from the Hyde Collection who's coming to take a look, he says. Hopefully, they'll be able to remove one layer of paint without damaging the other, underneath.

"Last thing," says LaRochelle. Late last night, the BCI received a complete list from someone on staff of all the guests on the grounds, and a complete list from T.J. Hewitt, the camp director, of all the campers and staff. He holds up a stack of manila folders. He's xeroxed these documents for everyone. Those who've already been interviewed have a check mark next to their names. The rest, says LaRochelle, will be talked to methodically, either in person or—in the case of the chil-dren who've already been picked up by their parents—over the phone. Today, every investigator sitting before him will be assigned one segment of the camp's population to pursue.

He passes out the folders.

"I want good notes today," he says. "Legible notes. I want signed statements, if you can get them. And I want fast work. It's already been more than twenty-four hours since Barbara Van Laar went missing."

He pauses in front of Denny Hayes. "Hayes," he says. "You're working the lead desk from now on."

He gives the last folder to Judy. But when she looks at the papers inside, she can't find her name next to any segment of either list. She wonders whether to say something. Before she can, LaRochelle speaks.

"Investigator Luptack," he says. "Your job today is to make a map of the house and the grounds. And to label every structure and every room with the name of its occupant during the hours of Barbara's disappearance."

Denny Hayes catches her eye before she leaves the Command Post.

"Hang on," he says. "I'll walk with you."

Together, they head for Self-Reliance, Judy's new possessions tucked under her arm. She drags her feet, just slightly.

He glances at her. "Tired?" says Hayes.

"No."

"You know, you don't have to get here so early," he says. "No one's giving you extra points for that."

"Okay," she says.

"You live with your folks, you said?"

"I do."

"Whereabouts?"

She hesitates. She's never actually told any of her new colleagues how far she commutes, and she's worried that revealing the gravity of the situation will make them worried about her ability to do her job.

She settles on an answer: "Schenectady. But I'm in the process of moving."

Denny whistles. "Schenectady? No wonder you were falling asleep in there."

"I wasn't—" Judy hears the defensiveness in her tone. Starts over. "I'm all right. I've never needed much sleep."

Denny looks skeptical. "Okay."

They walk in silence for a moment, and then Judy asks Hayes something she's been wondering since their morning meeting.

"How'd McLellan get released before the counselor did? Louise?" asks Judy, and Denny says, "How do you think?"

Connections. Money. A lawyer father. Hayes has found out something else: in addition to serving as chief counsel for the Van Laars' bank, McLellan Sr. is, in fact, the attorney who personally represented the family during Bear Van Laar's disappearance in 1961.

Judy frowns. "Isn't that unusual?" she says. "For a corporate attorney to get involved in a criminal case?"

Hayes shrugs. "People are legally allowed to be represented by whoever they want. I've seen some represent themselves," he says. "The arrogant ones."

Both of them look up, toward the great house ahead of them.

Then Hayes says: "Who do you like?"

"Who do I think did it?"

"Yeah."

She thinks. "McLellan."

"He's my guess, too."

She'd had less than an hour to look at the 1961 Van Laar files before Hayes arrived at the station, but it was enough to pique her interest on one point.

"I was wondering something," she says. She stops, rephrasing. "Yesterday, when the investigator asked about Jacob Sluiter?"

"Yeah?"

"Well, I looked through the Bear Van Laar files this morning, and I saw he was considered as a suspect in that case too."

Hayes stops walking. Judy faces him.

"Just seems like a coincidence," she says.

For a moment, Judy thinks Hayes is going to dismiss her. What was it LaRochelle said the other day? *Don't look for a zebra.*

But instead Hayes sighs.

"It does," he says. "I've been thinking that too."

Then he says, "Between us? I'm the one who pulled those files on Bear. The ones you were apparently looking through. I'm the one who wrote his name up on that board. And I think LaRochelle's completely wrong, completely out of line, to consider Bear's case closed. All of us in that room—*except* for LaRochelle—are thinking the same thing."

Judy looks at him.

"Why do you think LaRochelle's thinking differently?" she asks.

"LaRochelle was a lieutenant on that case," says Hayes. "He was the one who pushed the theory the family and the press ended up buying. Solving the Bear Van Laar case ended up being career-making for him. Led directly to his promotion to captain. He probably doesn't want to see that work undone.

"Besides," says Hayes. "The Van Laar family's happy with the outcome on that case. As in, they think they got the right guy. They're at peace with it, you know? It's hard to go back on that."

Judy nods. She gets it—sort of. But if she were the Van Laars, she would want to know the truth. She says as much to Hayes.

"They're a strange family," he says. "Too many generations with too much money. It addles the brain. You ever notice how the children of rich people are never as smart as the parents? Never as ambitious, never as successful? You gotta have something to strive for in life. What I think, anyway."

They keep walking.

"You know," says Hayes, "I'll tell you something else. I don't like that LaRochelle's on-site every day. I should be the one running the show. And I'm not saying that out of ego. It's just not good practice to have someone at his level running daily operations in a case like this."

"How come?"

"Some of the guys at LaRochelle's level are smart," he says. "But they're middle management now. Out of practice. Lot of 'em haven't really worked cases in a decade. It might reassure the family when the big guns come in," he says, "but it's risky."

Hayes turns back around, heading for the Command Post, where he'll get to work organizing and numbering their leads.

Judy's on her own to make her map.

Above her head, a helicopter is circling, its occupants scanning the terrain for any sign of life. To her right, a dive team is getting ready for a search of Lake Joan.

*   *   *

She approaches the main house. Outside it, she takes a knee, balancing the pad on the other one. She sketches the house from memory, placing inside each room the guests she interviewed yesterday.

When she's finished, she stands up and walks past the front entrance of the house.

Yesterday, she spent her day talking to the guests; it's time now, thinks Judy, to talk to the people who serve them.

For the first time, she knocks at the kitchen door. A small woman in an apron answers, holding a floured rolling pin in her hands.

"Good morning," says Judy. The woman wipes her hand on her apron slowly. Says nothing.

"Are you all right?" says Judy.

"Are you a police officer?" the woman asks.

"Investigator," says Judy. "I'm Investigator Luptack."

"But," says the woman. "With the police?"

Judy nods.

The woman walks back toward a counter, sets the rolling pin down.

"Do you have a moment to talk?" says Judy.

Again, the glance around. "I do have a moment," says the woman lowly. "Only it has to be your idea to talk, not mine. And it can't be in here."

Judy leads her through the kitchen door. Stops near the side of the house.

"Keep going," the woman whispers. "The windows are open."

They walk twenty paces more, until they are right at the edge of the lake. Then Judy takes out her notepad.

Above them, the circling helicopter has begun making announcements over its loudspeaker: *Barbara, your parents miss you. Barbara, move to a clearing. Barbara, get to high ground. Barbara, yell if you hear this.* The sound makes her shiver.

The woman looks at her expectantly. "Aren't you going to ask me questions?"

"Oh," says Judy. "Name?"

"Jeannie Clute."

"Date of birth?"

"June twelfth, 1947."

"Occupation?"

This gives her pause. "Temporary cook, at the moment," she says. "Prior to that, homemaker."

Judy glances up.

"Do you have children?"

"Yes. Three. A fourth on the way."

Judy glances down, briefly, at the woman's still-flat stomach.

"A husband?"

"Yes."

"What made you take this job?"

The woman turns her face away. Suddenly, tears come to her eyes and spill over. She swipes at them. Angry.

"Foolishness," she says. "I was wrong to take this job."

Judy pauses. A sensation is beginning in her lower belly that she's never felt before: some feeling that one piece of a larger puzzle is about to fall into place.

"Why not?" she says.

"They're bad people," says Mrs. Clute.

"How so?"

"They let the wrong man take the blame when their son disappeared," she said. "They let his name be ruined."

She's finished crying. A hard look has replaced her tears, and she looks into Judy's eyes with conviction.

"What's his name?" asks Judy.

"Was," says Mrs. Clute. "He's dead."

"What was his name?"

"Stoddard," says Mrs. Clute. "Same as mine."

Judy's mind works. It's a name she knows from the bankers box she went through earlier this morning. "Carl Stoddard was your—"

"Father."

Judy writes in her notepad. Truthfully, she doesn't know what words she's forming there—but she needs time to formulate her next question carefully. To avoid frightening her off.

"Clute's your married name?" she says.

The woman nods impatiently. She's looking back at the house now, growing nervous, waiting to be noticed.

"Do they know you're a Stoddard?" Judy asks.

"God, no," says Mrs. Clute.

"Why did you take this job?"

She shifts. "Desperation," she said. "Mouths to feed. You heard the shirt factory closed."

Judy hadn't. She doesn't know what shirt factory Mrs. Clute is talking about. Still, she nods.

"Well, there's no other work in Shattuck. It was this or move," says Mrs. Clute. "And where would we go?"

"Does the rest of your family know? The Stoddards, I mean."

Mrs. Clute nods.

"My sisters understand," she says. "But my mother isn't speaking to me. Said the whole family was rotten. That I'd regret it." Mrs. Clute looks out at the lake. "Turns out she was right."

"Mrs. Clute," says Judy. "Do you have any idea where Barbara Van Laar has gone?"

This, the woman answers quickly. "No idea," she says. "Truly. But I bet you her family does."

Again, that sensation—instinct, thinks Judy.

"Why?"

"I'm speaking out of turn here," says Mrs. Clute, "but when Bear Van Laar went missing, the family bungled the whole search from start to finish. First thing was they didn't call searchers in until hours after the boy first disappeared. By then there were footprints all over the place, and it had rained, and any hope of tracking him was lost. For the hounds, too, it made the work more difficult."

She holds out the thumb of her right hand, as if preparing to tally all the ways the family had erred.

"Next," she says, "they let us Shattuckers help, but after a week they sent us off. Flew in a team of searchers from the Sierra Madres, instead. Chartered a private plane and everything. Paid them hand-somely, from what I heard."

"Did they pay the local searchers, too?"

Mrs. Clute scoffs. "Hardly," she says. "They were treated as if they worked for the family already. Even those that didn't, those that missed their jobs to help. And the irony is, those searchers from California had no idea what they were doing. They'd never seen terrain like ours before. Never seen underbrush so thick. They turned tail and left without finding a single trace of the boy."

She smiles, almost in triumph, and then becomes aware of herself.

"Now listen," says Mrs. Clute. "I feel terrible for the family. If they're innocent—which they very well might be—it's an honest sin, what they went through. But what I'll never forgive them for is not clearing my father's name. After he died, they just let it be—*presumed* that he was the one who killed Bear. And that they'd most likely not find the boy, because you can't ask questions of a dead man."

She glances over each shoulder, and then continues. "I've seen someone on the grounds who was here before, when Bear went missing. LaRochelle's his name. I remember him from when they were making the case against my father. He's a liar. I wouldn't trust him, if I were you."

Judy keeps her head very still. To nod, even slightly, seems incorrect. But she understands what the woman is saying.

Mrs. Clute says, "Do you have children?"

"I don't."

"All right. Well, if you ever do, remember this conversation," says Mrs. Clute. "Remember my words. And ask yourself—would you stop searching as early as they did?"

Judy looks down, embarrassed suddenly by the depth of emotion in Mrs. Clute's gaze.

"Would you ever?" she says, once more.

Both are silent for a pause.

"I'll have to go back inside now," says Mrs. Clute. "Lots to do."

Judy nods. "Is there anything else you'd like to tell me? Anything else I should know?"

Mrs. Clute thinks. "Only thing I can think of is no one in that family likes that little girl. Barbara. Neglect, is what I'd call it. Before she went down to the summer camp, she used to wander into the kitchen for something to eat. Lost-looking, in her own house. I'd feed her whenever I could. Her mother didn't like it. Used to tell me to stop giving her food. I'd nod and pretend to be listening, but I always liked her visits. Barbara's an odd girl, dresses strangely, but she's the only one here who took the time to learn my name. She's a good soul, is what I think."

"Thank you," says Judy.

Mrs. Clute nods.

Judy remembers Hayes's words from earlier. She's been making good notes, but she wants to be certain she's gotten her facts correct.

"Mrs. Clute, would you mind if I did my best to write up everything you told me? You could look it over, and sign it if it's correct."

The woman looks at her, horrified. "Never in a million years," she says. "I don't regret telling you what I told you. But that's the only help I can give."

This, Judy thinks, feels more important than the map does at the moment. She walks down to the Command Post, looking for Hayes at the lead desk. Outside, two investigators are sitting on the steps, writing out statements on their clipboards.

"Hayes inside?" asks Judy, and one of them nods.

"Wouldn't go in there if I were you," he says. "LaRochelle's been letting him have it for ten minutes."

Judy pauses. Muted yelling, through the door.

There's no good place for her to sit.

"Would you tell him I'm looking for him when they're done?" she asks.

"Sure, honey," says the other. Not looking up.

"I'm Investigator Luptack," says Judy.

"Great."

While she waits for Hayes, Judy wanders the grounds of Camp Emerson, doing the work that LaRochelle assigned her that morning. She brings her pad of paper and her pen with her. She stops in front of every building she can spot, sketching its footprint, as if from above. She labels the ones whose use is clear.

When she's finished, she turns northwest, toward a set of farm buildings that are no longer in use.

They've been searched thoroughly, she knows. And to the best of her knowledge, they aren't used to house anybody.

Still—with nothing else to do until Hayes and LaRochelle are finished—she walks in their direction, pad of paper tucked under her arm.

*   *   *

There are four structures. Judy knows nothing about agriculture, but one seems to have been a dairy barn, its large doors open to the air outside. Inside, the standing stalls still have that animal smell, though they seem to have been abandoned long ago. Above the barn is a hayloft; a rickety ladder lets Judy climb high enough to poke her head into it, take in the remains of several hay bales standing against the walls.

She descends.

Next to the dairy barn is a small building set up on legs, window-less. Whatever its original purpose, it has since become home to rusting farm equipment. She enters it only briefly, then moves to the building to its west.

The interior of this third building, too, puzzles her at first: its floors are concrete and angle downward toward a drain. Perhaps, she thinks, this was where horses were sponged after exercise? There's a smell in here she can't identify, but it sets her on edge.

Then she looks up.

Five metal bars run from one end of the ceiling to the other. From these bars hang dozens of hooks in straight lines.

At last the smell makes sense to her: this was a slaughterhouse.

She stands there a moment longer, her body tense.

Then comes the noise: above her head, the sound of footsteps.

Tracy

1950s • 1961 • Winter 1973 • June 1975
July 1975 • August 1975

Survival Trip was never announced in advance. It was, instead, sprung upon them in this way: with an air horn, at 5:30 in the morning, just after sunrise.

All summer, they'd been coached. When the air horn sounded, they would leap out of their bunks and into their clothes, no shower in between, and run as fast as they could to the flagpole.

Whoever arrived first was given extra provisions; whoever arrived last was given nothing at all.

Barbara was up and dressed before anyone else in the cabin.

"Put warm clothes on over your uniform," she whispered to Tracy, and then she was gone.

Tracy was not last in her group to the flagpole, but she was close to it. And therefore she received, inside the backpack a counselor handed her, only four cans of beans, and a full water canteen. She looked around: Barbara and Lowell Cargill were inspecting tarps, compasses, Swiss Army knives. And the two youngest in her group, who arrived at the very end, opened their backpacks to find them entirely empty. Tracy watched their faces: they were trying to be brave, but their chins were tight with stopped tears.

T.J. Hewitt stood at the base of the flagpole, overseeing the chaos impassively. Once every camper was holding a backpack, she shimmied a small way up the pole and, planting the thick sole of her Danner boot on the cleat, lifted a bullhorn to speak.

"Survival Groups," she said. "Your leaders will come to you shortly. But remember: they're there only for emergencies. They will not help you in any other way. In general," she said—here she looked around the meeting grounds for so long that it seemed as if she was trying to catch every camper's eye—"you're on your own. Good luck."

From the center of the group, counselors began making their way outward toward the groups they had been assigned. Tracy scanned them, wondering who would come their way.

But it was T.J. Hewitt herself who approached.

"You're with me," she said.

Five minutes later, they set off.

T.J. was in the lead. Next came the youngest campers in their group. They fell in line like ducklings behind their leader, who looked back at them every so often, as if surprised or annoyed by their presence.

"Pretend I'm invisible," she kept saying—and they'd drop back next to the rest of the group, only to return to T.J.'s side a moment later.

Barbara and Tracy and Lowell and his friend Walter—the oldest—walked four abreast. Tracy glanced sideways at Lowell from time to time, remembering what it had been like to sing in harmony with him, then blushing furiously at the thought of it.

Walking north, they crossed in front of the main house, Self-Reliance. In the windows, Tracy thought she could see people moving, and she said so to Barbara, who shrugged, looking straight ahead.

"They're getting ready," she said.

"For what?"

"They're having a party. It's the house's hundredth birthday."

"Are you invited?"

Barbara shook her head.

"I don't want to go anyway," she said.

They crossed the main road, and hiked an hour more, until finally T.J. stopped them.

"This is good," she said. And then she walked away.

It was Barbara who broke the silence. "Open your backpacks," she said.

Between the twelve of them they had: sixty-two cans of various foods, twelve bags of gorp, twelve water canteens, four small bottles of iodine tincture, nine tarps, four can openers, various knives, a roll of snare wire, ten ropes, and—the last item to come out of the last bag, and the item that drew the biggest sigh of relief—one box of matches.

Barbara stood up, inspecting the goods, making calculations about how to use it all. Then she glanced at T.J., who was leaning against a tree, one knee bent, the sole of her boot resting against its bark.

"Don't look at me," said T.J. "I'm invisible. I'm not here."

She turned and hoisted her backpack onto her shoulders, then walked thirty feet up a slight incline, where she found a relatively flat place in the earth and began to set up her tent. In a flash, she'd made her own fire, strung a hammock between two trees, and begun reading a book while boiling water for coffee.

By noon, the campers had set up too, with Barbara leading the charge. Not for the first time, Tracy marveled at how well she moved, how much she knew about the woods. She was the one to locate running water in the form of a nearby stream, to lead a small group to refill their canteens, with an iodine topper; she was the one to use ropes and tarps to make primitive tents, to clear a patch of ground, to frame a large circle with rocks. Then she sent the children off to find the driest wood they could find, and kindling too.

She was not much older than the rest of them—in fact, she was younger than Walter and Lowell—but to Tracy she seemed, that day, like a grown woman.

On the nearby rise, T.J. glanced up from her book from time to time, watching impassively, saying nothing.

When she was not following Barbara's orders, Tracy sat on the ground and played a game invented by one of the younger children, a boy named Christopher who seemed sweet-natured and sort of frightened. He was eight years old: the youngest of the bunch. "The youngest in the whole camp," he noted glumly.

At night, after dinner, they told ghost stories—avoiding any mention of Jacob Sluiter, or Slitter—who felt too real to be fun. Lowell told the one about Scary Mary, the gray-haired woman, a favorite ghost on the grounds. "Boy in my cabin said he saw her just the other night," said Lowell—until one of the younger girls began to cry, and Lowell recanted. They sang camp songs instead, and then Lowell sang, a cappella, a beautiful mournful song about a sailor lost at sea.

Something wild was happening: Tracy could feel it. Yes, T.J. was just up the hill, but she was making good on her promise of invisibility.

The children were in charge, then: all of them, but Barbara the most. In the absence of adults, they came into themselves in a way that made Tracy proud.

The tarp tents were assigned by Barbara. Tracy and Barbara would be in the first; Lowell and Walter would be in the second; the four youngest boys would be in the third—when they briefly protested the injustice of this, Barbara stared at them until they quieted—and the four youngest girls would be in the fourth.

At ten in the evening, it was chilly away from the fire.

That morning, following Barbara's instructions, Tracy had put on sweatpants, a long-sleeved shirt, and a heavy sweater over her uniform before running to the flagpole. Most of the campers had also gotten that message from counselors and friends who'd tipped them off, but Christopher, the youngest, was shivering in his shorts and T-shirt.

Spying him, Barbara stripped off her sweatshirt and tossed it to him. "Put it on," she commanded.

It looked like a gown on tiny Christopher, but he grinned inside it, comforted.

There would be no sleeping bags on this trip; not a single camper had received one. Part of their job was to survive with a certain amount of discomfort.

"Listen up," said Barbara. "If you wake up in the night and see that the fire's getting low, it's your job to stoke it, or load it with new fuel." She paused to demonstrate, to point out where the makeshift woodpile was. She'd wrapped it in the one remaining tarp, in case of rain. "But don't go wandering," she said. "If you get lost in the dark, that's bad for everyone."

She paused, thinking.

"Another thing," said Barbara. "Stick together. I mean keep your bodies touching overnight. You'll be a lot warmer if you do."

A few of the younger boys groaned.

"Fine," said Barbara. "Freeze if you want. I don't care."

Someone giggled, and they all looked in the direction of her extended arm.

Christopher, the youngest, had curled up into a ball on the ground, his knees inside Barbara's sweatshirt. He was fast asleep.

Barbara clapped. "Everyone who's not me, Tracy, Walter, or Lowell," she said. "Go to your tents. Bedtime."

The camp settled. Even T.J., up on her crest, seemed to have retired: she'd let her campfire dwindle, apparently warm enough inside the sleeping bag she'd packed.

When the four oldest campers had finished tidying the site, Walter waved them toward him, toward the tent that had been designated his and Lowell's.

"I brought something with me," he whispered. In the dim light of the fire, Tracy could see the glint of his braces as he grinned.

Inside the tent, they sat up in a small circle, shaking with cold. Tracy's teeth chattered anytime they were not clenched. She could only imagine how Barbara was feeling, down one layer, having donated it to Christopher.

Walter, a wiry, young-looking fourteen, apparently noticed too, for he removed the sweatshirt he was wearing and handed it to Barbara.

"No," said Barbara.

"Take it," said Walter. "I've still got this shirt on." He pointed to the long-sleeved shirt he was wearing underneath.

"Besides," he said, "I can just cuddle with Lowell tonight."

And he slung an arm over Lowell, who grinned and shoved him off.

"What did you want to show us?" said Barbara.

Walter removed his arm from Lowell's shoulders and lifted his remaining shirt. Underneath it was a flask he had strapped to his flank.

Tracy recognized what it was immediately. Her own father had a flask that he brought with him to the track. He kept it in an inner pocket of his jacket, nipped from it occasionally with no self-consciousness. Once, after a horse of his had won a race, he had offered it to Tracy, and she had been curious enough to take a sip. She still remembered the burn of it as it went down her throat.

"Impressive," said Barbara.

"Thanks," said Walter. He unscrewed the top of it and swigged.

"What's in it?" asked Barbara.

"Crème de menthe," said Walter. "It's the only booze my dad doesn't keep track of."

He passed it. All of them drank. Tracy took a small sip at first, and then a larger one. It was sweeter than what her father drank, and also more disgusting.

She coughed.

"*Shhhhh*," said Barbara. She grabbed the flask from Tracy and took a long draught, wiping her mouth with the back of her hand.

Within minutes, the tent had become warmer. Tracy grinned in the dark. All the worries she had ever had suddenly seemed several yards farther away.

Barbara was to her right; Lowell was opposite her; Walter was next to him. Tracy inched her foot, inside its sneaker, in what she suspected was the direction of Lowell's, though she could not see. She was picturing what it would be like to feel his mouth on hers. When her sneaker reached his, she left it there, and it felt like putting a plug inside a socket.

"I'm bored. Let's play a game," said Walter.

"It's pitch black in here," said Tracy. She was thinking of cards, or checkers, or the pick-up sticks she had created for Christopher.

"Not like that. Truth or dare," said Walter.

Barbara laughed softly.

Tracy knew what this was only from books and shows. She understood it to be a game that people her age played at things like sleepovers, but the only sleepovers she had had were with her cousins on her mother's side, or with Debbie Finley, a neighbor girl whose mother worked nights. Those sleepovers hadn't felt anything like this one.

Part of the feeling came from danger: all of them, Tracy felt certain, had at the back of their mind the image of Jacob Sluiter at the edge of the campsite, recently escaped, hungry and angry. But none of them would say his name: to say it felt disrespectful to Barbara. To the memory of her brother, the rumors that Sluiter was somehow involved in his disappearance.

"I'll go first," said Tracy, feeling reckless. She put her hand out for the disgusting crème de menthe.

"Truth or dare?" said Walter. The words felt like an incantation.

"Truth," said Tracy, drinking.

"Who do you like?" said Walter.

And she understood immediately that she would lie. She thought about all the boys in her grade at her school in Hempstead.

"Philip DiGiacomo," she said, naming the boy who was widely considered the cutest.

"Aw, that's not fair," said Walter. "Who do you like at this *camp*."

"Too late," said Tracy happily. "Your turn. Truth or dare."

"Dare," said Walter.

Tracy thought for a moment. She wanted her dare to be creative, to be funny. She wanted to make the others laugh.

"All right," she said. "Walter: I dare you to walk up to T.J.'s tent and make bear noises outside it."

The boys fell into quiet laughter. Next to her, she could feel Barbara's head turn swiftly in her direction.

"That's not a good idea," said Barbara.

"Why not?" said Lowell. "That's hilarious."

From Barbara: a long measured pause. And then: "She's got a gun."

The other three fell silent.

"She almost definitely has a gun," said Barbara.

"For what?" said Lowell.

"For exactly that reason," said Barbara. "For bears and things."

"Or for Slitter," said Walter.

There was a long pause.

"Do you think that's why they sent the counselors along with us this year?" said Walter. "Because he's on the loose?"

"No," said Barbara. "I think it's just because so many parents complained. T.J. says this generation is different from earlier ones. She says the parents are just more scared."

More silence as the four of them considered this. Tracy didn't think her own parents would be scared. But when she remembered the mothers of the other girls—in their patterned wrap dresses, their Weejuns—she believed that they would be.

"Well," said Walter. "Not doing that. Any other ideas?"

Tracy racked her brain. She thought of having him finish off the flask—but she wanted more. She thought of having him kiss one of the others, or strip down and streak around the campsite, but she was worried about the precedent this would set—being terrified, herself, of being asked to remove any article of clothing whatsoever—and so instead she said, "I dare you to tell us Lowell's biggest secret."

She could not see anyone's face well, but she could tell Walter was thinking about how to respond.

"That's easy," he said finally. "When he's at home, he sleeps with the light on because he's scared of the dark."

He turned to Lowell. "But don't worry, pal," he said. "I'll protect you."

Tracy understood two things immediately: that this was not Lowell's biggest secret; and that Walter would be loyal to him at all costs. Her heart sank. She had not meant to be unkind.

Thirty minutes passed. An hour. All of them were tipsy and warmer than they had been. Tracy's good mood had been restored by the intimacies they had swapped: after running out of acceptable dares, they turned instead to truths, and in the small amount of time that had passed they'd learned more about each other than they had all summer. It was wonderful, thought Tracy, having friends like these, who seemed to see the parts of yourself you worked hardest to hide, and bring them into the light and celebrate them with a sort of tender ribbing that uplifted more than it put down. Lowell, she had learned, really *was* afraid of the dark; Lowell, despite his physical gifts, hated sports, to the horror of his football-playing father; Walter was terrible in school, had something called *dyslexia*, had a father who'd gone to Harvard and expected nothing less. She, Tracy, had disclosed how few friends she had at home, how the girls she went to middle school with were nothing like her; how her father had left her mother for Donna Romano, a cocktail waitress at the Adelphi Hotel; how her mother had become quieter, less boisterous in the wake of this event.

Each time a truth was told, they cheersed, they drank. They took turns stoking the fire when it got low.

The only person who seemed at all reserved was Barbara. She laughed quietly with them; she was engaged; but when it came time for her to tell her truths, Tracy sensed that they were censored.

It was so freeing, thought Tracy, to trade intimacies with friends in this way; she felt almost bad for Barbara that she was having a different experience. And so, when it came time for Tracy to participate, she chose Barbara. And Barbara chose truth.

Unswervingly, Tracy asked the question she'd been wondering all summer.

"Who's your boyfriend?"

Silence.

In the background, the fire popped loudly, and Tracy jumped.

"The truth is," said Barbara finally, "that I can't tell you the truth."

In her voice there was anger: whether it was directed at her, or at the boyfriend, or at the world, Tracy wasn't sure.

Barbara grabbed the flask from Walter and tipped it vertical. She finished it.

Then she said, "Lowell. Truth or dare."

Lowell thought. Opted at last for a dare.

"I dare you to kiss me," said Barbara.

At the base of her neck, Tracy felt a cold sensation that she recognized as fear.

In the dim light from the fire, she could see Lowell's broad shoulders, his forearms crossed one over the other on top of his tucked-up legs. He took one arm down and then the other, and then, with purpose, he got up onto his knees and leaned toward Barbara. He put his hands on either side of her face, and then he put his face toward hers and kissed her, and Tracy understood immediately that he had kissed many girls before; and that this was not a perfunctory, command-following kiss. This was instead a kiss with feeling, with desire. She wanted to turn away; she didn't. This was her punishment, Tracy thought, for letting down her guard. She deserved it. She took it.

Walter made a little *Oooh* sound when the kiss ended, but that was all.

Then Barbara said she was tired, and Lowell agreed, and the four of them split up abruptly: the boys to tend the fire one last time; the girls in the direction of their tent.

Inside, Tracy was cold again. She shook. She turned onto her side, tucked her knees up into her sweatshirt, lay there curled up like a baby.

After a beat, she felt Barbara move closer to her, and then Barbara put her arms around Tracy's side, hugging her from behind.

"Don't," said Tracy.

"I'm sorry," said Barbara. "I don't know what I was thinking. I'm sorry, Tracy."

She didn't want to cry, but suddenly she was crying. It was out of shame more than anger: shame for ever thinking someone like Lowell Cargill might possibly be interested in her.

"Don't cry, Tracy," said Barbara. "Please. I'm sorry."

Tracy closed her eyes. She was warmer now, at least; Barbara was correct that putting their bodies together was useful for retaining heat.

"Do you like him?" Tracy whispered.

"No."

"Why did you do it?"

Barbara paused.

"I do bad things sometimes," she said. "I have that problem. I think—what would be the worst thing I could do in this moment? And then I do it. Almost like I can't stop myself."

Against her will, Tracy understood what Barbara meant. She, too, had had those thoughts—the difference was that she was too afraid to act on them. She imagined that most people were.

"You should get that examined," said Tracy, and Barbara laughed a little. Tracy smiled. Despite everything, she liked to make Barbara laugh.

"Oh, I have," said Barbara. "My father has made me see a shrink since I was five."

"The same one?"

"All different. Every year there's a new one. This year's is Dr. Roth. I call her Dr. Sloth, because that's what she looks like. She talks like one, too. Like this," said Barbara—and she did an impression of someone sluggish and dull.

"At least she's a woman," said Barbara, after a beat. "I like women better."

"Me too," said Tracy—though she wasn't actually sure that this was true.

"What does Dr. Roth think is wrong with you?"

"Impulse control," said Barbara. "I don't have enough of it, according to her. My father agrees."

"You don't get along with him."

"Hah," said Barbara. "The understatement of the year."

"Is that why you came to camp this summer?" said Tracy. "To get away from him?"

"Partly."

"What's the other part?"

Barbara was quiet.

"To get away from all of them," she said. "They're having that party this summer, and I just didn't want to be there for that. All their terrible friends. I don't like any of them."

Tracy had another theory.

"Is it easier to see your boyfriend from camp?"

Barbara nodded. Tracy could feel her chin moving up and down against the back of Tracy's head.

"Easier to sneak out," said Barbara. "Up at the house, someone's always awake."

"What about your mother?" This was the most they had ever talked about Barbara's family. Normally, she changed the subject. "What's she like?" Tracy said, pressing on.

A pause.

"She's useless," Barbara said. "She barely functions."

"What happened to her?"

Barbara's arms slackened a little around Tracy.

"My brother went missing," she said quietly. "And he never came back. That's what happened to her, I think. Because I've seen pictures of her from when she was a teenager, and she looked okay. She looked like a different person."

Tracy put her hand over Barbara's. She squeezed it. She could feel herself sobering up in the cold. She had the feeling that she would be embarrassed by some of this, or all of this, tomorrow; that it would be difficult to look at Lowell and Walter and Barbara. But for now, she used what remained of the bravery the alcohol had given her to lace her fingers through Barbara's and pull her arm more tightly around herself.

"Did you know that, about my brother?" Barbara said. "Does everyone know that?"

Tracy nodded. "I'm sorry," she said.

Silence.

"My mom thinks he'll come back," said Barbara. "But that's a secret from my father. She only says that stuff to me. My father gets mad when she even mentions Bear."

"Do you think he will?" said Tracy.

"No," said Barbara. "I don't."

In the dark, Tracy could hear Barbara opening and closing her mouth.

"What is it?"

"I think about him a lot. I wish he hadn't gone away," said Barbara.

"Do you wish you could have met him?"

"No. I mean, that's part of it," said Barbara. "I've seen pictures of him and he looked like a good person. Everyone says he was."

She paused. Tracy held her breath, not wanting to break the spell.

"When I was younger," said Barbara, "I used to have these imaginary conversations with him. I used to pretend he still lived with us, that I had an older brother who looked out for me. Protected me from my parents when they fought, or when they got mad at me."

Tracy nodded. She—an only child—had had similar daydreams.

"But also," said Barbara, "if he hadn't disappeared."

She did not finish the sentence.

"Then what?" said Tracy.

"Then I wouldn't have been born," said Barbara. "That would have been better, I think."

They were quiet for a long time.

An adult, Tracy knew, would have registered alarm, would have protested that life was worth living. But Tracy, at nearly thirteen, read the statement not as a cry for help, but as a statement of fact. And so she said nothing, and the two of them breathed together for a long time, until each one thought the other had fallen asleep.

Suddenly, Barbara spoke again.

"What time do you think it is?"

Tracy held up her watch, angling it so that it caught the light from the fire.

"Midnight," she said.

"Shit," Barbara whispered.

"What?"

"I have to go."

She sat up abruptly.

Beside her, Tracy sat up as well.

"*Go?*" she said.

Barbara was rummaging in her backpack, feeling inside it.

"Where are you going?" Tracy asked.

"Same place I go every night."

She pulled out a small flashlight.

"Where did you get that?"

"I brought it with me from Balsam."

"But how will you know where you're going?" asked Tracy, incredulously.

But Barbara scoffed.

"Don't worry about me," she said. "I know every inch of these woods."

And then she set off, past the fire, heading downhill. Tracy watched until she could see only the beam from the flashlight. Until even that was gone.

Tracy

1950s • 1961 • Winter 1973 • June 1975
July 1975 • August 1975

Tracy slept fitfully, woken by cold and sometimes by the sound of one of the other campers tending the fire.

At some point, she opened her eyes to find that it was light out, and that she was still alone in the tent.

Tracy sat up quickly, afraid now. Everyone else was still sleeping. She tiptoed to Lowell and Walter's tent, and leaned down next to Lowell, whispering his name until he opened one eye.

"Barbara's not here," she said. "She's gone."

Lowell blinked in the sunlight, rubbed his eyes, stretched.

"What are you talking about?" said Lowell. "I just saw her. She was getting more wood."

Sure enough: from behind a little copse of trees came Barbara, arms full of branches, gathering kindling to fuel their morning fire.

She grinned at Tracy. *Good morning*, she mouthed.

Their plan for the day was to set up simple squirrel poles, which T.J. had taught them to do in their outdoorsmanship classes. Barbara, of course, oversaw.

By evening, the squirrel traps were empty of both bait and squirrels. Someone had found a small patch of berries, but the walk to retrieve them had no doubt cost more energy than the berries themselves would provide.

The mood had changed. With nothing to do, they waited for dinner, for the small portions of canned beans and gorp that Barbara had reserved for the night's meal. The younger campers were complaining of hunger; the older ones were annoyed.

Barbara, determined, set off one more time into the woods to check the traps. And in a moment, they heard a yell.

Tracy stood up. Across the campsite, she could see Lowell standing too. And then he took off in a run toward Barbara's voice.

The two of them emerged a minute later, grinning, shouldering two of the squirrel poles between them. From the poles hung the corpses of three red squirrels, swinging as they walked. One of them, Tracy saw in horror, was still twitching and scrabbling.

"Barbara!" she cried out. "Barbara, one's alive!"

Barbara nodded.

"Grab a rock," she said.

"*Me?*" Tracy said.

"Yes, you."

Tracy looked around the campsite. She quickly spotted a solid-looking one, and held it up over her head for Barbara's inspection.

"Good," said Barbara. "Now take off one of your socks and put the rock inside it."

Tracy felt her stomach lurch.

"Do it," said Barbara. "Come on, Tracy. If I have to put the pole down, he'll get away."

Something in Barbara's gaze told Tracy that this was a test, that to fail it would be catastrophic for their friendship. And so she complied, sitting down on the earth, removing a shoe and then a sock, putting the rock inside it.

With one bare foot she hobbled toward the frantic squirrel. The rest of the campers were quiet. She aimed her weapon, swung it like a bat toward the skull of the red squirrel until it no longer moved.

Raising her head at last, she saw that she was being watched: not just by her peers, but by T.J. Hewitt, up on her ridge, hands on hips, smiling down at her in approval.

"Good job," she called.

These were the only words she had spoken since declaring herself invisible.

Then, swiftly, she turned her back on them and crouched down to return to her tent.

Barbara was the one to butcher the squirrels, bending forward to work on a tarp on the ground.

When she was nearly finished removing the pelt, she shifted a squirrel carcass onto her lap and began to work off the remaining skin with a paring knife.

The rest of them watched.

Later, no one would be certain quite how it happened—not even Barbara—but suddenly she was sitting very still, and on her right knee was the half-skinned squirrel, and inside her left thigh was the tip of the small knife she had been using.

Her hand was still holding its hilt. Reflexively, she extracted it in one similarly swift motion, and then said, "I shouldn't have done that."

Sure enough: the wound lay dormant for three seconds, as if hesitating, and then from it a small pool of blood surfaced and then spilled.

"I shouldn't have taken it out," Barbara said, again. "I should have left it in there."

Barbara had been wearing shorts, and so her leg was in full view. Rivulets of blood were spilling down the inside of her thigh, splashing onto the soil beneath her.

Some of the other campers backed away, heads in hands; others approached.

"We should tell T.J.," said Lowell.

"No," said Barbara quickly.

"Why not?" said Walter. "She said to. She said the only reason to get her was an emergency."

"It's not an emergency," said Barbara. "I can handle it."

She looked around. The blood dripping from her leg was making a *pat-pat* noise on the ground.

"Christopher," she called. He had run away at the first sight of blood. From his tent, now, he emerged, timid.

"I need my sweatshirt back," said Barbara. "I'm sorry."

He stripped it off hastily, ran it to her. With her knife, she severed one sleeve and wrapped it firmly around her leg. The fabric of the sleeve went quickly from white to pink.

For an hour or two, Barbara wore it, going about her business as before, seemingly unperturbed.

They ate squirrel for dinner, each given approximately one bite of meat, which boosted everyone's morale, even if it did not lessen their hunger.

By late evening, Tracy noticed that Barbara seemed quieter than usual. She had no doubt lost a lot of blood; the sweatshirt sleeve had needed replacement twice with other fabrics.

"Are you all right?" Tracy said.

"I'm fine," said Barbara.

But her face was very pale. Tracy looked at her one beat too long. "What?" Barbara said.

Behind her, Tracy could feel the gazes of the other campers turning in their direction. The campsite was silent.

"We have to tell T.J.," said Lowell. He looked down at Barbara, inspecting her face. "I'm serious. You've lost too much blood. It's not safe."

"I'm fine," Barbara said again, weakly.

But Lowell wouldn't hear it. He strode off in the direction of T.J.'s campsite. Barbara called after him, once, but her voice was too quiet to be heard.

Ten seconds later, T.J. came running down the small incline between her campsite and theirs, carrying a large pot before her. She knelt down in front of Barbara, who was now on her back, apparently unable to hold up her head any longer.

After inspecting her charge, T.J. popped up onto her feet and looked around, assessing everyone.

Then, correctly identifying Lowell Cargill as the person most likely to be helpful in a crisis, she held out the pot in her hands, instructing him to stoke the campfire, and then to boil water over it. She, meanwhile, scooped Barbara swiftly into her arms, and then walked as quickly as she could back up the hill.

"Shout when the water's boiling," she called.

Then she and Barbara disappeared inside her tent.

By nightfall, Barbara was cleaned, sutured, fed, watered, clothed in warmer clothing, and much pinker in the face. She was also back with her peers at the campsite, already downplaying the severity of what had transpired.

Later, in their tent, Tracy and Barbara huddled together as before.

"Barbara," said Tracy.

"What?"

"I'm glad you're okay."

Barbara scoffed. "I would have been fine."

"I don't know," said Tracy. "You didn't look good."

"I could have taken care of myself. I would have walked back to Camp Emerson if I'd gotten any worse. I would have walked all the way there and all the way back. No one needed to get T.J. involved."

Strangely, Tracy believed her.

"Where'd you learn all that stuff?" said Tracy.

"What stuff?"

"You know. Trapping and putting up tents and all. Taking apart those squirrels. First aid."

"Same place as you," said Barbara. "T.J.'s classes."

Tracy shook her head. "I don't know what you know. I don't think anyone does."

Barbara was briefly quiet. "My family," she said.

They were quiet then. There was more to the story, Tracy could tell. She didn't press.

"Are you leaving again tonight?" said Tracy, whispering.

"I don't think I can," said Barbara. She shifted a little. "I don't think my leg will let me."

She sighed.

"Is it all right that you don't?" said Tracy.

She said this carefully: not wanting to repeat her mistake, to anger Barbara by pressing an issue she clearly did not want to talk about.

Barbara was silent so long that Tracy assumed she had fallen asleep. The extra clothes she'd been given by T.J. lent warmth to both of them, and Tracy felt herself growing sleepy, as well.

Then, in the dark, she heard Barbara exhale.

"Probably not," she said quietly. "It's probably not all right."

Alice

1950s • 1961 • Winter 1973 • June 1975
July 1975 • August 1975: **Day Two**

On the second day of Barbara's absence, Alice wakes, her mouth a desert.

She's slept all night on her stomach. A patch of wetness has spread outward onto the bedspread from her mouth.

She knows something bad has happened. The feeling of it hovers; the fact of it hasn't arrived yet. She sits up. Reaches for the tumbler of gin on her nightstand. Drinks painfully.

She stands.

Barbara.

There it is. Her daughter has been missing since yesterday morning.

Five minutes later, Alice stands in the sunroom. She watches from the window: more parents arriving to retrieve their children, one week earlier than they'd planned.

Some—those who live in Albany or Niskayuna or Vermont—came yesterday to retrieve their children.

Others—the West Coasters, the Coloradans, those who had to catch a flight—are only arriving today, and they pull onto the Preserve with urgency in their rented or hired cars, horrified that their children have had to spend an entire night in a place where another child went missing less than twenty-four hours earlier.

She understands. She remembers feeling this way about Bear: that she would do anything to protect him. That she would physically harm anyone who dreamed of harming him. He needed her—that was the thing. He needed her, when no one had ever needed her before. He clung to her—a habit that Peter pathologized. But she had never been anyone's protector before, and she enjoyed the feeling, indulging it in secret, whenever they were alone.

* * *

Behind her, someone enters the sunroom.

Without turning, she knows who it is.

She'll be taken to Albany today, she understands. The Peters are getting her out of the way, as usual.

That's all right. She likes being in Albany.

She can hear her son's voice better there.

Alice

1950s • **1961** • Winter 1973 • June 1975
July 1975 • August 1975

Bear was bouncing with anticipation. Alice watched him through the sunroom glass: the day that the Blackfly Good-by was due to begin, he always stationed himself on the front lawn, eager for company to arrive. Now, he was turning cartwheels and throwing a baseball up in the air over and over again. He was singing a song Alice didn't know, something he must have picked up at school. It struck her as funny, sometimes, that he had a whole life outside the home that she didn't know about. He's become such a *person*, lately, she said to Peter; and Peter rolled his eyes, as if he didn't know what she meant. But he did. She knew he did.

At age eight, he was delightful, intelligent, curious, funny, and increasingly independent. It went beyond what she had hoped for; now she sometimes missed him, his constant presence next to her, his high clear voice calling *Mamma* eighteen times in a minute.

But Peter was thrilled. It was all that he hoped for the boy: self-reliance. And one of the best parts of all of it was the way it had brought Peter and Alice together. Now they could sit still together, watching their son like a show. They began to enjoy one another's company in a way they hadn't before. She was older, for one thing: Alice was twenty-six that year. A respectable age, at last.

At times, now, she had the thrilling idea that her husband was falling in love with her—for the first time, actually. She was sad for the younger Alice, the eighteen-year-old who hadn't known anything about the world; but she was happy for herself in this moment. It was funny, she thought, how many relationships one could have with the same man, over the course of a lifetime together.

Peter and his father had invited more guests than ever to that year's event: thirty-seven, by Alice's count. Every bedroom was assigned, and every room in every outbuilding as well. Due to the number of single men and women who could not share a room, they'd even had to commandeer some of the Staff Quarters; for the staff members they'd displaced, they rented two unoccupied summer homes five miles to the south, and provided them with cars.

The first guest pulled in, and Bear ran toward the driveway to say hello. Alice, from her place in the sunroom, recognized the car immediately as her sister Delphine's.

It had been three years since George's death, and Delphine had continued to come alone for that time, always arriving in the same practical Buick that she staunchly refused to sell.

"Bear!" said Delphine. Through the glass, Alice could see the word as her mouth formed it. She and the boy had always had a special bond, a nice friendship. At each summer party, she treated him as an equal, brought paper and paint for him, sat with him for hours, talking with him about what he was learning in school.

Alice walked into the hallway, into the main room, where Peter and his parents were reading by the central fireplace.

"Delphine is here," she said.

The crowd that year was eclectic. The usual suspects were there: the families of Peter and Alice; the Southworths, who would bring their toddler daughter, Annabel; the McLellans and their children; and also a handful of clients, and the obligatory artists.

Everyone complimented the food. Everyone complimented everything, actually; the decorations, and the flowers, and the musicians they had brought in, and the outfits that Alice wore, and Bear's intelligence and good humor, and his handsomeness, too.

Throughout the week, Peter seemed different to Alice: his best self. He was happier, more enthusiastic. Relaxed, even. At times, she found him sitting on the lawn, reading a paper. Other years, he had seemed not to sit down at all.

One day, when most of the guests had gone for a hike up Hunt Mountain, Alice stayed behind. She was tired from a late night; she would take a short nap, she thought.

She went to her bedroom and stopped short.

Peter was there in her bed—awake.

He looked up at her. Surprised at first. Then he smiled.

"No hike?" he said.

"No," said Alice. "I thought I'd rest for a bit."

She waited, slightly nervous. The word *rest* was anathema to Peter; he didn't enjoy resting himself, and didn't appreciate it when anyone around him did either.

But he surprised her: "Come rest with me," he said.

In the first year of their marriage, sex had been something requisite. There was always a mild embarrassment about it, on both their parts: from their first moments alone together, she had never truly felt his desire, but something more akin to duty, or a sort of condescending charity.

When Bear turned one, Peter had had rooms furnished for her that were separate from his, in both their Albany house and at Self-Reliance. He didn't include her in this decision; merely presented both rooms to her, saying his insomnia required it.

Since then, she had slept alone.

Alice, still a young woman, sometimes felt desire so strongly that she did not know what to do with it. She lusted after friends, after strangers in the street. But, after a handful of rejections from Peter so brutal that they left her crying, she stopped making any attempt to engage him in that way. Attended to herself, instead, wondering if any other woman on the planet did what she was doing.

That day, though, Peter reached for her with a tenderness she had never felt before. He was gentle and forceful, all at once. She lay in bed with him afterward, astonished.

She cried: something she rarely let herself do in front of Peter.

"What is it?" he asked her kindly.

She was crying, she said, because she loved him. And she did, in that moment: she loved him, and the life they had built together. But she was also crying because of all that she'd been deprived of to that point.

"Silly," he called her, yet there was affection in his voice. And she let herself sink into him.

This, she thought, was what she had been wanting her whole life. At last, it was here.

*   *   *

Everything was different. For the rest of the week, the two of them mooned after one another. Every moment they could, they sought one another out. Peter slept in her room—the one he had made for her. He went to his, on the other side of the hallway, only to change and dress in the morning.

Even Bear noticed: he came to them once, taking both of their hands in his, grinning as he looked into their faces, as if he could sense their love.

Usually, the Blackfly Good-by took place from a Saturday to a Saturday. That year, at their annual farewell dinner—a clambake put on by the staff in the traditional manner, on the beach—Peter stood up and called for everyone's attention.

"Don't leave tomorrow," he said. "Stay an extra day."

He looked around then, as if only just realizing the implications of his idea. "Warren!" he called—the name of the cook in those days. "Warren, we have enough food for tomorrow, haven't we?"

Hesitantly, Warren nodded. It would mean more trips to town, Alice knew; it would mean a change in plans for all the temporary staff who had initially been contracted to work just the week.

But Peter had already made his decision. The guests had already cheered.

The dinner looked set to proceed, until someone on the periphery spoke up.

"Is that all right?" said Delphine. Everyone turned in her direction. "Warren, did you have other plans?"

Silence.

The impropriety of this exchange was obvious to everyone on the beach. What right did Delphine—a widowed woman, alone at the party—have to directly address a member of the Van Laars' staff?

Suddenly, Peter's father—who generally let his son run the show— stood up from the deep Adirondack chair he'd been sitting in with a spryness that would have been surprising in any other man of his age.

He addressed the group as a whole.

"Warren will be happy to accommodate you all," he said. "As will we. Thank you for your concern, Mrs. Barlow."

*   *   *

In bed that night, Peter's good mood was gone. A quiet fury had replaced it.

"What was she thinking," he said, over and over. *She*, Alice presumed, was Delphine.

"She means well," said Alice. "She's just—she's always been different. Ever since we were children."

Peter was silent.

"She has good qualities, too. She's very good with Bear," said Alice—thinking frantically of anything she could say to mollify her husband. "She's always been kind to him. She sits with him, you know. She brings him toys every time she comes."

"The presumptuousness of that woman," said Peter. "I know she's your sister, Alice, but I'm not certain we can keep inviting her."

He turned over, away from Alice.

Tentatively, she put a hand on his shoulder. He shrugged it off. Then he stood up. He put his robe on. He walked out of her room, across the hallway, and into his.

She didn't want the spell of the week to be over. She didn't want to go back to the way they'd always been.

She hadn't had as much to drink that week as she normally did; she'd been happily distracted by Peter's attention. But the final Saturday of the Blackfly Good-by—when she realized Peter would not be coming out of his room—she took a glass of wine at lunch, and continued to refill it in the kitchen whenever she had a moment to herself.

By four o'clock, the smell of the air had changed. Rain was coming, everyone said.

The staff had been busy all day, bringing bags of groceries back from town.

At some point, somebody proposed an outing on Lake Joan: it would be their last chance to boat before the storm. And so the decision was made, and everyone retreated to their rooms to change.

Bear would enjoy that, thought Alice. And she set off to find him.

For most of the week, he'd been running here and there with John Paul and Marnie McLellan; she could go long stretches without seeing him. She'd never paid so little attention to him as she did that week;

she'd never had anything to distract her the way that Peter had. It was all right, she told herself. Bear, too, was having fun.

Tessie Jo Hewitt was part of their group as well. Slightly older than the rest, she seemed to be their leader. Alice wasn't certain, but she thought it possible that Vic Hewitt had assigned his daughter the task of acting as babysitter for the other children.

Alice didn't find Bear in his room, or in any of the McLellans' rooms.

She looked down at the beach, and in the boathouse, where two of the staff were readying several watercraft for that afternoon's excursion.

"Have you seen Bear?" she asked them, but they hadn't.

She saved Peter's room for last. For one thing, she thought it unlikely that her son was there: Bear and his father had become closer, lately, but really he was hers alone. Peter seemed always to look at him from a distance, even when they were in the same room.

She walked down the carpeted hallway of Self-Reliance, listening for children's voices, for the voice of her son.

She stood outside Peter's room, her ear to the door.

And then, hearing nothing, she turned the knob.

Judyta

1950s • 1961 • Winter 1973 • June 1975
July 1975 • August 1975: **Day Two**

Inside the now-abandoned slaughterhouse, Judy stands silent. She listens: more footsteps. Five, six, seven in a row.

Toward the back of the shadowy room, she sees a staircase leading upward into darkness. If she were in a movie, she thinks, she'd head in that direction. But all of her training tells her not to go solo toward a potential threat, and so instead she backs out of the structure.

In the daylight, headed in the direction of Camp Emerson, she breaks into a jog.

Fifteen minutes later, Judy stands next to Denny Hayes and Captain LaRochelle on the dirt driveway. Across from them, a squadron of six state troopers—guns drawn, backs to walls—enters the structure two by two.

"This feels unnecessary," whispers Judy, and Denny turns and shushes her.

"Captain's orders," he says.

When the last of the troopers has disappeared out of sight, Judy feels the weight of what she's done.

For three long minutes, she looks up at the sky. Down at the ground.

How many footsteps did she actually hear? Just a few, she thinks. And were they loud? Not particularly. Could they have been something else? A tree, tapping on the roof. Acorns falling. Dozens of possibilities occur to her, until at last the troopers file out of the slaughterhouse, relaxed now.

The two at the front cross the dirt road to talk to Captain LaRochelle.

"Found the culprit," says one.

"Family of squirrels," says the other, grinning.

LaRochelle clears his throat. "That's it, huh? You sure?"

"Yeah. We searched the whole upstairs."

LaRochelle says nothing. Then, not looking at Judy, he turns to Hayes.

"I was interrupted during a conversation with Mr. Van Laar," says LaRochelle. "So I think it best that I return to him now."

He strides off.

Judyta

1950s • 1961 • Winter 1973 • June 1975
July 1975 • August 1975: **Day Two**

Back at the Command Post in the Director's Cabin, Denny Hayes positions himself at the front of the room, preparing to pick up where he left off with the small group of investigators gathered before him.

The superintendent, he says, is not happy with their efforts so far. The Adirondack Search and Rescue Team—a crew of civilian volunteers—is being dispatched to do a Type Three search today in the surrounding woods, after EnCon's failure to locate anyone, or anything, yesterday.

"Any leads from this morning?" Hayes asks.

The other investigators glance around. The looks on their faces are clear: not much.

One says: "Couple kids have said they've seen a woman in the woods in the past. This summer and other summers, too. Apparently she's a local legend. Ghost-story type of thing."

Hayes blinks.

"Ghost story about a woman. Noted," says Hayes. "Anyone able to tell us more about what this ghost looks like?"

The same investigator says, "Older woman. Thin. Gray hair. That's all I got. Aside from what they call her."

"Which is?"

The investigator, chagrined, makes a display of inspecting his notes. Reads it off: "Scary Mary."

"Scary Mary," says Hayes.

The investigator nods.

"Anyone else?" says Hayes.

Silence.

"Everyone says Barbara was well-liked," says another investigator. "No quarrels with anyone, that I've heard about."

Hayes looks more despairing than ever.

Still feeling humiliated from her earlier mistake at the slaughterhouse, Judy weighs whether to produce in this moment the information
provided by Mrs. Clute, the cook. Already, she imagines, she's being
talked about on the grounds. Being called incompetent. She'd prefer
to tell Denny Hayes in private. But Hayes looks poised to break up
the meeting, and so she raises her hand.

"Put your hand down, Judy," says Hayes. "You're an investigator,
not a student. Go ahead."

She flushes.

"There's a cook up at the house who had something to tell me,"
she begins. "Turns out she's the daughter of the man said to have
abducted Bear Van Laar."

For a beat, no one says anything.

Then an investigator who hasn't spoken yet says: "Carl Stoddard?"

Judy nods. She recognizes him: he's the oldest investigator in the
room. The one who, yesterday, asked LaRochelle whether Jacob Sluiter
was under consideration for Barbara's disappearance.

"I worked that case," the man says. Confirming what everyone
assumed.

Judy makes a note to talk to him, whenever she can get him alone.

"Why on earth," says Hayes, "would Carl Stoddard's daughter be
working for the Van Laars? That doesn't make sense. In either direction. They wouldn't want her here, that's certain. And she probably
wouldn't want to be here either."

"She uses her married name," says Judy. "Clute. She said the Van
Laars don't know who she is. Said she took the job out of necessity,
after her husband lost his. They've got a lot of kids. Another on the
way."

"And what did she have to say about Barbara's disappearance?"

Judy thinks about how to phrase this. "She said Barbara's family
never treated Barbara well. Neglected her, sort of. But she didn't have
any theories about where she might have gone."

"Anything—inappropriate? Anything beyond neglect?" asks Hayes.

"Not that she mentioned," says Judy. "But I guess she might not
have known everything. This is the first summer she's been here."

"And what did she have to say about her own father?"

The room feels as if it's holding its breath.

"She said Carl Stoddard was framed," says Judy. "Said there's no way he did it. But he died of a heart attack before he could be exonerated, and the Van Laar family just sort of let it be assumed that he was the one responsible, based on only a few pieces of evidence." She pauses. "I guess Captain LaRochelle agreed. And that's the story that was presented to the public, too."

Quiet.

Judy glances at the investigator who worked the original case.

"Goldman," says Hayes, and the investigator turns. "What do you think?"

Goldman thinks.

He glances over his shoulder—looking for LaRochelle.

"I never liked Stoddard for it," he says. "But don't ask me that in front of the captain."

"Did Mrs. Clute sign a statement?" asks Hayes, turning to Judy. "Will she go on record?"

"No," says Judy quickly. "She practically ran away when I asked her."

"Still," says Hayes, "thank you, Investigator Luptack. That's the most interesting thing I've heard today. She must have trusted you to tell you that."

He holds her gaze. Then: "Anything else? Anyone?"

The door swings open suddenly. In walks Captain LaRochelle.

Immediately, the mood in the room changes. Goldman busies himself with files. Two of the other investigators head outside. And Judy realizes that all of them have made a silent decision: they won't say anything in front of LaRochelle again—not without telling Hayes privately first.

Captain LaRochelle doesn't ask any questions about what's transpired since he's been gone.

Judyta

1950s • 1961 • Winter 1973 • June 1975
July 1975 • August 1975: **Day Two**

The Adirondack Search and Rescue Team, LaRochelle announces, has found something up by the observer's tower at the top of Hunt Mountain. Inside and outside the nearby cabin, a huge number of beer bottles have been collected. And from these, usable fingerprints have been taken. And from these, five have been matched with John Paul McLellan.

But there's more.

Someone called an anonymous tip into the station at Ray Brook: apparently, John Paul McLellan was known to be staying in the vicinity of the Van Laar Preserve—not just for the weeklong celebration at the house—but for the whole summer. Making it probable that the boyfriend Barbara Van Laar was going to see in the observer's cabin each night was, indeed, McLellan.

"So that's it," says Goldman. "Between that and the bloody uniform. McLellan's our guy?"

There's a hitch, says LaRochelle. Because McLellan and his lawyer father have made a separate allegation: it was Louise Donnadieu, Barbara's counselor, who asked McLellan to dispose of the bag.

The contents of which, adds LaRochelle, are currently being analyzed for blood type by forensics.

"So we're pointing at McLellan," says Goldman. "And McLellan's pointing at Donnadieu?"

"And a kid named Lee Towson," says LaRochelle. "Kitchen worker. McLellan says he and Donnadieu were a pair."

Around the room, a clearing of throats.

"Anyway," says LaRochelle. "Until we get the blood analysis back, let's just keep following the leads we have."

Around the Command Post, investigators stand. LaRochelle leaves to return to the main house.

Slowly, the room clears. When it's empty, Denny Hayes turns to Judy.

"Let me see that map," he says.

Judy retrieves the pad of paper from the wall she's leaned it against. Hayes takes it, inspects the several pages she's drawn on: the house, the camp, the outbuildings. Names above the buildings she was able to populate.

Hayes asks for a pen. Writes *Unoccupied* above the farm buildings. Judy's face reddens. For a long while, he says nothing. Then he points to a northern spot on one of the maps. "Let's add the observer's cabin here," he says. "We can add McLellan's name to it."

"Why wouldn't Louise Donnadieu have known McLellan was on the grounds all summer?" says Judy. "Weren't they together?"

"No idea," says Hayes. "Maybe he lied to her."

"Where does she think he was?" asks Judy.

"I'm not sure," he says. "But we can find out. She's still in Wells until they remand her to Albion. I'll stop in."

Judy nods. "What about McLellan himself?" she says. "Do you have tabs on him?"

Hayes confirms that they do. One investigator from every shift has been assigned to sit in the parking lot of the hotel he's staying in, keeping a lookout for him and his parents.

"The problem is," says Hayes, "no matter how much evidence we stack up—without a body, or the living girl, he's unarrestable. All we have him on are fairly minor charges. A DUI. Possession. With a lawyer father, that's not gonna keep him in our sights for long."

"But the uniform," says Judy.

"Still maintaining the Donnadieu girl asked him to dispose of the bag that held it."

At nearly 7 p.m., exhausted, Judy finally walks to her car.

She points her Beetle down the long dirt driveway of Self-Reliance, then left onto State Route 29, heading south. Now that Judy is alone, there is nothing to distract her from her earlier humiliation, and she presses her eyes closed against it, briefly. Says *Goddammit* several times. All those state troopers. Captain LaRochelle himself. Hayes. All of them watching her, skeptical. Laughing, even.

If she had just walked up those stairs, she thinks. If she had just listened longer.

Her eyes are heavy. It's been a long day in the heat. When she was promoted to investigator, she hadn't realized how much more human interaction she'd be tasked with. As a trooper, she'd enjoyed the long stretches of solitude that came with sitting at the edge of the highway, waiting.

She turns up the radio as loud as she can take it. Van McCoy commands her to *Hustle*. Sleepily, she tries to comply.

Judy wakes up with a jolt. It's full dark. She's still on Route 29. Her hands are in her lap. The car is turned off. She's still alive.

But apparently, she pulled to the side of the road and fell asleep, without having any memory of doing so. Without locking her doors.

A sudden rush of adrenaline and fear.

Imagine, thinks Judy—imagine if she hadn't pulled over.

Wide awake now, Judy puts her blinker on, checks her blind spot, and pulls back onto the road.

Up ahead of her, she notices a sign: *Shattuck Township, 6 miles*. Beneath it, two small icons: food and lodging.

Judy makes a right at the foot of the off-ramp. After a minute, she spies a tiny roadside motel: neon sign outside it; in-ground pool nearby.

The woman at the front desk is reading a novel. She looks up when Judy enters.

"I was wondering if there might be a room available?" says Judy. The woman nods.

Judy feels self-conscious, suddenly. She isn't sure how often single women check into motels around here, but she imagines the ones who do are a certain type.

So she volunteers, unasked: "I'm a police officer. An investigator. I'm working on a case nearby."

"Okay," says the woman. But she looks slightly more interested than she did before.

"Are there phones?" Judy asks.

"There are," says the woman, "but the ones in the rooms only connect to the front desk. If you wanna call out, you gotta use the pay phone over there." She points.

Her mother answers.

"Judyta?" she says, without waiting.

"Hi, Ma."

"Judyta, I've been worried sick. Please tell me you're all right."

The sound of her own name in her mother's voice—her mother, who came over at fifteen, who worked so hard to drop any trace of an accent, who refused to speak Polish to her children, who despite all of this still bears the weight of strangers clocking her as *foreign*—suddenly makes Judy want to cry.

"I'm all right, Mama. I'm just tired. Long day today."

She can hear her father in the background, asking, *What time will she be home?*

"Ma," says Judy, "I know Daddy won't like this. But I have to move out. I can't live at home anymore. Not with this job."

Silence. "Where are you now?"

"I'm at a motel. It's called"—Judy checks the sign above the counter—"the Alcott Family Inn. It's close to the case I'm working."

"At a *what?*" says her mother. "Judyta Luptack, did you just say you're at a—"

"Don't tell Dad," says Judy. "Please."

In the background: *Where is she? At a what?*

Her mother sighs lengthily. Then she says: "She's at a friend's house, Marty. Someone who lives closer to the case she's working."

A pause. *What friend of hers lives all the way up there?*

"Honey," says her mother. "Just be safe, all right?"

"I will be, Ma," says Judy.

The room is perfectly adequate: flowered bedspread, flowered curtains, framed pictures of flowers on the wall.

She collapses into bed without taking her clothes off.

Judyta

1950s • 1961 • Winter 1973 • June 1975
July 1975 • August 1975: **Day Three**

She wakes up to the sound of knocking on the door. She wakes slowly, trying to remember where she is. Then she grabs the clock on her nightstand, terrified that she's overslept.

It's only 6 a.m. Judy is relieved—and annoyed.

She stands, still wearing her suit, now rumpled, and goes to the door. Through the peephole, she sees a middle-aged man, his hair combed into a neat side part. He wears a short-sleeved dress shirt, tan, and a brown tie. He holds an umbrella above his head.

She looks past him, into the parking lot beyond the covered walkway outside all the rooms, and sees that it's pouring. Bad for the search, she thinks, automatically.

She opens the door, keeping the chain lock on.

"Hello," says the man. "Are you Miss Luptack?"

"Yes."

"My name is Bob Alcott," says the man. "Can I trouble you for a second?"

From behind the cracked, chain-locked door, she nods.

He glances over his shoulder, into the downpour soaking the parking lot. "I wonder—you mind if I come in?"

"I do mind."

He pauses. Explains: he's the husband of the woman working the desk, he says, and a co-owner of the Alcott Family Inn. He's also a history teacher at the nearby central school.

"Beatrice said you were a detective," he says. "And that you're working a case nearby?"

She nods.

"Is it the Van Laar girl?" he asks her.

She keeps her face still.

"It's all right," he says. "You don't have to answer. But if you are, I've got something to tell you."

"I'm listening," says Judy.

"It's about her brother," says Bob Alcott. "Bear."

Louise

1950s • 1961 • Winter 1973 • June 1975
July 1975 • August 1975: **Day Three**

Louise, in Wells, awaits her transfer. She'll be sent to Albion, hours to the west, near Rochester—farther away, in fact, than Louise has ever traveled.

She can't see the rain outside, but she can hear it. She closes her eyes. Imagines Barbara in the woods: pictures her alive, then dead. Wills herself back to the cabin called Balsam, the night before Barbara Van Laar went missing. Pictures falling asleep in her little cot there, the faint lapping of Lake Joan in the near distance, the cool sharp air of evening. Camp Emerson, she realizes with a twinge of sadness, is the place she has felt the most at home in her life.

She wishes Jesse could go there. Just one summer, she wishes he could go.

"Donnadieu," says a voice, and Louise gets to her feet. Ready for her transfer.

Instead, the officer unlocks the cell door.

"Somebody posted bail for you," he says.

Tracy

1950s • 1961 • Winter 1973 • June 1975
July 1975 • August 1975: **Day Three**

Back in her father's rental in Saratoga Springs, Tracy Jewell stands in the living room, a book in her hands. She is alone for the first time in three days, her father and Donna Romano having finally gone back to the track.

Now she lowers the blinds halfway and opens the windows halfway and points all the fans in the house in her direction. The pleasant smell of new rain comes in. She prepares an elaborate snack for herself, places it on the floor beside her. Two months ago—before she had ever heard of the Van Laar Preserve, or Camp Emerson—this was the way she anticipated spending her summer. Today, it feels like a letdown.

For an hour, her book goes unread.

She's thinking of Barbara Van Laar, running through every exchange they had, racking her brain for evidence that might help to bring her home.

There is one memory she returns to over and over. In early August—just after their return from the Survival Trip, the week before Barbara went missing—Tracy and Barbara had been walking back from a woodsmanship class to begin their free hour, when Barbara had an idea.

"Follow me," she said.

"Where?"

But Barbara only grinned, and veered east, toward the beach.

The day was one of the most beautiful of the entire session. Barbara didn't stop at the beach, but swerved northward, toward the woods that bordered the beach, passing the boathouse along the way. The sun came through the pines in golden shafts, casting spotlights here and there across the ground. At a certain point, Tracy understood where they were going. Under normal circumstances she would have felt afraid—she was typically a follower of rules—but at Camp Emerson, under the influence of Barbara, she had begun to feel reckless.

At the conclusion of their brief, silent hike, they were facing a parking area, full of cars; beyond it, the southern wing of Self-Reliance. A side door was propped slightly open; through it strode a maid in uniform, wheeling a cart of laundry around a corner, out of sight.

It took Tracy a moment to notice movement on the lawn that sloped down to the lake, but a handful of voices drew her eye in that direction. A large number of people sat on chairs and chaise longues. They held glasses in their hands, and their voices were loud and merry. This, Tracy realized, was the hundredth-anniversary party that Barbara had mentioned.

Tracy withdrew immediately behind a tree.

"*Barbara*," she whispered.

"Relax," said Barbara. "It's happy hour. They're definitely sloshed."

She strode forward, turning only when she realized Tracy hadn't followed.

"Come on," she said. "The only people we have to watch out for work for my parents. And they won't tell even if they do see us."

They entered the house through the open side door. Along the hallway were two rows of doors. In the ones left open, she could see made beds, framed paintings, animal skins, and mounted heads.

Every so often she took several running steps to keep up with Barbara, who was walking with intention toward what Tracy thought would be her room—but instead she led them into an enormous kitchen.

She opened the refrigerator and brought out several good things to eat. Then, setting it all before them on a nearby counter, she commenced.

"Dig in," said Barbara. "Are you hungry? I'm always starving."

Tracy followed suit, more cautiously. She had never before seen a girl eat with the abandon of Barbara Van Laar, who shoved food into her mouth with an open palm. She chewed loudly and swallowed vigorously. Tracy watched, fascinated.

When Barbara had taken her fill, she left everything out on the counter—"They won't know it was us," she said—and then retraced her steps down the same hallway through which they had entered.

Suddenly there came two voices, male and female. Unswervingly, Barbara opened a door on their right and pushed Tracy into a small broom closet. It was so small that there was only room for one.

"*Stay cool*," said Barbara, closing the door behind her. Through the crack beneath the door, Tracy could see her shadow move away, and then the sound of a door hinge creaking softly someplace down the hall: Barbara taking shelter elsewhere, she supposed.

Tracy breathed as quietly as she could. She was terrified of being caught, being punished. If at the start of camp she had wanted to be sent home—well, that feeling was gone now, replaced by a firm desire to remain at Camp Emerson for the duration of the session. To learn everything she could learn from Barbara Van Laar.

The footsteps that accompanied the voices were growing louder. She held her breath, listening. Had they gone? She waited thirty seconds. Longer. Then, just as Tracy searched fumblingly for a doorknob in the dark, she heard one name, uttered by the woman: *Peter*. In her voice Tracy heard what she assumed must be desire.

More noises, inscrutable to Tracy, and then the quick continued patter of those footsteps, one perhaps chasing after the other, and then true silence for some time.

She jumped when the door swung open. Bright daylight made her squint. There was Barbara, standing before her, gesturing with her head in the direction of the side door.

She was holding a paper bag in her hands.

She looked enraged.

What happened? Tracy mouthed, but Barbara only shook her head furiously and strode off.

Tracy followed her silently, glancing left and right, gulping the house with her eyes.

She wanted to see Barbara's room. She wanted to see the rest of the house. She wanted to know more about what she had heard, those whispering voices.

But Tracy's curiosity about all of these things was overruled by her discretion. She understood instinctively that Barbara would not appreciate questions along these lines, and so she said nothing, even after they'd reached the woods. Tracy panted as she walked. At a certain point—right before they reached the beach—Barbara finally stopped and turned.

"They painted my room," she said. "Those motherfuckers painted my room."

The word felt like a slap. Tracy had read it, but she'd never heard it spoken.

"I'm sorry," she said—though she didn't fully understand.

"All that *work*," said Barbara. "All that work."

She sank down into a squat. Put her face in her hands.

Slowly, Tracy lowered herself as well.

"What work?" she said, after so much time had passed that her knees had begun to throb.

But Barbara only continued with her rant.

"That's probably why they let me come to camp," said Barbara. "So they could get in there and paint it over without my permission."

She stood up and set off again abruptly.

"*Pink*," she said. "They painted my damn room *pink*."

"Why do you think they did it?" Tracy asked. She was, once again, running a little to keep up with her.

"Oh, for their guests," said Barbara. "For the party. God forbid someone witness any *creativity* in that house."

She spun around again. The bag she was holding in her hands had become a weapon, swinging at the end of her arm like a bludgeon.

"The funny part is," said Barbara, "they invited all these artists and writers and actors. But they're the entertainment. The decoration. No one takes them seriously."

They reached Balsam moments before the end of free hour. Louise and Annabel were waiting to lead them to the commissary for dinner.

So grateful was Tracy not to have been caught that it took her several hours to remember something. After lights-out, she lay in her bunk, growing more and more curious, until finally she couldn't stop herself. She leaned her head over the side of the bunk.

"Barbara," Tracy whispered. "What did you bring back in that bag?"

There came a little pause.

And then: "What bag?" whispered Barbara, in the dark.

Louise

1950s • 1961 • Winter 1973 • June 1975
July 1975 • August 1975: **Day Three**

Louise, freshly bailed out of jail, once again finds herself in a car with Denny Hayes—in the front seat, this time. Though she has tried to persuade Hayes otherwise, he's driving in the direction of her mother's house.

One of the conditions of her pretrial release is that she will remain at one known address, and adhere to a six o'clock curfew. The only address Louise could provide upon being taken into custody was her mother's.

Now, they ride in silence toward that house.

Abruptly, Louise says, "Do you know who bailed me out?"

Denny looks surprised. "Don't you?"

"No. All I heard was a lady did it. That's what the trooper told me."

"Your mom?" Denny asks.

"I guess so." She doesn't want to let herself be hopeful. She's barely seen her mother outside the house for several years. She's never known her mother to have more than five dollars in her billfold at one time.

"You've changed a lot since you were a kid," says Denny.

She tenses. To her, it feels like the opening of a come-on. Alone in a car with any man, she feels a threat in her body.

But he continues, reassuring her. "You were such a happy little thing. Always had the sunniest smile on your face when I came around."

They're approaching the crest of a hill that's familiar to Louise from all of her trips home. The small center of Shattuck comes into sight, briefly, and then disappears once more.

"You remember when I took the two of you to Storytown?"

Louise is startled.

"You must have been six years old," he says. "Thereabouts. I picked you and your mother up and we drove down to Lake George together. Your mother was quiet. But you were so happy. You were jumping up and down. Bought you an ice cream and it fell off its cone. Bought you another one straightaway. Couldn't stand the look on your face."

Sharp tears come to Louise's eyes and she wills them to be gone. Why, she wonders, is she crying? And the answer comes to her: it's the idea that anyone in the world ever took care of her, Louise, rather than the other way around.

She does remember that day, though she didn't know it was Denny Hayes. In her memory it was just another one of her mother's boyfriends, someone whose name she avoided using because she didn't want to mix it up with anyone else's. Of all the men who ever came around to see her mother, that one was the only one who ever did anything nice for her without demanding a favor in return.

Out front of her mother's place, Louise regards the house alongside Denny Hayes. Two of its shutters are missing altogether; another one is hanging at an angle. So much mail has piled up in the mailbox that a stack of waterlogged envelopes now sits on the ground beneath it, the postman having given up.

She'll have a talk with Jesse about taking responsibility for that. At least he should be bringing in the mail.

"Looks just the same," says Denny charitably.

"Thanks for the ride," Louise says, and gets out of the car. She hopes he'll leave. But he, too, exits, stands, adjusts his shirt and pants.

Louise rattles her key loudly in the lock, letting anyone inside know she's about to enter.

She hopes Jesse isn't smoking anything upstairs; her first sniff of the kitchen tells her he isn't.

"Mom?" she calls out. "Mom, I've got some company here."

A pause.

"Who is it?" Her mother's voice is creaky with disuse.

"Denny Hayes," calls Louise.

She waits. She can very easily imagine her mother saying—*Who?* It's been years, and the years have been hard.

"Just a minute," her mother calls, instead. And Louise hears her ascending the staircase, slowly.

"Is Jesse home?" Louise calls, but there's no answer.

When her mother comes down again, she's fully dressed. She's wearing makeup for the first time in years.

Shameless, Louise thinks, but secretly she is reassured to find her mother still capable of making this effort.

Denny's face changes upon seeing her. Softens. "Well, hi, Carol," he says to her. "Been a long time, hasn't it?"

The sound of her mother's Christian name awakens something hurt inside Louise. She hasn't heard the word said aloud much in recent years.

Louise's mother looks back and forth from Louise to Denny.

"You a cop now, Denny?"

"I was a cop back when I knew you," says Denny. "Don't you remember? A state trooper."

She thinks.

"I guess I do remember that."

"I'm a senior investigator now," says Denny. "I got promoted, and then promoted again."

"Well, congratulations," says Louise's mother.

Then, realizing something: "What's my daughter done?"

Louise tenses.

"I thought—" says Louise. But she stops herself. She blinks rapidly, willing unexpected tears back into her skull. After all these years, she thinks; how could she have let herself hope that her mother would come through with bail?

"Denny?" says her mother.

Denny glances at her. "Well," he says, "I guess I'll let Louise tell you about that. Being that she's over eighteen."

Her mother is still, sharp-eyed. She looks more sober than Louise has seen her lately; whether this is intentional or a coincidence of timing, Louise isn't certain.

"Carol," says Denny, "would you mind if I had a few words with Louise? In private?"

"I guess that'd be all right."

Her mother retreats to the other room.

Alone together, Louise and Denny face off.

"Louise," says Denny. "I gotta ask you two things before I go."

She waits.

"You know I'm an old friend," he says. "And I hope you can trust me to do the right thing. I don't think you're guilty of anything to do with Barbara Van Laar. And I want to help you get out of the mess you're in. Do you believe me?"

She keeps her head still. She does and does not trust this man.

Unbothered, Denny proceeds. "First question. Where did John Paul McLellan tell you he was staying this summer?"

"All over the place," says Louise. "He was visiting friends. He wanted to spend the year traveling before going to law school."

Denny nods. "What if I told you, instead, that for a large part of this summer he was most likely staying right at the top of Hunt Mountain?"

It takes Louise a moment to process the information.

"I'd believe anything about him now," she says.

Denny nods. Sympathetic.

"What's your other question?" Louise asks.

"How well did you know Lee Towson?"

Louise flushes. The name alone brings desire into her body.

"Not well," she says.

"Were you, y'know. Together?"

"No."

"You have any idea where he might have gone?"

"No," she says. In fact, she's been wondering this too.

"You're sure."

"Why?"

"Well," says Denny. "Normally I'd keep this to myself. But because you're an old friend, I'll tell you."

Louise waits.

"Apparently," he says, "Barbara was sneaking out of the cabin every night to meet someone she called a boyfriend. You know anything about that?"

She shakes her head. Truthfully, she doesn't.

"There's more," says Denny. "Did you know that Lee Towson was incarcerated once?"

She'd heard a rumor about that. It's one of the many things that have been said about Lee at Camp Emerson; it only added to his allure. Hesitantly, she nods.

"You know what it was for?"

"Dealing grass?" she says.

"Statutory rape," says Denny Hayes.

She freezes. She doesn't know what *statutory* means.

As if reading her mind, or expression, Denny continues: "Intercourse with a girl sixteen years of age or younger."

Louise says nothing.

"So you're sure you don't know where he is?"

"I'm sure," says Louise.

"Well, if you think of anything else. Here's my card."

She takes it into her hands.

"Guess I'd better head out," he says. She pictures him going home to his family, his wife and children. She feels suddenly jealous. If she had had a father like Denny Hayes—or a mother, hell—she might have made something more of herself.

"Anything else you want to ask me or tell me?" says Denny.

"Yeah," says Louise. "If you find out who it was that bailed me out. Will you let me know?"

"I will," says Denny Hayes.

Tracy

1950s • 1961 • Winter 1973 • June 1975
July 1975 • **August 1975**

The evening of the final dance, the girls of Balsam got ready together in an elaborate ritual that served as the culmination of all the grooming skills they'd taught one another over the course of the months they'd been combined. Buckets of water were brought out to the porch; legs were shaved. Outfits were selected from among the several each camper had brought for occasions like this one. Finally, makeup was applied, with precision, by the undisputed master: Barbara Van Laar herself.

Louise and Annabel, who'd been getting ready in their small separate room, emerged and gasped loudly when they saw their charges. How grown-up they all looked; how different from the start of the summer.

Tracy understood. They were different, it was true: they'd grown a year in two months. They'd formed an alliance.

In the Great Hall, Tracy danced with everyone in Balsam, and everyone who'd been on her Survival Trip, and most of all with Barbara. Mitchell, the swim instructor, had brought in three friends from Schenectady, and together they served as a mediocre band. Lowell Cargill was someplace in the room, she knew, but it wasn't until Mitchell and his friends played "I Honestly Love You" that the frenzy in the community room slowed and then stopped, and Tracy became aware, suddenly, that the people around her were pairing off. Even Barbara, who had so far been her constant companion, had been asked to dance by someone else: a boy named Crandall who was widely considered to be, aside from Lowell, the most sought-after male camper at Camp Emerson.

Suddenly alone in the middle of the dance floor, Tracy panicked. And then, quickly, she ran to the periphery and stood by the food table.

She didn't actually see Lowell anyplace. Perhaps he had gone outside for fresh air.

"I hate slow songs," someone next to her said.

She turned her head.

There next to her was someone she recognized as a kitchen worker, a good-looking twentysomething man she'd seen walking, from time to time, with her counselor Louise. Lee, his name was.

"Me too," said Tracy.

"They're so embarrassing," said Lee. "One minute you're out there having fun with your friends, and then the band decides to make things difficult for everyone by slowing it down. It's sadistic, actually."

Tracy wasn't certain she knew what *sadistic* meant, but she nodded anyway.

"I gotta get back to the kitchen," said Lee. "You look great, by the way. Cool dress."

"Thank you," said Tracy. And then he was gone.

It was only after he left that she saw Lowell, across the room, wearing the type of absurd broad-collared polyester suit that the boys brought for dances and that still, despite everything, made her heart speed up.

He stood still as a statue against the opposite wall. He was looking at a couple in the center of the room: Barbara Van Laar and her partner. And on his face was an expression of pain.

Outside. That's where she wanted to go. Out to the fresh pine and the soil and the smell of the lake. Out to the light of the moon on water.

When no one was looking, she seized her moment, and left.

She walked into the dark. There were surprisingly few lights across the grounds of Camp Emerson at night.

Suddenly, in the dim night, there was movement. Someone walking across her path—someone she recognized. Annabel, their CIT, dressed in her clothes for the dance, was heading north.

There was nothing up there, thought Tracy, except the main house. Barbara's house. Annabel's parents were staying there this week, Tracy knew; maybe that's why she was heading in that direction.

Tracy for a moment considered calling out—Annabel was supposed to escort them back to Balsam at the end of the dance—but the determination in her stride gave Tracy pause. Better not to say anything.

And then her own name was called, interrupting her thoughts.

She turned. Walked in the direction of the voice that was repeating her name.

On the beach, in the moonlight, she saw Lowell's best friend. Walter. He was sitting on the sand, looking dejected.

She sat down next to him, lowering herself toward the earth. Until that summer, she had never felt at home in the house of her body. Never felt graceful, like Barbara, like the Melissas, like Lowell Cargill.

"You too?" said little Walter. His arms were around his knees; his chin was on his arms.

"Me too what?" said Tracy.

"Sad?" says Walter.

"Oh," said Tracy. "No, not really. I'm fine."

Walter was silent.

"Are you?" said Tracy.

He nodded. She could barely make it out. But she knew, without asking, why he was.

"You know," said Walter, "he asked Barbara to the dance. But she said no."

Tracy sat very still, letting his words settle over her. She had known ever since the Survival Trip that Lowell wasn't interested in her, whatever she might have thought before. It was Barbara whom he loved. Still, hearing it knocked the breath out of her all over again.

"He was torn up about it," Walter continued. "When she said no, I mean. People like Lowell aren't used to being rejected."

He wasn't trying to be cruel; Tracy was certain of this. Most likely, he assumed that Barbara would have told Tracy already. They were, after all, a pair at Camp Emerson. Just like Walter and Lowell were.

The silence between them persisted awhile, until Tracy heard Walter sniff loudly, once. He was crying, she realized.

"He's amazing," said Walter. "Isn't he."

Louise

1950s • 1961 • Winter 1973 • June 1975
July 1975 • **August 1975**

She saw everything. She sat on the edge of the stage that overlooked the community room, watching her campers in all of their triumphs and failures, the ones having genuine fun, the ones pretending to have it.

If she believed in a God, it was in one who functioned something like Louise in this moment: rooting for her charges from afar, mourning alongside them when they were rejected, celebrating every small victory that came their way. She noticed the lonely ones, the ones at the edge of the crowd; she felt in her heart a sort of wild affection for them, wanted to go to them, to stand next to them and pull them tightly to her side; and yet she also knew that to intervene in this way would disrupt something sacred that—at twelve and thirteen and fourteen years old—they were learning about themselves and the world. And this, too, was how she thought of God.

At a certain point she began to play a game in her mind, counting each one of her charges, picking a name and scanning the crowd until she found the person in question. With every name she chose she was successful, until she got to Annabel.

She couldn't find her counselor-in-training anyplace in the room.

In retrospect, this would make a different kind of sense to her; just then she chalked it up to her suspicion, that session, that Annabel had met a boy.

Earlier, she had noticed that Annabel was getting ready with particular care. In theory, the dance was for the campers, but in prior years Louise had often seen counselors and CITs pairing off there, too. Going out into the dark woods for a few minutes, or an hour. Coming back flushed.

This, she suspected, was where Annabel Southworth had gone. And from her place on the stage she smiled, happy that Annabel, too, had found love, or at least infatuation, at Camp Emerson.

Judyta

1950s • 1961 • Winter 1973 • June 1975
July 1975 • August 1975: **Day Three**

"Who's *everyone*?" asks Denny Hayes.

It's noon already, and this is the first time she's seeing him. He's half in and half out of his car when she launches into her updates, the new theories she's formed since this morning.

"The whole town," says Judy, now. "Every person in Shattuck thinks the wrong man was blamed when Bear disappeared. And that the Van Laars were too quick to accept it."

Hayes tilts his head in the direction of the Command Post in the Director's Cabin.

"Come on," he says. "I need coffee."

Together, they walk. He glances at her.

"Judy, were you wearing the same outfit yesterday?"

She flushes. "Don't remember," she says.

It's still raining, on and off, and her hair and clothing have gotten soaked and partially dried several times over. She must look like a drowned rat, she thinks.

"Judy," says Hayes. "Where exactly did you hear this about Bear Van Laar?"

She tells him what happened last night, and early this morning.

He raises an eyebrow. They've reached the Director's Cabin now, and he holds the door open for her. Judy goes inside first. Reflects for a moment on the time-capsule decorations, the World War II–era kitchen appliances, all of which clearly predate the director herself. Judy has seen her only a few times, wandering about the grounds. Each time, she's looked beside herself with anguish. More distraught, thinks Judy, than the Van Laar parents themselves.

Hayes pours himself a mug of coffee. Holds one out to her, as well.

She takes it. She's never been much of a coffee drinker—it's something she associates with older people, with her own father—but since being on the Van Laar Preserve, she's begun appreciating its bitterness and warmth, which now cuts through the wetness of her hair and clothing.

She sips. Grimaces. Sips again.

"So who does the town of Shattuck think is to blame?" says Hayes. "If Carl Stoddard was innocent."

"Well, according to Mr. Alcott, there are two prevailing theories."

"I'm all ears."

"The first," says Judy, "is that Jacob Sluiter did it."

He looks at her. "Weren't you the one asking me about Sluiter yesterday?"

"Well, yes," says Judy. "But—it makes sense, doesn't it?"

"Good old Slitter," Hayes says. "The bogeyman of the North Woods. I've heard him blamed for every death—accidental or intentional—from here to Rochester."

He leans against the counter.

"It's not crazy," Judy says. "Think about it. The majority of Sluiter's killings took place not far from here. And all of them in the early sixties, right when Bear disappeared, and right before Sluiter was caught."

"True."

"And now," she says, "he's escaped, right at the same time that Barbara Van Laar goes missing. Am I saying something wrong?"

She stops, annoyed. Hayes is laughing.

"You've got the bug," he says.

"What bug?"

"It's a good thing," he says. "We've all got the bug. Go on."

"The second theory is more popular in the town," says Judy. "And it's one you won't like to hear."

"Why not?"

"Well, it's more—controversial, I guess," she says. "It'll make more waves."

"Go on."

She sips from her coffee, steadying her nerves.

"Mr. Alcott says that the majority of people in Shattuck—the ones who don't think Sluiter did it, anyway—think that Bear's grandfather is to blame."

She expects him to scoff. Instead, he turns and looks out the window, his hands on the counter next to the sink. He's quiet for long enough that she gets worried.

"Are you all right?" she says.

"I remember that theory," says Hayes. "I remember it being spoken of, when the boy went missing."

Judy stares at him. Why hadn't he mentioned this before? She had—*interviewed* the man, her first day here. According to Hayes, he was a minor player. Someone above suspicion. Frantically, she searches her memory for anything he said that sounded suspicious, but all she can remember is his demeanor: Dismissive. Impatient. Unkind.

"What happened?" Judy asks. "Was he interviewed back then? Did anyone in the BCI think he did it, too?"

"According to the records I've been going through," says Hayes, "some did. But no one pursued it."

"Why didn't they?"

Hayes pauses. "Well," he says. "Couple reasons. Carl Stoddard seemed pretty suspicious to everyone, according to some of the guys here who've been around long enough to remember. He was the last person to see Bear. There was some carving that was found—a whittled bear—that Bear had apparently been carrying just before he disappeared. That was the only trace of the boy that was ever located. Turned out Stoddard had been the one teaching him to whittle. Everyone thought he had a kind of obsession with Bear."

Judy waits.

"Second," he says, "the Van Laars' attorney liked him for the crime. And he was aggressive from the start."

Now it's Hayes's turn to wait for Judy to catch up.

"McLellan," says Judy.

He nods.

"Senior," says Judy.

Hayes nods again.

Judy thinks. "Can I take this lead?" she says.

"Bear's grandfather?" says Hayes, and Judy nods. She can talk to people like him, she thinks. She knows how.

"All right, as long as you don't scare him off," says Denny Hayes. "He's right up there at the main house, as far as I know."

*   *   *

Before she can set off, there's a knock on the front door of the Director's Cabin, and Investigator Goldman comes in, panting, shirt untucked.

He looks from Judy, to Hayes, to Judy again.

"Either of you any good with kids?" he asks—doing his best to phrase the question neutrally—but his implication is clear. Judy, as a woman, will take this one.

Judyta

1950s • 1961 • Winter 1973 • June 1975
July 1975 • August 1975: **Day Three**

Outside the Director's Cabin, a tiny boy is waiting with his parents. "Mr. and Mrs. Muldauer," says Hayes. "This is Investigator Luptack. She'll be speaking with Christopher, if that's all right.

Mrs. Muldauer—brown-haired, bespectacled, nearly as tiny as her son—looks nervous. "May we come along?"

"Of course," Judy says. "Come on in."

Hayes stands outside the Director's Cabin, serving as a guard while Judy works.

Inside, Judy pulls forward a downtrodden sofa that's been shoved against a wall; she offers this to the family, and pulls up a hard folding chair to face them. As he sits between his parents, Christopher's legs stick straight out into space.

Judy takes out her notepad and pen.

"What brings you here today, Christopher?" she says.

He's silent. He looks down at his knees.

"Go ahead," says his father.

Nothing.

"How old are you, Christopher?" Judy tries.

Nothing.

"Twelve? Thirteen?" she says. She smiles a little. Joking.

"I'm eight," he says, in a voice so low she can barely hear it. "I'm the youngest camper at Camp Emerson."

"Did you like camp?" Judy asks.

"No, I hated it," he says. Above his head, his parents glance at one another.

"Chris," his father says, refocusing him. "Can you tell the lady what you told us? She has other things to do."

"That's all right, Mr. Muldauer," says Judy. "Christopher can take his time."

And he does. Thirty seconds pass. A minute.

"Is there a reason you don't want to tell me what you told your parents?" asks Judy.

"I don't want to get them in trouble," he says.

"Your parents?"

"My friends."

There is pride in his voice as he says it. This is a boy, Judy understands, who doesn't have many of those.

"Who are your friends, Christopher?"

"Barbara and Tracy," he says, so quietly she isn't certain she heard him right.

"Barbara and Tracy?"

He nods.

"Christopher," says Judy. "The most important thing right now is finding Barbara and bringing her home. If she did something bad, we can address that some other time. But anything you can tell us will help us to keep Barbara safe."

A pause.

"We all went into the woods together," says Christopher.

"When?"

"For Survival Trip."

He explains it to her. Lists all the people in his group. Explains how their campsite was laid out.

"We were there three nights," says Christopher. "And I have this problem that keeps me awake. So two of the nights I saw Barbara go out of the tent she was sharing with Tracy, and it looked to me like she was walking into the woods. But then a weird thing happened."

"What was it?"

"Well, she turned around," says Christopher. "I watched her. Her flashlight would go off and it was like she'd wait awhile, out in the dark. And then a while later, her flashlight would go back on, and she'd walk back in our direction. The first night I thought she'd just gone to pee or something. But she walked past our campsite, all the way past it."

"Where was she going?"

"Into T.J. Hewitt's tent," says Christopher.

"T.J.? The camp director?"

He nods.

That same low thrumming begins in her abdomen. The feeling she got when she was talking to Mrs. Clute. *The bug*, Denny Hayes calls it.

"And how long did she stay there for?"

"I don't know," said Christopher. "I always fell asleep before she came out. In the morning, she'd be back at our campsite."

"Thank you, Christopher," says Judy. "This is really helpful. Is there anything else you'd like to tell me?"

"She got hurt on that trip," says Christopher.

"Barbara?"

He nods. "She was skinning a squirrel. She had an accident with the knife. She hurt herself bad. T.J. was the one who fixed her."

"Anything else?"

"It kept happening," says Christopher. "Even after we got back. I saw Barbara going to T.J.'s cabin every night."

This he says quietly, with a certain resignation. At eight, he already understands the implication of what he's saying—or at least that it isn't right. For a child to go to the abode of an adult, late at night, in secret.

He looks as if he might cry.

"You've done a really brave thing, Christopher," says Judy. "You're a brave person. Thank you. I only have one more question for you."

"Okay."

"What's the problem you have?"

He looks at her. Doesn't understand.

"The problem you have, that keeps you awake?"

"Oh," he says. His face turns a deep red. "Oh. I wet the bed." He's practically whispering now. The father puts his hand on his son's shoulder.

"It happens," says Judy. "You know, I wet the bed when I was a kid too."

"You did?"

She didn't. "I did."

"If I can stay awake long enough," says Christopher, "I can go to the bathroom one last time, after everyone else is asleep. Usually that helps."

"I bet it makes you tired, though," says Judy, and Christopher nods, with dignity.

Just before the Muldauers leave to go home, Mrs. Muldauer pulls Judy aside. She speaks in a whisper.

"We heard from a friend that this camp was the best around. And heaven knows the people who attend have good taste. But," she says—inclining her head toward Judy's, seeking out her eyes—"if I had *seen* the camp director in advance, I might have had second thoughts."

Judy keeps her face very still.

"Especially if I had a daughter. Do you understand what I mean?"

Judyta

1950s • 1961 • Winter 1973 • June 1975
July 1975 • August 1975: **Day Three**

I'll work the lead on the grandfather," says Hayes. "You go talk to T.J." To his credit, he can tell that momentum is on Judy's side.

"We need good notes," Hayes reminds her, before walking away.

Judy nods, and then she walks toward the Staff Quarters, to which T.J. Hewitt has been relocated, ever since her house became the Command Post for the BCI.

T.J. Hewitt, her short hair disheveled, swipes at her face, as if she's just woken up from sleep. She wears a white undershirt and cutoff blue jean shorts. She's barefoot.

"Sorry," says T.J. "I'm out of it. I haven't been sleeping much." She stretches.

Then, perhaps noticing Judy's expression, she goes still. Sits up straighter.

"How can I help you, Investigator Luptack?" asks T.J.

Judy thought about her opening question on her walk over. Something open-ended, she decided; something neutral.

And so she begins: "Miss Hewitt—"

"T.J."

"Excuse me. T.J. Can you tell me about your relationship to Barbara Van Laar?"

T.J. shifts. "Pretty sure I told Investigator Hayes all about it already," she says.

"Well, would you mind telling me?" says Judy. "I'm trying to catch up."

T.J. clears her throat. "I've known Barbara since she was born."

"How old were you at that time?"

"Fourteen."

Her voice is quiet. She looks just to the left of Judy's head as she speaks, so intently that Judy turns her head briefly to see if something, or someone, is behind her. But the only thing she sees is the unfinished wood of the wall.

"And did you spend much time with her prior to her arrival at Camp Emerson?"

"I did."

"Can you describe the time you spent with her?"

T.J. looks down. "At first I was her—babysitter, I guess you'd call it. From the time she was born."

"Here?"

"Here on the grounds, yes," says T.J. "All summer long. Every summer. It's what I was paid to do."

"So you've been here your whole life?"

T.J. nods. "It's my home."

"What brought you to the Preserve to begin with?"

"My father was groundskeeper and camp director," says T.J. "I took over both jobs when he began to lose his memory."

Judy notes this.

"What about when the Van Laars were in Albany?" she asks.

"Well, I was in school for Barbara's earliest years," says T.J. "So I stayed here. But I never went to college or anything. So I was pretty free starting at seventeen, when Barbara was three. I'd travel with the family. Go down to Albany when the parents had to go out of town."

"And you were close with Barbara."

T.J. nods.

"We are. Yes."

"Was Barbara a difficult child when she was young?"

T.J. laughs a little. There is a sort of ruefulness on her face, in her voice, that Judy suddenly finds unsettling.

"God, no," says T.J. "She was the best kid. She and her brother both. Just nice, nice kids."

Judy pauses.

"So you were close with her brother, too?"

"Yup. We were closer in age. I was twelve when he," says T.J., and then stops. "When he disappeared. He was eight."

It's warm outside, but Judy suddenly feels cold.

"How would you describe the Van Laar children's relationship with their parents?" asks Judy.

"Depends which kid you're talking about. And which parent," she adds.

"Let's start with Bear."

"Well, his mother loved him," says T.J. "Loved him more than anything. Never been the same since he left."

"And his father?"

"His father," says T.J. "Now his father, that's a hard one."

She seems genuinely to be thinking of how to phrase something.

"You know, his father loved him too, in his way," says T.J. "But it was like Mr. Van Laar thought of him as one of his bonds. Something only worth having around because of what it'll become later. If that makes sense."

Judy makes another note.

"What are you writing?" T.J. asks. "Are you writing about me?"

"Well, I'm writing down what you're saying."

"Who's gonna see that?"

Judy hesitates. "For now, just me," she says. "And possibly my colleagues in the BCI. But eventually, it's possible that it could be used as some kind of evidence. And that would be a public record."

T.J. nods. For a moment, Judy wonders if she's going to clam up, stop talking.

She puts the pen down. Instantly, T.J. looks comforted.

"What about Barbara's relationship with her parents?" says Judy.

T.J. thinks for a long time.

"I don't know if *nonexistent* is the right word," she says, at last. "But it's close."

Judy pauses. Stalling for time.

"Is that the reason she got close to you?" Judy asks quietly.

She knows better than to show her whole hand, at this point. She wants to see what T.J. will say on her own.

"Maybe," says T.J.

"How close would you say you were?"

"Well, that's difficult to describe."

"Let's start here," says Judy. "I know she came to camp this summer. Was that her idea, or yours?"

"Hers," says T.J. "All hers. She wanted to get out of the house. Didn't want to go to the big party they were planning."

"Why do you think that was?"

T.J. takes a deep breath. "You know how much money the Van Laars have, right?"

"I have some idea of that. Yes."

"You know they sent their daughter off to boarding school last year with two outfits and no winter coat? You know they give her no spending money?"

"Why do you think that is?"

"Either they don't remember," says T.J., "or they don't care. I'm the one who comes around. I bring her extra food for the weekend, bring her books and records she likes. I drive down there anytime I can. I take care of her. No one else does."

"While she was at camp," Judy says, "how many times did you see her?"

"Well, every day," says T.J. "I saw all the campers every day. I'm always around, you know. Always fixing something, planning something, whatever it is."

"And at night?"

T.J.'s gaze goes back to the wall to the left of Judy's head.

For some time, there's quiet in the cabin.

"Investigator Luptack," says T.J. "I think I know what you're implying."

T.J. scoots to the edge of the bed, puts her hands on her knees. Leans forward, looking directly at Judy now.

"I know what people say about me down in the town. Maybe they've even said it to you during your investigation."

Judy keeps her face blank.

"I'm not sure what you mean."

"I dress a certain way, is what I mean. I talk and walk a certain way."

"All right."

"Barbara is like a little sister to me," says T.J. "Prob'ly the closest thing I'll ever have to a kid of my own, if you want to know the truth. I love her. But not in the way you're implying."

Judy lets T.J.'s words sit in the air as long as she can.

Then she says, quietly, directly: "We have an eyewitness willing to testify that they saw Barbara going into your cabin in the middle of the night. Every night."

It's the first time, as an investigator, that she has ever challenged someone she was interviewing.

It's also the first time she's ever bluffed; she has no idea whether Christopher will go on the stand. Whether his parents will let him.

For a moment, T.J. turns red; her whole face flushes, and then her neck, and then the top of her chest.

And then she stands. She walks across the room, kneels down next to her brown boots, begins lacing them.

"T.J.," says Judy.

"I'm not dumb," says T.J. "I know what it means when someone's got a theory they're working, no matter how wrong they are. And I also know I have no legal obligation to stay here and talk to you. So come back to me when you've got a warrant for my arrest."

She stands up and walks out of the room.

Judy, increasingly desperate, stands too, and calls after her down the empty hallway.

"What's your theory?" asks Judy. "Do you have a theory about where Barbara went?"

T.J. stops. Puts her hands on her hips. Turns, reluctantly.

"Can I tell you something?" she says. "Woman to woman? Something you'll keep out of that notebook?"

Judy lowers it to her side.

"John Paul McLellan is your man," says T.J. "I can't tell you how I know that. But I do."

Jacob

1950s • 1961 • Winter 1973 • June 1975
July 1975 • August 1975: **Day Three**

Overnight, he'd retraced his steps along the river, walking downstream this time. Toward dawn, it had begun to rain.

Normally he slept outdoors in daytime, but today he wanted the comfort of a home, a bed, a meal under a roof. And so at some point he found a promising house, apparently empty, and went into it.

He'd gone to the pantry first. Found it disappointingly empty, but for a large container of Quaker Oats that he cooked into a porridge on the electric stove.

Next he went into all of the bedroom closets. This, in his experience, was where people tended to keep their arms and ammunition, tucked on high shelves in bedroom closets, out of reach of children. And there they were: two double-barrel shotguns, three boxes of shells.

Too bad, thought Jacob. He would have preferred a pistol; the shotgun would be hard to carry. But it came with an ammo sling, which he loaded with the shells. Loaded a gun up, too.

It's four in the afternoon, now, and he's slept all day. He rises from the bed, loaded shotgun in his hands. And suddenly he hears the creak of a floorboard.

He stills.

As quietly as he can, he moves to the far side of the bed and gets down behind it. From there, he points the shotgun at the bedroom door.

He's familiar with this position. It reminds him of hunting as a child.

The door swings open. Unswervingly, he fires—but no one has been hit. No one, apparently, ever intended to walk through the threshold of the bedroom.

Was it a trap? Jacob can't be sure.

And then, from behind him, a voice says, "Don't move."

He freezes.

Through the open window by his head, a police weapon is pointing in his direction.

Judyta

1950s • 1961 • Winter 1973 • June 1975
July 1975 • August 1975: Day Three

S he walks up the hill, her head filled with new information from
T.J. to pass on to Denny Hayes.

Good notes, she thinks, were all he asked for—and she has none.

So she goes around to the lake side of the house, ready to find
herself an Adirondack chair, to sit down and write everything T.J. said
before it leaves her mind.

She is disappointed, when she arrives, to find that one chair is already
occupied.

From behind, the woman in it looks unfamiliar. But she turns, and
Judy recognizes her suddenly: it's Mrs. Van Laar Sr. Barbara's grand-
mother. The wife of the man who had spoken to her so dismissively
during her first hour on this job—the man who has, as of this morning,
become one of their top suspects.

"Sit down," says Mrs. Van Laar. "Don't let me stop you."

Judy complies. She bends her head to her notebook, feigning work.
But in her mind, she formulates question after question—anything
that might illuminate some aspect of this woman's husband.

Mrs. Van Laar speaks before she can.

"Beautiful view," says Mrs. Van Laar.

"It is," says Judy.

"This is my favorite place to sit on the whole Preserve. And my
favorite time of day," says Mrs. Van Laar.

Judy nods.

"I imagine the view brings back memories for you," says Judy.

Mrs. Van Laar pauses, as if thinking. Then she says, "Not really."

Judy is still shuffling quickly through ideas for an opening when
Mrs. Van Laar stands from her chair and sets off toward the main
house.

"Mrs. Van Laar," says Judy, unwanted pleading in her voice.

Slowly, the woman turns. Her expression is still pleasant.

"I just—I haven't had a chance to speak with you since our first day here," says Judy. "Is there anything further you've thought of that you'd like to add?"

Mrs. Van Laar opens her mouth. Closes it. Looks back over her shoulder, as if making a decision.

Then she says: "Have you had a chance to interview Vic Hewitt?"

The name stops Judy. *Hewitt* she knows, of course; it's the first name that's unfamiliar.

"Is that—" she says.

"Tessie Jo's father," says Mrs. Van Laar. "The first director of the camp."

Judy frowns. *Tessie Jo.* She scans the notes she just took, searching for what T.J. had said about her father during their interview.

Memory loss, she wrote.

"I didn't realize he was," says Judy.

"Still alive, yes," says Mrs. Van Laar, reading her mind. "Perhaps you should interview him. He's such an interesting man. And he'd like the company, no doubt."

"Where can I find him?" asks Judy.

"These days he lives in the Director's Cabin with his daughter," says Mrs. Van Laar. "She cares for him."

Judy shakes her head. "We've taken that over, ma'am," she says. "It's our Command Post now."

Mrs. Van Laar looks directly at Judy. "Well, dear," she says, "I suppose you'll just have to investigate. Isn't that what you do?"

She turns and disappears inside the dark, cool house.

VII

Self-Reliance

Alice

1950s • **1961** • Winter 1973 • June 1975
July 1975 • August 1975

Alice, still looking for Bear, took a breath before turning the doorknob to her husband's room.

It wouldn't have been so bad if it had been anybody else.

If it had been one of the girls on the grounds that week—an actress or a singer or a model. Somebody young and frivolous, somebody difficult to take seriously.

Or, thought Alice, one of the staff: if it had been one of the temporary staff, she would know with certainty that Peter was simply blowing off steam. He'd never pursue anything further with someone in his employ.

But it wasn't an actress or a singer or a member of the staff in Peter's bed.

Inside Peter's bed was her own sister. Delphine.

Someone she believed Peter reviled. A woman he considered *intelligent*—which was, according to Peter's stated system of beliefs, a waste.

She'd been wrong about all of it.

She could tell, from their position, that their closeness was not new. Connections and inferences began to form in her mind. Delphine's familiarity with the staff—her insolent question to Warren, yesterday, about whether he was prepared to accommodate the guests. As if *she* were the mistress of the house.

Peter's trips to Manhattan—two or three times a month, always on business, he said. Always to meet with the bank attorney, McLellan.

Her mind reeled. How long had Peter and Delphine been doing this? For years? Since Delphine's first visit to Self-Reliance, as Alice's chaperone?

Before that?

Delphine had always, always been afforded more respect than Alice had. Even as Peter complained about her, there was a certain admiration in his voice.

Perhaps it had all been a ruse.

Perhaps they had always known: Peter's mother and father. All of their friends.

Perhaps Peter and Delphine and McLellan and his wife all went to dinner together, in Manhattan. Perhaps it was excused. Perhaps they came here together, to Self-Reliance, in moments when Alice was in Albany—and perhaps this was the reason she knew the staff so well.

Could it be that Peter and his father had chosen Alice not *in spite* of her youth and inexperience—two qualities they often lamented aloud as deficits that Alice had to work to overcome—but because of them? Because she would do whatever they commanded her to do, all of the time. Because she wouldn't be difficult.

Because it would not occur to her that a woman like Delphine was the type of person Peter really wanted.

The two of them were asleep, unclothed. Delphine had her head on Peter's chest. His arm was curled around her shoulders. Her hair fanned out behind her on the bed.

Peter and Alice had never slept like that.

When she was eighteen years old, when she was newly married to a man more than a decade her senior, living away from her childhood home for the first time in her life, pregnant and uncomfortable and frightened: never once had Peter held her so tenderly. Instead, citing insomnia, he had rolled to the opposite side of the bed and lay straight as a pencil while she, Alice, curled onto her side and held a pillow for comfort and missed her friends back in New York City and her sister and her father and even her mother.

Alice stood there watching them a while longer. She thought for a moment of waking them—slamming the door, shouting, making certain that they knew she knew—but then it would change, all of it. Her whole life would change.

Alice personally knew only one couple who had ever gotten divorced: people her parents had been friends with.

These days the man was still in their group, with a much younger wife. The woman had all but disappeared. It was said that she no longer lived in New York; she had moved to Connecticut. From the way she was spoken about, it felt as if she had died.

Alice asked herself: Could she live this way, always pretending? Could she walk out of the room, into the hallway; could she close the door gently, and face Peter and Delphine at dinner, and pretend to have seen nothing, for the rest of her life?

Yes, and yes, and yes, she thought.

As long as she had Bear—the answer would be yes.

She closed the door as gently as she could.

She walked to the sunroom, where she found the tumbler of gin. She poured a tall glass of it and drank it in several swigs. She deserved this, she reasoned. She poured another. Drank from that.

As she drank, she let herself cry.

By the time she finished, she wasn't standing up well.

She had had nothing at all to eat that day.

She walked out of the sunroom, the hallway spinning, the ground coming up to meet her. She walked into the great room, where the rest of the party was gathered—the senior Van Laars, and the McLellans, and the actresses, and the clients. And there, by the fireplace, Tessie Jo and Bear. All of them had been drawn to the great room by boredom; all of them were deciding what to do next.

They stopped when she entered. She swayed slightly; she caught herself with her back foot.

They looked at her, their faces masks of judgment.

None of them mattered to her. She spoke only to Bear.

"Come here," she said, trying to smile, holding both hands in his direction.

An uncomfortable silence.

"Where are you going, Alice?" asked Peter's father. He furrowed his brow.

"Bear's been asking to go out in the rowboat," she told him. Her father-in-law frowned, as if he hadn't understood her. Surely, she thought, she hadn't been slurring that badly.

She tried again.

This time, Bear stood up, unsteadily; his grandfather gestured for him to sit back down.

"I'm afraid Bear and I already have plans," he said. "We're about to set out on a walk." He turned to his grandson. "Bear," he said. "Are your boots on?"

Bear, tense, looked back and forth between his grandfather and his mother. Alice loved this about him: loved the care with which he handled others. The concern he had for their well-being. He thought frequently of how to make people happier; he picked her flowers from the garden. Drew love notes for her in school.

A generous impulse in Alice told her to free her son from his predicament. "It's all right, Bear," she said. "We'll go boating another time." Too late, she realized that her voice had cracked with emotion as she spoke. She turned on her heel and tottered out of the great room, then walked down the hallway and through the southern door.

Outside, the sky was darkening. A few drops of rain pattered onto her face, rousing her briefly from her stupor. Giving her permission to cry outright.

She'd go out in a boat by herself, she thought. She'd escape from the party, from her sister and husband. She pictured it: she'd row out into the middle of the lake, and lie in the belly of the boat, and simply float like that awhile, letting herself be rocked by the water in perfect solitude until she had gathered herself.

Then she'd return to the party.

Fifty feet before the boathouse, she tripped badly, falling to her knees, skinning the palms of her hands. She stood. Brushed them off. Continued.

She opened the door.

The boathouse was shadowy, darker even than it normally was. Spectral watercraft stood on stands in three neat rows. She moved to the aluminum rowboat. She'd never before tried to lower it from its stand on her own, but she thought she could do it.

Several tugs. A clatter. One oar skittered over the ground.

She dragged it, with effort, to the ramp that led down to the lake. She was sweating, despite the cold wind that was blowing up from the water. Her movements were clumsy, disjointed.

From behind her, suddenly, the sound of the boathouse door.

Alice

1950s • **1961** • Winter 1973 • June 1975
July 1975 • August 1975

She didn't know where she was. She opened her eyes. Her mouth
was so dry that she couldn't swallow. Above her, the room rotated
slowly, the overhead light making slow arcs in the air.

She had the sensation of being unable to form words. Even her
thoughts were wordless. *Water*, she thought—but it was an image, not
a noun. She looked around the room for a sink, turning her whole
torso in one direction and then another. Her neck was stiff, as if she
had not moved her head for days.

There were windows in this room, but they were darkened by closed
shutters with tight slats and exterior latches. She couldn't tell if it was
day or night outside.

The bed she was on was so firm that it felt like a plank of wood.

She stood up from it unsteadily. She was wearing a dress, she saw.
Its material was stiff, as if soaked and then hung out to dry.

Toilet, she thought. The image of one. The urge to urinate was
suddenly so powerful that she doubled over.

Where was she? She had the sensation that the answer would come
to her shortly, and with it some terrible knowledge that perhaps she
did not want. Slowly, she straightened again.

There was no toilet. Only a few meager trappings that indicated
she was in someone's bedroom, long disused. A sturdy dresser. A bowl
for water. A mirror: this she avoided completely.

She saw a door. She moved to it, pushed against it: locked. She knew
somehow that it would be.

She lay down on the floor, barring entry to the thought. Something
terrible had happened, she knew. If she went back to sleep, she wouldn't
have to learn it.

She closed her eyes.

The door opened.

Through it came Peter's father.

Judyta

1950s • 1961 • Winter 1973 • June 1975
July 1975 • August 1975: **Day Three**

It's nearing the end of her shift. She has to find Hayes; she can't risk talking to anyone else about what Mrs. Van Laar told her. She can't afford to be wrong in front of LaRochelle again; not after yesterday.

Perhaps you should interview him. He's such an interesting man.

When she reaches the Director's Cabin, two investigators, smoking outside, tell her that Hayes is gone for the day.

"Shit," she says, and the investigators straighten.

"You got a mouth on you," one says.

She doesn't reply.

"Anyway," says the other, "he left this for you." Begrudgingly, he holds out a piece of paper with a phone number on it. *Denny. Home*, the paper says.

"You two got something goin' on?" the first investigator says. His buddy smothers a grin.

Judy ignores them. Pushes into the house.

Alone, she feels better.

There's a long hallway that runs to the back of the house from the main room. At the end of it is a bathroom—practically destroyed, now, by its constant use over the past few days.

But there are other rooms, too. And according to Mrs. Van Laar—one of them is, or has been, Vic Hewitt's.

Judy walks down the hallway, toe to heel, making as little noise as possible.

She tries the first door. Inside is a neatly made bed, a stack of reading material on the nightstand, a magazine called *Camp Life*. She opens the closet door; inside she finds several articles of androgynous clothing and a neat row of fishing hats.

At this point, Judy has no guess as to whether she's in Vic's room or T.J.'s. She walks to a dark wooden dresser and pulls open one of the two small top drawers.

Here, at last, is her answer. The undergarments are distinctly female: high-cut briefs, one brassiere with tags still on it. One pair of woolen stockings that look similarly unworn.

She moves across the hallway. Opens another bedroom door. There is no doubt, this time, as to whose room she's in: a metal cane leans against a wall. A straight row of men's walking shoes is lined up against another. Most curiously, a pair of dentures swims in a tall glass of liquid on a bedside table.

Which raises the question: If Vic Hewitt's dentures are here—then where is Vic Hewitt?

Judy moves toward Vic's dresser. But instead of clothing, she finds what looks like a trove of black and white photographs. Most are of children: T.J. when she was young. Barbara, too. And Bear: so many of them are of Bear Van Laar, in various poses, fishing, swimming, standing sturdy on cross-country skis.

The one that intrigues her most is a group shot. She squints, trying to recognize anyone she can in the photograph. She knows for certain that two are Barbara's grandparents, the elder Mr. and Mrs. Van Laar. They stand in the back row. She smiles; he doesn't.

The youngest boy in the picture, she guesses, is Bear.

The woman looking down at him, lovingly, is his mother, Alice; the man standing to her right is his father.

And standing off to one side, a part of and apart from the rest of the group, are T.J. and her father, Vic.

Judy turns the picture over. On the back is written, in light pencil: *Blackfly Good-by. 1961.*

The year of Bear's disappearance.

Judy shudders. Puts the photos back in the drawer. Walks out into the main room again.

It's time, she knows, to tell someone about the tip Mrs. Van Laar gave her. She fishes a piece of paper out from her pocket, goes to the phone in the Command Post, and dials Denny Hayes's home phone number, as instructed.

A woman answers. His wife, no doubt. In the background, Judy can hear children's voices.

"Hi," says Judy. "Is Investigator Hayes there, please?"

A hitch in the woman's voice. "May I ask who's calling?"

"This is Investigator Luptack," she says. "I'm—I work with him."

"I didn't know he had a lady—coworker," says Mrs. Hayes. "I didn't know they let ladies be investigators."

"Well," says Judy, "they do."

"Anyway, he's not home yet," says Mrs. Hayes. "You can leave me a number if you want."

"Will you tell him I'm staying at the Alcott Family Inn in Shattuck, New York?" says Judy. "I'll be there in twenty minutes or so. He can call the front desk and they'll find me."

A long, skeptical pause.

"Sure," says Mrs. Hayes. "I'll do that."

But Judy can tell, already, that she won't.

It's full dark when she pulls into the inn. It's mid-August, the time of year when high summer becomes late summer. She sits still in her Beetle for a moment, listening to the pings of the cooling engine, then gets out and locks it. Walks to her room. Pulls out her key.

Then, from behind, she hears her own name said aloud.

She knows who it is before turning.

"Daddy," she says. "What are you doing here?"

He strides toward her, looking as angry as she's ever seen him. "What are *you* doing here, Judy?" he asks. "You think this is safe for a single girl? Place like this? Coming home late at night, when it's dark out? I don't think so."

"How'd you find me?" says Judy.

"Your mother was worried sick," says her father. "She couldn't sleep last night. She couldn't eat today. She told me the name of the place."

Judy sighs heavily.

"Don't you blame *her*," says her father. "She's looking out for you. She did the right thing by telling me. Seedy place like this? You're lucky nothing happened to you already."

He walks back to his car. Opens the passenger door.

"Come on," he says. "I'll drive you home. I'll bring you back tomorrow to get your car."

He's not looking at her. He expects her to get in, no questions asked. As a child, Judy and her siblings had obeyed him religiously. He never hit them—but he was a big man, and he yelled.

For a moment, Judy imagines going to him. Getting in. Keeping the peace with her family. Doing what's expected.

Instead, she says, "It's not seedy."

"What isn't?"

"This hotel."

"Motel."

"This motel. It's run by a very nice family. The Alcotts. The husband is a history teacher. The wife reads books."

Her father is looking at her.

"I'm going to stay here tonight," says Judy. "Because I have to be at work very early in the morning. And I'm tired."

"Judy," says her father. "Get in the car."

"I'm going to keep staying here as long as I work this case," says Judy. "After that, I'm going to find an apartment closer to BCI headquarters in Ray Brook. I can afford it, because I got a raise."

"Judy."

"When I was promoted," she adds, for emphasis.

Slowly, her father closes the passenger door. For an instant, she feels almost bad for him. She pictures him on the drive home, alone, his face a mask of sadness and anger. This will be the first time in her life that she's gone directly against his wishes.

"Your mother's been crying," says her father. "Because of you, she's been crying."

"I'm twenty-six years old," says Judy. "I'm a woman now, Dad. I can take care of myself."

He says nothing. He gets into his car—his ancient car, a Fairlane Skyliner from the late 1950s that Judy still remembers him buying and proudly bringing home—and pulls backward into the night, one thick arm thrown over the passenger's seat, where her mother would normally be.

Then Judy is alone.

Judyta

1950s • 1961 • Winter 1973 • June 1975
July 1975 • August 1975: **Day Four**

In her room at the Alcott Family Inn, Judy turns the boxy television on as she gets ready. The anchor is telling her about the weather: sunnier today, cool for August. She likes this new routine: waking up alone, at a reasonable hour, with no brother shouting at her from the other room.

She turns on the shower as hot as she can take it. Stands in it for far longer than her mother would allow.

At last, reluctantly, she steps out. Turns off the water in time to hear the news anchor say, in the other room: *in custody at this time.*

Towel clutched to her front, she runs quickly into the bedroom, where she sees an image of Jacob Sluiter on the screen.

From there, the newscast cuts to an interview with the superintendent of the New York State Police, who confirms, from state police headquarters in Albany, that Sluiter was captured at a private home near North Creek.

At work, Denny Hayes has been tasked with leading the morning briefing; LaRochelle, he says, is up at the house, speaking again with Barbara's father.

"Well, if you haven't heard already," says Hayes, "you're about to."

After filling everyone in on the events of last night—a distant neighbor who spied Sluiter as he walked past his home; a police stakeout while Sluiter slept—he makes a few things clear: the first is that Sluiter is in custody, is uninjured, and is in good health.

The second is that he seems willing to talk.

The third is that—yes—there is one possible timeline that would have enabled him to reach the Van Laar Preserve four days ago, just in time to capture Barbara Van Laar, and then double back to North Creek, heading south. But that seems unlikely; and they have no evidence of it, yet.

The last is that it's up to Hayes to decide who'll get the first crack at interviewing him.

For a moment, Judy thinks Hayes is going to call on her. He even looks right at her—but then he looks away.

"Goldman," he says. "Did you have contact with him when you worked the Bear Van Laar case?"

Goldman shakes his head. No.

"Would you be up for it now?" says Hayes.

This makes sense. Judy tries not to let herself feel disappointed. Goldman is steady, fatherly, unthreatening. A good detective, everyone says; the rumor about him is that he's never accepted the promotions he's been offered because he likes the legwork that an investigator undertakes.

Judy holds her breath. Wonders if Goldman will say no.

"Yes," says Goldman.

Hayes nods. Then, one by one, he assigns the rest of them their work for the day—including Judy, who's given the names of some parents to track down.

Then he dismisses everyone, sending them out of the cabin.

Judy stalls. Waits until everyone else has gone before approaching Hayes.

"I called your house last night," she says. "I left a message with your wife."

Hayes frowns. Then sighs.

"She didn't tell you," says Judy.

He shakes his head.

"Did you talk to the grandfather yesterday?" Judy asks.

"Couldn't find him anyplace," says Hayes. "Everyone gave me a different story about where he was." He pauses. "You?"

"Not him, exactly," says Judy. "But I've got a new lead for you." And without waiting for him to respond, she describes her afternoon: the tip Mrs. Van Laar Sr. gave her. Her search for Vic Hewitt. The cane, the dentures. The empty bedroom.

"You can see for yourself," says Judy, nodding in the direction of the hallway. "It's right there."

"What did T.J. say when you interviewed her? About where her father was?"

"That's the funny thing," says Judy. "She didn't mention him at all, in the present tense. Just said he had been camp director until his memory began to fail. I had no idea he was still living in the Director's Cabin."

"Until he wasn't anymore," says Hayes.

"Right."

Hayes thinks. "All right," he says. "Forget what I said before. Your task for the day is to set eyes on Vic Hewitt."

Judyta

1950s • 1961 • Winter 1973 • June 1975
July 1975 • August 1975: **Day Four**

Camp Emerson, these days, is deserted of everyone except troopers and rangers and investigators. The counselors and campers and staff are all gone. The only employee who should, in theory, still be on the grounds is T.J. Hewitt.

But when Judy returns to Staff Quarters, to the place she last saw T.J., she finds the door to the room she was in not only closed, but locked with a hasp and padlock. Newly installed, by the looks of the wood shavings on the floor.

Despite the external lock, Judy still knocks at the door, gently and then firmly.

No response.

She spends the next several hours asking anyone she encounters if they've seen T.J., but no one seems to have—not since yesterday. Her truck, too, is nowhere on the grounds.

She is not a person of interest in this case—not officially, anyway. She has the right to come and go as she pleases. Still, the absence of both T.J. and her father feels suspicious—especially in the wake of yesterday's conversations—and Judy has an unsettled feeling in her stomach.

At noon, she returns to the Director's Cabin to find lunch. When she enters, Denny Hayes is hanging up the phone.

"Investigator Luptack," he says. "You're just the person I was looking for."

"Me?" says Judy, and Hayes nods.

"I've got a favor to ask you," he says—but he stops himself. "Any progress on Vic Hewitt?"

"No," says Judy. "And now it seems like T.J.'s gone, too."

A pause.

"I'll get someone else on that," says Hayes.

"Who?" Judy asks. And then, realizing: "What's the favor?"

Hayes sighs.

"He wants to talk to a lady," says Hayes.

"Who does?" Judy asks.

"Sluiter. Goldman did his best, but he got nothing. Sluiter wants to talk to a lady."

"Okay," says Judy.

"There's one female investigator in the BCI," says Hayes delicately.

"Right."

"I argued against it," says Hayes. "I don't know that it's right to give him what he wants. And I have no idea what he might say to you. Could be all kinds of perverted garbage, for all I know. But it's out of my hands. LaRochelle's given the okay."

"It's all right," says Judy. "I'm not scared."

She's scared. Two hours later, Judy stands outside one of Ray Brook's interrogation rooms, gazing through a one-way mirror at Jacob Sluiter himself.

He's tall and thin. Receding hairline. At fifty, now, his arms are ropy and his body looks spry; she can imagine that Sluiter in his thirties— the age he was when his original string of homicides took place—would have been even more difficult to overpower. A sparse beard looks as if it's been growing in the whole time he's been on the lam.

She's been prepped over the phone by a forensic psychologist who's familiar with the case from Sluiter's initial spree in the early 1960s.

"He hates his father," said the psychologist. "The father abused him badly. Don't mention anything about his father, or parents in general."

"All right," Judy said.

"He's sexually violent," said the psychologist. "He might say certain things, looking to get a rise out of you. Try not to give him the satisfaction."

"All right."

Now, Judy clenches her jaw to prevent her teeth from chattering. She hopes this will give her an appearance of toughness. From her solar plexus outward, she vibrates with nerves and cold. The window-unit air conditioners at Ray Brook are set so high that she's been bringing a jacket to work, in August. But to mention anything about it would feel like an announcement: *I am weak.*

A small crowd has gathered behind her. Hayes is there, of course, and Goldman. So are Captain LaRochelle and two of his lieutenants.

She tries not to look back at them. As usual, she feels both her age and her gender acutely. Hayes stands beside her, glancing at her.

"You sure this is all right with you?" he asks.

"I'm sure."

Judy walks in alone. There are microphones in this room, she knows. They feed both a speaker and a recording apparatus on the other side of the one-way mirror. The idea of being listened to in real time makes her self-conscious. She wishes for more privacy.

Jacob Sluiter, who has been leaning back in his chair, sits up straighter when she walks in.

"Mr. Sluiter," says Judy. "I'm Investigator Luptack." She's trying to keep her voice light.

For a moment, Sluiter says nothing. Then he says: "Are you cold?"

She hesitates only for a second. The psychologist has told her to show no sign of weakness; this, he says, is what Sluiter gets off on. With a woman, his goal will be to intimidate. Only one person escaped Sluiter in the early 1960s; that woman relayed that he had asked her to beg him for mercy, and that she had declined.

"No," says Judy. "I'm fine."

Sluiter looks almost disappointed.

"How old are you?" he says.

"How old are you?"

"Almost fifty-one. My birthday is next week."

"Well," she says. "Happy birthday in advance."

She smiles at him.

Sluiter regards her, reading something.

"You look very young," he says. "Do you live at home with your parents?"

Judy blinks. Willing every part of her body and face to be still. "No."

"Are you married?"

Judy is silent.

"I don't see a ring on your finger," says Sluiter. "That's why I asked."

He smiles, crosses one leg over the other. "Didn't mean to offend you, or anything."

"Mr. Sluiter," says Judy. "Can you tell me a little about your where-abouts since you left Fishkill?"

"Oh," says Sluiter. "I have no idea where I've been. I was just walking north."

"I see," says Judy. "Did you have a particular destination in mind?"

"No."

"Did you encounter anyone? While you were moving north?"

"No."

For the first time since she entered the room, he looks bored. He turns his face away from hers, toward the one-way mirror, as if he knows he has an audience.

"Would you tell me a little bit about your—habits? Where you slept, what you ate?"

"I don't really remember," he says.

For a time, they continue in this way: Judy asking questions, Sluiter dodging them, until she begins to grow worried. She thinks of the men standing outside the room, listening. Imagines them glancing sideways at one another, as doubtful as she is about her ability to extract any information whatsoever from this man. Why did he ask for a woman investigator if he'd give her no more than he gave Goldman?

She hears the psychologist's voice in her head. *No sign of weakness.* She ignores it.

"You know," she says. "I *am* cold. This building is the coldest building I've ever been in."

She puts her arms around herself. Shivers a little.

He turns his face toward her again. His eyes, on the other side of his glasses, narrow a bit, as if bringing her more clearly into focus.

"Investigator Luptack," he says. "May I ask you something?"

"Yes."

"Are you a virgin?"

Judy feels a rush of humiliation. The blood comes to her face, as if she's been slapped. At twenty-six, she is, in fact, a virgin. She wants to deny it, but thinks of the microphone in the room, the speaker just outside it. She thinks of the four men, her colleagues, standing there and listening to every word.

She says nothing.

"I'm sorry," says Sluiter. "Have I embarrassed you?"

"Yes," says Judy. "I feel embarrassed."

He smiles. Shifts in his chair.

"You won't tell me?"

"I'll trade with you," says Judy. "I'll tell you if you'll tell me a few things first."

"What's that game called?" asks Sluiter.

"Truth or dare," says Judy.

He grins. Adjusts his glasses, as if readying himself for some fun.

Judy does not recognize anything about this version of herself. She's playing a part. She has no experience with men, or women. When she was twelve years old—already aware of her place in the middle of things, as someone not *too* pretty, but pretty enough—her father had given her one piece of advice about dating: *Don't write boys checks that you don't want to cash.*

She had found the phrase grotesque. But it stuck with her. Perhaps it's one of the reasons she now dresses as she does, in garments designed to obscure. Perhaps it's why she hunches her shoulders, lowers her head around men she doesn't know or trust. Which is most of them.

Today, for the first time in her life, she sees her sexuality as something useful. She wants a confession. Wants it as badly as anything she's ever wanted in her life.

"Truth or dare?" Sluiter says.

"Truth."

"Are you a virgin?"

"Yes," says Judy. "I am."

In her mind, she blocks out the image of those men, her superiors, in the other room. Her hope is that they'll let her work awhile, that they won't come barging in too early, mistaking her acting skills for genuine distress.

He clears his throat. "I could tell that about you," he says.

"My turn," says Judy. "Truth or dare?"

"Dare."

"I dare you to tell me about everyone you ever killed or kidnapped."

A heavy silence fills the room, and she wonders immediately if she's gone too fast. Quickly, she contorts her mouth into a small smile—something meant to convey insouciance.

After a long beat, Sluiter matches her smile, wags a finger in the air. "No, ma'am," he says. "That's cheating."

"Why?"

"The word *dare* implies action," he says. "Not confession."

"I can dare you anything I want," says Judy. "There's no rule against it."

He clears his throat again. "Didn't you do your research?" he says. "I've never killed or kidnapped anyone." He grins. Flirting. Her stomach clenches: nausea, or nerves, or both.

"You never *confessed* to it," says Judy.

"That's right. I never."

"But now," says Judy. "With all the evidence. The second time you've been caught. Isn't there anything you'd like to get off your chest?"

She can feel, for the second time during this interview, that she's boring him.

She tries again. "Mr. Sluiter, are you a religious man?"

He scoffs. "Hardly. My father was that sort, though."

"So you're rational," says Judy. "So you believe in the power of deduction and evidence."

"Depends," says Sluiter.

"On?"

"On who's gathering the evidence. On whether they can be trusted."

Judy is surprised to find that some part of her understands what he's saying. Agrees with it, even.

"What about me?" she asks him. "Would you trust someone like me?"

"I would," he says. "Now, if that was your question—it's my turn now."

"It's not your turn," says Judy. "We're still negotiating our terms here. On the meaning of the word *dare*."

Sluiter frowns.

"Fine," he says. "One more question. Then I've got a good dare for you, if you'll take it." He grins.

Judy pauses, giving herself time to think. One more question, before she can escape the room. She isn't certain she has permission to mention Barbara Van Laar by name, but she senses she's on the verge of something. She wants to prove something to the men in the other room, but mostly she wants to prove something to herself.

"We're looking for information on a girl," Judy begins. "A missing girl."

"Barbara Van Laar," says Sluiter.

A chill goes down her back.

"You know her name," she says—careful not to phrase anything as a question.

He nods. Looks down at the table. Is it remorse she senses in his posture? She tries to slow her breathing.

"Mr. Sluiter, have you been in the vicinity of her home in recent days? Have you—did you have anything to do with her disappearance?"

He looks at her, calculating.

"That was two questions," he says. "You have to choose one."

"Fine," says Judy. "The first."

Slowly, he nods.

"I have been," he says.

"In the vicinity of her home," says Judy.

"Yes."

Judy opens her mouth to speak, but Sluiter holds up a finger. "My turn to ask you a question," he says.

She says nothing. Watches.

"Are you a virgin by choice? Or because no one wanted to fuck you?"

Before he finishes the sentence, the door behind her opens. She turns: Hayes and Goldman and Captain LaRochelle.

"Wait," says Judy, but already they're speaking over her.

"Thank you, Investigator Luptack," says Captain LaRochelle.

Sluiter glares at them, his face darkening.

"We weren't finished," he says.

We weren't finished. Judy wants to say it too—to yell it out—but she understands that her job, now, is to comply with the order being given silently to her by LaRochelle's firm gaze.

Reluctantly, she stands up from her chair.

Goldman gestures to the door; he accompanies her out.

Behind her, she hears Sluiter's voice, his tone unreadable, hovering between mocking and earnest.

"Investigator Luptack," he says. "You did a good job."

*   *   *

Outside the interrogation room, Judy's whole body goes limp. It takes all of her strength not to let herself sink to the floor.

"All right there?" asks Goldman, concerned.

"I could have gotten him to say it," says Judy. "I could have done it."

"I know," says Goldman, consoling her. "I do. They just—weren't certain if what he was saying was useful anymore."

"I could have gotten there," says Judy.

He raises a hand as if to pat her back, and then thinks better of it. Clears his throat.

On the other side of the two-way mirror, now, Judy watches as Jacob Sluiter angles himself away from Hayes and LaRochelle. As he folds his arms, like a petulant child, over his torso, even as the investigators begin to speak.

Louise

1950s • 1961 • Winter 1973 • June 1975
July 1975 • August 1975: **Day Four**

Since Louise returned home yesterday, her brother Jesse has been nowhere to be found.

Louise's mother doesn't have a clue where he might be.

"How long has he been gone?" Louise asks, increasingly panicky.

"Oh," her mother says, "no more than a day. I think I seen him in the kitchen yesterday."

He's eleven, Louise wants to say. But if she has to live with her mother for a time, she's going to do everything she can to keep the peace, to keep herself calm by simply not engaging.

At noon, just as Louise is finally about to walk to the center of town to inquire there, Jesse walks through the front door, stopping short when he sees her in the kitchen.

"Where were you?" Louise asks him—willing herself to speak calmly.

"At my friend's house."

"What friend?"

"Neil. You don't know him."

"Why didn't you tell anyone?"

"I did!" says Jesse, indignant. "I told Mom. I told her Neil's mom'd pick me up and drop me off, too."

Louise stares at him. Without shifting her gaze, she calls into the other room: "Mom, did you know Jesse was at his friend Neil's last night?"

A pause.

"I guess I did know that," says her mother.

Louise drops her head. Jesse grins in satisfaction.

"I'm sorry," says Louise. "I worry about you."

"I know you do," says Jesse.

She opens her arms, and he walks uncertainly toward her.

When she was fourteen and he was three, she held him just like this:

his face, turned sideways, on her shoulder. The weight of him draped over her. Today he is taller than she is, for the first time, but still he finds a way to relax his bones and muscles onto her bones and muscles, and for a moment—before he comes back to himself—the two of them breathe like that, unselfconsciously.

"Jesse," she says. "Don't get anyone pregnant."

"Stop," he says.

Then he stands up straight.

"You're home?" Jesse asks her.

"For now."

The two of them watch TV with their mother. *Kojak*: a show that Jesse loves.

At a certain point, both Jesse and her mother fall asleep, and Louise makes her way back into the kitchen, where she opens a cabinet. Yesterday, she noted with some satisfaction that Jesse had done what she asked him to do on the phone. He got some provisions. He's growing up.

She's dipping a spoon into a jar of Cheese Whiz when a knock comes at the door.

Outside is a person she doesn't, at first, recognize.

All she sees is that it's a woman, and that the woman has gray hair.

Judyta

1950s • 1961 • Winter 1973 • June 1975
July 1975 • August 1975: **Day Four**

When Denny Hayes finds Judy, she's pacing in circles around her desk like a defeated boxer.

Hayes watches her sympathetically.

"Goldman said you were upset," he says.

With effort, she sits in her chair. "What'd you get from him?"

Hayes pauses. "Nothing," he admits. "He clammed up when you left. Didn't say another word."

Then—looking over his shoulder, lowering his voice—"LaRochelle was the one who made us go in. Outside the room, he was telling us he was concerned that Sluiter was playing with you. That he wasn't giving you the truth. But what I think it really was," he says, "was that LaRochelle wanted to be able to say he finished the job himself."

Judy's shoulders sink.

"I would have let you keep going," says Hayes.

Judy nods. "I know."

"If it makes you feel better," says Hayes, "conservator from the Hyde Collection is on her way to the Preserve right now to see about removing that paint from Barbara's room."

Judy has been so focused on Sluiter that it takes her a moment to remember.

When she does, a question comes to mind: "How did the parents react?" Judy asks. "Are they okay with it?"

"Good thought," says Hayes. "I was wondering the same thing. But I heard from the captain that they're fine with it. The father is, at least. Didn't hesitate."

This, in Judy's mind, could mean one of two things: it could be a mark in favor of the innocence of the Van Laar parents. Or it could be that there was never anything interesting on those walls to begin with.

Before she leaves for the Preserve, Judy makes a request of Hayes:

"Will you tell me what happens today with Sluiter? Will you call me, even if you're not at the Preserve?"

Hayes nods.

The conservator is a tall young woman, maybe as young as Judy. She wears large glasses and white coveralls. In her right hand is a bucket; in her left is a drop cloth.

Her name is Anna, she says. She's here to look at the paint.

Judy, being the one to come up with the idea, is also the one to oversee it.

She leads Anna into the main house, and then down the hallway to the pink room.

Anna the conservator enters the room first, puts her bucket down. Takes in the very pink walls, the neatly made bed, the surprising square footage of the room.

"Any idea which wall I should start with?" she asks.

"I think it's the one behind the bed," says Judy, thinking of the picture Barbara drew. The plan for the mural.

Anna moves with confidence. Spreads her drop cloth on the floor. Kneels to the ground and reaches into her bucket, removing from it a metal container of acetone and something that looks like a large Q-tip.

She dips the Q-tip into the acetone, applies it to a tiny spot in a corner.

When she takes it away, a tiny patch of green blooms through the pink.

"Well," says Anna. "That's a good sign. Looks like oil paint underneath. Which means I might be able to remove the latex paint on top without damaging the underlayer."

She returns to her work, making her tiny circle a tiny bit larger. Yes: there's green, and some black next to it.

Anna glances back over her shoulder at Judy.

"You know this is going to take me a really long time, right?" she asks. "I mean days."

Toward the end of the afternoon, a young investigator comes up the hill to find them in the main house. He looks flustered.

"Are you Luptack?" he says to Judy. She nods.

"Captain LaRochelle is on the phone for you. He says it's urgent."

When Judy reaches the phone in the Director's Cabin, she finds Denny Hayes has reached the grounds as well. He's the one holding the phone. Around him, a little crowd of curious onlookers has formed. She takes the receiver into her hands, angles her back to them.

"I'm here in the room with Mr. Sluiter," says the captain, someplace between serious and chagrined. "He says he'd like to speak with you. He's agreed to allow me to remain in the room with him as he does so."

She glances at Hayes, who has no idea what's going on. As a courtesy, she covers the mouth of the phone with her hand. Mouths to him: *Sluiter's asking to talk to me.*

He raises his eyebrows. *The call will be recorded*, he mouths back to her.

"I know," says Judy.

"What do you know?" asks Sluiter, on the other end of the line.

Jacob Sluiter makes no small talk, this time. Speaks clearly and directly.

"I don't know anything about Barbara Van Laar," he says. "I'm telling you the truth."

"How did you know her name?" Judy asks. "When I asked you about her, you said her name before I did."

"I seen it in the papers," says Sluiter. "Same as anybody else." He's grinning, triumphant. She can hear it through the line.

Judy waits. There's more, she thinks; there must be more.

She can hear Sluiter breathing: a wet sound that turns her stomach. At last, he continues.

"I do know where her brother is, though."

Judy closes her eyes briefly. "Will you tell me?" she asks. She can almost taste the answer. She wants it badly.

"No, I won't."

Be quiet, Judy tells herself. *Wait.* Through the telephone line, she silently wills LaRochelle to shut up, too.

It works.

"But I'll show you," Sluiter says, at last.

Louise

1950s • 1961 • Winter 1973 • June 1975
July 1975 • August 1975: **Day Four**

L ouise opens the door.

She knows this woman. She can't remember how.

The woman wears her gray hair in a long low ponytail, one that nearly reaches her waist. She wears a long cotton dress. Socks inside walking shoes.

For a while, they look at each other, unmoving.

Then the woman says, "Louise?" and it's only upon hearing her voice—distinctive, low-pitched—that Louise puts together who she is.

"Mrs. Stoddard," says Louise. "Are you all right?"

Mrs. Stoddard—once a Sunday school teacher, a fixture in the town, the mother of Antonia Stoddard, one of Louise's classmates from kindergarten through the end of school—has, since her husband died, rarely been seen.

For more than a decade, there have been more rumors about her than facts.

Like Louise's mother, Mrs. Stoddard is said to be a shut-in. To have had a "nervous breakdown."

But unlike Louise's mother, Mrs. Stoddard has a clear reason for her rumored break with reality: she lost her son and then her husband in cruelly quick succession. And her husband was so disgraced in death that she couldn't even mourn him properly—in public, at least.

"May I come in, Louise?" asks Mrs. Stoddard.

Louise steps back, making way. She gestures to a chair; Mrs. Stoddard accepts the offer, placing her purse in her lap, clutching its handle tightly, as if afraid someone will take it.

"Can I get you something to drink?" she asks Mrs. Stoddard. "Tea?" She has no idea if there's tea in the house.

"I'm all right," says Mrs. Stoddard.

"How's Antonia?" asks Louise.

"Oh, fine," says Mrs. Stoddard. "All the girls are fine. I'm a grand-mother five times over."

She sits up straight in her chair, proud. But something tells Louise she should not pry further into Mrs. Stoddard's family—that, perhaps, they are not much in touch.

"You must be very proud," says Louise.

"I am."

"I remember Antonia played piano really well. Sang well, too."

"She did, didn't she?" asks Mrs. Stoddard.

A long and awkward silence ensues.

Suddenly, the woman leans forward in her chair.

"I know what they're trying to do to you," she says.

Louise blinks. "You do?"

Mrs. Stoddard nods. Her eyes fill sharply with tears. She reaches one thin hand across the kitchen table, palm upward, and Louise has no choice but to place her hand there, on top of Mrs. Stoddard's.

"But don't worry," she says. "I won't let them do it again."

She opens the purse in her lap, then rummages inside it, searching for something.

She pulls out a wrinkled document, places it on the table between them, and smooths it with a fist.

"There," she says. "Take it. It's for you."

With some hesitation, Louise pulls a set of stapled pages toward her.

She doesn't know what she's looking at, at first. It's a carbon copy of something, the text so faint she has to squint in places. At the top of the document are words she does not understand: *Collateral Receipt and Informational Notice.*

At the bottom is a signature: *Maryanne Stoddard.*

"Did they tell you it was me?" asks Mrs. Stoddard.

"Did who?"

"At the magistrate's office. Did they tell you it was me who bailed you out? I put my house up," says Mrs. Stoddard, excited now, her hands trembling slightly. "Look," she says. "Look at the next page."

On the next page is a promissory note, the address of the Stoddard house listed at the top. On the third page is a xeroxed copy of the deed.

"Mrs. Stoddard," says Louise. "You shouldn't have done this."

"Why not?"

"It's so kind of you," she says. "But it's too much."

"Nonsense," says Mrs. Stoddard, forceful now. "I've spent the past fourteen years of my life trying to clear my husband's name for a crime he didn't commit. I'll be damned if I let the bastards do the same thing to someone else."

Louise is still looking at the paperwork. Scrutinizing the signature at the bottom of the page.

"Do you know," Mrs. Stoddard continues, "how many hours of my life I've spent in the woods around Hunt Mountain? It's practically all I've done. My children think I'm crazy. But I always think—if I could just find something—some of the boy's clothing, or—" She goes quiet for a moment, weighing how honest she should be. "Or the boy himself," she says finally. "Poor soul."

Louise is listening intently. Everything that Mrs. Stoddard is saying is confirming a theory that she's formed over the past few minutes. She squints at the signature, parsing it.

"Mrs. Stoddard, I don't mean to be rude. But your first name is Maryanne?" she says.

"It is."

"And you've spent the years since Bear Van Laar's disappearance searching in the nearby woods?"

She nods. "Since my husband's death, while he was in the custody of the police," she says. "To be precise. But yes."

Louise waits. Afraid to ask.

"Scary Mary," says Maryanne Stoddard. "You can say it. I've heard they call me that."

Judyta

1950s • 1961 • Winter 1973 • June 1975
July 1975 • August 1975: **Day Four**

Judy sits in the belly of a canoe, being rowed across Lake Joan by two EnCon rangers who paddle in long unified strokes, silent and calm, barely disturbing the water.

Two more canoes flank the one that Judy is in. One contains Hayes and a medical examiner from Schenectady.

The other contains Sluiter and an armed guard.

It took several rounds of negotiations with Sluiter's state-assigned attorney for this plan to be permitted by a county judge. The concern, said Denny Hayes, was Sluiter's history of bolting. His ability to manipulate those around him.

An escape risk like Sluiter would have to be shackled at the ankles, his hands cuffed to a waist belt. This, therefore, is his situation as he and his guard are propelled by rangers sitting fore and aft.

Judy wills herself to keep her gaze straight ahead. If she turns it, she fears she'll see Jacob Sluiter looking back at her.

They're heading for the opposite bank of Lake Joan, to the small stretch of rocky land at the center of a bay that appears inaccessible by foot. Steep rocky outcroppings come up from the water and frame the inlet on either side.

On approach, it becomes clear that they'll have to wade. There is no beach here, only boulders that impede entrance to the forest beyond. One by one, they disembark, holding each canoe steady as they go. Sluiter—hands bound together at his front, as if in supplication—must be helped out of the canoe by the burly guard assigned to him. As he walks toward the bow, body low, the canoe wobbles, threatens to tip. The guard opens his arms and Sluiter falls into them.

The forest beyond the rocks is brutally dense. Away from the shoreline, not much sunlight reaches the earth.

Walking in a line behind Jacob Sluiter, the terror of the North Woods, Judy scans the ground beyond his figure.

Earlier, on the phone, Sluiter had described what they'd be looking for: a cairn. A little stack of rocks, one atop the other, meant to mark a spot.

Now, Judy wants to be the one to see it first—if Sluiter's telling the truth, that is, which remains to be seen. Part of her believes that he simply wanted a field trip: one last chance to see the outdoors before being remanded to a federal prison for the rest of his life.

After several minutes of bushwhacking, the quiet of their march is interrupted, at last, by the sound of Sluiter's voice.

"Look up," he says. They do.

They've reached the steep rock face they could see from shore. Ten feet above their heads, there looks to be a cavern, an open mouth of unclear depth.

"Look down," Sluiter says, and bows his head. "There he is."

At his feet, on the bare earth: a little tower of rocks.

A cairn.

Beneath that marker, says Jacob Sluiter, they will find the boy.

Louise

1950s • 1961 • Winter 1973 • June 1975
July 1975 • August 1975: **Day Four**

Louise stands in her childhood bedroom.

She's been avoiding it. Last night, she slept on the couch. She doesn't like to go in there, full as it is of the artifacts of her promise, of Louise Donnadieu at seventeen, the salutatorian of Central High, off on a full scholarship to Union.

Now, though, she'll have to come to some sort of truce with the space: she may be here for weeks or months until her hearing.

She turns in a full circle and then begins to clear the walls of their adornments. Down come the National Honor Society certificate, the photograph of Louise in her cap and gown, shaking hands with her high school principal; down comes the last report card she ever received, filled with A's and A-pluses.

She was the one who put them up. At fourteen, sixteen years old. No adult in her life ever cared enough to do so. Embarrassing, she thinks. Pathetic.

Her graduation photograph is the last to go. The girl in it is smiling, but her brows are furrowed, as if she's seeing into the future.

Louise makes a pile on the floor of all the documents, then gathers them into her arms. She's walking to the kitchen door to take them to the garbage when she hears Jesse speaking to someone outside it.

She picks up her pace.

"Who's asking?" Jesse says, but Louise can't hear the response.

Jesse turns to her, scowling: an expression that means it's most likely a man.

He closes the door before asking.

"You know someone named Lee Towson?"

Three minutes later, Louise stands out front of her mother's house, facing Lee Towson in the flesh. She's made Jesse swear to stay inside; she'll be damned if she has this conversation in front of an audience.

It's only been four days since she stood opposite Lee in the hallway of Staff Quarters at the camp. It feels like a month. She can still hear Denny's phrase in her ear: *statutory rape.* She looks down at the ground when she speaks.

"How'd you find me?"

"Phone book," he says. "Not too many Donnadieus in Shattuck, New York."

"But how'd you know *I* was here?"

"I've got friends in the area."

She considers the implication of this. She has always disliked being gossiped about. But in a town as small as Shattuck, she guesses it's inevitable.

"You know they're looking for you?" Louise asks him.

"I heard that."

"Where've you been?"

"Here and there."

"You hiding?"

"Kind of, I guess. I've got a plan to leave, anyway."

Louise looks up at him, finally. Then past him. There are only two other houses on this cul-de-sac, both of them seemingly shuttered for the night. There are no streetlights on the side streets of Shattuck; she can see his form only by the glow cast forth from her mother's house.

"Louise?"

"What?"

"I've got something weighing on my mind," he says. "Had to tell you before I go."

Louise's heart skips several beats. In her mind, she makes guesses, all of them far-fetched.

"Oh?" she says—trying to sound casual.

"Your boyfriend," says Lee Towson. "Your fiancé. Excuse me."

"What about him?"

"He was sleeping around."

Louise closes her eyes.

"How do you know?" she says.

"I supplied him. And I saw him a couple times with another girl. Same one."

"Not," says Louise.

"Not Barbara. No. He was up at the main house. On the beach behind Self-Reliance. He was with a girl he called Annabel," says Lee.

Louise closes her eyes. The world around her fades; her understanding with it. Other things come into focus now: Annabel's declaration, early on, that her parents had someone in mind for her to marry. The Southworths and the McLellans, longtime friends, staying together at Self-Reliance. John Paul's staunch refusal to bring Louise anyplace in its vicinity. His absence throughout the week. And—last, most brutal—Annabel's departure in the middle of the camp dance. The same night as Barbara's disappearance.

"Annabel's seventeen," says Louise.

Lee says: "Normally I'd mind my own business. But I thought you needed to know that, in case."

"In case what?" says Louise.

"In case it—proves anything. In case it's helpful to you. I know what charges they laid on you. But I bet they're interested in you for something else. That's how they work," he adds.

"Why do you care what happens to me?" says Louise abruptly. It sounds more bitter than she meant it to. Everyone, she believes, has an agenda.

"Well," says Lee, "because I like you."

She says nothing. She closes her eyes.

A long pause. Then: "Louise. Why don't you come with me?"

"What?" says Louise—distracted now. "Where?"

"I'm going to Colorado tomorrow. To a town called Crested Butte. Buddy of mine lives out there, says it's heaven."

"I'm not allowed to leave my house," says Louise stiffly. "My mother's house. I'm out on bail. They got me on possession charges. For some drugs that weren't even mine."

"Ah," says Lee. "Well, there goes that idea. Unless you feel like pulling a Bonnie and Clyde. Hide out awhile, till things cool off."

Louise shakes her head. "Anyway," she says, "that's where they think you're going. So you should prob'ly choose a different place."

"Who does?"

"The police."

Lee pauses, considering.

In the silence, Louise says: "I heard about you. I heard about why you went to jail."

Lee inhales and exhales. Then, as if suddenly tired, he seats himself on the ground. "Who told you that?"

"My mom's friend." She doesn't feel like telling the whole truth.

Lee gives a long sigh.

"I was nineteen," says Lee. "She was sixteen. She was the daughter of the family I cooked for. Rich family. Had a place in the Catskills, okay? Not quite as nice as the Van Laar place, but something like it."

Louise listens, considering.

"Her dad caught us. Freaked. He called the cops. Said I forced her. She's screaming in the background that it isn't true. It wasn't true."

Louise, still standing, sits down now, next to Lee.

"Louise? Do you believe me?"

"I don't know," she says. And she doesn't: feels her instincts are all wrong. Always have been. How, she wonders, can she fix her instincts about people? About men?

"I'm done working for rich people," Lee says. He's talking to himself now, more than to her. "I can't believe I ever did it again. That's why I hid. Minute I heard what was happening with the Van Laar girl, I split. With my record . . ." He trails off. Continues. "Anyway, there's a new thing happening out there," says Lee. "It's 1975. You gotta go west, is what I hear."

In her left hand, Louise is still holding the papers and photographs she took down from the walls of her room. She looks down at them. She listens to the voice of another man, making her another promise that won't come true. How many times in her life has she said yes to a boy or a man just because it was the easiest thing to do? How many times has she let a man take what he wanted, instead of taking something for herself?

She places the papers delicately on the ground. Glances back over at Lee, whose forearms and hands she has dreamed for a whole summer about touching.

She does so now. Places her left hand on the inside of his elbow. He looks up at her, curious.

"You want to mess around a little?" says Louise.

He says nothing. Sits very still as Louise brings her body around to face him, kneeling before him on the ground. She glances up toward the lit house; knows she won't be seen outside in the dark. She lifts her shirt over her head.

"Jesus," he says. He reaches forward, puts his hands around her waist.

"No," she says. "Yours." She lifts his shirt off, too, and then leans into him, her skin on his skin, on top of him as he lies back onto the ground.

She'll take what she wants from him, a moment of pleasure in the middle of all this dark, a washing-away of John Paul and the McLellans and the Van Laars and the grand house she was never going to be invited into, ever, no matter what she did.

Tomorrow, Lee Towson will leave for Colorado. She won't follow.

Alice

1950s • 1961 • Winter 1973 • June 1975
July 1975 • August 1975: **Day Four**

S he's been shipped back to Albany. Her parents—who have, during this ordeal, largely kept to their room—were the ones assigned to oversee her transport. From Albany, they decamped to Manhattan, with mumbled assurances that Barbara would be found.

Now she is alone.

She's out of everyone's hair this way, she thinks, and her shoulders shake a little with laughter. Today, like every day, is a very bad one, and so with Dr. Lewis's blessing she has been advised that she can take three pills when needed.

She takes them now, her brain ahead of her body, sighing with relief when the pills come out of their home in the glass bottle, anticipating the chemical surge. She chews them up to get there faster.

She closes her eyes. Her mind relaxes, bringing her, unexpectedly, back to the Dunwitty Institute.

To her sister Delphine, her only visitor the entire time she was there.

I'm sorry, she'd said. And then she said more: that she'd been in free fall since George died. That it had not been the first time, with her and Peter; that they'd been intimate, too, when they were young. All the way back when she first introduced Alice to Peter, for her coming-out party.

Was introducing Alice to Peter simply a way for Delphine to stay close to him? Setting him up with her guileless, stupid little sister? Making Alice the brood mare while Delphine and Peter—intellectual matches—carried on together every time Peter went down to New York?

"It's nothing like what you're imagining," said Delphine. Reading her mind. "George and I loved each other very, very much. But we were never interested in a traditional marriage. He was free to do as he pleased. As was I. I'm not sure if you'll recall this, but I tried to warn you of it, once," said Delphine. She leaned back. "About how you should—*have some fun*, I think I said. Did you ever try it?"

Alice said nothing.

"It was wrong of us, Alice. All of us," said Delphine. "We've treated you abominably."

Silence.

"Will you leave him, Alice?" said Delphine. "You could, you know."

Silence.

"Alice," said Delphine. "Alice, are you sleeping?"

At last, Alice smiled. In a way, she thought, she was. She was having a waking dream—the same one she always had.

In this dream, she was locked in a room she didn't recognize while the search for her missing son went on without her. And someone—she didn't know who—was standing just outside the door.

In Albany, Alice opens her eyes. She doesn't like being here by herself. The house is cold in summer, and all of Albany seems desolate, abandoned. The government workers are taking vacations in places farther north or south. In this city, Alice feels somehow like the only survivor of a plague.

Three pills in her blood now. Her body goes slack.

This, this is how she hears him best: on the other side of the veil, in the other world. The one where Bear lives.

Once, while playing a game of Dictionary, Alice came across the word *nonsecular*, and this is the word that comes to mind when she thinks of the liminal space between life and death in which she encounters her son.

The space in which she lets herself acknowledge what she did is *nonsecular*. The space in which she doesn't work so hard to stop the slivers of light and memory that come at her from time to time, in unexpected moments, so sharply that she feels as if she's been stabbed, is *nonsecular*. In this world, when those memories come, she accepts them, examines them impassively, opens herself to them instead of willing them away.

Alice blinks now. Coming back to life.

Outside a window, the sun is going down now. How long has she been sitting in one chair? She isn't certain.

She stands up, goes to the toilet, relieves herself. And then she drifts, in a dream, toward the room that used to be a nursery. Another nonsecular space.

I'm here now, she says. *I'm here.*

She listens, awaiting his reply.

Judyta

1950s • 1961 • Winter 1973 • June 1975
July 1975 • August 1975: **Day Four**

She has seen dead bodies before. She has seen her own grandparents, three of them, in open caskets. She has seen the freshly deceased, victims of vehicle accidents, during her tenure as a state trooper on highway patrol.

She has never before seen skeletal remains.

The medical examiner issues directives as the forest rangers, with gloved hands, gently lift a small intact skeleton from where it has rested for more than a decade onto a plank for observation.

Out of respect for the dead, Jacob Sluiter has already been led away by the armed guard.

Now: a sort of impassive interest in the medical examiner's voice as he begins. "I wondered," he says, "whether the skeleton itself would have deteriorated. But it looks like the soil here isn't highly acidic, probably due to its proximity to water."

He kneels down next to the plank, produces a measuring tape, holds it to various points on each bone.

"I'd say this was a child," he says. "Probably between seven and eleven years of age.

"Do you know if it's male or female?" asks Hayes.

"In immature skeletons there's room for error," says the examiner. "But right now, I'd say male."

Back at the Command Post, Denny Hayes holds his finger over a magnetic tape player, ready to listen to the recording of the phone call between Jacob Sluiter and Judy. The one in which he directed them to the body of Bear Van Laar. A copy of the call has been made and transported from headquarters at Ray Brook, where Sluiter is being held, to the Van Laar Preserve.

"You believed him?" Hayes says, before listening. "You believed his story?"

Judy nods. She did. She does.

"Why?" Hayes asks. "He's a known liar. He's never admitted to anything before."

"Just my instinct," says Judy. "He had no reason to help us out with this. But he did."

Hayes presses play. Jacob Sluiter begins to talk, his voice crackling.

I know where Bear Van Laar is, says Sluiter, on the tape.

But I didn't kill him.

Judyta

1950s • 1961 • Winter 1973 • June 1975
July 1975 • August 1975: **Day Five**

At morning briefing, LaRochelle confirms it: the dental records are a perfect match. The skeleton was definitively Bear Van Laar's.

Then he asks Hayes to give a summary of Jacob Sluiter's story.

"Shouldn't Investigator Luptack do that?" says Hayes. "Being that she's the one he told?"

LaRochelle frowns.

"Whatever," he says. "Somebody. Go."

Reluctantly, Judy turns and trades places with Captain LaRochelle, walking to the front of the room while he walks to the back. There, he holds his gaze steady on Judy as she speaks.

According to Jacob Sluiter, the Van Laar Preserve is his ancestral land.

The Sluiter family—Dutch immigrants to Albany as far back as 1700—first settled in the North Country during the logging boom in the 1820s. A Sluiter ancestor purchased the tract of land on which the Van Laar Preserve was later built. He and his sons logged the first-growth forest clean, making a good living in the process. But in the 1870s, when politicians began to grow wary of what logging might do to the water supply downstate—threatening to ban it altogether within the future Adirondack Park—the Sluiters sold their land.

The man who bought it was—Judy allows herself, only briefly, to pause for dramatic effect—Peter Van Laar the First.

Bear and Barbara's great-grandfather.

It is no coincidence, therefore, that each time Sluiter is on the lam, he finds himself in this area. He says he's pulled to it; his own grandfather used to take him here when he was a boy, sneaking him onto property that was no longer theirs, pointing with resignation toward the grand house and camp as evidence that fortune favors some over others. That they, the Sluiters, had always been cursed with bad timing and bad luck.

The land had a secret, though, that even the Van Laars seemed not to know about.

On Lake Joan's opposite shore—deemed impassable by most due to its steepness and rockiness, by the density of its trees—was a series of natural caverns. The Sluiters had discovered them the first time the land had been logged, and the knowledge had been passed down through the generations; it was a place that Sluiter's grandfather still took him to, a marvel one had to see to believe.

According to Sluiter, during his time on the run from the authorities in 1961, he sought refuge in these caverns for the length of that summer, when the homes he relied on in winter were occupied by their owners.

It was a perfect spot: approachable only by water, hidden by thick trees, sheltered from the rain. He swam back and forth across the lake to reach his makeshift shelter; he fished and trapped and scavenged for food.

One afternoon, said Sluiter, he woke in his cavern to the sound of what he recognized as human footsteps.

At first he feared capture. The police, he knew, were on his trail. But to his ears, it sounded as if only one man was approaching. And so, curious, he moved to the front of his cave, keeping close to the shadows to avoid being seen.

Eventually, a man came into view. He was carrying something that Sluiter couldn't see, at first.

Eventually, it became clear: it was a child. A boy. Lifeless in the man's arms.

The man knelt to the ground. Weeping, he laid the child before him, and began to dig.

Sluiter, silent, ten feet above them in his cavern, watched it all.

Judy stops. For a moment, the room is quiet, until someone asks the question she knows will be next.

"What did the man look like?" someone asks finally, and all the heads in the room swivel in the direction of Goldman, the oldest investigator, who has called out from the back.

"Most of the description Sluiter gave was generic," says Judy. "Tall, brown hair, middle-aged."

She pauses. Considers her next words carefully. "But he did say that the man looked like a local, as opposed to someone in the family."

Someone in the back speaks up. "What'd he mean by that? Something the man was wearing?"

"He didn't explain," says Judy.

Another hand goes up. "Why didn't Sluiter tell anyone? After he was apprehended the first time?"

"He thought no one would believe him," says Judy. "That he wasn't the one who killed the boy in the first place. Later, when he heard about Bear's disappearance in the news, he put two and two together, figured out who the boy was. But he had no incentive to talk."

A pause.

"Well, do we?" asks Hayes. "Believe him?"

Judy does. But she won't say it aloud—not yet.

"Why did he tell us now?" someone asks.

Hayes turns his gaze to Judy. "Investigator Luptack," he says. "Any thoughts?"

Judy clears her throat. Is she actually expected to answer?

"Go ahead," says Hayes.

"Well," says Judy. "He said he trusted me."

Someone in the room snorts. Someone coughs.

"All right, all right," Hayes says. "The whole story sounds implausible. Correct. But there's one thing to acknowledge: the boy would be an outlier for Jacob Sluiter. He's different from any of Sluiter's other known victims. He's a sex predator, but his targets are women. Grown women. Young boys have never been his interest, that we know of. So let's work this theory for a little bit. Say Sluiter didn't kill Bear Van Laar. Say he's telling the truth. Then who did? How did his body end up buried where it's buried?"

LaRochelle, in the back, says: "Why not Carl Stoddard? He was a local. If what Sluiter's saying is true, he'd fit the profile."

Hayes pauses, diplomatic. "Maybe. Yes," he says. "But I think it's worth looking into other ideas, at this point, sir."

"Such as?" says LaRochelle. Testy.

For a moment, everyone is silent.

Then Hayes says: "Has the family been notified, sir? Of Bear's discovery?"

LaRochelle looks away. "They have."

"May I ask how they reacted?"

LaRochelle frowns. "I spoke only to Bear's father. He received the news—stoically, I would say. He's gone back to Albany for the present, to relay the information to his wife in person."

He looks distracted. Then abruptly, he straightens.

"Excuse me," he says, and walks out of the cabin, tapping a pack of cigarettes into his palm as he goes.

Hayes catches Judy's eye.

The case will be reopened. Everyone knows it, including LaRochelle.

After LaRochelle's departure, Hayes turns to face the investigators left in the room.

"Here's what I don't understand," he says. "Why didn't any of the searchers see it? A new patch of disturbed earth, just across the lake? Marked with a cairn, no less. Huge crew of people on-site for weeks. You'd think they would have searched the periphery of the lake first thing."

"Maybe they were misdirected," says Judy.

Hayes looks at her. "By?"

"The family, I guess," says Judy. Then she turns to Investigator Goldman. "Was that the sense you got? When you were working the case?"

Goldman hesitates. Looks down.

"I did always have the strange sense that they didn't want to find him. Yes."

"You think someone in the family killed him?" Hayes asks.

But this, apparently, isn't a claim Goldman is prepared to make. He goes silent.

"What if it was an accident?" Judy says.

"Then why let Carl Stoddard take the fall? More than that—why actively indict him?" Hayes says.

Judy looks around, pausing to see if anyone else will chime in. But for a moment, there is silence.

"How did Carl Stoddard die?" someone asks.

"Heart attack," Goldman says. "He had a heart attack and died while in police custody, awaiting questioning."

Judy is forming a theory.

"What if it was convenience?" says Judy. "What if it was just easier for the family to let everyone think it was Stoddard who did it? He was dead, after all," she said. "They probably thought they weren't hurting anyone."

"All right," says Hayes. "Maybe. But that would still mean they had something to cover up."

Silence.

"Which was?" says Goldman.

Judy is looking at something on the wall.

"Judy?" says Hayes.

"Investigator Goldman," says Judy. "Who was the person running the search for Bear?"

"Well, the family was," says Goldman.

"No," says Judy. "The person providing direction. The person actually overseeing the search."

Goldman looks down at the floor, thinking. Then he looks up. "I think it was the former camp director, actually," he says. "The father of the current one. Vic Hewitt was his name."

For a moment, Judy goes silent.

Then she walks down the hallway, toward the bedroom she now knows to be Vic's.

When she returns, she proffers the group photo she found to Denny Hayes.

"Look," she says, pointing to the pencil on the back. *Blackfly Good-by. 1961.* She flips it again to its front side. "Look again."

A small group of investigators gathers around, looking at the photo.

Everyone in the picture is formally attired, children and adults alike, in dresses and suits. The women wear small hats. Even in black-and-white, she can see their lipstick and mascara.

Only two people stand off to one side, dressed differently: T.J., a young teenager; and her father Vic. Middle-aged. Bearded. Wearing a fishing hat with a floppy brim, and a plaid shirt rolled at the elbows, and corduroys patched at the knee.

Judy puts a finger to the girl. "That's T.J. Hewitt," she says. "Right? Doesn't it look like her?"

Hayes nods.

"Which makes him," says Judy, and Hayes says: "Vic Hewitt."

She moves her finger back toward the larger group. "I'd describe them as summer people," she said. "Based on their clothes. But how would you describe Vic?"

Hayes looks at her. "A local," he says.

He turns to an investigator. Hands him the photograph. "Take this to Jacob Sluiter," he says. "Ask him if he recognizes anyone in this photograph as the man who buried Bear Van Laar."

A knock at the door interrupts them.

Anna, the conservator, stands blinking in the bright sunlight, exhausted.

LaRochelle, taking the last few drags on his cigarette, stands behind her.

"Anna, did you ever go home?" Judy asks her.

"No. I got excited."

She turns and walks in the direction of the main house. Judy glances over her shoulder at Hayes, who glances at LaRochelle. Then the three of them follow her, trotting to keep up with Anna's long strides.

With both Van Laar parents back in Albany, and most of the guests now gone, the house is almost empty.

Together, Judy and Anna walk to the pink room. Inside, the exposed mural is in plain sight.

Judy's first reaction is to be surprised at the quality of the artistry. Barbara Van Laar could paint; that's certain. The wall is covered with a set of icons Judy doesn't understand: safety pins and flags and odd-looking faces with odder-looking haircuts. Music notes abound, as well.

A river makes its way from the upper left-hand corner of the wall to the lower right-hand corner.

Judy takes the whole thing in, scanning it rapidly to see if anything catches her eye.

"Do you see it yet?" says Anna.

Judy's heartbeat quickens.

"See what?" says Captain LaRochelle, his head moving in quick circles as he takes the whole wall in.

"I don't blame you," says Anna. "The whole thing is overwhelming. But come closer."

She walks to the river. Its waves, she realizes, are not just waves. They're letters.

BVL + JPM, they spell.

The way that children, for decades or centuries, have memorialized their love.

"Barbara Van Laar plus John Paul McLellan," Hayes says.

He's asked for the Director's Cabin to be cleared. As senior investigator, he has that authority. Now Judy sits opposite him in a folding chair, elbows on knees, gaze on ground.

"I think that'll hold up as solid evidence," says Hayes. "With any judge. We'll start the process of getting a warrant for his arrest. The only question now is—where'd he stow the girl?"

"That's not the only question," says Judy.

"Oh?"

"The other one is: Did Vic Hewitt kill her brother Bear?"

Hayes looks at her. Then he slaps his knees and stands up.

"That's your assignment, Judy," he says. "Forget the grandfather, for now. Forget Jacob Sluiter. I'm on the lead desk, and that's the lead I assign you. In the meantime, I'm driving down to the hotel McLellan's staying in myself. I don't trust these troopers to keep good tabs on him."

Judyta

1950s • 1961 • Winter 1973 • June 1975
July 1975 • August 1975: **Day Five**

She spends hours looking for any sign of either Hewitt. She goes back to Staff Quarters; she searches the commissary, where T.J. must be eating, to see if she can find her there. She asks the staff up at the main house; no one has seen her, and no one seems to know her well enough to speculate about where she might have gone.

Either that, thinks Judy, or they're not talking.

At 4 p.m., just before the end of her shift, Judy is seated outside the Director's Cabin, gazing at the lake, when the sound of a vehicle draws her attention.

It's T.J. Hewitt, in her truck. She drives by without turning her head in Judy's direction. Pulls to a stop out front of Staff Quarters, a hundred yards away.

Judy watches as T.J. brings a bag out of the vehicle. Then lets herself into the building.

Judy follows.

Inside, she finds the padlock on the door unlocked, and the door standing open. She knocks anyway.

T.J., inside, jumps.

"Sorry to startle you," says Judy.

"You didn't," says T.J.

"Have a minute?"

"For you?" says T.J. "Sure." She smiles, and Judy is momentarily disarmed. Then she gathers herself, and walks over the threshold of the room.

"What's going on?" says T.J.

"How come you didn't tell me your father was alive?" says Judy.

"Didn't I?"

"No. You talked about him as if he was dead."

T.J. sits down on the edge of her small bed. "Well," she says, "I guess that's what it feels like. He's not himself these days."

Judy nods. Remains standing. "Where is he now?" she says.

"With family."

"With family."

T.J. nods.

"Why?"

"You needed to use our house as your headquarters," says T.J. "I didn't have a better place for him to go. He needs to be looked after, all the time."

Judy glances back into the hallway. "Lotta empty rooms in this building," she says, but T.J. is shaking her head.

"You don't understand," she says. "He's not familiar with this place. He'd wander off. He needs to be—watched."

T.J. looks out the window.

"What family is he staying with?"

"What? Oh," says T.J. "With his brother."

"His brother?"

"Yes," says T.J.

For a moment, silence. Then Judy takes out her card. Hands it over.

"Miss Hewitt—T.J.," she says. "I don't know why, but I have the feeling that you're not telling me the whole truth. If you want to, you can call me anytime."

Judyta

1950s • 1961 • Winter 1973 • June 1975
July 1975 • August 1975: **Night Five**

Judy can't sleep. She lies in her room at the inn, turning one way and then the other. She turns on the television, and then she turns it off. She ruminates on the facts of the day: Vic Hewitt. T.J. Hewitt. The results from the analysis of the blood on the uniform in McLellan's car: Type A positive. A match for Barbara Van Laar, though not definitive proof.

An hour goes by. Another.

It takes her until midnight to realize she never had dinner.

Defeated, she rises from her bed, pulls a wrinkled suit back on, and extracts several quarters from her wallet. Then walks under the portico toward the main building of the inn, where she'll get something from the vending machines.

The front door is unlocked, but the desk is empty. Under the fluorescent lights of the lobby, Judy inspects her choices. She'll get a Milky Way bar, she decides—her mother's favorite. But when she makes her selection, the bar gets stuck against the glass on its way down.

Judy curses. Kicks the machine once, twice.

Three times.

With her hand, she pounds on the glass.

"Miss?" someone says, and Judy spins, panting.

It's Bob Alcott—the owner of the inn.

"I'm sorry," says Judy, twice. "Did I wake you?"

"No, no," says Mr. Alcott. "I was up anyway." He's fumbling for something in his pocket, and she sees that it's a set of keys. He takes the smallest one out, inserts it into the vending machine, and opens the door.

Immediately, the Milky Way falls to the ground. Judy stoops to retrieve it, feeling foolish.

"Take another," says Mr. Alcott. "Take whatever you want."

"That's all right," says Judy, but already Mr. Alcott is silently collecting a small assortment of candy and snacks from the machine.

"Here," he says. "Least I can do."

Then he closes it, and locks the door.

Judy regards him. "Mr. Alcott," she says. "You're a history teacher, right?"

He nods.

"How much do you know about the history of the Van Laar Preserve?"

"Oh," says Mr. Alcott. "Just about everything there is to know."

He straightens as he says it. This, Judy understands, is his life's work.

"Miss Luptack, would you like to come in for a cup of tea?" says Bob Alcott. "To go with your Milky Way bar."

"Won't it disturb your wife?" Judy asks, and the man shakes his head. "Oh, no. She's up too. We're both night owls, now that the kids are grown."

"That's very kind of you," says Judy.

Then she excuses herself briefly to retrieve her notepad from her room.

In the Alcotts' apartment, just off the lobby, the couple sits across from Judy at a table.

Judy lets her pen hover for a moment over the paper before her. Then she dives in.

"Mr. and Mrs. Alcott," she says. "Here's my first question. Do you know when the Hewitts came to live on the Preserve?"

"Oh," says Mr. Alcott, "that's easy. Same time as the Van Laars. In fact, it was the Hewitts who guided them to the land. Dan Hewitt was Vic's father. He was born into a guiding family about an hour north, up near Saranac Lake. The first Peter Van Laar made his acquaintance when he was scouting land for his estate. It was Dan who knew about a piece of land a bit farther south that a family of loggers was looking to sell. He pointed Peter the First in that direction."

"What family was that?" asks Judy.

"The ones who sold it to the Van Laars, you mean?"

She nods.

"Funny you ask," says Mr. Alcott. "It was a family called Sluiter. You might have heard of their son."

"Yes," says Judy. "I have."

"Anyway. Peter Van Laar—the first one, I mean—took such a shine to the land that he felt indebted to Dan Hewitt. Brought him along to what became the Van Laar Preserve to serve as the family's personal guide."

Alcott stops. Sips his tea.

"A decade went by. The first Peter Van Laar met and married his wife, and together they had a son—the second Peter, still alive today. Dan Hewitt, too, met a woman named Clara, who gave him twin boys. But Clara didn't live long after that, according to my research. So the boys were raised by their father until they were about fifteen—which is when he died too. They became orphans, living on the land of the Van Laar Preserve. Mr. Van Laar, the First, was the one to take them in. He brought them from the cabin they'd been living in, right into the Van Laar house. They even lived in Albany with the Van Laars during the year."

Judy considers this.

"What was the age difference," she asks, "between Peter II and the Hewitt boys? Were they older than him, or younger?"

"Only a handful of years younger," says Mr. Alcott.

"Six, I think," says his wife.

"Six years. And the rumor in the town was that Peter II never liked the Hewitt boys. His father favored them. Took them on daily walks. Gave them the run of the place. He was kind to Charlie Hewitt—always spoke well of him. But it was Vic he really loved. Treated him like another son. Adopted him, basically, though that was never made official.

"In theory," Mr. Alcott continues, "the Hewitt boys should have been like brothers to Peter II. But he was jealous, I think. Still is, maybe."

Judy is writing as fast as she can. Still, it's not fast enough. Mr. Alcott notices, and pauses.

"Camp Emerson was Vic's idea," says Mr. Alcott, when Judy looks up again. "He was the one did all the work for it. But Peter I supported it from the start. By the end of his life, he described it as his greatest accomplishment. He saw it as a way to teach generations of children about the importance of the land. The beauty of it. He never gave a damn about the money he made banking—always seemed surprised by how much he had, in my opinion. He used to come into Shattuck and greet everyone by name. He was different from his offspring. More like a Hewitt than a Van Laar, if you ask me. Because the rest of his family always saw Camp Emerson as a folly. They wanted nothing to do with it. Still don't."

Mrs. Alcott stands. Puts the kettle on again.

"The problems between the Hewitts and the Van Laars began when Peter I died. I hate to gossip, and I'm telling you honestly that I have no way to know, but the rumor is that Peter I left Camp Emerson and its operations entirely to Vic Hewitt. Divided the Preserve in half. The main house and the farm would go to the Van Laars; the camp to the Hewitts. In theory, it was a plan that might have worked. But," he says.

"But?"

"He made a mistake. He made his own son, Peter II, the trustee of his will—thus granting him the power to distribute funds for the camp as he saw fit, until his death."

"And after he dies?" says Judy.

"Then the camp'll go to Vic," says Mr. Alcott. "Or more likely to his daughter, Tessie Jo."

The kettle whistles. Judy looks up.

"But as I said," says Mr. Alcott. "This is all rumor. Speculation. Which—as a history teacher—I should know better than to propagate."

"I understand," says Judy. "I'll look into it myself."

She stands. Thanks Mrs. Alcott for the tea. At the door, she turns back.

"I do have another question," she says.

"Go ahead."

"Vic Hewitt's brother," she says. "Charlie. What happened to him?"

"Oh, he died a decade ago, at least," says Mr. Alcott.

"Two decades ago," says Mrs. Alcott.

"Two decades ago. Before Bear disappeared. That's right."

"How did he die?"

"Natural causes," says Mr. Alcott. "Nothing suspicious."

"What did he do on the Preserve?"

Mr. Alcott frowns. "Now, I have to think about that," he says. He puts his head down, as if trying hard to remember. "I guess—if I'm remembering right, I think he ran the farm. I think he oversaw the farm that supplied the main house with all its provisions, back in the day."

"And he lived," says Judy—though she already knows how he will answer. *Where is he staying?* she'd asked T.J., and T.J. had said: *With his brother.*

"He lived above the slaughterhouse," says Mr. Alcott. "In a little apartment up there. That's if I'm remembering right," says Mr. Alcott, again.

Judy thanks him. Walks back toward her room, to get her car keys. And her gun.

Within five minutes she's driving, headlights pointed north toward the Preserve.

Judyta

1950s • 1961 • Winter 1973 • June 1975
July 1975 • August 1975: **Night Five**

She's never been on these grounds except in daylight. Now, the moon lends the long dirt driveway a different aspect. The pines on either side of it stretch like giants toward the sky. The farm buildings, in the glow cast by her headlights, look even more decrepit and decayed.

Judy pulls to the side of the driveway. Cuts her engine. Cuts her headlights, too.

She sits for a moment in the vast dark of the Preserve, letting her eyes adjust. This is the month of the Perseid meteor shower in the Adirondacks, and the sky is bright with stars.

She opens and closes the door to her Beetle as gently as she can. Opens the trunk to retrieve the flashlight from her emergency kit.

Then, holding her flashlight forward, she walks toward the slaughterhouse.

She approaches it the way she used to dive into cold water as a child. Quickly, confidently, without thinking too much.

If she stops and considers her actions, she knows she might falter.

Inside, she walks straight to the back, where a staircase rises toward the second floor. She ascends. The beam of the flashlight trembles slightly in her hand.

Halfway up, she pauses.

She hears something.

Voices, maybe: a man's voice. And then, suddenly, music. She can't make out the lyrics, but the music itself is old-fashioned, something she believes her grandparents might have listened to.

She continues up the stairs. At the top, in the beam of her flashlight, she sees a closed door. It's held shut by a hasp and a padlock—the same kind she noticed on T.J. Hewitt's room in the Staff Quarters building.

She hesitates for a moment. And then, carefully, she draws her gun. With her other hand, she raps at the door.

"Mr. Hewitt?" she says. "Are you in there?"

The radio goes off.

"Mr. Hewitt," she calls. "My name is Investigator Judyta Luptack. I'd like to ask you a few questions."

Silence.

"Mr. Hewitt?" says Judy.

She feels so close to the truth. Her heartbeat quickens.

"Mr.—" she begins, and then at last she hears him.

"Barbara?" he says.

Judy shivers a little. "No, Mr. Hewitt," she says. "My name is Judyta—" she begins, but Vic Hewitt cuts her off.

"Barbara," he says. "You're not supposed to be here."

"Mr. Hewitt," calls Judy, "I'm not Barbara. Is Barbara inside with you?"

Silence.

"Mr. Hewitt?"

She feels the weight of the gun in her hands. Considers her options. She could retreat; could walk or drive up to the Command Post; could bring yet another fleet of troopers to this structure. Could risk being seen as a fool yet again.

Instead, she says, "Mr. Hewitt, stand back from the door."

She aims her pistol sideways at the padlock, ensuring that the bullet won't make its way through the door. She braces her arm. Fires.

The padlock falls with a clunk to the floor, and Judy opens the door.

Inside a sparsely furnished room, an old man lies in a twin bed. A blanket covers him from his chin to his feet. His body is small; his expression confused.

"Who," he says, over and over again.

Instantly, Judy feels guilty.

"I'm not here to harm you," she says. "I just need to ask you some questions."

But Vic Hewitt only lets out a series of sounds that Judy can't comprehend, and at last, she recognizes that she's in a situation she can't get out of: with the padlock broken, she has no way to lock the door again; with the state this man is in, she has no way to bring him outside. And she has no way to bring others to him either, without leaving him alone.

Judy looks straight down at the ground, between her feet. Maybe, she thinks, this wasn't the right line of work for her after all. Maybe she would have been better off remaining a trooper.

Then, from the bed, there is movement.

"Oh," says Vic Hewitt. "Oh. Oh. I guess you're here about Bear."

His voice is remorseful—but also younger, more energetic, as if he is returning in his mind to another time in his life.

Judy hesitates. She isn't certain whether statements from those with *infirm minds*—the term she learned at the academy—are admissible in court. But her own personal curiosity, in this situation, wins.

"Yes," she says. "I'm afraid I'm here about Bear."

Vic Hewitt is struggling, now, to sit up in bed. Judy bends down, places a hand on his back. Helps him. Then sits on the edge of his bed. Upright now, Hewitt gazes directly at her, and she sees his eyes are filled with tears.

"I only helped," he says. "I only helped."

"You didn't kill him?" Judy asks.

"*Kill* him? God no," says Vic Hewitt.

"Who did?" Judy says.

And then, from outside the door, the sound of footsteps on the stairs. Judy goes quiet. Draws her gun. Walks swiftly toward the wall next to the threshold, and puts her back to it.

"Oh no," says Hewitt. "Oh no."

The person stops outside the door. Judy can hear breathing. She will fire this gun, she tells herself, only if necessary.

At last, T.J. Hewitt takes one step into the room, looking in Judy's direction already, as if she knows who will be there.

She looks Judy up and down. Looks directly at her gun.

"I've got one of those too," she says mildly. "But I don't draw it on people."

"Lie down," Judy says. And then she adds: "Please."

T.J. sighs. Takes her time. She gets down on her knees, looking up at Judy all the while as if demonstrating the ridiculousness of the exercise. Then lowers herself, in a slow push-up, to the ground.

Judy, gun still drawn, pats her down.

"All right, listen," she says. "You and I are going to walk toward the Command Post together."

"Toward my house, you mean," says T.J.

"Sure."

"Well, that won't work."

"Why?"

"I can't leave my dad here. He wanders. That door has to be locked."

Judy sighs, exasperated. "Can he come with us?"

T.J. gives a half laugh. "Hardly. Look at him. I had to carry him up the stairs to get him here."

For a moment, Judy and T.J. look at each other. Then T.J. says: "Tie us up."

Judy blinks. "With what?"

"There's rope downstairs. All kinds of stuff. Tie us up. I'll help you."

She hesitates. It feels like a trap; and yet there is no other option, in Judy's mind, that doesn't involve leaving at least one of the Hewitts alone.

And so she does it: she follows T.J. down into the slaughterhouse, and then around the side of it toward another building T.J. calls the granary, and from here they extract the rope, and back upstairs, in the little apartment above the slaughterhouse, Judy ties the Hewitts together, back to back on Vic Hewitt's bed. Then she ties the rope itself to the bed frame.

Fifteen minutes later, she returns, with four investigators and five state troopers.

Thirty minutes later, she's sitting in the passenger's seat of a patrol car. The Hewitts are in the back.

Victor

In the Director's Cabin, Vic was speaking with a recalcitrant twelve-year-old boy, a child who had been shunned by his peers and had recently converted his embarrassment at this development into physical aggression.

In the middle of their conversation, the boy had stopped suddenly to point through a nearby window.

"What is it?" said Vic, turning.

"Something's in the lake," said the boy—his tone changing from bitter to unsettled.

Sure enough: in the middle of Lake Joan was a white-bellied object that looked at first like a surfacing whale.

Vic stood and walked to the window.

It was a rowboat, capsized.

"Stay here," said Victor. "Don't get up out of that chair."

Outside, Vic broke into a run. A bad thunderstorm had just come through, sending counselors and campers inside, and the grass was slick with new rain. He stumbled, once. Fell to his knees. Then stood again.

The grounds felt empty. He swung his head around, but saw no human forms.

Even up the hill, at Self-Reliance, it was quiet—for the first time in a week, it seemed. The Van Laars had been having their annual party on the grounds—to which Victor, who used to be included when Peter I was alive, had not been invited in years.

Upon reaching the beach, Vic stood with his hands on his hips, observing the upside-down boat. One of the guests up at the main house, he thought; someone had capsized it and then left it to sink. They were always pulling stunts like this, drunken antics that resulted in more work for everyone else on the grounds. He scanned the shores, looking for movement, seeing none.

Then, sighing, he turned and jogged up the hill, toward Self-Reliance.

The thought occurred to him that he had not set eyes on Tessie Jo since morning. Normally, this wouldn't have concerned him overmuch. All summer, she was given free rein to run about the grounds—usually with Bear on her heels. Her relationship with the Van Laars was different from her father's; they accepted her as a playmate for Bear, as someone who could keep an eye on their adventurous son. She went freely in and out of Self-Reliance with the boy; Victor, meanwhile, avoided the house entirely.

Now he steeled himself, and squared his shoulders, and knocked at the front door of the Van Laars' house.

It opened immediately.

On the other side was Peter II, Bear's grandfather, who looked as if he'd been standing guard.

His face was stiff and pallid. His hair was wet.

"Everything all right?" said Victor. "I saw a boat—"

Peter II grabbed his shoulders swiftly. Manhandled him away from the threshold. The blackfly doorknocker clacked once in their wake as the door closed.

"Follow me," Peter II commanded. His voice was low and urgent.

"I need to find my daughter," said Victor. "I need to make sure she's all right."

"She's fine," said Peter II. "Bear's not."

Victor looked at the man: his nominal brother. His enemy. At that moment, Peter II's entire face was trembling slightly, his mouth down-turned, his eyes bulging in what looked like an effort not to shout, or faint, or cry.

He set off toward the boathouse. Wordlessly, Vic followed.

Halfway there, he heard a noise that stopped him in his tracks. He listened, alert, his whole body still.

A fox, he thought—he'd heard that sound in the night, an eerie throttled cry that raised the hair on his neck.

But foxes were nocturnal; this was no animal.

It was, he realized at last, the sound of a woman wailing.

Victor

1950s • **1961** • Winter 1973 • June 1975
July 1975 • August 1975

Together, the two men stood in the threshold of the boathouse, looking out toward the lake and the sinking, upturned rowboat.

Peter II had been the one to find Alice. After her embarrassing entrance into the great room—after his attempt to divert the boy from boating with his obviously incapacitated mother—Peter II had gone outside to where he'd told his grandson to meet him for a hike, and found him absent.

Thinking at first that he might have gone ahead toward Hunt Mountain, Peter II had walked in that direction awhile, until the rain began in earnest, at which point a terrible thought occurred to him.

The boy would not be at the trailhead. He would be at the lake, with his mother. He was devoted to her; he would have noticed her distress, when she stumbled into the crowded great room and issued him the invitation to go boating.

"At which point I ran," said Peter II to Vic Hewitt. His face, as he looked toward the lake, was still. His formality would not waver, even in that moment.

When he reached the boathouse, the storm was receding. And there before him, climbing up the ramp, a terrible vision: Alice, waterlogged, hysterical, screaming incomprehensibly. In the far distance, the rowboat, overturned.

"Where's Bear?" he said to her, urgently, but she made no noises he could understand. Only pointed in the direction of the water, doubled over as if in physical pain.

He had scanned the water, and the shore. Just as he was doing now. He hadn't seen Bear.

"I sat Alice down," said Peter II. "I commanded her to be still. Then I dove in."

He was hoping, he said, to find the boy alive, under the hull of the boat. He was praying for this.

But when he reached the rowboat, and dove under, he was met with a terrible sight: his grandson, lifeless.

His clothing hooked to the oarlock.

"I pulled him to shore," said Peter II. "He had no pulse."

Did you breathe into his mouth? Vic wanted to ask. *Did you pump his chest?* It was a technique his father had taught him; that his grandfather had taught his father.

To ask these questions aloud felt cruel, and so Victor was silent.

Peter was too. For a while, neither spoke; Peter II cleared his throat several times in a row, and Victor turned to him: this man he had known since birth. Peter I had told Vic, on his deathbed, that he hoped they would come to see one another as brothers. But for all those years of acquaintance, he had never once felt any sympathetic impulse for the man, until now.

Tentatively, Vic put one hand on his shoulder.

The look that Peter II cast in his direction—imperious, appalled— made him withdraw quickly.

"Alice can't know," said Peter II, after a short pause. "Peter's with her now, trying to keep her calm. But we have both decided that she can't know what happened."

Vic furrowed his brow.

"Where is she?"

"In one of the farm buildings, I think," said Peter II. "In your brother's old apartment. Far enough away that she won't be heard."

This didn't seem right, or useful.

But it was not, he knew, Alice's well-being that concerned them. It was theirs. And the bank's.

To have their name in the papers for anything other than success was anathema to the Peters. And a scandal like this one—Bear's mother, drunk, taking her son out boating in a storm—something that would affect their business, shake the confidence of their clients in the entire enterprise—well, they wouldn't let it happen. That much was obvious.

A long silence ensued, until Peter II said, "Look."

He pointed in the direction of the rowboat. Only the faintest trace of it was visible now, the seam of its white belly facing up toward the clearing sky.

Together, they watched as it sank beneath the water. Then it was gone.

Before Victor lay two clear paths. One was to disagree with the Peters. He could tell them that he would not lie; he could say to them that an untruth as large as this one would have consequences they couldn't foresee. His own father had taught him this well, when he was learning to guide: in the woods, each decision you make is irreversible, and sometimes catastrophic. A forgotten compass. A wrong turn. A fire lit in defiance of a drought. He could tell them he would not stand for it, and leave.

But in the process, he would lose the trust of the overseer of his inheritance. Lose the camp. His livelihood.

If Victor were deciding for himself alone, this was the path he would go down, surely. He reassured himself of this. Nodding once, as if to seal the thought inside him.

But he wasn't deciding only for himself: there was Tessie Jo to think of, too. His daughter, who loved the land as much as he did. Whose unusual demeanor and appearance and comportment had already drawn stares in town. With the camp, her future was secure: she would never be required to marry, not if she didn't want to. She could live, without restriction, what he thought of as an *unconventional* life.

Every choice would be open to her. This was what he told himself, as he took one step down the other path that lay before him: to hide the truth, at the command of the Van Laars.

"How can I help you?" said Victor.

He thought of his own father, holding a compass in his hand, watching its needle wobble, and then calm.

Victor

Together, they lifted Bear's body from its place on the floor of the boathouse and into the bottom of a red canoe. Vic stood guard while Peter II walked up to the slaughterhouse to switch places with his son. Then Peter III came, white-faced, and asked for a moment alone.

Outside the boathouse, Vic froze. From inside came the muffled sounds of a grown man crying. Trying not to be overheard.

Five minutes passed. Ten. And then Peter III emerged, red-faced and red-eyed, looking straight ahead, away from Victor.

"Do what you must," he said. And then he walked away.

Vic pushed the canoe into the lake. In its belly, beneath a blanket, was the body of Bear Van Laar. Next to it, a shovel.

He sat in the stern, keeping his eyes ahead, trying hard not to look down at the small figure he was ferrying across the water to a permanent repose.

When he did, it was not revulsion that he felt, or fear, but tenderness.

He, too, had loved the boy.

As gently as he could, he moored the boat on a rocky bank, on the opposite side of Lake Joan. He lifted Bear's small strong body from the boat. It was so strange to see it still: the boy had been in motion, always, from the time he could walk. Tessie Jo's shadow, following her wherever she went.

Vic took the shovel from the boat. Cradled the boy in his arms. Thirty feet inland, he laid the boy down at the foot of a sheer face of rock, and began to dig.

At Self-Reliance, he knew, the Peters would be making the announcement to the guests, who would be rising lazily from an afternoon nap, or looking up from the books they had brought out when it became clear that the storm would keep everyone inside.

"We need your help," they would say. "Earlier, Bear went for a walk with his grandfather. Now it seems as if he might be lost."

This was the plan they'd created while, above the slaughterhouse, Alice Van Laar slept, stupefied by a dose of Valium that bordered on dangerous.

"Vic Hewitt is already scouting the area," they'd say. In case anyone saw him out in the canoe.

"We're calling the fire department now," they'd say.

Victor's face betrayed his doubt.

It would work, the Peters insisted.

Now, with Bear safely inside the ground, Vic bade him farewell and began the work of filling in the hole. When he was finished, he began to walk away—and then thought better of it.

He gathered a cache of stones.

He built a cairn.

He'd visit the boy from time to time. He'd bring Tessie Jo, too, when she was old enough.

For now, she would not have to know the truth.

Victor

1950s • **1961** • Winter 1973 • June 1975
July 1975 • August 1975

What he didn't count on was that Tessie Jo would have seen.
Her absence that day made him assume that she was busying herself someplace, finishing one of her projects elsewhere on the grounds. And he was glad for it—glad that he would not have to explain things to her, while she was still so young. There would be time for that eventually, he thought.

But then—after the firefighters arrived, after he had persuaded them to wait until morning to begin their search in earnest—Tessie Jo had come tearing out of the forest, her mouth wide, her face white, her long braid damp.

He had managed to corral her, before she could speak. He had managed to hustle her down a hallway.

"Tessie Jo," he said, when they were alone. "What is it?"

She'd seen the overturned rowboat. Her curiosity had brought her to the south side of the boathouse. From there, she overheard her father speaking with the Peters; had overheard what the Peters wanted to do.

From there, she saw her own father row the red canoe to the other side of the lake, and she saw him return from it, too.

She knew what they had done.

Now, as Vic made his request of her—to stay silent, forever, about what she had seen; to join him and the Peters in their great untruth—she looked back at him, her large eyes narrowed, her eyebrows furrowed.

Her doubt made him doubtful, too.

But a girl of her age couldn't understand her own future the way he did. She couldn't understand how limited her opportunities would be, if they defied the Peters, told the truth.

Their future rested upon this lie.

"Trust me," said Victor.

Reluctantly, his daughter nodded.

Victor

1950s • **1961** • Winter 1973 • June 1975
July 1975 • August 1975

His assignment, overnight, was to keep watch over Mrs. Van Laar, in her temporary residence above the slaughterhouse. It was important to keep her apart from the other guests, said the Peters, until she could be calmed.

At two in the morning, Mrs. Van Laar was asleep again, finally. It had taken four pills—the most they had authorized him to dispense at one time.

On a little chair, he sat across from her, watching her. He didn't dislike Mrs. Van Laar, though she had never been particularly kind to him. He found her to be pitiable. Someone the Peters had identified as *useful*.

This was also, no doubt, the way they thought of him. When they didn't think of him as burdensome.

When Mrs. Van Laar was finally permitted to be conscious—whenever the Peters deemed it safe—she would be broken beyond repair to learn the truth of what had transpired that afternoon.

What she had done.

Each time she woke—in between doses—Mrs. Van Laar asked the same question, increasingly desperate: "*Where's Bear?*" Over and over she asked it, the words blurry at their edges.

For anyone else, it might have been difficult to understand what she was saying. But Victor knew: they were the same words she asked him, daily, whenever she ran into him on the grounds.

"Where's Bear?" she asked him, anew, and again he spoke the line he was told to speak.

"He went for a walk with his grandfather. We'll find him soon."

"But the boat," she said.

"There was no boat. That was a dream."

Again and again, the same exchange. Then she would quiet, until: *Where's Bear?*

This was the question she would ask for the rest of her life, seeking her son without end. In keeping the truth from her, Victor thought—the truth that they told him she could not abide, that they insisted would send her to an early grave—the Peters were simply taking away the grief of loss and replacing it with the grief of uncertainty.

This, he realized, was the very thing from which he was attempting to protect his own daughter. He believed, on most levels, that he had little to give her, without the Van Laars. And so he bent to their collective will, telling himself that at least, in doing so, he was giving his strange and wonderful daughter the certainty of meaningful work. An income. Freedom from the sort of life the Van Laar women had been assigned at birth.

Next to him, Mrs. Van Laar now moaned softly in her sleep. A thin film of sweat dotted her brow. He opened a dresser drawer. Took out a towel. Gently, he placed it to her head.

In the morning, he would face a larger crowd of searchers.

He would tell them the same story he had told the firefighters, and his daughter, and himself.

Bear went for a walk with his grandfather.

He turned back for a pocketknife.

He was not seen again.

Alice

1950s • **1961** • Winter 1973 • June 1975
July 1975 • August 1975

Each time she surfaced from sleep, she was greeted by the same set of images:

Bear, opening the boathouse door.

And then:

The boat on the water.

The oncoming storm.

The darkening sky.

The face of her son as he sat in the bow of the boat, smiling tightly, his small brow furrowed, while she rowed. How he'd looked toward the shore, and then the sky, and then his mother, seeking her reassurance at the first clap of thunder.

The rain came on so quickly that she could see it moving toward them like a curtain, east to west across the lake. When it reached them, it had filled their boat.

She tried to bail with her hands. She clawed at the water.

The boat tipped, and the two of them spilled out.

The far gunnel came crashing down with a slap on something hard. A human form.

She shouted the name of her son.

Judyta

1950s • 1961 • Winter 1973 • June 1975
July 1975 • August 1975: **Day Six**

"She'll sign a statement?" says Hayes.

"She will," says Judy.

They're standing outside an interrogation room at Ray Brook—the same one in which Judy first met Jacob Sluiter. On the other side of the mirrored window, they watch T.J. Hewitt, who sits as still as stone, both hands on the table before her.

"You know what she told me?" says Judy. "That time I heard noises up above the slaughterhouse? She said that was them. The Hewitts. That when I left, T.J. hustled the two of them off the property, knowing that I'd return with backup. So when the troopers climbed the stairs," she says.

"It looked empty."

"Right."

"Thing I don't get," says Hayes, "is why choose this moment to confess? Why keep the secret for fourteen years, only to give it up now?"

"I've got a theory about that."

"I bet you do."

They pause, watching T.J., who closes her eyes for such a long time that Judy wonders if she's asleep. Then she opens them.

"I think she was afraid the Van Laars were right on the cusp of framing an innocent person again. Just like they did with Carl Stoddard."

Hayes turns to her, frowning. "McLellan?" he says. "She thinks McLellan's innocent?"

"No," says Judy. "She thinks he did it. But McLellan, Junior, is the Van Laar's godson. He'll take over the bank someday, according to his sister—since the Van Laars have no son. And McLellan, Senior, has a lot of sway over the family, and the bank. T.J. was afraid the McLellans would convince the family that Louise Donnadieu was the culprit."

Hayes pauses.

"So the Hewitts came forward to save Louise Donnadieu's reputation?"

"And Carl Stoddard's. All these years later."

Hayes nods.

"Never too late, I guess," he says.

Together, they watch as T.J. Hewitt turns her face toward the one window in the interrogation room. It's too high to give any view of the buildings outside, or even of the trees; but still she searches it, her eyes moving rapidly. She breathes deeply, face turned toward the bright sky.

What will she do now, wonders Judy, if the Hewitts lose the camp? If the Van Laars cut them out entirely, as they'll no doubt do, snapping the thin thread that has stretched for decades between the Hewitts and Peter the First?

And she answers her question herself: They'll be fine. The Hewitts— like Judy, like Louise Donnadieu, like Denny Hayes, even—don't need to rely on anyone but themselves.

It's the Van Laars, and families like them, who have always depended on others.

Judyta

1950s • 1961 • Winter 1973 • June 1975
July 1975 • August 1975: **Day Six**

Technically, her shift is over. But now that she no longer has to answer to her parents each night, Judy can stay as long as she likes. Until her work is done.

Hayes, on the other hand, has to get home to his family.

Before he leaves, he claps her on the shoulder. "Good work," he says. "I mean it."

In the wake of the Hewitts' revelation about the Van Laars, Investigator Goldman is on his way to obtain arrest warrants for both Van Laar men—Peters II and III—and also for John Paul McLellan Sr., on charges of criminal conspiracy for their role in lying to the police in the 1961 drowning of Bear Van Laar. Vic Hewitt may be formally charged as well; but given the state of his health, it's unlikely he'll serve time.

Tonight, at a press conference, Captain LaRochelle will announce the discovery of Bear Van Laar's body. He will also announce that the case has been reopened, with more information forthcoming to the public as soon as he can disclose it.

Within a week, she suspects, Carl Stoddard's name will be publicly cleared; and his wife, Maryanne, can at long last retire from haunting the grounds of the Van Laar Preserve, looking for any evidence that might restore her husband's innocence.

The Van Laars, on the other hand, will finally suffer the consequences of their actions.

All of these developments should, in theory, give her a feeling of peace.

But instead, the feeling she has is that there's more work to do—another whole case to solve.

Because Barbara Van Laar—or Barbara Van Laar's body—still hasn't been found.

* * *

In the parking lot at Ray Brook, she gets into her Beetle. Drives south on the thruway, toward Shattuck. These days, she does her best reasoning in her car.

The most logical conclusion, she thinks, is that Barbara was killed by John Paul McLellan. All of the evidence points in this direction: the bloody uniform, most damningly; but also the mural, the references Barbara made to an "older boyfriend," her nightly excursions up Hunt Mountain, the fingerprints, pulled from beer bottles, that indicate that John Paul had been living there for some time.

Given all of this evidence, Judy feels as if she should be more certain of John Paul's guilt.

But something isn't sitting right with her.

More than that: without finding Barbara—alive or otherwise—they still can't make an arrest. And this means that John Paul McLellan will go free.

Over and over again, she goes through the pieces of the puzzle, willing a final piece to land in place.

But it doesn't, and doesn't.

For a while, Judy drives in silence, until her stomach rumbles so loudly that she laughs.

Last night, she ate dinner in Shattuck's only restaurant, which was more like a bar.

At the bottom of the exit off the thruway, she squints into the darkness, looking for the sign.

There it is: *Driscoll's.*

Judy, still in her same wrinkled pantsuit from a long day of work, turns right, and then right again, into the driveway of Driscoll's Pub.

Louise

1950s • 1961 • Winter 1973 • June 1975
July 1975 • August 1975: **Day Six**

Put on a shirt," says Louise. "A real shirt."

By this she means a shirt with a collar. Her little brother has been wearing the same Led Zeppelin T-shirt, thin from use, for a year.

"I don't have one of those," says Jesse. So she gives him her own: a white Camp Emerson polo, unisex enough to make him unashamed.

"I'm taking you out to dinner," says Louise.

At Driscoll's, the air is smoky, the atmosphere one of disuse.

Several men Louise vaguely recognizes play pool in the middle of a side room. The dining room, where Louise and Jesse sit, is empty but for a woman sitting at the bar.

Louise hands Jesse a menu.

"Get anything you want," she says.

Jesse regards her. "Louise, you know I'm okay?"

"What do you mean?"

He looks down. Touches each corner of the menu. Fumbling with it.

The waitress—Connie Driscoll, eighty years old if she's a day—comes to take their order.

"Get a steak if you want," says Louise, but Jesse orders a burger and fries.

"I'll have a steak, please, Mrs. Driscoll," says Louise. "Medium rare. Thank you."

Connie Driscoll vanishes into the kitchen, her sneakered footsteps silent on the wall-to-wall carpet that covers the floor.

Jesse and Louise fall into silence.

"What were you saying?" says Louise. "About being okay?"

"Oh, I don't know," says Jesse. "I just know you worry about me. But I'm actually fine. Mom's tough, but I've got friends who look out for me. And half the teachers in my school. They liked you and they look out for me because of it."

Against her will, Louise smiles.

"You're welcome," she says.

"No, I'm serious," says Jesse. "I'm fine. I'm almost twelve years old. I can look out for myself."

"Jesse. C'mon," says Louise.

"Well, then let Mom look out for me for a change," he says. "It doesn't always have to be you."

Louise looks down. Unwilling to break the news to him: their mother will never watch over him. Not the way Louise does. No one will.

"I worry about you too, you know," says Jesse. "If you took care of yourself a little better, that would help me out. If you really wanna help, I mean."

"Took care of myself how?"

Connie Driscoll returns with a Shirley Temple for Jesse. A Coke for Louise.

"On the house," she says.

He sips.

"Started dating better guys," he says. "For one thing. Or no guys," he adds, as an afterthought.

Louise nods. It's painful to hear, but it's true. When, Louise wonders, did Jesse become the person in front of her? In her mind she sees the version of her brother who, when tired, used to drape his small body onto hers, place two of his own fingers into his mouth. Time, she thinks, moves differently in Shattuck from how it does at the Preserve.

"And also," says Jesse, "you should get a different job."

"Like what?"

"I don't know, Lou. You're really smart. You can do anything you want. You could go back to Union."

"On whose dollar?" says Louise.

"I dunno. Borrow it from a bank. Isn't that what they do?"

It sounds exhausting. She feels as if she's at the base of a mountain, looking up.

But she's climbed mountains before. She's run up mountains, even.

They eat their meal in comfortable silence, listening to the clack of pool balls, the warbly music coming over the speaker system.

Connie Driscoll asks them if they'd like anything else, and Louise orders dessert. Why not? she thinks. She has enough saved in her bank account to support herself, and Jesse, for a little while.

Tonight, she thinks, she's taking a break from worry—a little respite while she awaits her hearing.

Someone puts a nickel in the jukebox, and the music changes. The Everly Brothers, singing about dreams. Then, beneath their close hypnotic harmonies, Louise hears the squeak of a barstool being pushed backward. The lone woman who has been sitting there stands, digs out her wallet.

When she turns, Louise sees that the woman looks familiar, but she can't quite place her. She's wearing a suit with some stains on it. Her hair is short. She looks young: Louise's age, or a few years older.

She also looks, if not drunk, then like she's deposited two beers into a body not used to alcohol.

Louise knows, before she hears it, what the woman will say. "Excuse me?"

But when Louise turns, the woman is looking not at her, but at Jesse.

"Do you go to Camp Emerson?" says the woman. She's holding a finger out in Jesse's direction, pointing to his polo shirt, which bears the camp's green logo.

Jesse looks suddenly frightened.

"No," says Louise, rising, standing in front of him. "He doesn't. But I'm a counselor there."

The woman turns her gaze toward Louise.

"I recognize you," she says.

Tracy

1950s • 1961 • Winter 1973 • June 1975
July 1975 • August 1975: **Day Six**

Tracy leans her head against the window of the Stutz Blackhawk. Her father's car is the first she's ever ridden in that has air-conditioning. The car he'd had for years prior was a Chevy, a practical four-door pickup that was also strong enough to tow a horse trailer.

She misses the Chevy. More than that, she misses the version of her father that drove the Chevy.

The house in Hempstead is exactly as Tracy left it at the start of the summer. Silver front gate, astroturf lawn, artificial flowers in plastic window boxes beneath each of the two front windows.

And her mother—her mother is sitting on the front steps, head high, waiting for the two of them to arrive.

The Blackhawk roars to a stop in the driveway, and Molly Jewell stands up.

Tracy jumps out of the car, and runs to her mother—her kind, funny mother, who has always been exactly herself, who makes no attempt to be anyone or anything she isn't.

With a jolt, Tracy realizes whom she reminds her of.

"Oh, Tracy," says her mother. "I'm so sorry about your friend. It sounds like she meant a lot to you."

"She does," says Tracy.

How, wonders Tracy, will she ever explain to her mother how her life was changed by a person she knew for two months?

Her father, having unloaded the car, now clears his throat awkwardly.

"Good to see you, Molly," he says. She nods.

He hugs Tracy, and then he is gone, leaving Tracy and her mother standing in the driveway with all of her things from Camp Emerson. This, she understands, is how things will be for the rest of her childhood: the two of them, together. The two of them, alone.

She'll see her father again at his wedding to Donna Romano, and at holidays where, for each of the three years afterward, a new baby half-sibling will appear. She will make conversation. She'll be polite. But they won't be her family, not anymore. The only family she has left stands beside her.

"Mom," says Tracy. "Have you ever heard of punk music?"

"No," says her mother. "Will you tell me about it?"

The sky above Hempstead is growing dim. Tracy thinks of Barbara Van Laar. Wonders if she's alive, if she's seeing the same sky, three hundred miles to the north.

She pictures Barbara's strong limbs, her upright steady head, her skillfulness in water and in woods. She pictures Barbara as she was on the Survival Trip: building a tent, building a fire, bringing back food for them. Keeping everyone alive.

And she knows—or believes, at least—that Barbara is still in the world.

Judyta

In her Beetle, Judy pulls into the driveway of her parents' home in Schenectady. She sits for a moment, preparing herself.

It's a Saturday, and she knows precisely what they'll be doing: Inside, her mother will be vacuuming while her father dusts. Her brothers will be changing lightbulbs, or doing other odd jobs that their parents have requested of them. It's the same thing they've done every Saturday for as long as she can remember. For years, she would have been working alongside them, folding laundry, making beds. Only this Saturday, Judy is, for the first time, a visitor.

A month ago, she moved all of her things out of her childhood bedroom and into a tiny rental a few miles from headquarters at Ray Brook. She had no help doing so; her father, upon her arrival, had nodded once in her direction, and then left the house.

Now she gets up out of the car. Closes the door. The noise brings her brother Leonard to the door.

Seeing her, he calls backward into the house. "Ma."

Judy enters the house, and Leonard hugs her.

The sound of the vacuum, ceasing. "What is it?" her mother calls.

Leonard grins.

"The Nation's First has returned."

Ten minutes later, all the Luptacks sit at the kitchen table. Her mother has set out tea. Her father, the last to arrive, stirs sugar into his cup, clears his throat. All of them are silent, until Leonard says, "We saw your name in the paper again."

Judy looks up.

"You did?"

Leonard nods. Stands up from the table. Returns with a sheet in his hands: another clipped article from the *Times Union*.

She takes it into her hands, and reads.

Van Laars Indicted, reads the headline. Beneath it, a subhead: *Original Suspect Posthumously Cleared.*

The story continues.

Alice Van Laar, who would no doubt have been charged originally with vehicular manslaughter in the death of her son, will go free: the statute of limitations has run out.

But Peters II and III will be charged with criminal conspiracy to obstruct justice. Their ongoing lies to the police about the fate of Bear—including those made in the wake of Barbara's disappearance— make the charge timely.

At the moment, they're out on bail, awaiting trial. Their attorney, the journalist notes, will no longer be John Paul McLellan Sr.

A picture accompanies the article.

In it, the Stoddard family—Maryanne, her three daughters, her sons-in-law, her grandchildren—stand together, posed formally in front of a neat house in Shattuck, their faces solemn, their posture straight.

Justice restored, reads the caption.

Judy hands the article back to her brother, who hands it to his father, who folds it along its original creases and tucks it into his shirt pocket.

"Did you see your name?" her father says. "It's right there in the second paragraph."

Judy smiles. "I did."

"I always knew that family did it," says Judy's father. "Back when it happened. Everyone knew they had something to do with it. We just didn't know exactly how."

Judy's mother, who has been silent this whole time, suddenly takes Judy's cup from her. Pours her more tea. She is a visitor in their home, now; a guest. The realization makes Judy feel proud and sorrowful at the same time.

"What about the girl? Barbara," Leonard says. "Any leads there?"

There are. But she can't tell her family about them—not yet—and so another curtain is drawn between them.

"Nothing substantial," she says.

On the way back to Ray Brook, Judy watches the pines become taller and denser. She reaches her exit, turns onto 73. Climbs up and up in her Beetle.

In the car, she lets her mind wander again to the most recent developments in Barbara Van Laar's disappearance.

Most interestingly: Annabel Southworth—Louise's CIT—has come forward with a confession. She was with John Paul McLellan the night of Barbara Van Laar's disappearance: once at 10 p.m., during the community dance; and again in the early hours of the morning. She has provided him with an alibi; her parents, Katherine and Howard, have verified her story as well. The two families—the Southworths and McLellans, both good friends of the Van Laars—are supportive of the new relationship, despite Annabel's young age.

They're very compatible, said Katherine Southworth, in her signed affidavit.

The only other charges they had against John Paul—driving while intoxicated, and felony possession of a controlled substance—have been resolved. The bloody clothes—which John Paul maintains were planted—are not admissible as evidence without a charge. He'll do no jail time; instead he's been commanded to perform one hundred hours of community service work by a judge who seemed, to Judy, particularly chummy with John Paul's father.

Judy is surprised by none of this: only slightly disappointed at the outcome.

But since then, there's been something new. Although they may never be able to charge John Paul McLellan with anything related to the disappearance of Barbara Van Laar, they will be able to charge him with something else: second-degree aggravated assault.

The victim: Louise Donnadieu.

After some discussion with Judy, Louise has agreed to come forward with a complaint. Even better: several people have agreed to testify on Louise's behalf. Judy has done the legwork of tracking down the witnesses who were there in John Paul's shared house near Union College, the night of the attack: his roommate, Steven, along with three girls Steven named as guests of theirs on that occasion.

She thinks of the boys she went to high school with. The girls, too. Would they have been so brave? She isn't certain. But it's 1975 now, she tells herself. The world has changed.

"So what's your theory?" her brother had asked, at the kitchen table. "If you can't give us any new details—give us your hunch."

"About?"

"Barbara Van Laar," said her brother, and to her right her mother had made the sign of the cross. *That poor child*, she muttered lowly.

Judy looked out the window.

"I think she's all right, actually," said Judy.

Leonard furrowed his brow.

"How do you know?"

"I don't know. I just have a feeling," said Judy.

The night she ran into Louise Donnadieu at Driscoll's Pub, Louise said one thing that has echoed in Judy's mind for weeks.

On a whim, Judy had asked Louise about T.J. Hewitt. Because, despite her belief in T.J.'s innocence, she could never shake the story that the boy—Christopher—told her.

Why on earth, thought Judy, was Barbara going into T.J. Hewitt's tent at night? What could she have been doing there, aside from something—incorrect?

And so, with two beers in her belly, and her inhibitions lowered, she floated this idea to Louise Donnadieu. Making sure she was out of earshot of her brother before she did.

Louise had laughed.

"What?" said Judy.

"There's no way," said Louise.

"Why?"

"A lot of people think T.J.'s strange," said Louise, "but she's harmless. She's better than harmless. She's a good person. All she wants to do is hunt and fish and be alone. Her family's got a place on an island up north. I think she'd move there now if she could."

Louise flagged the bartender down. Ordered a beer for herself.

"She just needs money first," said Louise.

Judy watched her.

"Where exactly?" she said.

Louise furrowed her brow. "Where what?"

"The island. The house."

"Oh, I don't know the name of it," said Louise. "But she's got a map of it on the wall of the Director's Cabin. Last time I looked, there was a pin where the cabin is."

She drank again.

And then, slowly, she looked up at Judy. Realizing.

It would be career-making for Judy. Finding Barbara Van Laar—finding her *alive*, no less—would mean a promotion. Maybe two. It would set her on a path for success. And it would resolve the question that's hovered over her head since she began her work as an investigator, the one that every male investigator she's encountered has thought upon seeing her. Are women cut out for this work?

Captain LaRochelle, she knows, would find Barbara if he could. Every investigator would—but none of them would take into account Barbara's preferences, or her safety.

Instead, they'd sacrifice Barbara's well-being to better their own lot in life.

This, in fact, is what Captain LaRochelle did do, in a way, when Bear Van Laar disappeared, and when Carl Stoddard became a convenient suspect: he let Stoddard, voiceless in death, take the fall, while LaRochelle took the promotion that came with a closed case.

Judy disagrees with many of the things her parents have taught her, but one thing she respects them for is this: their belief in putting others before themselves.

If Barbara Van Laar has chosen to hide in the woods, of her own volition—if she is safe, and protected, and fed, and self-reliant—who is Judy to drag her back into the world she abandoned?

Still, she wants to be certain that her theory is correct.

And so, from her small apartment in Ray Brook, she makes plans: she'll go back to the Van Laar Preserve; she'll go back to the Director's

Cabin where she spent so many hours. Her guess is that it will be abandoned; the Hewitts, after all, have cut ties with the Van Laars. She'll open the door, which has never had a lock.

She'll pray that the map is still tacked to the wall.

If it is, she'll make a note of the spot that a pin, or pinhole, marks:

The site of the Hewitt family's cabin, way up north, in the middle of the High Peaks of the Adirondacks.

Barbara

1950s • 1961 • Winter 1973 • June 1975
July 1975 • August 1975: **Day One**

The bed is empty.

In the moonlight, in the threshold of the cabin called Balsam, Barbara Van Laar takes a last look over her shoulder, saying goodbye in her mind to Tracy, to her bunkmates, to Camp Emerson.

She's leaving later than she'd agreed upon with T.J., who'll be pacing her cabin, buzzing with nerves. But Barbara's counselors stayed out much later than she'd predicted; she had to wait for them to return, one after another, and then wait some more, until the sound of their movements quieted, until the sound of their breathing steadied.

Then she stood up, as silently as she could, and tiptoed to the doorway, where she now stands.

Her bag. She's forgotten the paper bag she brought back from the main house—the one that almost gave her away.

What's in the bag? Tracy had asked her, last week, and she pretended not to understand.

Outside, the air is fresh, the moon so bright that she doesn't need the flashlight she brought along.

Her other things are waiting for her in T.J.'s cabin: her backpack, loaded with fresh food that should hold her for a week, at least. Her warm clothes, her hiking boots, into which she'll change as quickly as she can.

Sure enough: when she steps onto the porch of the Director's Cabin, the door opens swiftly. There is T.J., checking her watch. It's almost three in the morning, says T.J.; they'll barely make it.

"Should we wait a day?" asks Barbara, but T.J. shakes her head, fast.

Tonight's the last night of the party up the hill. It's tonight—while the guests are on the grounds—or never.

And *never* means being sent away to Élan in the fall. *Never* means not seeing T.J. or Vic—her true family—for years.

In silence, they walk to T.J.'s truck, a canoe strapped to its roof; as quietly as possible, they close both doors. Then T.J. starts the truck, and it rumbles up the hill, past Self-Reliance on its right, past the parking lot full of cars.

"Were you able to get into it?" asks Barbara—gesturing toward John Paul McLellan's blue Trans Am.

T.J. nods. "Clothes're in the trunk now," she says. "He won't see them. But the police will, when they search it."

"Why will they search it?"

T.J. grins. "That's not all I planted in the car," she says. "When he's apprehended—they'll have probable cause to perform a search."

Once they reach the thruway, they continue for an hour. T.J. drives as fast as she can without risking the attention of the police: nine miles over the speed limit, exactly. She glances up at the sky as she drives, which is lightening with every minute that passes.

On the way, T.J. quizzes her.

What do you do about water? she asks.

Build a fire. Boil it. Use iodine.

What do you do if you're sick?

Use the medical guidebook you've put on the shelf. Look for medicine in the cabinet.

The same instructions they've been over, again and again, during the nightly training sessions T.J.'s been giving Barbara all summer. Preparation for life in the woods—not forever. Just until she turns eighteen—at which point she'll be legally allowed to make her own decisions.

Then, she can do as she pleases, without fear of her parents imposing their rules. Or their punishments.

If at any point she changes her mind: all she has to do is emerge. It's Barbara's decision, completely, T.J. says.

Barbara glances at T.J., taking in the contours of her profile, her kind face. When Barbara was a baby, a small child, it was T.J. who tended to her most. T.J. who helped her and taught her. The word *motherly* is not one that applies to T.J. Hewitt, and yet T.J. is the only mother Barbara has ever known. Her own, though living, has been unreachable for all of Barbara's life. A walking shell.

"I put tea in your pack," says T.J. "The kind you like. Some chocolate, too, for a treat at night."

Then: "Will you have enough to read?"

Barbara nods. "I will," she says. "And I'll write if I run out."

"I'll be able to come to you soon," says T.J. "In a month or two. I just have to be certain I'm not being followed."

She glances at Barbara, pats her knee. "I know you can make it until then."

"I can," says Barbara—reassuring T.J. as much as herself.

But in truth, she does feel ready. T.J. has made her so. All of their training, every night; all of the preparations they made.

The one thing she'll miss is music: this, she has had to leave behind.

Both of them fall into silence again. And then, just before the sun rises, T.J. pulls off the highway.

Two headlamps light their way as they dismount the canoe from the roof, and then portage it for a half mile through the woods.

T.J., Barbara knows, is growing nervous: the whole plan will fail if she isn't back on the grounds of Camp Emerson before the rest of the staff wakes up. And so Barbara picks up her pace, despite the fact that her lungs are burning, despite the fact that the backpack she carries is weighing her down.

"We're almost there," says T.J., again and again.

The sun is rising as the two of them row quietly over the surface of the lake, toward an island in its middle. As they approach, Barbara can see—just beyond the tree line—the flat surface of a man-made structure.

"Remember there's deer here," says T.J., climbing out of the stern of the canoe and onto the shore. "You can always hunt for deer. There's two guns in the house, and plenty of shot."

Barbara has a sudden flash of her own mother following her, ghost-like, about the house—admonishing her not to eat so much. The opposite, always, of T.J., who throughout her life has fed her every chance she got—even coming to Barbara's school from time to time to hand-deliver coats and clothing and other treats she knew Barbara liked.

She used to sneak in and out a window to do so.

It was never a problem, until the one time she was seen by the house mother from behind, and Barbara—flustered, in a panic—said that T.J. had been a teenage boy.

From there, things went terribly wrong.

"I'll remember," says Barbara, now. "I remember everything you taught me."

They've reached their destination. For a moment, the two of them regard each other.

"Go," says Barbara.

"You'll be fine," says T.J.

"I'll be fine," says Barbara.

Now Barbara stands on the shore of the island, watching T.J. move away in her canoe. She waits until she can't hear the dip of the paddle into the lake, until T.J. disappears, at last, into the forest on the other side, turning back with one last wave before she goes.

Barbara closes her eyes. She listens, waiting for a sign: and a hermit thrush answers with its beautiful song.

She walks to the cabin that the Hewitts built, many generations prior. Inside, it's cool and shadowy and stocked with the supplies that T.J. has been ferrying over for months, in anticipation of her stay.

Something new is in the corner: an acoustic guitar. A beginner's instruction book. A way, Barbara realizes, for her to make her own music.

She sets her heavy pack down gratefully on the ground. At the top is the paper bag she brought with her from Self-Reliance.

She opens it, pulls out the one nonessential object she permitted herself to transport today: it's a framed picture of her brother, Bear.

He, too, will have a home here.

She sets the picture on the rough table at which she'll eat her meals.

You're safe now, she tells her brother, in her mind.

Judyta

1950s • 1961 • Winter 1973 • June 1975
July 1975 • August 1975 • **September 1975**

At the edge of a lake fifty miles north of the Van Laar Preserve, Judy Luptack stands with her hands on her hips, squinting toward an island in the distance. She has brought no boat with her.

She's trying to estimate the distance between the shore and the island. Half a mile; maybe slightly more. She's never been a strong swimmer, but she takes off her shoes and dips a toe in nonetheless, testing the water.

It's freezing. For a moment, Judy rethinks her decision. She has no evidence that she'll find anything on the other side. It's a Saturday. Her day off. She could go home, back to her rental in Ray Brook; she could go to the grocer and buy food for dinner. Already, she's learning the names of the people in the town. She could be doing anything she wants. Instead—pulled by a hunch that she hasn't been able to shake, ever since she spoke to Louise Donnadieu—she strips down to her bathing suit. Plunges into the cold water before her.

She has no idea how long the swim will take her. You can always float, she tells herself. If you get tired, you can float.

As she swims, she thinks. If she's right in her theory—*if* she's right, which remains to be seen—she can understand the logic at every step: the bloody uniform that resulted from what Christopher Muldauer described as *Barbara's accident* on the Survival Trip. The sudden realization, for T.J. and Barbara, of how useful it might be. Planting those clothes in John Paul McLellan's trunk would serve a dual purpose: not only would they throw investigators off the scent of where Barbara had really gone—but they would function as a neat form of justice. Justice for Louise Donnadieu, who had once gone to T.J. with fresh injuries, inflicted on her by John Paul. Justice for Carl Stoddard, who was himself framed after death by two families—the McLellans, the Van Laars—who wished to preserve their good reputations. To avoid a scandal, at the expense of an innocent man. Justice, too, for T.J. Hewitt's own father—who had entered into the sort of agreement that went against his own set of ethics. Reduced him to something no better than the Van Laars themselves.

With two simple actions—revealing the truth about Bear, and helping Barbara to hide—the Hewitts have redeemed themselves. They've retraced their steps to their last wrong turn, and taken a different path instead.

It's difficult to know how much time has elapsed since Judy left the opposite shore. Sometimes, she takes her own advice and floats, looking straight up into the blue September sky. She closes her eyes. Lets herself be cradled by the water. Then goes on.

At some point, the shore in front of her is closer than the shore behind. She stops, treads water. If she squints, she thinks she can see a trail of smoke rising into the sky, as if from a chimney.

At last, she makes land. And in the near distance, she sees a figure peer out from behind a tree.

Barbara Van Laar.

Judy would recognize her anywhere, though she's never seen her in the flesh.

From the water, Judy raises a hand in the air, tentatively. Barbara won't know who Judy is; she was gone long before the state police descended on the grounds. Judy has the feeling of looking through a one-way mirror, knowing far more about Barbara than Barbara understands. In her bathing suit, trembling with cold, Judy must look slightly ridiculous, amateurish: an especially adventurous hiker or camper, who didn't expect to be seen.

Across from her, Barbara stands still, both hands at her sides.

"Are you all right?" Judy calls out.

"Yes," Barbara says. Then—"Are you?"

Judy nods.

"Do you want me to leave you alone?" says Judy.

For an instant, Barbara hesitates.

Then she says, with finality: "Yes."

The swim back feels longer and slower than the swim there. Judy is so cold that her teeth clack. Still, fifty feet into her journey, she pauses, turns back toward the island to take a last look.

There she is: Barbara Van Laar, standing straight and strong. At home in her body, at home in the woods. Something about her looks immortal, thinks Judy: a spirit, an apparition, more god than child.

Judy keeps swimming until, at last, she reaches the opposite shore.

When she looks back to the island she sees only the pines, drawn closed like a curtain around the girl.

Acknowledgments

Thank you to Bob and Kelly Nessle, Kevin Gagan, Kevin Hynes, Kathleen Bower, Anna Serotta, Jean Dommermuth, Max O'Keefe, Rebecca Moore, and Steve Williams, for granting me interviews on various subjects that informed the writing of this novel. All fictionalization of the (procedural, medical, legal, geographical) facts is entirely my doing.

Thank you to the authors of the following publications, which provided invaluable information as I wrote: *Woodswoman*, by Anne LaBastille; *Lost Person Behavior*, by Robert J. Koester; "Self-Reliance," by Ralph Waldo Emerson; *Walden*, by Henry David Thoreau; *Creem* magazine; *Adventures in the Wilderness; or, Camp-Life in the Adirondacks*, by William Murray; *Adirondack Album*, volume 2, by Barney Fowler; *Adirondack Explorations: Nature Writings of Verplanck Colvin*, edited by Paul Schaefer; and *At the Mercy of the Mountains*, by Peter Bronski.

Thank you to Seth Fishman, Rebecca Gardner, and the Gernert team; to Sarah McGrath, Alison Fairbrother, and the Riverhead team; and to Sylvie Rabineau, Hilary Zaitz Michael, and the WME team, for your professional guidance and your friendship, too.

Thank you to Don Lee, Cara Blue Adams, Jena Osman, Pattie McCarthy, Rich Deeg, the late Dr. JoAnne Epps, and all my colleagues and students in Temple University's MFA program.

Thank you to Alex Gilvarry, Mac Casey, Christine Parkhurst, Stephen Moore, and Rebecca Moore for reading and discussing early drafts of this novel.

Thank you to Murph Casey, Mike Casey, Kelly O'Hara, Abby Bailey, Sarah Lanzone, Jessica Geller, Maggie Casey, Adriana Gomez-Juckett, Asali Solomon, Jessica Soffer, Kiley Reid, Alexandra Kleeman, Scott Cheshire, Christy Davids, Crossley Simmons, and The Claw for the moral support, friendship, child care, and many long talks.

Thank you to those ancestors who made a home of the Adirondack Mountains, most especially Cheryl and Gerald Parkhurst.

Thank you to Mac, Annie, and Jack, for reminding me why I write, and also for giving me the best reason in the world not to write all of the time. I love you.